BLUE WATCH

Lee !

Read and enjoy.
It aint all fiction

A-Je

Gwg
m

BLUE WATCH

by

Gwyn Fford-Osborne

DIADEM BOOKS

Published by Diadem Books
Distribution coordination by Spiderwize

For information, please contact:

Diadem Books
16 Lethen View
Tullibody
Alloa
FK10 2GE
Scotland

www.diadembooks.com

ISBN: 978-1-908026-02-6

Table of Contents

The Greener Gun

IFFOR LOOKED BACK AT THE TRAIN, glad to see the faces of his newly-made friends smiling at him through the carriage window. He turned, and raised his bottle of what was now a very flat Castle beer, in a drunk's salute, and with a slight bow, acknowledged the returned salutes. He placed the bottle by the side of the dirt track which served as a road, knowing that even now, a sharp eyed African lad was already homing in on it anxious to claim the tickey the local store would give him for it.

The sign read 'Kensington' and the dirt track gave way to tarmac leading into town. Having drunk and spoofed the night away, all he wanted now was some breakfast and a decent hotel room. As he walked into town, he reflected on his train journey; just my luck, he thought, to choose the same train as the one taking troopies back to the war. Still, he had made many friends, drunk many beers and lost many pounds playing spoof with experts. He walked slowly along the pavement, enjoying the fresh morning sun and the fragrance from the jasmine trees. It was still quite early, so apart from the Indian shopkeepers busy opening their shops, there were few people about.

Iffor stopped outside one shop; above a large lattice window was a sign, 'PREMJI EMPORIUM'. Standing just inside the doorway was a tall bearded sixty-something Sikh. On seeing Iffor, the Indian smiled and nodded. "Good morning," Iffor said. The Indian's smile broadened, exposing gold-capped teeth.

"Mr Premji, I presume."

The Indian stepped from the coolness of the shop doorway onto the pavement. "And good morning to you sir," he responded. "No, my grandfather was Premji, I'm a Patel."

"Well, Mr Patel, perhaps you can direct me to a decent hotel?"

"Step inside out of the sun and join me for a cup of chai, and I will give you the directions you require." The Sikh made it quite clear there could be no refusal.

Iffor left the shop an hour or so later with directions to a small family hotel owned by a Mr Patel (whose grandfather also just happened to be Premji.), his head buzzing with the history and latest gossip of Kensington and stories of the Punjab that would put Kipling to shame. The tea had been very refreshing, but now Iffor needed a real drink. The vision of a cold Castle beer sent his taste buds into turmoil. He quickened his step; surely his host at the hotel would take pity on him; then Providence stepped in. Across the main road, built by the early pioneers and wide enough for a wagon drawn by eight oxen to complete a U-turn, Iffor spotted a sign above what was obviously a clubhouse. A Moth club, The Memorable Order of Tin Hats, the sanctuary of all ex-servicemen in Africa.

A glance at his watch suggested someone should be on site; he just hoped that person had a good sense of humour. It wasn't that he just needed a drink; he felt he needed to touch base with someone, let people know he was in town. He walked into the lobby past the two brass-jacketed, highly polished Vickers machine-guns, one either side of the imposing front door, and was confronted by a wall covered with the plaques and shields of various military regiments. On his right was a cloakroom and a door marked Snooker Room; on his left was a door marked Bar and Clubroom.

Iffor was conscious of the Brno pistol holstered on his hip; he'd broken his rifle down and stowed it in his Burgan. In this part of the world it was normal practice to wear a pistol at all times, but it was also etiquette to leave one's weapons in the room provided before going into the bar. However, it was out of hours, so he poked his head around the door and coughed to announce his presence.

Dressed rather formally in safari jacket, shorts and long socks, a tall slim built man with close cropped hair, aged about forty, was seated at a table counting what were probably the weekend's takings. Standing behind him with a Greener gun, the butt of the weapon tucked into his armpit in the ready position, was a uniformed Askari. The sight of the Greener gave rise to some concern for Iffor: a twelve-bore shotgun, probably loaded with buckshot; single twenty-inch barrel; Martini action, the most basic of all shotguns but highly favoured by police forces throughout Africa, and devastating in the right hands.

The man at the desk looked up and frowned with annoyance. Iffor got in first:

"Just got off the train and looking for a friendly face," he said, putting on his best hangdog look. The man relaxed, which was more than could be said for the Askari; his eyes didn't waver from Iffor's face, and the muzzle of the Greener moved a little higher than the forty-five degree angle.

"Come in, dump your kit and grab a beer," he nodded towards the bar. "Give me a couple of minutes to finish this, and I'll be with you." Iffor dropped his Burgan to the floor, unbuckled his pistol belt and laid it on the Burgan, then smiled at the Askari who acknowledged the smile by lowering the muzzle of his weapon slightly. Iffor lifted the counter hatch and went behind the bar to the cold shelf. Without turning, he said," Lion or Castle?"

"Lion for me, please. Leave it on the counter. I've just about finished here."

"And how about your minder?" asked Iffor, knowing what the answer would be.

"On duty," came the reply. Iffor poured the beers and sat on a bar stool, savouring the anticipation of the cold lager, resisting the urge to drink until his host joined him. The clubroom was typical of all Moth clubs, with weapons, various animal heads and tusks, and pictures of historical battle scenes on the walls. Iffor studied his host, who was now completing his task by putting the cash bags into a well-worn Gladstone bag, and saw, for the first time, two silver pips on each shoulder indicating an Inspector in the BSAP, the famed British South African Police.

The Inspector pushed his chair away from the table, revealing an Uzi across his lap.

"Can't be too careful these days," he said, standing up with the sub-machine gun in his hand. He crossed the room to the bar and offered his hand. "Pete Saxon; welcome to Kensington."

"Meredith—Iffor Meredith," Iffor said and shook his hand warmly. "Sorry to barge in on you like this, but I knew I'd find a friend here."

Pete smiled and drank his beer. "You're very welcome. Now, tell me about yourself; I am a policeman after all, a bit like the local sheriff, always suspicious of strangers in town. Ex-military?" he asked.

"60th Rifles and Airborne Forces; yourself?" Iffor said. He did not want to get involved in telling his life history at this stage.

"16/5th Royal Lancers," Pete replied, then asked, "Para Reg?"

Iffor was much more at ease now and sat back on his stool, feeling relaxed. He noticed that the Askari was now sitting down, but still had both hands firmly grasping the Greener. "No," he replied, "I was Para Sappers; much more fun."

"I know what you mean." Pete drained his glass. "That's why I went for tanks; you can cause much more havoc and mayhem in a tank." He stood up. "Got to turn you out, old boy," he said. "Got somewhere to stay?"

"Premji's," said Iffor, walking over to his Burgan.

"Ah, you've met Mr Patel." Pete stood up and beckoned to the Askari to pick up the Gladstone. "Good family the Patels, they'll look after you." Pete put the sling of the Uzi over his shoulder and took the Gladstone bag from his escort, leaving the African free to use both hands to cause total mayhem, should he have to use the Greener. "By the way," Pete said, "Meet my shadow, Sergeant Timothy Banda."

Iffor studied the African's face for a few moments, then said, "You're a Nyasa, aren't you?"

The African smiled for the first time. "Indy, Bwana," he said, and took Iffor's hand in the thumb-palm handshake, the common greeting between African friends.

Iffor picked up his Burgan and pistol belt, and followed Pete into the street.

"In case you're wondering," Pete said, "the club made me treasurer because I can provide my own escort when I take the cash to the bank. I'm also responsible for entertainments, which brings me to another point; what are you like at darts?"

Iffor thought back to when he last played. "Brilliant," he said, trying hard to look confident.

"Good," said Pete, "we've got a grudge match against Blue Watch tonight and I'm a player short."

"Blue Watch?" Iffor slung his Burgan onto his shoulder. "They sound like a bunch of queers to me."

"Far from it," said Pete. "They are our proud and efficient fire brigade; although any serious fires or problems are now handled by the mine fire and rescue people." He went on: "We used to have two 'Watches' or teams, Blue Watch and Red Watch, but all the youngsters have been called up, so the older blokes that were left formed themselves into just one team, Blue Watch. We retain them to deal with minor fires and to support the mine team. Here, my friend, is where we part company, until this evening, that is?" Pete made it sound like a question.

"I'll be there," Iffor replied,

Pete went on: "Your hotel is about two hundred metres on the left, my bank is just opposite." And then as an afterthought, said, "Is that pistol your only weapon, or have you got others lurking in your Burgan?"

"Glad you asked, I need to lodge them somewhere safe." He went on, "I've got a Ruger Carbine broken down and a 22 Snubby."

"And that pistol in your belt holster, a Browning?" said Pete with authority.

"Close; it's a Brno, very similar."

"Either way," Pete said stepping onto the road, "introduce yourself to Agnes at my police station; she'll look after you... oh, and you can hang on to your pistol while you're in town, just keep it safe."

Iffor made his way up the main street towards the hotel. The pavement was wide and well-maintained, with a jacaranda tree offering shade to a street vendor selling warm, fresh samosas. He was tempted by the smell of the samosas but he guessed the hotel would provide something more substantial for him. That establishment was all Iffor could have asked for, cool, clean and comfortable, typical of colonial days. His host, Mrs Patel, was waiting to greet him having been warned he was coming. She took his Burgan and put it behind the reception desk, assuring him that it would be quite safe, then steered him into the small but adequate breakfast room. He sat down at the table offered him by his host while she opened the large French windows that overlooked the patio, letting a welcome breeze into the room. She hadn't asked him what he wanted for breakfast, nor had she shown him a menu, so he steeled himself for what he knew she would be preparing for him. A short while later she was back with his meal. As expected, it was a very large plate of *Boereworse*, slices of thick bacon, fried eggs and mushrooms and a huge teapot. "You must be starving," she said, "I'll be back later with some more eggs."

An hour or so later Iffor staggered to his room where his Burgan was waiting for him. He stripped and collapsed onto the bed. Then he glanced at his watch—ten o'clock. He set his body clock for midday and fell into a deep sleep.

He awoke soon after twelve, refreshed and happy. He showered, shaved and dressed in clean shorts, faded khaki shirt and sandals. He didn't bother to unpack; he knew Mrs Patel would do that. He took the Carbine from the Burgan and assembled it; then he unloaded the Brno and put it back into its holster; the Astra 22 in its thumb-break holster, he threaded onto his belt and positioned it in the small of his back under his shirt. Gathering up the Ruger, magazine pouches and pistol belt, Iffor left the hotel and made his way to the police station for his meeting with Agnes. The police station, typical of such a town, had a large reception area with the obligatory counter and various desks, high windows and a corridor at the rear leading off to the cells. As Iffor entered the room, his way was barred by a five foot square female police constable, who smiled comfortably. He already liked this woman.

"Constable Agnes, I presume," he said.

She offered a huge grin showing perfect white teeth.

He went on: "Inspector Saxon asked me to lodge my weapons with you."

She waddled to a desk and without being asked, Iffor followed. She sat down, opened her Arms Register and began writing in his name and hotel. She looked up at him, smiled again and said, "You can put your weapons on my desk, and, starting with the rifle, prove the weapons and read out the serial number."

Iffor did as bid, with the Ruger and the Brno, then, playing his trump card to gain favour with this woman, said, "I'm carrying a pistol. The Inspector said, if you agree, I can hang onto it."

She saw straight through him. "If the Inspector said you can keep it, then you can keep it; just let me see it and record the serial number."

Having seen his weapons taken off to a cell for safekeeping and having obtained a receipt, Iffor stepped out into the street; things to do, places to see, people to meet.

The sign above the entrance said 'BOONS BAR', and experience told Iffor that this was the best place to tour and discover the town without actually leaving the bar stool.

A tall, well-built Matabele dressed impeccably in white uniform and red fez, standing in the entrance hall, was being confronted by a young woman with a small child. The butt of a Sten gun protruding from her shopping basket identified her as a farmer's wife. "I know my husband is in here," she said, "I dropped him off and watched him come in."

The African looked straight ahead. "I think you may be mistaken, madam," he said, and smiled at the child who shyly smiled back at him.

"But I can hear him laughing in there."

"He is not here, madam."

"Can't I just go inside and look for myself?"

"I'm sorry madam; men only."

"Look," she said, "just go inside and tell him I'm here."

"I'm not allowed to leave the door, madam."

Exasperated and defeated, she said, "If you see my husband, tell him I'll be waiting for him at the hotel." Then looking hard at Iffor, added, "You bastard men, you're all the same, you seem to think life's a game." And taking the child's hand, she strode away.

Iffor picked up her shopping basket with the Sten in it. "Excuse me," he called out, "haven't you forgotten something?"

She came back, took the basket without a word and walked quickly away.

As Iffor entered the bar, a man pushed past him and thrust a pound note into the Matabele's hand. "Thanks old chap," he said, "I'll do the same for you one day." Then, talking to no one in particular said, "The problem with women is they just don't realise the seriousness of a game of Max and Jacks, a chap simply can't be disturbed." As they walked into the bar, the man back to the game with his mates and Iffor to the bar, Iffor surmised that this was the husband, obviously a farmer, well-worn shirt and shorts, boots with no socks, bush hat, which in all probability never came off his head, and a Browning Hi- Power holstered comfortably on his hip.

Safely settled on a bar stool with a glass of cold Lion in his hand, Iffor now let his gaze wander around the room. A group of four men, probably all farmers who'd brought their wives into town shopping, were seated round a table playing Max and Jacks for the privilege of buying the next round. To avoid being interrupted by wives, they would have bribed the Matabele on the door to tell enquiring spouses their men were not at home. Against the far wall of the room, under a window, too high for curious onlookers, was a high-backed wooden padded settle with a small table in front. Sitting on the settle he saw a short stocky man in his sixties, of military appearance, dressed rather formally in safari jacket, shorts, long socks and highly polished shoes with a Royal Air Force cravat about his neck. Beside him, with eyes fixed firmly on Iffor, was an orang-utan. Nothing unusual about that, mused Iffor; in England, yes, but this was Africa. Glass in hand, Iffor walked over to the pair, curious and eager for conversation. "Don't tell me, his name's Cheetah, right?"

The man smiled. "Yes, you're right, but only his friends call him by name."

"So..." Iffor spoke slowly and deliberately; he knew his next question was going to cost him money... "How do I become a friend?"

As if to answer the question, the ape extended his arm and open palm towards Iffor.

"Just give him a ticky for an egg and he'll be your friend for life," the man said, looking quite bored; he'd probably made the same statement many times before.

Iffor reached into his pocket retrieved a ticky and placed it in the ape's hand, then watched in amazement as the animal clambered off the settle, crossed the room to the bar, climbed onto a stool and exchanged the ticky for a hard-boiled egg.

The man stood up and extended his hand. "Please join us," he said. "I'm David Jones; most people call me Davy. I was a Warrant in the Royal Air Force."

Iffor shook his hand, introduced himself and sat down. The ape, peeling the shell from the egg, joined them.

"New in town?" asked Davy.

The question took Iffor by surprise and he had to think for a minute; could it be that it was only that morning he had got off the train? It seemed like an age.

"Yes," he replied, "arrived this morning." Anxious to avoid questions, he said, "Tell about the town."

"Tell about the town?" Davy repeated, looking intently at his empty glass.

Iffor got the message. He collected two more beers from the bar.

Davy poured his beer, settled back in his seat and began to reveal all the places of interest in the town, which, as Iffor duly noted, comprised all the main watering holes: the mine club; the two hotels with bars, the Elephants head and the Impala; the theatre club; flying club and the Moth club.

A commotion in the hallway caused Billy the barman to leave the bar and join the Matabele at the front door. Moments later he came back into the bar. "It's your wife again, Ian," he said, "and this time she ain't taking prisoners; time to go."

Without a word, the young farmer stood up, squared his shoulders, settled his bush hat firmly on his head and left the bar to join his irate wife.

"That," said Davy "was young Ian Dix. He and his brother own the Lamumbwa farm about sixty miles north of here. There was another brother who farmed further north up on the border; he was one of the first farmers to be murdered by the terrs."

Iffor drained his glass and stood up. "Thanks for the info, Winco," he said, smiling at his own little joke. "See you again no doubt."

The ape extended an arm with open palm, "Do I shake hands with him?" Then, as if to answer his own question, said, "Give him a ticky, right?"

Davy just smiled and nodded.

PART TWO

If only, if only

REFRESHED, HAVING HAD A SLEEP, a shower and a plate of Mrs Patel's sandwiches washed down with yet another gallon of hot sweet tea, Iffor entered the MOTH club where Pete was waiting.

"If you're carrying a weapon, you can lodge it in our cloakroom," he said, indicating the far side of the lobby.

Iffor smiled his thanks and walked over to the cloakroom, followed by his host. At the counter he reached for the holster under his shirt in the small of his back and pulled out the Astra 22 which he unloaded and exchanged for a cloakroom ticket with the African behind the counter.

"That," said Pete, raising his eyebrow quizzically, "is a pretty little piece, chromed with mother-of-pearl grips. That's what's known as a lady's pistol in these parts."

"Don't let looks deceive you," said Iffor as they walked towards the bar. "Loaded with nine stingers, it's pretty formidable at close range and it comes complete with a Hunter thumb-break holster which makes it a useful bit of kit." As they entered the main clubroom, they were confronted by a man who, in the British army, would have been referred to as being built like a brick bog: well over six feet, about fourteen stone and a menacing crew-cut.

"Ah," said Pete, "Mad Harry. Harry, meet Iffor Meredith."

"Mered-ith," Iffor corrected him.

"Sorry; Mered-ith," said Pete. "Anyway Iffor, this is Mad Harry; Harry, this is Iffor, arrived in town this morning." They shook hands and Iffor wished they hadn't.

10

"God," he exclaimed, "I thought *I* had a strong grip," and he looked down at his hand, watching the colour slowly returning.

A man standing just behind Mad Harry stepped forward, hand outstretched. "And I'm the other Harry," he said, "although I prefer Henry; but since everybody calls me Harry, Harry it is."

The man, though younger, was only a shadow of Mad Harry and Iffor had some satisfaction in watching him wince as they shook hands. This time Iffor had the stronger grip by far.

"The two Harrys here are both members of Blue Watch," Pete explained. "We tell them apart by calling one of them Mad Harry."

"I'm glad you told me that," said Iffor, looking at them both, one a giant of a man, the other slim, much shorter and obviously very effeminate. "I would certainly never have been able to tell them apart."

They moved to a nearby vacant table and sat down. The clubroom was rapidly filling up now, all men; women only ventured into Moth Clubs by very rare invitations. The darts team members were warming up on the board and the score board was being wiped clean ready for the start. Looking at the standard of the players, Iffor began to wish he hadn't volunteered himself for the match.

"Get the beers in Harry," said Mad Harry, "and you had better include Evil—he's heading this way."

A tall thin man with long flowing hair and a Latin South American appearance joined them.

"Iffor, meet Jesus, we call him Evil Jesus. He's a Dago."

"Let me guess," said Iffor, "you call him Evil Jesus because there are two of them, right?"

"Almost," said Pete. "His name is J-E-S-U-S, pronounced Hay-sous, but the Africans can't get their head around that one. The Jesus they know about is good and holy while our Jesus here is, well, different, so they refer to him as Evil Jesus."

Jesus took a seat at the table while Harry returned with the beers and sat down. They spoke for a while about the forthcoming darts match and asked politely about Iffor's train journey and was his hotel comfortable; but as Iffor finished his beer, he knew what was coming next. The four men seemed to close in on Iffor. Just like the bloody inquisition, he thought, and sure enough, Pete said, "We are all curious as to why you came to our town—it can't be for a holiday."

"It's no big secret." Iffor raised his empty glass and peered into it. Mad Harry glanced at Harry and raised an eyebrow. Harry stood up and without a word collected more beers from the bar. Iffor slowly poured his beer. "As I said, it's no big secret. I've just completed a contract with the Zambian Army." He paused, letting the words sink in. Zambia was not a friendly nation, and seeing their concern, went on, "For the past couple of years my battalion was bush bashing, trying to prevent the terrs infiltrating into Rhodesia, but when the army started to support the terrs, I decided to move on, and since there is nothing for me in England to go back for, I decided to stay in Africa. I'm in Kensington on a sort of pilgrimage." Iffor paused for a drink, then went on. "An old British army buddy of mine who had left the army to come out here to run his family farm was murdered by the terrs before I had a chance to catch up with him, so I'm here to look up his wife and child."

"Helen Dix!" exclaimed Mad Harry. "You're here to see Helen, aren't you?"

"Right first time," said Iffor, "and the rest of the family."

"Young Ian Dix was in town today," said Harry, looking important with this news.

"I know," said Iffor, "I was drinking with him in Boons Bar, but I didn't know who he was until after he had left."

The darts match was a complete disaster for Iffor. He walked back to the table with Pete.

"You told me you were an expert," Pete said. "You couldn't hit a cow's arse with a banjo!"

"I lied," grinned Iffor.

The shrill of the telephone at the end of the bar effectively ended the evening. The barman answered it and rather formally called, "It's for you, Inspector." Pete took the phone.

"Saxon here." The men in the room kept a respectful silence, allowing Pete to hear what was being said. They were well used to him receiving routine calls from his station, but the look on his face told them this was something serious. He rapped out orders down the phone: "Advise army at New Epsom of unconfirmed contact, give grid and tell them we probably have friendly casualties, then, give the duty constables a warning order, standard operating procedures, no move before first light." Pete put the phone down and turned to face his silent audience. His policy had always been to keep this small community well informed of terrorist activities. "Gentlemen, I'll tell you what I know; Ed Dix phoned my station earlier this evening and reported that young Ian and his wife and daughter hadn't arrived at the farm as expected after their visit into town. He asked us if we could confirm that he had collected his rifle and logged out of the police station. When my station eventually phoned Ed back confirming that Ian had left town, Ed then told my constable that he had heard gunfire, including machine-gun fire in the distance earlier; so it looks as if young Ian might have had a problem. Now, if you will all excuse me, I have to get back to my HQ and get a sitrep off to army."

Iffor looked into the bottom of his empty glass and reflected on his visit to Boons bar that afternoon: if only Ian had gone with his wife when she first asked him; if only he hadn't stayed to finish his silly drinking game; if only he hadn't stayed for another beer. The terrorists didn't like operating when there were still hours of daylight left; they preferred early evening and darkness when the army helicopters couldn't find them. If only Ian had gone home sooner, if only, if only… "What now?" said Iffor, once more seated with his new friends.

"Well," said Jesus, indicating that he had some knowledge in these matters, "Pete will meet up with the army in the morning and sweep the area until they find the point of contact, then the army tracker will follow the spoor in the hope of catching up with the terrs; but they are on a hiding to nothing—this bunch of terrs just seem to melt into thin air. The army puts stops on the border and sweeps the area with helicopters, but there is never any trace of them after the attack."

"Has this sort of thing happened before?" asked Iffor.

"Two police patrols, one mine security patrol and of course Jamie's murder further north, and in every incident, the terrs just seem to melt away without trace." Jesus raised his hands to emphasise the point.

"I presume these were our local ZAPU terrorists," Iffor said.

"ZAPU, ZANU, what's the bloody difference? I don't even know what ZAPU stands for," Mad Harry said.

"ZAPU," said Iffor, "stands for Zimbabwe African Peoples Union, while ZANU, N'komo's hooligans, stands for Zimbabwe African National Union. And just beware gentlemen, if these two groups merge…" He preferred to leave this statement unfinished. "…the outcome would be unthinkable." He went on: "ZAPU are our local lads while N'komo's hooligans operate in the south-west of the country."

In spite of the bad news, Blue Watch were obviously going to make a night of it, but Iffor had had a long hard eventful day. He gave his excuses, collected his Astra, and made his way back to the hotel, his bottle of Glenffidich and bed.

Iffor got in first. "Just tea and toast this morning, Mrs Patel, on the patio if you don't mind, and a morning paper, please."

Mrs Patel opened her mouth as if to say something, thought better of it and scurried off to the kitchen, wondering what she was going to do with the *Boereworse* and bacon already cooked. Iffor, dressed only in shorts, shirt and flip-flops, finished his breakfast and settled down on a sunlounger under an umbrella to read his newspaper, enjoying the silence and scent of the jasmine and jacaranda trees and quite soon, typical of a soldier with nothing to do, fell into a deep sleep.

He was awake and alert moments before Mrs Patel touched his shoulder to tell him of his visitor. Pete Saxon stepped onto the patio. A very different Pete Saxon from the one he was drinking with last evening. He was dressed in typical Rhodesian army combat shirt and trousers, the canvass 'six-magazine' vest worn by most farmers and favoured by police to tell them apart from army who wore 58 equipment. He carried his G3 rifle with the butt resting on his hip and muzzle pointed to the sky. Iffor noted with some satisfaction that there was no sling on the rifle. The soldier studied his guest for a few moments, then said, "For a policeman you look like a damned good soldier."

Mrs Patel insisted they took their tea in the small gazeboo; she had an idea what they would discuss and wanted to ensure both shade and privacy.

"I'm afraid it's as bad as we thought." Pete took off his equipment and laid it down beside his rifle as he spoke. "Ian and the child are confirmed dead." Then, looking hard at Iffor, he said, "No sign of the wife; they either killed her and took her body away, or..." His voice trailed off. "Either way, the fact that she was not found at the ambush site will cause a lot of fear and anguish among the white women in the area; they know what the terrorists would do to her if they took her alive."

Having confirmed the bad news, Pete continued with a more formal debrief. "When the police arrived at the ambush site, the army were already there, but were only able to confirm the terrorists' firing point and the fact that an RPD machine-gun had been used. They already had trackers out looking for spoor, and now that the police had arrived to begin their investigation and arrange for the bodies to be removed, began to fan out into the area in the vain hope of a contact or at least finding the woman's body."

Pete stood up and collected up his rifle and equipment. "Sorry to be the bearer of bad news, but I thought that being a friend of the family, you should hear it from me before the rumours started."

When he had left, Iffor went back to the sunlounger and his paper. Mrs Patel, who seemed to know exactly when to appear, went off to his room in response to his request: "Be an angel and fetch my Glenffidich and a glass from my room." He had a lot of thinking to do. First and foremost, he had to get out to Lamumbwa farm to see what he could do to help.

Late afternoon he made his way to the police station, to be met once again by Agnes. No smile this time; the murder of whites by the terrs was no different from the murder of black Africans. Everyone in this small community was affected. She led him to the Inspector's office.

"Can you spare a minute or two?" Iffor noted maps and reports on his desk; this was not a good time.

"Come in, come in, sit yourself down. I've been expecting you; I imagine you'll be wanting to get out to the Dix's place."

"Soon as possible; I hope you can tell me where I can hire a car." Then Iffor went on, "Something decent, a Land Rover or something similar."

"I can do better than that," said the Inspector. "I've got a Rhino going out to the farm tomorrow; you can ride shotgun." The thought of travelling in the armoured Rhino appealed to Iffor. The Inspector went on, "I've formally identified the bodies myself; I brought them back from the ambush site this morning; they are with the undertaker now. I've spoken to Ed Dix; they're both going in the same coffin, then back to the farm for burial in the family plot. One of my constables, Elias Abraham, is taking the coffin to the farm; you can go with him, stay overnight and he'll bring you back next day. On parade 1200 hours, we'll have the coffin loaded and ready for the off. Questions?"

"No."

"Good; fuck off, I've work to do."

Iffor made his way back to the hotel, planning his evening, a leisurely bath, then dinner at the Elephants Head with a bottle or two of a decent wine, then, who knows.

This time Mrs Patel was ready for him. "Your breakfast is on the table," she said.

No chance of tea and toast today, Iffor thought. She went on, "You'll need a decent meal for your journey." Iffor frowned at her in annoyance, "So much for secrecy," he commented. It was standard procedure not to discuss travel arrangements outside town. He added, "I won't be back tonight." She smiled, indicating she knew that as well.

After a hurried breakfast, Iffor returned to the police station to collect his weapons; then back to his hotel room to prepare for his journey, to what he knew would be a sad and fraught meeting with the Dix family. He stripped, cleaned and oiled the carbine and the pistol, unloaded and cleaned the magazines, then reloaded them. Although the chances of a terrorist attack so soon after the ambush were remote, Iffor had always adopted a standard operating procedure of being prepared for any eventuality.

He presented himself at the police station five minutes early, and this time it was the Inspector who was impressed. He was wearing a British army floppy hat, faded khaki shirt and shorts, desert boots with socks rolled over the top, his Brno held securely in a comfortable shoulder rig. The web belt around his waist supported two magazine pouches, one on each hip, each containing two thirty-round magazines, while a pouch at the front of the belt held two fifteen-round mags for the Brno. He carried his Ruger in one hand, and in contrast, a shopping bag borrowed from his host, containing washing gear, sleeping bag and change of clothing in the other hand.

Pete introduced Iffor to his travelling companion, a tall, gangly thin man in his early twenties, dressed in camouflage uniform but wearing his police peaked cap. This, Iffor thought, gave him his authority. He carried a Stirling sub-machine gun slung over his shoulder in place of the normally favoured G3 rifle. Iffor looked at Pete who answered the unspoken question, "Constable Abrahams here couldn't hit a cow's arse with a banjo let alone with a rifle; however, with the Smg on full auto he's got half a chance of hitting somebody." They made their way into the yard behind the station where stood Pete's pride and joy, the Rhino. "Chassis and engine of a long wheel-base Rover," Pete spoke with some authority. "The cabin, the mine workshops knocked up for us; it's got double-skin armour on the sides to give some protection from RPG's and you've got sliding panels in the roof and bottom in case a mine blows you onto your side." He paused, letting that invaluable information register with Iffor, then said, "It gives you a chance to defend yourselves if you're lying like an upside-down tortoise in the middle of the road."

The coffin had already been loaded into the Rhino with a foot or so protruding from the back doors, stout cord holding it in place. Iffor let his mind dwell for a few moments on the father and daughter lying together asleep, in peace; then, setting his mind to the task ahead, took his seat next to the constable who was already sitting behind the wheel with his Smg, butt folded, across his knees.

PART THREE

But in Africa, it's perfectly acceptable to be seen drinking with a Catholic priest, Davy Jones and an Orang-Utan named Cheetah.

T HE JOURNEY TO LAMUMBWA FARM was uneventful until they reached a place some two miles from the farm. Elias stopped the vehicle and turned to Iffor. "This is the spot of the ambush," he said, and leaving the engine running, got out of the Rhino. Iffor followed. Elias described the ambush as best he could. "The Land Rover was stopped where our vehicle is now and," he pointed to a ridge some fifty metres from the road, "that was the firing point—we think five men and an RPD machine gun; we recovered the spent cases."

"Can we go and take a look?" asked Iffor. The African nodded and cocked his weapon. Iffor did the same; the dead ground on the other side of the ridge could hold some unpleasant surprises. On reaching the ridge and the firing point, Iffor could not conceal his amazement and disbelief. "Are you sure this is the spot?" he asked.

"This is where we found the empty cartridge cases, and look, you can see where the legs of the machine-gun marked the ground." Elias pointed to the ground.

Iffor surveyed the area and looked to the African for an answer. "But there is no cover, no lying up point, no secured escape route; they must have got here very shortly before Ian; it was mid-afternoon, they couldn't afford to be seen and they couldn't just vanish after the ambush."

"But they did," said Elias, "they did. Come, it's time to go."

They drove slowly into the farm and stopped outside the farmhouse where the family were gathered. Iffor got out of the vehicle, suddenly lost for words and wondering how to introduce himself, until help, in the form of Helen, arrived; she dashed from the group and flung her arms around his neck. "Iffor, oh Iffor, I'm so glad to see you." She hung on to him for a few moments, quietly sobbing into his chest, then, grabbing his arm, said, "Come and meet the family," and with a wave of her arm, rattled out their names: "Meet Ed, wife Joy, daughter Verity; and this young man," she said putting her arm around the boy's shoulder, "is my pride and joy, Jamie junior," adding with a smile, "Your godson, in case you'd forgotten." Iffor looked down at Jamie's son, longing to hug him, but since he was eleven or twelve, offered a hand instead.

Elias joined them. "We've unloaded the coffin," he said. As he spoke, six farm hands were placing the coffin onto trestles on the veranda. Iffor guessed that the six labourers were probably the pallbearers; the farm, after all, was a family, providing homes, school and clinic for the workers, so the workers would want to be involved in the proceedings.

The Constable took Ed to one side; there were forms to be filled in and signed. Helen took Iffor's arm. "Let me show you where Jamie is," she said. "You can leave your rifle here." She nodded at a table which held the family's weapons: Ed's FN; Joy's Sten Gun and Verity's Weatherby, weapons that had to be within easy reach at all times. Iffor went through his 'make-safe' drills: magazine off; working parts to the rear ejecting the live round from the chamber; looking inside at chamber and breech; working parts forward; point weapon into the air; squeeze trigger, safety catch on and replace magazine.

She led him to some high ground about seventy metres behind the Dix's bungalow, the family plot. She held on to his arm with both hands. "How's that for a view?" she said. The ground fell away into a deep valley with the Lamumbwa River snaking and winding through its centre. The late afternoon mist swirling among the m'pani trees gently dimmed the setting sun. "It's so beautiful," she said, but Iffor could only think, what a great position for a fire section of an RPD and RPG in the event of a terrorist attack.

They stood looking down at the gravestone; the name stood out: Jamie Dix M.M. "I asked him once how he won his M.M.," she said. "He told me that some idiot had got himself into a bit of trouble and he had got him out of it."

Iffor turned to face her. "In case you hadn't already guessed," he said, "that idiot was me; someday soon I'd like to tell you and the lad what happened." They turned again to face the gravestone, silent in their thoughts, Helen's on her life with Jamie, his on that time many years ago in Cyprus fighting Eoka... and the ambush. The terrorists had opened fire from prepared positions on the high ground looking down on the road

The concentrated fire disabled the Land Rover, killed the driver and a bullet smashed Iffor's femur. Jamie, realising that the only hope for them to survive was to get out of the killing ground, away from the Land Rover and into cover, fixed his bayonet on to his Sten and charged up the hill at the nearest enemy position occupied by three young Eoka terrorists. Firing short bursts from the hip as he ran, he killed one terrorist and forced the other two to take cover behind the stones of their position. Jumping into their position, he kicked one of them in the chest as he brought his rifle to bear and bayoneted the other; then, having an empty magazine, bayoneted the first one.

Pausing only to change magazines, he ran back to the Land Rover and, grabbing Iffor and the driver's magazines, dragged and carried Iffor to the terrorists' position. While Iffor swapped shots with those remaining, Jamie made up an improvised Thomas splint with the dead men's rifles for Iffor's leg, and together they held their enemy at bay, until help in the form of two ferrets from the Life Guards arrived to save the day.

The sound of a car engine backfiring and lacking an exhaust, brought the pair back from their thoughts. "That," said Helen, "is Father Sean arriving. He is going to conduct a simple graveside service at sunset." She went on, "You'll like Sean, he runs the monastery; it's a retreat for Catholic priests." They made their way back to the house. A black, battered V.W. with a church cross painted in white on both doors was standing parked next to the Rhino. A cleric, tall, muscular, wearing a short sleeved grey shirt and a dog-collar, walked purposely towards them. He spoke in a soft but distinct Southern Irish accent.

"Helen, please accept my profound condolences." He hugged her, touched the young lad's head, and turning to Iffor said, "You'll be Iffor, I've heard all about you." The two men shook hands; then the priest said, "Do you know, I feel I've known you for many years even though we've never met." Words that would come back to haunt Iffor.

At sunset the cortege, led by the priest with the farm labourers carrying the coffin, made its way to the prepared grave where Ian and his beloved daughter were finally laid to rest.

Joy had laid out a buffet on the veranda; it was far too nice an evening to eat indoors. Elias had excused himself and gone off to visit friends within the farm compound, with a promise to return before everyone had turned in for the night.

Leaving Helen in deep conversation with Joy, Verity and the priest, Iffor was able to take Ed to one side for a chat. They moved to the table where the weapons were.

A cold box packed with Castle beer appeared, courtesy of the Dix's houseboy, followed by two chairs. Like most African domestic staff, he had the ability to read minds. They sat, and Ed poured the beers; the two men touched glasses without a word. Ed broke the silence. "Not quite the reunion you expected."

Iffor shrugged his shoulders. "I'm so very glad to be here. I think Jamie would have wanted me here at this time. I just wish there was more that I could do."

Ed leaned forward and touched Iffor's arm. "Just being here has meant a lot to Helen and the boy." Then, changing the subject he asked, "Has anybody told you any details of the attack on Jamie's farm?"

Before Iffor could answer, Elias joined them. "Elias my friend, come join us, have a beer," and turning to Iffor said, "Elias and I are old friends. His brother is my dairy manager."

The African remained standing. "I think sir it would be best if I patrol the area; that is my job." Then he turned and walked into the darkness.

Ed watched him go and muttered softly, "With men like him in this country we've half a chance." He continued: "They hit the farm late afternoon." He paused and knocked off the top of two more beers "They were-mob handed, ten or twelve of them with at least one RPG; Jamie managed to get Helen and the boy into the priest hole he had built in the kitchen. The walls were lined with steel plates; one of them opened into a tunnel which Helen was able to lock behind her. The tunnel led to a chamber in the orchard where Helen stayed until the security forces arrived." Ed went on, "It would appear that although badly wounded, Jamie managed to get into the priest hole himself. In the confusion and darkness the terrorists threw a couple of grenades in after him and probably thought they had killed Helen and the boy—that's why they didn't go looking for her." They were interrupted by the priest and the constable, Abrahams to tell them he would be sleeping in the Rhino, the priest to bid them goodnight.

"I'll be in town tomorrow afternoon, probably in Boons, if you fancy a beer or two." The priest extended his hand to Ed and Iffor.

"It would be churlish of me to refuse," smiled Iffor. He was beginning to warm to Sean.

In spite of Ed's protests, Iffor refused a bed, preferring to sleep in his sleeping bag on the veranda. Dawn found him awake and very much alert, and like all good soldiers, 'standing to' as the sun rose.

Arriving back in Kensington at midday, Iffor bade farewell to the Constable, lodged his weapons with Agnes, and made his way back to the hotel for a shower and change of clothes, ready for his meeting with Father Sean.

He found Sean in deep, meaningful conversation with Davy Jones and the ape, and judging by the empty bottles and eggshells on the table, had, to coin a phrase, 'had a couple'. Collecting three beers and an egg from the bar, Iffor joined them. "Have you two decided how to save the world, or do you want my help?" he said, sitting down next to the ape, who gratefully accepted the egg. As if in gratitude, the ape leaned to one side and farted.

One of the drinkers on the next table turned and pointed an accusing finger, "You bastard Davy, you can't blame that one on the priest! That was definitely the chimp."

Iffor fancied he saw a plume of green haze appearing from the ape's behind; it seemed to remind him of gas attacks in the First World War, a thought confirmed by the acrid smell of sulphur and chlorine and partly digested pickled eggs.

Billy shouted from across the bar: "That's it Davy; in future, only one egg each visit." If Davy looked glum, the ape looked positively mortified.

Iffor burst out laughing. Davy said, "I don't see what's so funny, Cheetah's quite upset."

"What is so funny," Iffor said leaning towards Davy, "is that here I am drinking with a Catholic priest, Davy Jones and an evil-smelling Orang-Utan called Cheetah."

"Ah," said Sean, "but this," he waved a finger, "but this, my boy, is Africa."

PART FOUR

The smile reveals the culprit.

IFFOR COLLECTED TWO CASTLES and joined Pete who was sitting alone. It was early evening and the Moth club was quiet, just how Iffor liked it. His friend was looking thoughtfully into an empty glass; Iffor took the glass from his hand, filled it and placed it in front of Pete. He poured his own beer and enjoyed a few moments of silence before Pete lifted his glass and said, "Cheers."

"Still in uniform I see; bad day at the office?" Iffor sensed his friend wanted to share a problem.

"Had some bad news to deliver; some of our local lads on call-up were involved in a fire-fight and we had casualties. I had to break the news to the families."

"How bad?" Iffor asked.

"One dead and two wounded, but the wounded should recover and with luck we'll fly them back to Kensington in a few days. The army Beaver will fly them down, or we'll send the Islander to collect them."

Anxious to change the subject, Iffor said, "I used to jump from an Islander in the British Army; I didn't know there were any in Rhodesia."

"There are one or two." Pete looked happier now. He went on: "Our Islander belongs to the mine. They keep it on the airfield with the crew and fitters; they are quite happy for the military to call on it if required. Before the war took our youngsters away we had a thriving parachute club; we still have, it's just that no-one uses it anymore."

"Pity, it would have been nice to jump again for old times' sake." Iffor drank the last of his beer.

24

"You still can if you want to; your drinking mate runs the club."

"My drinking mate?" Iffor looked puzzled.

"Davy Jones; he looks after the club and all the equipment, has done for years."

"But he was Air Force," said Iffor, wondering when Pete was going to get the beers in.

"Survival equipment was his trade. He maintains and repairs the parachutes and teaches parachute packing." As he spoke, Pete was on his feet, heading for the bar to collect two more beers. When he returned to the table, Iffor took up the conversation. "Thanks for the lift out to Dix's farm."

It was Pete's turn to pour the drinks. "On the contrary, you did me a favour; it's my policy not to send my constables out into the country alone." Then he went on, "I imagine you'll be wanting to stay a few days at the farm."

"Ed suggested that, and I will probably take up his offer, but I'm expecting a letter from Salisbury which might well change my plans. By the way, I asked for the letter to be sent to the police station, since I wasn't sure where I'd be staying."

Pete leaned forward in his chair. "I'm intrigued. Tell me more; you might just as well since I'm going to read it anyway."

"I've applied to join the Rhodesian Army."

"Now that is good news, tell me more."

"Not much to tell; they've got my discharge papers from the Zambian Army, but I imagine they might be having problems getting information about me from the British Army under the circumstances. Salisbury are probably suspicious about my leaving before my time was up."

"Well, come on, tell me why did you leave?" Pete adopted the pose of a terrier.

"It's no big deal," began Iffor.

Mad Harry joined them with three beers and a glass in his hands. "Ah, Harry," said Pete, "You're just in time for another chapter of Iffor's life story, he's just got to the 'It's no big deal' bit."

"That sounds familiar," said Evil Jesus, joining them with four beers and a glass for himself. "Carry on, I'm all ears."

"Like I said," Iffor continued, "It's no big deal; Jamie Dix and I were involved in an incident with the IRA early on in the troubles." He emptied his glass trying to catch up on the beers stacked up on the table.

"Go on," said Harry.

"Well, the IRA had developed a new way to amuse themselves; they started hi-jacking the workmen's buses, the single-deck type, shooting anyone they didn't like; then they would set fire to it at a busy road junction. Needless to say, this upset the RUC and the army, and they decided on countermeasures, which involved putting a team of two soldiers disguised as workmen on selected routes. Since young twenty-year olds would be too obvious, older, more mature soldiers were tasked with the job. Hence, Jamie and I found ourselves dressed as farm labourers on the workman special from Lisburn to Downpatrick or some such place."

Harry stopped Iffor there and dispatched Evil to the bar on an errand of mercy. Iffor went on: "Our plan was simple; we took it in turns, one to sit behind the driver, ready to zap anyone trying to stop the bus, the other to sit opposite the door to discourage terrorists from boarding the bus, or to be more specific, to kill them.

"On the day in question, I was up front behind the driver and Jamie was opposite the door; we each had a Browning Hi-Power. We had just pulled away from a bus-stop, when a man wearing a balaclava and carrying an M16 stepped in front of us and pointed his rifle at us. I shouted, 'Contact Jamie,' pushed the driver's head to one side and fired through the windscreen, dropping the terrorist before he had a chance to fire his weapon. I heard Jamie open fire and turned to support him, but he had already killed the two terrorists who had tried to board the bus; one had a pistol and the other a Thompson.

"We whistled up the RUC and RMP to tidy things up and returned to base to be debriefed. We each got a pat on the head from our OC, and that night in the mess the sergeant-major gave us both a tube of smarties and we thought that was the end of the matter. However, it would appear that the three men we shot were all members of the same family, two brothers and a cousin, and that family were, understandably, a little more than upset; so much so that the IRA swore revenge.

"Jamie and I were not concerned until the British press published our names, and a few days later our photos." Iffor paused and took a drink. He looked across at Pete, who nodded; having been a soldier he understood the situation. Iffor went on: "This didn't bother me because my wife, sensible girl, had long since left me, but Jamie had a wife and child, and they had to be protected. Anyway, the army in its wisdom decided to send us both back to mainland UK. We swapped our red berets for green berets. I went back to Greenjackets and was posted to a TA company at Duke of York's Chelsea, while Jamie re-badged to Intelligence Corps and went to Beaconsfield to learn to speak Chinese."

"Clever bastard," said Evil.

"Not really," said Iffor. "He just wanted to be able to show off when we went to the chinkie." He didn't mention, however, how much he admired his friend for taking on such a difficult task. He finished his beer, relieved that he had caught up with the others, and walked to the bar for more beers aware that they, hanging on his every word, were anxious to hear the end of the story. Having sat down and poured his beer, Iffor went on, "We kept in touch; he came over to the mess at Duke of York's, and I spent the odd weekend at Beaconsfield staying with him and Helen. The army didn't want us to be seen together in local pubs; that would pose too much of a risk."

Pete nodded. He had experience himself of the IRA and he knew just how long their arm could be. "So, just how did you come to be in Africa?" he asked.

"Jamie phoned me at work one day and said he had some news for me and would I care to meet him at the Lifeguards' mess at Combermere Barracks where we both had friends from our Cyprus days, and somehow I guessed that this visit was to say goodbye. It was quite a coincidence, since I had received a letter that day from my Regimental Colonel who now worked at the Crown Agents, asking if I was interested in a contract with the then Northern Rhodesian, soon to become Zambian army. Jamie's news, sad, but not unexpected, was that his father had died, and the family were assuming he would take over the farm at New Epsom. Since Jamie had decided that 'duty called' and he had to return to Rhodesia, my decision was made for me. We persuaded the army to release us before our twenty-two were up, which was not difficult under the circumstances, came to an agreement over our pensions and within a month we were both in Africa. Like I said, no big deal."

They drank and talked well into the night, discussing the escalating war and the town's latest casualties. At long last, and to Iffor's relief, Pete announced, "Time for bed," tried to stand; then abandoned all hope of standing and walking on his own, relying instead on Mad Harry to get him to his bed, which, Iffor was informed, was a contingency bunk in the club storeroom. As Pete lurched onto his feet, he pointed at Iffor, "I've got a little job for you in the morning; my office nine sharp!"

"Dress?" enquired Iffor.

"As before; you know where you're going."

In spite of the previous evening's hard drinking, Pete appeared 'bright-eyed and bushy-tailed', which was more than could be said for Iffor, and immediately got down to the briefing. Pointing with his swagger stick at the map on the wall, he said:

"GROUND: Lamumbwa farm and area;

"SITUATION: Ed Dix considers it is not safe for his dairy manager and family to remain where they are currently living and wants to bring them into the farm;

"MISSION: To transfer Mr Abrahams and his family to Lamumbwa farm compound;

"EXECUTION: Constable Abrahams and Mr Meredith will drive to Lamumbwa farm in the Land Rover, where they will meet up with Mr Dix, who will have a Land Rover and trailer. The party under command of Mr Dix," Pete paused, and continued, "It is his property after all, will then proceed to Mr Abrahams' kraal where, we hope, Constable Elias will be able to persuade his brother to see sense and move into the farm.

"SERVICE AND SUPPORT: I'm afraid you're on your own until you meet up with Dix. Constable, have you drawn first line ammunition?"

"Yes sir," the Constable answered, "five thirty-round mags."

"Iffor?"

"Five thirty-round magazines plus my pistol mags."

"Questions?"

None were necessary; the briefing had been thorough.

As they walked to the station yard and the Land Rover, Iffor said, "You make this sound like a military operation."

Pete laughed, "Believe me, getting Abrahams and his family to move into the farm will be one of the most difficult ops you've been on."

A couple of hours later they drove into Lamumbwa farm where Ed Dix was waiting. He opened a cold bag and offered Iffor a chilled Lion lager, which was gratefully accepted. Then Ed turned to the Constable, who answered even before Ed could invite him to have a beer, "Thank you sir, but I am on duty."

Iffor savoured his beer, wondering if he would be offered another before they moved off. "I can understand why we are bringing this chap Abrahams back to the farm," he said, "but why was he living so far away in the first place?"

"Because," said Ed, zipping up the cold bag, "that's where the cattle are." He explained further, "The cattle are on lush ground close to the river, only a dozen or so animals. Abrahams milks the cattle in the evening, then the following morning, when he and his family are collected and brought into the farm to work, he brings the milk with him in churns; then he and his wife distribute the milk in smaller containers to our African families. His kids go to the farm school while mum and dad are working; everyone's happy."

They drove in convoy the three miles to the Abrahams' kraal, Iffor with the constable, neither of them speaking, each one anxiously watching the surrounding countryside. They stopped a hundred or so metres from the kraal. Ed got out of his Rover and walked back to them, anxious and worried. "If you'll excuse the cliché," he said, "I don't like it, it's too quiet. Abrahams knew we were coming and normally the kids would be running up to meet us."

The soldier in Iffor came to the fore. "Quick fire plan," he said to the other two. "Elias, you go down to the kraal, stop about twenty metres short and call to your brother; Ed and I will take cover up here and form a fire section to cover you. If your brother doesn't answer and you think it is safe, call us down and we can look into the huts together."

The Constable nodded, cocked his Stirling and started to walk cautiously towards the huts. Ed and Iffor took up firing positions among the rocks. As Abrahams approached the family home he started calling to his brother, but instead of waiting for the others to join him, walked into the hut. As Iffor and Ed started down to join him they heard a wail of anguish. Elias came to the door and held on to the frame as if for support. They knew what they would find before they looked inside, but the scene waiting for them still came as a massive shock, even for the battle-hardened soldier that Iffor was.

On the floor, stretched out on their backs, were the bodies of Abrahams, his wife and two young sons, all bayoneted and all showing the signatures of their killers. The husband and the two boys had the lips cut away from their mouths leaving all three corpses grinning as if happy to see their guests. The smiles revealed the culprits; this was the calling card of the 'Comrades', the brothers from the bush, the saviours of Rhodesia. The mother had both her breasts cut away, probably before being bayoneted.

Ed and Iffor stood outside the hut, unable to speak, unable to talk, stunned and shocked by what they had witnessed; only the policeman, forever 'on duty', seemed to know what to do. Taking his notebook from his tunic pocket, he went back into the hut to start taking his notes, only to reappear moments later. He stood staring at the other two men, obviously trying desperately to compose himself, and looking directly at Ed said, "She's in there, under the bedclothes; it's Miss Susie—they've killed her as well." Susie! Ian's missing wife from the ambush.

While Ed went into the hut, Iffor's imagination ran riot. The terrorists, having kidnapped her, had kept her prisoner, a plaything, subjecting her to horrors and humiliation beyond belief, before bringing her to Abrahams' kraal, where she might have thought she was being released, only to be killed and in all probability having watched the family being tortured and bayoneted before her turn came.

Ed went back to his Rover to radio for help, either from New Epsom or Kensington. Iffor watched as Elias with shaking hand and tears gently running down his face, started to write in his notebook, and he considered taking a defensive position, but realised the terrorists wouldn't be back—he couldn't be that lucky.

Ed returned. "I managed to raise New Epsom. They've got a Patu team on standby—they should be here within the hour."

He took Elias's arm. "You know, we really should move the bodies back to the farm. We've got a cold-room in the dairy. It's refrigerated. We can keep them there until we can arrange for burial."

Elias took out his notebook again. "I will draw a sketch of their positions," he said. "Then you have my authority to move them."

Wrapping the bodies in blankets, they gently loaded them into the Rover trailer. As they finished their sad task a helicopter clattered out of the sky and unloaded the Police Anti-Terrorist Unit, the Patu, reservist police made up of farmers and game-hunters, people who knew the bush, people who could track and more importantly, people who could fight.

Their commander spoke to Ed. All he wanted were the basic details, then he inspected the bodies. "Who's the white girl?" he said abruptly. Then he softened and gently covered her face, as Ed said, "My sister-in-law, the girl kidnapped at the ambush on the Lamumbwa road."

Ed and Iffor returned to the farm with the bodies, leaving Elias to guard the crime scene until Pete could get out to start his investigation, which could only come to one conclusion—murder by terrorists.

Meanwhile the Patu team began the task of trying to pick up the spoor before darkness came, a task that would once again end in failure.

Morning came slowly for Iffor. He had slept fitfully through the night on the veranda, wide awake at the slightest sound, grateful for the sunrise. Ed came to him with two cups of strong tea laced with Cape Spirit. They stood silently together, sipping the hot liquid and savouring the beauty of the African sunrise. Ed broke the silence: "A beautiful sad, sad day; how can such a beautiful country create such havoc for its people?"

Iffor touched his mug to Ed's. "Amen to that," he said, as if making a toast. Then abruptly changing the mood, said, "If you don't mind, I'll take you up on your offer of a bed for a few nights."

Ed walked to one of two wicker-chairs and sat down; he patted the chair next to him and Iffor joined him. "I know you mean well," he said, "but you are going to be much more use to us in the army; besides, Guard Force, the village and farm protection people are posting a two-man team to me; they should be here later today."

Iffor marvelled over the speed at which the information about him applying to join the army had reached Ed.

Ed stood up. "Sounds as if Elias is coming."

Iffor strained his ears, hearing nothing. "If you say so," he smiled, and finishing his tea went to the bathroom. Elias would be clean-shaven, so must he. Having completed his ablutions, he joined Ed and the Constable on the veranda. To his surprise, Elias had accepted a cup of laced tea, grateful for the hot liquid coursing through his body. His debrief was short and expected:

The Patu team, having returned to the kraal before darkness and given their report to Constable Abrahams, had gone back in the helicopter to New Epsom. The terrs had taken Abrahams' cattle with them to destroy their spoor and confuse the trackers, and then, having reached the river, slaughtered the cattle. An army tracker team and a New Epsom police sergeant arrived at first light to continue the search and investigation. Elias had been advised that because of an incident at Kensington, Inspector Saxon and his small team had their hands full, so New Epsom took on the investigation. Elias hadn't been told what the incident was, but it could only mean bad news, and in spite of a tempting offer by Ed's wife of breakfast, Iffor and the Constable climbed into the Police Rover, anxious to get back to Kensington as quickly as possible.

The journey along the Lamumbwa road was in complete silence, neither of them knowing quite what to say. The signpost, 'Great North Road one mile', brought some relief; only an hour or so to Kensington; they might even meet up with a protected convoy to ensure their safety. Elias began to slow the vehicle as the junction approached. Iffor, for want of something sensible to say, said, "You'll be able to phone your parents on the police network when we reach the station," and looked to Elias for an answer, but the Constable was already unconscious from the blast that had shattered his legs and sent the front wheel of the Rover bounding along the road on its own.

MINE! Iffor recognised the smell of high explosives before the concussion hit him, before the explosion sent shards of glass from the windscreen into his face and chest and before the Rover lifted into the air then lazily settled on to its side amid a cloud of dust. Then came the aftermath—the complete silence.

The vehicle on its side, Iffor was held in his seat by the full harness, obligatory in all police and military vehicles; Elias was underneath him, still, and bloodied. Iffor allowed himself time to think, forcing himself to think. If he released his harness he would fall on top of Elias, probably causing more damage. He needed help. He forced himself to wait for a few minutes trying to formulate a plan, needed to think, he needed... The door which was now above him opened and a distinctly Australian voice said, "G'day sport, you look like you could do with a hand."

Iffor looked up, and wiping the blood from his eyes, saw a bronzed face with a digger hat firmly wedged on his head. Through the ringing in his ears, Iffor heard himself say, "Where the hell did you spring from?"

"Heaven! I'm your guardian angel, name of Digby, but everyone calls me Digger; now let's get you out of there, then we can get to your driver."

Digby came in through the rear of the Rover and supported Iffor while he released himself. Then they pulled Elias from the still smoking wreck. It was only when they were clear of the vehicle that Iffor saw the crop-spraying aircraft, propeller idling.

"We need to get the Constable to hospital, can you help?"

Iffor found himself looking at an aircraft with only one seat in a tiny cockpit and his hopes sank. To his relief, Digby said, "No wucking furries mate, all crop sprayers are modified for casevac, but I can only carry one."

While Digby collected the collapsible stretcher from the aircraft, Iffor examined Elias. He was still unconscious, which was just as well since both his legs from beneath the knee were missing; he wasn't bleeding, his blood pressure was already too low, so there was little Iffor could do for him. Digby came back with the stretcher and between them they loaded the constable into the rear of the modified cockpit and strapped him in. As Digby climbed into the aircraft he shouted back to Iffor, "I'll tell someone where you are", then turning the aircraft around, took off, turning as he gained height for Kensington.

PART FIVE

The first and foremost requirement of any fighting force is discipline.

IFFOR **WATCHED AS THE AIRCRAFT** gained height and became a speck in the clear blue sky. The feeling of guilt and remorse was beginning to overwhelm him; he felt he was responsible for this tragedy. Instead of sitting in the Rover wallowing in self-pity over the deaths at Abrahams' kraal, he should have been reading the road ahead, looking for evidence of mine-laying. He was a soldier, a former sapper, for Christ's sake, trained to sniff out mines. He drove all these thoughts from his mind, to what to do; it wasn't unheard of for terrorists, on hearing the blast, to return to the site to ransack the vehicle and finish off any survivors.

He collected his Carbine and the Constable's Stirling from the wreck; then, taking the magazine off his weapon, pulled the working parts to the rear, blowing and wiping the dust from the bolt. Satisfied that it was still functioning, he replaced the magazine and cocked the weapon, then did the same with the policeman's weapon.

Now he looked around for a defensive position, somewhere to make his stand if he had to. The Land Rover was no good, it was too big a target; all the terrorists had to do was direct their fire at the vehicle and sooner or later they would hit him. The ground around him was featureless, but a storm drain on the side of the road would have to do. Using the Rover canopy, he rigged up overhead cover to keep the sun off, careful to ensure he had all round vision. Now he turned his attention to himself and his own wounds. The reaction of closing his eyes when the blast occurred had saved his eyes from damage, but his face was peppered with fragments of glass from the windscreen and the cut above his right eye would eventually need stitching. A shard of glass had penetrated his left breast leaving an inch or so protruding from the skin, enabling him to carefully remove it. Making use of the first aid kit from the Rover, he applied a shell dressing to the wound over his eye and taped a smaller dressing over the wound on his chest.

Satisfied he had done all that he could do, he settled himself into his defensive position to wait. He knew it would take at least two hours before anyone would come for him. To take his mind from that awful feeling that he was responsible for the whole episode of the mine, Iffor allowed his thoughts to drift back to his arrival in Kensington and all the friends he had made and the many characters he'd met.

As he thought about Mad Harry and Evil Jesus and the rest of Blue Watch, an idea began to form in his mind, and the more he thought about it over the next couple of hours, the more he began to expound on it.

Movement on the road from Kensington brought him from his thoughts, and a few minutes later the police Rhino drew up and out jumped Sergeant Timothy Banda, complete with Greener gun. He was followed by two constables armed with G3's.

He was brief and to the point: "I've been ordered to bring you back to Kensington." Then, as an afterthought, said, "Safely."

Iffor climbed into the Rhino beside the Sergeant leaving the two constables to guard the Rover until it could be recovered. As they drove away, he watched them settling into his former 'fort'; they probably had a long night ahead of them.

If Iffor thought he would be taken straight to the hospital to have his wounds dressed, he was sadly mistaken. The Sergeant drove him to the police station and Pete's office. As if compensating for not being taken to the hospital, Pete offered him a chair and called to Agnes for some tea. On Pete's desk was the throwaway launcher of an M66 rocket. "That looks ominous," Iffor exclaimed, "you don't see many of those in this part of the world."

Pete got straight to the point. "I've heard about the killings at the Abrahams' kraal, but I'm short on detail. You can fill me in."

Iffor just said, "How's Elias?"

Pete looked a little embarrassed, ashamed. "Died in hospital," he said. "Apart from the legs, brain injury."

Iffor gave Pete a full and complete soldier's debrief of the past twenty-four hours. As Agnes poured him his third cup of tea, he added, "It was all my fault, Pete, I should have been reading the road, I should have seen the signs, they were there."

Pete got up from his desk and walked round it to his friend, placing his hand gently on Iffor's shoulder. "If anyone is to blame, it's me. If I had sent you out in the Rhino you would both be sitting here now, and besides, these people are experts at laying mines; you wouldn't have known it was there."

Picking up the M66 launcher, Pete said, "We've had another disaster, this time closer to home. The army Beaver bringing our two casualties back from New Epsom was hit by a rocket as it came in to land yesterday evening; all on board were killed. We found this launcher at the firing point."

Iffor shook his head in disbelief, "How in hell's name did the terrs get hold of one of those?"

"The church," said Pete, "the bloody South African church; they send crates of so called medical supplies to the various terrorists group on humanitarian grounds. This," he said, holding up the launcher, "was probably listed as bandages."

Iffor was kept in hospital overnight. He had needed six stitches in the wound over his eye, and two nurses had spent over an hour picking bits of glass out of his face and chest. The following morning the wonderful Mrs Patel arrived with clean clothes and a car to take him back to his hotel. This time he welcomed the breakfast she prepared for him, and even listened when she insisted he spent the rest of the day lazing in the garden.

Pete arrived late afternoon—in time for tea. Mrs Patel showed him into the garden where Iffor was still taking advantage of his enforced rest period. "Remember!" she wagged her finger at him, "No more than half an hour."

Pete drew up a chair while Iffor poured the tea. "I just thought I'd pop in and see how you are and bring you up to date."

"When's the funeral? I'd like to attend." Iffor put his hand to the dressing above his eye as if to establish a right to attend.

"That will be difficult; in fact, you can't," Pete adopted his policeman's pose. "Mr and Mrs Abrahams will be here tomorrow midday. They will view the body, then with an escort of my chaps they will take the coffin to Lamumbwa farm, have the funeral and bury him with his brother and family in the African cemetery Mr Dix has on the farm. Agnes will represent the police, only close friends and relatives allowed."

Pete went on, "I'll meet them from the bus and take them to Finch's undertakers to view the body. It's just a shame that old Elias didn't achieve his ambition."

"Which was?" Iffor interrupted.

"He wanted his mum and dad to see him in his uniform, wearing a medal."

"And he hasn't got a medal," Iffor said.

"No, the GSM is awarded to the army and air force, Guard Force and internal affairs force after twenty-one days in an operational area, but as yet, not to the police."

Mrs Patel appeared. "Time's up, Inspector and before you ask, no, he's not coming out to play tonight, he's having dinner with my family."

This was news to Iffor, but he gratefully accepted. As Pete got up to leave, Iffor said, "I need to speak to you—can you spare me an hour or so tomorrow morning?"

"Nine okay with you?" Pete asked.

"Make it half past," said Iffor. "I've got a little task to perform first."

Iffor's first mistake was waking up; the second was trying to clean his teeth.

After that, it was all downhill. No matter how hard he tried to put all thought of the previous evening's dinner, which had turned out to be a banquet comprising dishes from just about every region in India, from his mind, constant belching reminded him of his eagerness to try every dish Mrs Patel had put in front of him. To make the festivities go with a swing, Mrs Patel had invited her brother Imran, the Indian Iffor had spoken to when he first arrived. He came bearing gifts, two cases of beer, the name of which should have given Iffor fair warning, 'KRAIT'—Indian beer.

Iffor rummaged through his Burgan, found what he was looking for and with the cunning of a desperately wounded animal crept down the stairs and out into the street before Mrs Patel could force breakfast on to him. It had just turned nine and Iffor reasoned the undertaker would be open for business. Mr Finch was at the back of the shop when Iffor entered, but came to greet him, wiping his hands on his white apron. He had a pleasant smile and a firm, "Good Morning."

Iffor smiled and nodded. He liked this man. He came straight to the point, "Constable Abrahams, I believe you are preparing him for his funeral, I'd like you to do something for me."

Finch said, "Please will get you most things."

"Sorry," Iffor tried to look suitably embarrassed, "I've got a hangover to beat all hangovers and being blown up on a mine yesterday didn't help."

Finch said quietly, "It didn't do Elias much good either."

Iffor produced a small box from his pocket. "I'd like you to pin this medal on Constable Abrahams' tunic for me please, on his left breast."

"I know where it goes," said Finch, "Why?"

Iffor explained: "His main ambition in life was for his parents to see him in uniform wearing a medal. Unfortunately, the government haven't yet got around to giving the police the General Service Medal, so I'm giving him mine. It's the Northern Ireland medal but I don't think his parents will notice."

Finch took the medal from its case, unfurled the ribbon and fingered the oak leaf. "You got a mention?"

"Yes, first in the Naafi queue three days running."

Finch went on, "His parents will be here around midday to view the body. It is the custom that the coffin is then sealed; you won't be able to get your medal back."

Iffor responded, "I realise that, just do it for me please."

Finch said, "Why not do it yourself?" and led the way to the chapel. Iffor followed.

He arrived nine-thirty sharp at the police station where Agnes showed him into the Inspector's office. He flopped into a chair, his legs unable to support him any longer. "What in hell's name has happened to you? You look bloody awful." Pete looked quite concerned. "Can I get you anything?"

"Snake bite serum might help."

Pete now looked very concerned. "Don't tell me you've been drinking Krait with the Patels. Didn't anyone tell you they replace the alcohol with pure venom?"

A pot of Agnes's tea cleared Iffor's brain; time to get down to business.

Looking directly at the Inspector, Iffor said, "The terrorists are running rings around us, we are on a hiding to nothing, they are winning. We need to turn this situation to our advantage."

"I agree," said the Inspector, "but just how are 'we' going to do it? We've no army here—they are all up on the border trying to keep the terrorists out."

Iffor spoke with passion and determination. "We need to show resistance; we need to make the terrs more cautious when they are planning their attacks; we need to upset their little applecart; we need a small, well trained militia."

"And just where are 'we' going to get this force?" Pete queried. "All our young bucks are in the army up north on the border."

"What's the basic requirement of any fighting force?" Iffor answered his own question: "Discipline, and apart from your boys, what other force is trained and disciplined?"

Pete looked aghast. "Not Blue Watch! You can't mean Blue Watch. There's only eight of them and all over military age."

"The very same," said Iffor. "They are trained to be disciplined and to look after one another. Teaching them basic battle skills will be easy and can be concentrated into a short period of time, which is just as well since time is something we ain't got a lot of. If we can mount mobile vehicle check points, standing patrols and covert ops, it will give the farmers more security and confidence and who knows, we might even get lucky and meet up with this bunch."

Pete was silent for a few moments, then said, "What problems do we have to overcome to get this incredibly stupid idea of your up and running?"

Iffor sat back in his chair; he had sold the idea to Pete; they were now into the planning stage.

"Only two major problems; command structure, weapons and equipment."

Pete looked like the cat that had just got the cream. "I can resolve both those problems for you, my friend." He went on, "Your letter from army arrived today, you've been granted a short service commission, rank of lieutenant in the fourth Rhodesian Rifles, our local TA Battalion. You take over as training officer. Since you are now the military authority in Kensington, everyone else being away, as part of our emergency regulations, you can press into service or call up any one you like except African Rhodesians—they are exempt call-up and national service.

"And as for weapons and equipment, you have a drill hall here full of the stuff; get yourself down to the drill hall and introduce yourself to the CQMS. He's a good man."

Pete stood and extended his hand. "Congratulations, and welcome to the team. I know your Colonel well. I'll phone him and tell what you're up to. Questions?"

"Just one, where do I find the drill hall?"

Pete put his arm around his friend's shoulder, leading him to the door. "You can't miss it—it's behind this building, next to the fire station."

Iffor went back to the privacy of the hotel garden to read his letter from army.

He didn't mind that Pete had already read it; that's what friends do, he told himself.

The letter contained conditions of service, a copy of the posting order to 4 RR and an identity card for him to sign and insert a photo of himself. Time was of the essence; he knew the battalion would soon be rotated back to Kensington, and that would mean the army having priority on him. He had to put his plans for Blue Watch into operation as soon as possible. He formulated his plan for the day: first, get down to the drill hall, introduce himself to the Colour Sergeant and get himself kitted out; second, get Blue Watch together and tell them of his plans.

Having missed breakfast, Iffor gratefully accepted a sandwich and tea from Mrs Patel. He toyed with the idea of another Krait, but thought that might be pushing his luck a bit far.

Arriving at the drill hall about midday, Iffor pressed the bell-button marked 'caretaker' and stood back, admiring the double oak doors and the inscription in the concrete arch above the doors: NATEL MOUNTED RIFLES 1878. From the depths of the drill hall he heard, "Coming," and a few moments later the door opened and introduced Iffor to Colour Sergeant Bob Peterson. Iffor clumsily produced his identity card: "Sorry about the photo, I'm Meredith, the new boy."

"Heard you were coming, sir." He extended his hand: "Bob Peterson, I'm i/c rear party, comprising myself and five sick, lame and lazy riflemen. If you don't mind me saying so sir, you look bloody awful. We heard about the mine and the copper. I imagine you want to get kitted out and have a look around the place."

"If you're not too busy," Iffor replied.

The Colour Sergeant carefully locked the front door and led the way into the drill hall. Inside the main hall was a fortified sanger, the point of entry control. He followed the Colour to the QM stores, typical of every other QM store that Iffor had been in.

A counter, which none dared to venture behind except for the Colour-Sergeant, separated Iffor from row upon row of shelves and compartments and the overwhelming smell of mothballs. He stood one side of the counter, the Colour Sergeant the other. As he packed items of kit into a holdall, carefully ticking off each item on his kit list, he said, "You'll be replacing Captain Graham as training officer."

"Captain Graham?" Iffor queried.

"Yes, he was one of the two wounded being casevact back to Kensington; the terrs stuffed a 66 mil rocket into their Beaver."

"I heard, bad news."

"I expect you'll be joining the Battalion at new Epsom," he said as he handed Iffor a green beret, "Try that on for size."

"Not just yet awhile," said Iffor, "I've some unfinished business with some terrorists who tried to blow my arse off with a mine and have killed some very good friends of mine."

"Sounds interesting." The Colour pushed the kit list and a pen in front of Iffor, "Sign for your kit, I'll put the kettle on and we'll have a brew while you reveal all."

As Iffor signed for his kit, the Colour went to a drawer marked 'Badges etc', and took out the rifles' cap badge, crossed spears mounted on a buffalo-hide shield.

"While you're there, Colour, any chance of some para wings?"

Bob rummaged around and came back to the counter with badge and three sets of wings. "You're in luck sir, the Colonel is ex-para so we keep the wings in stock for him."

Iffor felt quite privileged. He was sitting in the Colour's small but comfortable office on the other side of the counter, drinking tea, compo tea; he recognised it instantly. Bob Peterson had listened intently to Iffor's plans. "I've been in this man's army, man and boy for sixteen years, and this has got to be the most ridiculous scheme I've ever heard; how can I help?"

Iffor had the Colour's undivided attention. "First tell me what the Battalion's orbat is."

"More tea?" Iffor shook his head. "Right, we have two rifle companies here plus Battalion HQ. Another two companies, B and C plus a tac HQ at New Epsom, then we have Support Company at Monza. Incidentally, Support is the first of our companies to be integrated with black Rhodesians, all volunteers; it's working well."

"And what's Support's role and Support's weapons?"

The Colour, pleased to be talking about military matters, went on, "They support the protected villages in the area; Guard Force are stretched very thin and Mwonza is a very hot area. The police station where Support is based is attacked so frequently that our squaddies are on Christian name terms with the terrorists. As for weapons, they have three-inch mortars and Vickers machine-guns."

"You're joking!" Iffor sat bolt upright, "Vickers? They went out after the Korean war!"

"Maybe," said the Colour, "but remember, we have an arms trade embargo against us; modern machine-guns, the general purpose and the MAG are few and far between, and since we have a considerable store of weapons left over from federal days such as the three-inch mortar and the Vickers, we use them."

They were interrupted by the phone ringing. The Colour answered listened and said, "He's here with me now sir," and handed the phone to Iffor. "It's the Colonel."

The message was concise, "Saxon's told me of your plans; you have my blessing, you can probably do more good down there than up here. Put the Colour back on."

The Colour listened for a while, making notes of the various tasks the Colonel wanted doing, then putting the phone down, smiled and said, "The boss says I'm to give you all possible assistance. Where do we start?" and sat back in his chair.

"First and foremost," said Iffor, "do I have an office?"

"Upstairs; I'll give you a key to your office and a key to the side door of the drill hall. You can come and go as you please."

"Accommodation?"

"For now, hotel; the army will pay. Where are you staying at present? I'll need your address."

"Premji's Hotel; Mrs Patel is looking after me."

"Premji's?" Bob looked concerned. "Whatever you do, don't let them give you any of their Krait beer; it's lethal."

"Too late," Iffor looked glum, "I've already been bitten."

He stood up. "You've work to do, Colour, so I'll get out of your hair. I'll formulate a training programme, bring in our new recruits to be kitted out, plus an introduction to the rifle and we'll start training first thing tomorrow morning. By the way, what transport can you let me have?"

The Colour shook his head. "None sir, it's all up with Battalion, our vehicle casualties are quite bad. However, Blue Watch have got an Austin Champ that pulls their tender, it's in good nick."

He shook hands with the Colour. "Thanks for your help; all I've got to do now is break my happy news to the innocents of Blue Watch and just hope they see the funny side."

PART SIX

Desperate times require desperate measures.

IFFOR MADE HIS WAY TO BOONS BAR hoping to find Mad Harry, and since he was feeling a little better, a cold Lion might not go amiss. Mad Harry was sitting with Evil Jesus, Davy Jones and the chimp, playing whisky poker for matchsticks. Iffor couldn't help but notice the chimp had the largest pile of matchsticks in front of him.

Iffor indicated four beers with his hand to Billy behind the bar, and sat down at Harry's table. Harry stared into his face. "God, but you look bloody awful!"

Evil nodded in agreement. "Shouldn't you be in hospital or a morgue?" he asked. "Have you seen the state of your face?"

Iffor remembered he hadn't seen his face that morning; it was too painful for him to shave and the Krait had left him with only partial vision.

"Look at yourself." Harry nodded at the mirror behind the bar.

He peered into the mirror, but an alien looked back at him. Bruising from the wound above his right eye had spread down to his cheek, while the rest of his face was pockmarked from the glass splinters. He touched the bruising; his cheek was numb but he put that down to the Krait.

Billy brought the beers across to the table and Iffor paid him. "Can the chimp have an egg?" he asked.

Billy didn't even smile. "No," he glared at the chimp who was doing his best to look innocent. "No eggs."

They poured their beers. Harry said, "Can you tell us what happened at Lamumbwa?"

Iffor took his time relating all that happened, the Abrahams' kraal massacre and the mine which killed the constable. He told of the events in every detail, describing the mutilations to the bodies and pulling Constable Abrahams from the wreckage minus his legs.

This was an opportunity to turn the disaster to his advantage. It worked.

"I feel so bloody helpless," Harry said. "If only there was something we could do."

"There is something you can do, something you and the rest of Blue Watch can do." Iffor chose his words carefully. "Harry, I need your help—you and the rest of your team."

Harry could see how serious Iffor was. "What can we do?"

"Get Blue Watch together and let me speak to them. Today will do."

"Five in the Watch Room at the station okay with you?" asked Harry. "We can go on to the Moth club for a sundowner when you've finished."

After a couple more beers, Iffor felt fit enough to make his way back to the hotel. He had an hour or so to kill before his meeting with Blue Watch, time enough to set in his mind what he was going to say to them. He had to be convincing.

As he walked into the hotel, Mrs Patel was waiting for him. He put the holdall containing his kit on the floor and started to explain about future bills. She cut him short and producing an envelope said, "There's your bill to date; I'll send future bills to the army. Now you go and rest in the garden while I take your uniforms up to your room." She picked up the holdall. "Anything special you want doing to your shirts?"

Iffor was still trying to fathom out how she knew about the bills and the fact that he was now in the army. "If you can make holes in the shirt epaulettes for my pips and sew my wings on, I'd be obliged," he replied as he went into the garden to consider his strategy for the meeting.

Only Mad Harry was waiting for him when he arrived at the fire station. "I thought you might like to tell me what this is all about before the others arrive."

"No big deal," Iffor smiled. "I'm going to turn your lot into soldiers and we're going to go hunting terrorists."

"And there was I thinking it was something serious." Harry walked across to a control panel and pressed a button. Immediately a siren began to wail, calling Blue Watch to their duty.

After a few minutes, men started to arrive. Mad Harry ushered them into the Watch Room assuring them there was no emergency to attend. The last man arrived some ten minutes after the alarm was sounded. "Don't ask me what I was doing when the alarm went," he said, looking flustered and a little embarrassed.

When they were seated, Iffor, without formal introduction, came straight to the point.

"In the past couple of months the terrorists have murdered three policemen, a mine security team, two farmers, a farmer's family, and constable Abrahams' brother and family and, of course, the Beaver carrying our wounded. The terrorists can attack with impunity, knowing full well that all our soldiers are guarding the border up north and by the time a quick reaction force can assemble and be lifted into our area the terrorists' spoor is cold and they just seem to melt away."

Iffor paused noting the concern on their faces, then went on: "We have a choice, gentlemen: do nothing and allow the terrs to get bolder and more active, or take positive action, which is where you lot come in. If you *all* agree," he emphasised the 'all', "I intend to turn you into a small mobile infantry section."

He went on: "I have the authority to arm and equip you and train you."

A couple of hands shot up. "Questions when I've finished, please." Iffor softened his tone. "If I tell you what I've got planned, it might help.

"TRAINING: a concentrated week of weapon training and basic battle skills in the drill hall; training in the field.

"OUR MODUS OPERANDI: mobile vehicle check points; standing patrols; showing the flag in the farms."

He paused, "Questions?"

Evil said, "Why vehicle checks?"

"The terrorists that brought the Beaver down with a rocket didn't walk into town," Iffor responded grimly.

Harry said, "It takes twelve weeks to train a soldier."

"They haven't got the discipline and technical knowledge you have," replied Iffor, "and look around at the quality of the men in this room. Believe me, when we commence operations a week from tomorrow, you'll be ready. Some of you may recall the British Home Guard were prepared to face the might of the German army with considerably less training than you will have."

Harry said, "They were fighting for the survival of their country."

"And just what do you think we'll be doing? Eight-thirty at the drill hall tomorrow morning and it's all of you or nothing." Iffor looked at his watch, "Time for a sundowner. I'm in the chair. Today I became a soldier again."

In the comfort of the Moth club Iffor spent the time getting to know his fledgling soldiers. Mad Harry, Harry and Evil, he already knew; the others he encouraged to give as much information as possible:

Shamus—a gentle giant, former RUC policeman forced to leave Ulster after threats to his family.

Phillip Hill—too old for service but kept on to man the ops room and comms.

Hennie Amos—South African, sensible, serious, would love to get involved fighting terrorists, but considered too old.

Mal Jackson—considered too old for call-up, former National Serviceman Middlesex regiment, served in Korea, previously a gamekeeper, good at tracking and stalking.

And finally, Alvin—quiet, educated and probably the brains of the bunch.

A little after 0800 hours Iffor arrived at the drill hall in uniform: shirt, shorts, boots with puttees and hose tops, wearing the Green Rifles' beret. It felt good.

The Colour Sergeant was waiting. "How many are we expecting?"

"All of them," Iffor replied, but with not much conviction.

The Colour took charge. "When they do arrive, I'll take them into the stores to start kitting them up; you can go upstairs to the main office, say hello to our civilian clerk and arrange for the necessary papers to be signed.

"Now sir, what kit shall I give them?"

"I think at this stage, combats: floppy hat and boots; a set of equipment, belt, cross-straps pouches and water bottle. I presume it will be '58 pattern?" Iffor asked.

"58, or if you prefer, I've got a few sets of '44 which might suit better," Bob answered, "and I've got enough to give them each two water bottles."

"Even better," said Iffor, exclaiming, "Ah, here come the troops!" as Mad Harry led Blue Watch into the drill hall.

Iffor found the door marked 'Bn orderly room', and politely knocked. Surprised, he heard a female voice say, "Come in" and entered the room. The girl at her desk watched as he closed the door behind him and walked towards her. "Mr Meredith, I presume," she said, in a lovely lilting Indian accent.

"Mered-ith," Iffor corrected her, "but please call me Iffor."

She smiled and offered her hand, "Josie Patel."

Iffor held onto her hand longer than etiquette demanded. "No relation to Mrs…"

"Her niece," she said and gently removed her hand from his. At least now Iffor knew that Mrs Patel was not clairvoyant. Iffor watched her as she explained the call-up procedure for Blue Watch. Thirty and a bit, slim, short boyish hair, no make-up, her natural complexion forbade the use of any additives, small mouth with gracious lips and, to Iffor's eyes, a perfect tilted nose, the sort of nose a man only sees once in a lifetime. But what took Iffor's breath away were her breasts. Full, firm, encouraging, inviting. She wore a plain frock, square cut at the top, and obviously a vest of some sort which tried in vain to hide her firm dark nipples.

She knew he was studying her and enjoyed the moment. Then she stood up and touched the dressing above his eye, "Either you're blushing," she said, "or your wound is causing you pain." Iffor muttered his thanks and feeling confused and embarrassed, left the office, envying Blue Watch who would have to stand beside her signing their call-up papers.

Outside, he paused and turned back into the office. "Sorry to walk out so abruptly, I was blushing; girls like you frighten the life out of me."

"Frightened? Of a plain Jane like me!" She smiled, looking into his pockmarked face. Iffor moved close and whispered in her ear, "A very beautiful plain Jane." As he straightened up he had some satisfaction watching the red blush appear in her cheek.

Downstairs, the Colour had completed the issue of kit and watched as Blue Watch changed into uniform and musketry order. Iffor looked them over. "I'm impressed gentlemen, very impressed. Now if you will go upstairs to the office, Mrs..."

"Miss," the Colour corrected him.

"Miss Patel will take you through the paperwork. We've made it simple for you; while you are in uniform you are in the army; when you are out of uniform, you are firemen again. They are the conditions of your call-up."

Iffor watched as Blue Watch crossed the drill hall to the stairs. Did he imagine it, or were they making an effort at marching? The Colour spoke to him, "What next?"

"Weapons."

"I'll get my keys and we'll go down to the armoury." Bob disappeared into his office and came back with a bunch of keys. "I've told my storeman to send your lot down to the armoury, when they've finished ogling Josie."

Iffor stood looking around the armoury. A row of rifle racks, which would normally contain A and D companies' weapons, were now empty, apart from a dozen or so self-loading rifles. He walked across to a rack containing some old Lee Enfield rifles. "Who do the Number Fours belong to? Not us, surely?"

"Intaf," the Colour replied, "Internal affairs—they store them here; the Uzis and Stens belong to the District Commissioner. He dishes them out to farmers and the like."

"No Mark Five Stens I see," Iffor commented.

"You know your weapons," Bob muttered to himself, then aloud, "Our special forces nicked them; they managed to get hold of conversion kits and converted them to..."

Iffor interrupted him: "Mark Five 'S', the Silenced Stens."

"Correct sir."

Iffor pointed to a transit chest marked 'Guns Machine Bren 0.303'. "Is there a Bren in there?" he asked.

"There is," the Colour replied, "it belongs to Intaf."

"Any ammo?" Iffor was aware the army had moved on to 308, or as the army called it, 7.62mm.

"Stacks," the Colour replied, "and in answer to your next question, yes, you can borrow it; and talking of ammo, I've got twenty or so 36 grenades to get rid of if you want them."

Mad Harry and his team began to assemble in the armoury. "Look sir, when I issue weapons to our new recruits, I prefer to teach the stripping and assembling and cleaning myself; do you mind? I was the skill-at-arms NCO before I took this job on."

Iffor was glad to be able to hand the first lesson to the Colour; he needed time to write up his training programme. He had already decided the training would have to be very basic: weapons; fire control and indication; fieldcraft and section battle drills.

Alone in his office, he began to think through his strategy, jotting down his tasks. He had eight men plus himself. The Champ could carry five. The trailer would carry sleeping bags, water, rations and the like and it would also give protection from an RPG up the arse.

He would rotate his team as and when: four in the field; two manning the Watch Room, radio and telephone; two resting and relieving the Watch Team.

The driver and Bren-gunner would remain as a team for the duration of the patrol which could last two days. The windscreen would be removed, allowing the Bren to be rested on sandbags, allowing it to be fired over the bonnet. The Champ would be in effect Iffor's fire-section, able to support the team searching vehicles, and on roads where ambushes might occur, Iffor and the other two riflemen would dismount and 'walk' the road, while the Champ held back away, ready to give covering fire.

He thought about visits to the farms in the area.

First and foremost he had to get as much information as he could and the locations from the police. In his mind, he envisaged arriving at the farm at first light, and either setting up a covert o.p. or even mounting an ambush on a likely approach to the farm. Then he would move into the farm compound at last light, set up a defensive position and operate a sentry watch throughout the night. That would give the farmer and his family a good night's sleep, probably the first they had had for some time.

He started to consider his standard operating procedure for farm visits:

It would be essential that farms were advised of his presence and arrival. That would be up to the Watch Room team, and of course, the whole operation would have to be secret.

Iffor fished around in his desk drawer for a piece of foolscap paper; he needed to get all his thoughts down on paper.

He looked down at the blank sheet, smiled, and wrote: 'OPERATION KRAIT.'

PART SEVEN

Whereupon, the bullet nips smartly up the barrel, hotly pursued by the hot gases.

IFFOR LOOKED UP AS THE COLOUR SERGEANT walked
through the open door of his office. "Thought you might want some
lunch." He carried a biscuit tin lid with two mugs of tea and a plate of
compo biscuits covered with meat paste on it. "I've sent the troops
home, they've done enough for one day."

"Thanks Bob, take a seat," and looking at his watch said, "God, is
that the time? I'm sorry, I didn't mean you to do all the work today."

The Colour sat down and pushed a mug of tea towards Iffor. "You
look as if you've been pretty busy yourself," he said.

Iffor gathered up the several sheets of foolscap and handed them to
Bob. "What do you think?" he said, and helped himself to a biscuit.

The Colour spent several minutes studying the training programme
and the orders for operation KRAIT. "I like that," he said, "sweet and
simple." He went on, "Is there a reason why I can't do all the training;
you've only got me down for fieldcraft and rifle."

"I appreciate your help Bob." He was quite pleased that the Colour
hadn't objected to him using his Christian name, "but it's essential that
these men know that I know what I'm doing; they must have confidence
in me; that's why I must be involved with the training, and besides, I
must select a good man for the Bren. If we are in the shit, he's the man
who will pull us through."

The Colour nodded his agreement. "Vehicle searches and ambush drills?" he asked.

"You can do the vehicle check points, and I'll do the ambush drills in the field, along with covert observation points and section battle drills."

The Colour had taken his beret off, as if to indicate he was now off duty. "You know, Iffor, when you first put this idiotic scheme of yours past me, my first thought was, what a cunt, but because of you, a few farmers are going to sleep easier in their beds."

"Me and Blue Watch," said Iffor, "and who knows, we might get lucky."

The two of them spent the next hour or so making up a list of training aids, stores, and the use of the rifle club range. At some stage the lovely Josie put her head round the door, "I'm off now. See you tomorrow."

The Colour said, "What a good idea, fancy a beer?"

The two of them walked across to the Elephants Head Hotel; they had things to discuss. Iffor selected a table away from the bar while Bob went and collected the beers. "Lion okay?" he asked.

Iffor took the beer and began to pour it. "You're about to piss all over my strawberries," he said, "I can tell by the look on your face."

Bob downed his beer in one and looked expectantly at Iffor, who indicated to the barman to bring two more beers to the table. "I just think your timescale is wrong; you can't possibly put these men into the bush against experienced terrorists with just a week's training."

"And we can't wait for our soldiers to get back to Kensington to protect our farmers. The terrorists will want to inflict as much damage as they can before our troops get on the ground, and besides," Iffor drained his glass, "I like a challenge."

"With other men's lives?" Bob didn't even look at Iffor; he knew what his answer would be.

"Either we risk our lives or a lot of innocent people lose their lives; we have an opportunity to do something about the situation."

Bob looked into the bottom of his empty glass, "If you, as you so aptly put it, upset the terrorists' apple-cart, when they realise there are only five of you, they will come looking for you."

"That's what I'm counting on. Another beer?"

Iffor spent the weekend relaxing and pouring over his training programme: the Colour was right, he needed to amend it.

He decided that Monday morning would be skill at arms; Monday afternoon and if necessary, evening, would be spent on the range.

On Tuesday... he couldn't think that far ahead, and wandered into town to buy a car. He needed to visit Helen as often as he could and he couldn't rely on Pete to give him a lift to the settlement. On Mrs Patel's advice, he went to 'Patels Garage and Used Cars' and bought a second-hand Mazda Pickup. In the back of his mind, he thought that sometime in the future he would ask the mine to weld some steel plates on to the vulnerable areas and fit roll-bars to the vehicle.

He dined alone at the Elephants Head that night, trying to imagine Josie sitting at the same table with him. This made him feel very guilty; if anyone, he should be entertaining Helen. He pondered over all she had been through—the death of Jamie, living in isolation on the Leper Commune. He knew that Ed Dix had asked her to move onto the farm, but she maintained, her place was with her patients.

When he got back to the hotel, Mrs Patel invited him to Sunday lunch.

With memories of the previous disastrous evening with the Patels, filled with curry and the dreaded Krait beer, Iffor began to make his excuses, until Mrs Patel told him Josie was also invited.

Lunch was an informal affair held in the garden. Other hotel guests, if there were any, were excluded. A traditional English roast was served by the Patel's faithful old retainer, Godfry, who would normally be found dressed in shorts and shirt doing odd jobs around the hotel, but was resplendent in white suit and polished shoes.

If Iffor thought that lunch would be dinner, sweet, coffee, then off to his room for a kip before an evening at the Moth club, he was sadly mistaken. The meal went on far into the afternoon, with the roast lamb, spotted dick and custard, followed by various Indian confectionery and delights, accompanied by exotic wines and liqueurs. Several times during the meal, Iffor attempted to make eye contact with Josie, but she simply smiled and turned her head. When the meal was finally finished, he sat in the shade on a double garden swing and invited Josie to join him, but it was Mrs Patel who came and sat beside him. She set the seat swinging. "So what does it feel like to be back in uniform?" she smiled. "I heard what you are doing with our firemen." He started to answer her question, but she went on, "Those firemen are far too old to be chasing terrorists in the bush, but I dare say they will take it in their stride, except for Henry; he's far too sensitive, and you must not let your plans interfere with his art and painting."

Iffor began to suspect that the invite to lunch with the delectable Josie as bait, was nothing more than a ploy to somehow get him to go easy on Harry, or Henry as she insisted on calling him. He decided to glean more information about this budding artist. "He didn't tell me he was into art," Iffor said.

"That is because he's very shy and he puts on an act when he's with men; he doesn't want too many people knowing about his other side, though most of his friends know."

"Are we talking about his art, or something else, something that I should know about since I'm going to have to depend on him?"

"He likes to dress as a woman; he and his friend Paul spend hours with me trying on my dresses and getting me to alter the clothes I give them or buy for them; they say that dressing in female clothes gives them the freedom they need to express themselves when they go off into the bush to paint."

By now, Iffor was quite concerned. "How often do they go off painting, and where do they go?"

Mrs Patel was now quite happy to tell Iffor all she knew. "About once a month, and they always go to Angel Falls, to the river and waterfall. They leave town dressed as men, change clothes when they get to the Falls and spend the day painting."

She put her hand on Iffor's. "Don't be hard on him, he's not homosexual, he's just a lost transvestite trying very hard to live in the world of men; you can trust him and depend on him. After all, Blue Watch have accepted him."

Josie got up to leave, and said her goodbyes. As Iffor rose to his feet, Mr Patel said, "I'll walk you home m'dear, I could do with some exercise."

Iffor sat down, cursing his luck and had to be content watching her lovely long legs and pert bottom disappearing through the patio doors.

He called out, "See you tomorrow." She waved a hand; he wondered if she noticed how husky his voice had become. Mrs Patel got up and followed her husband and niece to the front door. Iffor tried not to think of Mrs Patel hugging Josie; the thought of those large firm breasts pressing into his own chest destroyed all resistance. He beckoned to Godfry.

"Sir?"

"A cold Krait please."

Monday morning eight sharp found Iffor clean and bright and slightly oiled, standing in front of Blue Watch who were trying to resemble a straight line of sorts.

"Good morning gentlemen, welcome to the start of this week's training.

"The Colour Sergeant has, quite rightly, voiced his opinion that a week's training is nowhere near enough time to prepare for operations against terrorists. May I remind you of what I said at the beginning? This week's training will be bare basics; what we learn in the drill hall we will practise and hone to perfection on the hoof in the field.

"My second reason for haste is that the Battalion is to be rotated back to barracks in about three weeks' time.

"We know that the terrs are getting accurate information from this town, so if they don't know already, they soon will.

"It is unlikely that the terrs will continue their terror campaign while we have two companies of infantry available. My guess is they will disperse locally, or as a group cross into Zambia for a rest and reorg.

"But before this happens," Iffor paused to stress the importance of what he was about to say, "it is my firm belief that they will try to mount a significant assault on a prime target.

"This will impress their peers, give them confidence for when they return, as they will, and cause utter fuck among our farmers.

"Our mission gentlemen is to prevent this from happening.

"Questions?"

Hennie, the big Afrikaner, said, "We haven't got a snowball's hope in hell of bumping into them in the dark, and if we do, they outnumber us."

"Correct, that's why we're not going to be wandering about in the dark, as I have already explained. Apart from regular vehicle check points, we will carry out standing patrols on the four farms and the Leper Mission; with luck, that will keep them on the hop."

Mad Harry spoke: "If we upset them, they will come looking for us, especially when they find out how small a unit we are; what happens then?"

"Then my friend, Christmas will come early." They all knew what he meant.

Iffor waited for more questions; there were none. "Right gentlemen, the Colour will issue you with your personal weapon and five magazines. This morning will be spent cleaning, stripping, assembling and drills.

"This afternoon we will be on the thirty metre range zeroing our weapons."

As the week progressed, so did the training. More weapon training, fieldcraft, target indication and fire control orders and battle drills.

The Colour Sergeant was in his element, training soldiers instead of counting boots and tins of jam.

Wednesday was Iffor's turn. Blue Watch were in a half circle around a table on which Iffor had placed the Bren Gun.

"Gentlemen, may I introduce you to the Bren light machine-gun. This is the mark three version, weight nineteen pounds, calibre 0.303, which you will notice is different from the ammunition we use in our rifles, which is why we are able to get hold of it. The weapon comes complete with thirteen thirty-round magazines, and a spare barrel.

"Since the ammunition we use is rimmed, I will be stressing the importance of the correct loading of the magazines during training."

Iffor stripped the weapon into its three components parts and described the workings of the weapon, allowing himself to break the serious mood of the class with a phrase used so often with recruits: "Whereupon, the bullet nips smartly up the barrel hotly pursued by the hot gases." Then it was the drills: load, unload, make safe and the immediate actions; each drill repeated again and again until it was second nature.

Only when each man completed the tests on the weapon to Iffor's satisfaction did he fall them out, by then it was early evening.

Pete came into the drill hall as Iffor and the Colour were leaving. "Sundowner at the Elephant?" he asked.

"Not for me," said the Colour, "wife wants me home early tonight."

"Iffor?"

"Churlish not to."

They sat at a table in the balcony bar overlooking the main street, watching the town people hurrying home after work, the same people Pete and Iffor were committed to protect. They drank their first Lion in silence, then, as they poured their second, Pete said, "Helen's in town this weekend; we'd like you to have dinner with us Saturday night."

"Love to," and without thinking added, "Where's she staying?"

"Here with me, her and the boy, I have a suite here at the hotel, the government pay for it."

Iffor leaned forward in his chair. "You and Helen?" He was confused. "I didn't realise, I didn't know, it's only been a few months since Jamie…"

Pete cut him short. "I adore the girl and young Jamie; she is dedicated to her Leper Mission, but she would like to live a normal life here in town and be a family again.

"She cares for me and that's all I ask. As for the time element, we are going to wait for another six months before we marry. In the meantime, we are content to share the odd weekend together, either here or Kariba."

He allowed Iffor time to take all this in, realising it was quite a shock for him, then said, "Ed's going to give her away; we'd like you to be best man."

"This," said Iffor, "calls for a celebration; do they serve Krait here?"

Iffor slowly opened his eyes; the pain was minimal and he might even attempt breakfast. After a shower and shave he went in search of a newspaper; he didn't want the embarrassment of asking Mrs Patel what day of the week it was. He made a solemn promise to himself never, ever again to drink that dreadful Indian beer.

He went through into the breakfast room and picked a paper from the rack. As he tried to focus on the date, Mrs Patel came in with his breakfast. "It's Thursday," she said, "and you are on the range all day; I've packed some sandwiches and a flask for you."

Arriving at the drill hall, Iffor was surprised to find the police Rhino parked outside and Pete inside talking to the Colour.

The Colour saluted. "Good news boss, we've taken delivery of a Bedford three tonner. We can lift all the guys and stores to the rifle club range; my sick, lame and lazy are coming along to help out—we can fire rifle and Bren."

It was Pete's turn. He saluted and Iffor returned the salute. "I need a favour from the military, I'm going to Lamumbwa Leper Mission to bring Helen and the boy into town. I need an escort."

Before Iffor could answer, the Colour said, "I can handle the range—you go with Pete, you need a break."

"I'll have to get my weapons from Agnes."

"They're in the Rhino," said Pete. "Let's go."

They reached the turn-off to the Great North Road before Pete spoke: "Thanks for volunteering."

"Between you and the Colour Sergeant I didn't have much choice, but thanks for asking me. The Colour was right, I could do with a break and I intended to do a recce of the mission sometime soon."

"Don't let Helen hear you saying that; the Mission is neutral ground. She let it be known that if the terrorists need food and water or want their wounded treated they will be welcome, but after they have gone, she will tell the security forces, and so far, the terrorists have stayed clear of the place."

"Fear of leprosy will do that," said Iffor. "If they come looking for a soft target, her neutrality won't stop them."

"I'm aware of that," Pete said. "You didn't have to remind me."

Iffor regretted what he had said, but he pressed his point. "Like it or not, I intend to include the mission in my standing patrols and I'd like to see her armed and trained."

"Tried that, pistol and Uzi, but she refuses to carry a weapon or have a weapon at the mission."

"I suppose I could insist," Iffor went on, "but she's very stubborn as doubtless you have already found out." Iffor looked at Pete, who just smiled and nodded.

They drove in silence until they reached the Old Lamumbwa Road, the scene of the mine ambush.

The wrecked Land Rover had been recovered to Kensington and the crater filled in, but the feeling of guilt came back to haunt Iffor.

"Compromise," he said to Pete, "see if she will accept a compromise. Try her with my Astra, my little snubby, it's designed to be worn in the small of the back. If she wears a shirt outside her trousers or skirt, no-one will see it; it's a two, two with a two-inch barrel."

"What good will that be?..." After a moment's thought, he said, "Go on then."

"Look," Iffor said, "she won't use it to defend her perimeter against a gang of terrorists; the man she shoots will be five feet away, intent on raping her and then sticking a bayonet into her."

Iffor said quietly, "Think it over and discuss it with her. I'll drop the pistol and holster into your office."

The Leper Mission was typical; white-washed brick building with thatched roof serving as hospital, clinic and admin, surrounded by small residential huts where the patients lived in 'family' groups. A thatched roof on four poles served as the school during the day and community centre in the evening.

Pete drove into the compound and just about managed to reach the admin block before the crowd of delighted, curious boys forced him to stop.

As they climbed out of the Rhino, the more adventurous boys climbed in and for a few minutes forgot their disabilities as they imagined themselves driving the Rhino across the veld.

Iffor's thoughts went back to his early days in the Zambia Regiment:

He commanded the escort for the ammunition trucks travelling to Lusaka to collect ammunition to take back to the copper belt. En route, they stopped at a small town for a beer and to give the drivers a break. During one of these stops Iffor got chatting to a group of Africans who told him they worked at a mission for boys with leprosy, just outside the town. As they resumed their journey, Iffor looked out for the mission and was delighted to see groups of youngsters waving as they passed by what he now knew to be the mission.

On his next trip he was invited to visit the mission and meet the boys. He and his soldiers were given a reception which brought tears to the hardest of them, with the boys showing great interest in weapons and uniforms and vowing to become soldiers when they were old enough and if only their fingers and toes would grow back again.

At the Colonel's weekly meeting, Iffor mentioned the mission and the ambitions of the boys and asked if the battalion could help.

Since the battalion was stood down from operations, the Colonel tasked Iffor to do what he could to help.

A couple of days later, courtesy of the quartermaster, Iffor loaded a four tonner with 'written-off' uniforms, boots, tents and equipment and twenty-four hour ration packs, weapons, ammo and a section of enthusiastic soldiers, and headed off to the mission.

Within a week, Iffor had a mission cadet force with uniformed boys being taught military skills by the soldiers and Iffor conducting rifle shooting on a hastily built range.

Even boys with no fingers could fire the self-loading rifles, using the 'arctic' trigger.

Iffor's thoughts were interrupted by Pete saying, "Iffor, meet Grace, Helen's right hand man."

Grace, tall willowy and very much a lovely woman, smiled at Pete's little joke, took Iffor's hand and said, "Welcome to Lamumbwa Mission, and you really are most welcome." Her handshake was very firm and, being the same height as Iffor, she looked directly into his face.

"Matabele?" he asked.

"No, Zulu, and by the sound of your name, you're Welsh."

A firm friendship was established.

Helen appeared with young Jamie in tow. An African in a white coat, obviously staff, carried their overnight bags and stowed them in the Rhino. As Helen approached the two men, Iffor leaned closer to Pete, "You lucky bastard."

She was dressed in plain white skirt and matching blouse, flat shoes and to break the colour, or rather lack of it, a floral scarf about her neck.

Iffor was disappointed to notice that the blouse worn outside the skirt gave no indication of her small bust with generous nipples. Still, just to see her again was enough. She ran to Iffor who hugged her and lifted her off the ground, swirling her around to the delight of her watching patients. "I'm told I'm to be best man and I can't think of a better choice."

"Just get it right this time," she said, and Iffor winced at the memory of his efforts as best man when she married Jamie. "God, I'd forgotten about that."

"Well, I haven't," she frowned, then laughed. Her face just inches from Iffor's, he could smell her breath, sweet with a hint of mint. He remembered his own 'morning after' breath: at the Naafi club in Aldershot his breath could drop a crap hat, a non-para, at five feet.

Helen and Jamie sat in the front of the Rhino beside Pete, while Iffor stood on the step behind the driver with his head and shoulders above the cupola, Carbine at the ready in the event of an ambush. Iffor's fire might give them half a chance to get out of the killing ground. At the Great North Road turn-off, the site of the mine ambush, Iffor made Pete stop. "Better safe than sorry," he said and went ahead on foot, probing at any disturbed earth with his knife.

They arrived back in Kensington in time for Iffor to catch the Colour before he went home. He was anxious to find out how the range training went.

"Soldiers they ain't," Bob said, "but they shoot well enough to take on the terrs and their weapon handling is good enough."

"Who are the all-time greats on the Bren?" Iffor asked, nodding his satisfaction at the Colour's efforts. "Harry or Henry or whatever he calls himself. He was the best, he always seems to be trying to prove himself to be as good or better than the others.

"And the other is Evil, and that's exactly how he looks when he's carrying that Bren: he looks as if he can do serious damage given half a chance."

The Colour fumbled with his keys, waiting for Josie to come downstairs before he locked up. Quietly, Iffor said, "Thanks for everything Bob; without you we wouldn't have got this far."

Before the Colour could answer, Josie came gliding down the main staircase. Wearing a sari, she looked gorgeous. "Glad you're back, Iffor. Auntie would like the three of us to have a sundowner in her garden." The Colour looked at Iffor and shrugged his shoulders. They both knew this was not a request. As they left the drill hall Iffor asked, "Have you tried Krait beer, Bob?"

"Naughty," said Josie, scowling at Iffor.

Pete was already in the hotel garden, talking to Mrs Patel when they arrived. Like Iffor and Bob Pearson, he was still in combat uniform and looking tired and dusty.

Mrs Patel sat them around a large table in the shade of a jacaranda tree and beckoned to Godfry to serve drinks.

Under Josie's watchful eye, Iffor joined Bob and Pete in a cold Lion and like the other two, sat back in his chair, relaxed for the first time that day.

They talked about everything and nothing for an hour or so, until Helen appeared with her son at the French windows. The men stood as she paused for a moment, framed in the entrance. She looked fresh and cool, and with the bright light behind her, Iffor could not but help notice the outline of her legs and thighs through her skirt. She walked straight across to Iffor and kissed him on the cheek. He held her at arm's length, "My God girl, but you scrub up well."

She sat next to and close to Pete, holding his hand. Jamie drew up a chair next to his mother. Iffor thought he had never seen her looking happier.

Mrs Patel stood up, and as she did so her husband and several Indians and their wives appeared on the patio. "My friends," she said, "I welcome you here today for this very important announcement and presentation."

She sat down and beckoned to Pete who looked completely confused and bewildered. Helen whispered, just loud enough for all to hear, "I think it's about us."

Pete stood up and the Indian guests started to fill the tables in the garden. "This was supposed to be a secret," he said, "but with Josie and Helen being such good friends and Mrs Patel being Josie's auntie," he looked at Mrs Patel smiling, "we had no chance of keeping our secret." He went on, "I've asked Helen to marry me and she has said yes, so we are now officially engaged."

Mr Patel came forward holding a tray. "It's not quite official, but this should do the trick." He put the tray on the table in front of Pete and Helen; on it were two small boxes. "Peter and Helen," he said. Mrs Patel came and stood beside him, "On behalf of the Indian community of this town and with our gratitude..." He picked up the smaller of the boxes and opened it, "an engagement ring for you my dear, and..." He picked up the remaining box and opened it, "a signet ring for you Pete, both made especially for you by Indian craftsmen with Indian gold."

Everyone stood and applauded and a very embarrassed Pete tried to stammer his thanks, while Helen just sat looking demure and radiant.

Iffor looked round for Godfry, spotted him and thought, God, not another bloody mind-reader, as Godfry walked across the lawn towards him with a clean glass and a cold Krait on a tray.

The way that Iffor breezed into the drill hall next morning bore no reflection on how he actually felt. The previous evening he had asked the Colour to draw and issue personal stores: ammunition; ration packs; field dressings and medical kits, etc., giving him time to write up his orders and stores list.

He had given a warning order for his orders group: time and place, the lecture room 1000hours. This would allow Blue Watch the rest of the day to pack personal kit and load magazines and clean weapons, etc.

He had already decided that a full military briefing would not be appropriate; he would give the short SMEAC—situation, mission, execution, ask and confirm.

Blue Watch filed into the lecture room and sat in a semicircle around Iffor, standing at the blackboard. He began, "Gentlemen, good morning.

"Operation Krait.

"Situation: We have a group of terrorists responsible for several deaths operating in our area. Because our two infantry companies are committed up on the border, the terrs are unopposed. Until now.

"Mission: We will through aggressive patrolling and vehicle check points attempt to keep the terrs 'wrong footed', and with luck, we might even bump into one of their recce groups.

"Execution: In four phases:

"Phase one: Preparation. You will spend the rest of the day under command of the Colour Sergeant, drawing personal kit and ammunition while I and the Colour's riflemen will load the Champ trailer with the main stores: food, water sleeping bags, etc.

"The Colour has also scrounged two 31 sets for us so we now have comms, one in the Champ and the other in the Watch Room.

"Phase two: 0800hrs Monday morning, move out to the Great North Road and Kensington crossroads and set up a vehicle check point.

"Phase three: Drive up the Lamumbwa Road to the sight of Ian's ambush and set up an observation point. We will not be covert, but we will throw a cam net over the Champ.

"Phase four: Drive to Lamumbwa farm and establish a night routine."

Iffor went on: "I've chosen Lamumbwa farm because our security forces at the request of the Monastery and the Leper Mission have agreed to stay clear to ensure their neutrality with the terrs. However, I feel we should show the flag in that area to show we are active."

He looked at the Colour who nodded his approval.

"Next morning we retrace our steps with the observation point and vehicle check points, arriving back here last light Tuesday.

"Our order of battle known as 'Orbat': Myself, Mad Harry, Henry on the Bren, Shamus and Hennie.

"The other four will be the Watch Team working in pairs, four hours on, four off."

Iffor paused, letting the information sink in, then said, "Before I go over all this again and start asking questions, let me say that secrecy is of the utmost importance.

"On Monday morning Inspector Saxon will phone Ed Dix and tell him an army unit will be active in his area. Phillip, stand up."

Phillip Hill, by far the oldest in the group, stood up.

"Phil, you normally man the Watch Room, so you will be in command of the Watch Team. It is imperative that you contact Ed at the farm before last light and tell him we are moving into his farm at last light; we don't want his farm guards opening up on us as we walk in. You will advise me over the air on the 31 set that it is safe for us to move.

"Now say all that back to me."

Iffor completed his briefing answering questions, but more importantly, asking questions and confirming that each member of the team knew what his task was, then, handing the team over to the Colour, went in search of the corporal storeman.

By mid-afternoon, kit had been issued and packed onto the Champ trailer, weapons cleaned and checked by Iffor and magazines loaded.

"No point keeping the lads here any longer, can I dismiss them?" It was after all, so far as the Colour was concerned, 'poets' day.

"One more little task Bob; then they can knock off."

Iffor brought the blackboard and easel from the lecture room and stood it in the main entrance, so the team would have to walk past it on leaving. Then, without a word, wrote: 'IF YOU DON'T WANT YOUR ENEMY TO FIND OUT, DON'T TELL YOUR FRIENDS.'

Returning to the hotel, Iffor felt quite pleased with himself. He collected the Astra and holster from Mrs Patel's safe and made his way back to the police station.

He flopped into the chair in Pete's office and put the pistol on the desk.

"One Astra twenty-two, nine rounds in the pistol, nine in the loops either side of the holster, the rest is up to you."

Pete took the pistol and put it in the drawer of his desk.

"Thanks, I'm going to insist she wears it at all times, and when this is all over, wherever you are, I'll get it back to you.

"Now, don't forget tomorrow night, dinner with Helen and me at the Elephants head; Helen thought you might like to bring Josie with you."

Having collected his weapons and magazines from Agnes, Iffor returned to his hotel room to carry out his own preparations.

He stripped and cleaned the Ruger Carbine; then the Brno 9Mil and, having reassembled and oiled them, unloaded, stripped and cleaned the magazines; then loaded each of the five magazines each with thirty rounds and fifteen rounds in each of the three pistol mags he would carry.

He would travel light, shoulder holster for the pistol, web belt with water bottle and two by two magazine pouches, his overnight bag would go in the trailer.

When he dressed on Monday morning into his combats, he would put a twenty-round box of carbine ammunition in each of his breast pockets. One of the good things about his carbine was the size of the ammunition, 5.56 against 7.62 and a box of twenty rounds was about the size of a cigarette packet.

Having completed his preparations, he carefully locked the window and the door of his room and went down into the garden.

Just in time for afternoon tea, some sandwiches and a snooze on the sun lounger, he made a mental note to ask Mrs Patel how he could get in touch with Josie.

He awoke as Mrs Patel approached and started to clear the teacup and plate. "You have a visitor," she said and nodded towards the French window. Josie was walking towards him, this time dressed in western clothes; trousers, shirt and a scarf about her neck.

Iffor stood. "What a very pleasant surprise. Shall we sit in the shade?" He indicated the table under the jacaranda tree. He stood his ground so that she had to walk closely past him; he breathed in through his nose so that she wouldn't realise he was smelling her, then followed her to the table.

"I'm glad you came. I've been wondering how to get in touch with you."

"You see me every day at work," she said. "I'm in the next office to you."

Iffor leaned forward in his chair, moving closer to her. "You know exactly what I mean," he said.

"And what exactly do you mean?" She was playing with him now.

"I was wondering how I could get you alone under a jacaranda tree in a beautiful garden. I'd like to get to know you better, to know more about you."

She opened up to him. "What would you like to know?"

Iffor relaxed; he'd got over the first hurdle. "Well, first I'd like to know if you will have dinner with me tomorrow night. I'm meeting Helen and Pete at the Elephants Head."

"Love to," she said. "Next?"

"Where do you live? I need to collect you and deliver you home safely."

"I live here with Auntie. I have two rooms converted into a flat; I'm independent and quite comfortable." Her face hardened and she became serious. "I moved in with Auntie after the terrorists murdered my mother and father. They had been visiting my uncle in Zambia and were ambushed a few miles inside Rhodesia, round about the time of Jamie's murder and probably by the same gang. They were old, unarmed, an easy or what's known as a soft target."

The ensuing silence was broken by Auntie arriving with a tray of snacks and a large pot of tea. Josie came alive again. "Oh Auntie, you shouldn't have done, but I'm glad you did—I'm starving."

Like a couple of vultures, they set about the several dishes of different curries, samosas and nan bread. Iffor hadn't realised just how hungry he was until the delicious aroma of the spicy Indian dishes reminded him.

As they ate, Josie said, "My turn—married?"

"You know I'm not," Iffor said. "My file is in your office. No wife, no children, both parents dead; my family are, or rather were, Jamie and Helen and my godson little Jamie, who in years to come I will take great pleasure in teaching to drink, gamble, lust after women, start fights and generally make a nuisance of himself in pubs and weddings."

Mrs Patel made her way across the lawn to their table. "A man called Harry phoned to remind you, you were going to meet the boys for a drink tonight at the Moth club."

Before Iffor could answer, Josie said, "Go ahead. I'm going to wash my hair, have a bath, read a book and get an early night."

Only Mad Harry, Henry and Mal Jackson were drinking at the bar; the others, thought Iffor, were very wisely at home with their wives.

"Beer anyone?" said Iffor, nodding at Jacob, the club barman. Three empty glasses were pushed in his direction. Silly thing to say, he thought.

"Four Castles please Jacob."

"Well boss, what do you think will happen on Monday when we take to the bush?" Harry filled his glass while Iffor paid the barman.

"What I think will happen, my friend, is that we will annoy several drivers when we stop and search their vehicles; our observation points will be nothing more than a glorified picnic, but on the plus side, Ed Dix and his family will get a good night's sleep with us guarding him, but on the other hand…" He didn't complete the sentence.

Henry, the artist, the transvestite, said, "Do you really think we can make a difference to this war? Will my small contribution help in any way?"

"Oh yes, when this war is over, people will remember you for the very best of reasons." Little did Iffor know how poignant his words were.

Saturday evening saw Josie waiting for Iffor as he hurried down the stairs of the hotel; he looked anxiously at his watch. "It's okay," she said, "I'm early."

Relieved, Iffor wondered what her reaction would have been if he had been late.

She was dressed very simply in a pale blue sari with gold sandals contrasting her red painted toenails, for jewellery just a gold bangle and on her right hand, a gold wedding ring which Iffor suspected probably belonged to her mother. She carried a stole which she offered to Iffor to drape around her shoulders. As he did so, he breathed her fragrance and whispered in her ear, "You're gorgeous."

She smiled, "I know."

Pete and Helen were waiting for them as they were led to their table, Helen looking radiant, Pete looking like the cat that got the cream.

Throughout the meal, the two girls chatted, hardly pausing to eat, while Pete and Iffor were content to sit and watch them. At some stage, Pete attempted to draw Iffor into conversation: "All set for Monday?"

"Yup!"

"She's agreed to wear the Astra pistol."

"Good."

Both men became silent again, speaking only when the girls tried to involve them in their girl talk.

After the meal, they settled into the comfort of the lounge, enjoying their drinks. The girls had become quiet. Helen looked at Iffor, without speaking, inviting him to ask the question she knew he had to ask. "So you two," he said, "what are your plans after you are married? I hope I'm not going to lose you both; good friends are hard to come by and I've got to be around to teach my godson all my disgusting habits."

Pete and Helen exchanged glances. Pete said, "We haven't yet decided. I'd like to stay in Kensington; I've still got five years of my contract to run, but I've got to think of Helen and Jamie and their safety; we may even go back to England."

Those last words put the dampener on the evening. Josie stood up, "Time for me to go, Auntie will be waiting up for me."

Iffor hoped she was joking.

She wasn't.

PART EIGHT

Friendly fire is always more accurate than enemy fire.

NINE SHARP ON MONDAY MORNING Blue Watch were ready to move out. The Watch Keeping team had worked out their own rota and had completed a radio check.

Iffor had his team lined up in the MT yard behind the drill hall where the loaded Champ was waiting. Carefully, he inspected each one, checking magazines, water bottles, field dressings and weapons.

When satisfied, he stood to one side and gave the orders: "Prepare to load... Load!"

These two simple but significant orders somehow gave way to the final transformation of Blue Watch from firemen to soldiers.

They drove down the main street under a clear blue sky with a warming sun; Iffor revelled in the admiring glances of the few people in the town and made a mental note to get a pennant or a small flag for the radio aerial.

He felt quite satisfied with his small but potent force: Mad Harry driving, Harry beside him with the Bren resting on the sandbag in front of him and big Shamus and Hennie either side of him. He felt ready for anything.

They arrived at their first R.V., the Kensington, Great North Road crossroads. An hour or so later, before dismounting, Iffor said, "Quick Orders group, fellas.

"We are not interested in any documentation, we are only interested in any warlike items, weapons, explosives and any hand-drawn maps, and remember, when you are looking into the boot or engine of a vehicle, always ensure the driver is between you and the vehicle. That way, if there is an anti-handling device, he'll catch the blast before you do."

Iffor deployed his force. He uncoupled the trailer and placed it on the right-hand side of the road and a few metres back. He parked the Champ on the opposite side, ensuring that any passing vehicles would have to slow down to negotiate the two vehicles.

Then, he positioned Henry with the Bren in the storm drain at the side of the road, with a couple of sandbags to give him some cover and to allow him to fire the Bren standing up. The other two men took up positions beside the two parked vehicles ready to flag down oncoming traffic.

Satisfied, Iffor said softly to himself, "This is the bit I really enjoy," then shouted out, "Make ready all weapons," and thrilled at the sound of the weapons being cocked.

As an afterthought, he shouted, "Check safeties."

As he suspected, the seven or eight vehicles they stopped were African traders, lorries and vans going or coming to Kensington or Sinoia, all of them quite happy to be searched.

Among them, an old Volvo estate driven by a white woman with two children in the back; Shamus happily signalled her through the roadblock, waving at the children as she drove by.

As they climbed back into the Champ ready to move off to their second R.V. Iffor said, quite casually, "Anyone care to hazard a guess how many white people support our terrorist friends of ZAPU and ZANU?"

Shamus muttered, "Sorry boss, won't happen again."

The team's second R.V. was the Great North Road/ Lamumbwa road junction. Iffor showed them the scene of the mine ambush and his makeshift ridout. He allowed them to drink freely from the chagals of cold water hanging from the wing mirrors of the Champ; he'd already told them the water on their belts were for extreme emergency, like surviving an ambush and having to take to the bush to escape.

They set up their vehicle check point, but after an hour or so, as Iffor suspected, not a single vehicle appeared. Road signs in this part of the world advised Europeans against travelling after 2 p.m., and Africans were anxious to get home before curfew.

By the time they arrived at the site for the observation point, it was mid-afternoon; the site selected was the high ground the terrorists had used to ambush young Ian Dix.

Having concealed the Champ and trailer as best they could with the cam net, Iffor positioned his men in an all-round defensive position allowing them to brew up and break into their 24-hour ration pack.

As the men ate, Iffor stood guard surveying the ground with his binoculars, breaking the ground up into areas, near, middle and distant, looking for suspicious signs of shape, shadow, shine or sudden movement.

All basic but all very necessary.

He munched on a Mars Bar and gratefully accepted a swig of tea from Hennie, wincing as the tea laced with cane spirit hit the back of his throat. He made a mental note to have words with Hennie when they got back.

With the men in a defensive circle around him, Iffor began his lesson:

"Target Recognition and Fire control orders.

"The difference being, I give the fire control orders; anyone spotting an enemy gives a target indication order.

"Now all of you look to your front for a prominent object, a tree, bush or large stone at about three hundred metres; now imagine a terrorist to the left or right of that object; as I call your name indicate the target by shouting 'Three hundred, lone tree. Quarter left of tree', or whatever your target is."

When Iffor was satisfied the men had a fair idea of target recognition he went on to fire control orders.

"We will always use the same format GRIT, which stands for Group, Range, Indication, which for the benefit of those among us who have been drinking cane spirit means where to look, and T for type of fire.

"There are four types of fire control orders, but we shall only use two of them.

"Brief order: enemy front fire or enemy left or right fire.

"And a full order: Group, Bren or rifle or all.

"Range, probably within fifty metres.

"Indication, which is, Hennie?"

"Where to look boss."

"And Type of fire, which will probably be rapid but controlled."

After questions, they spent the next hour or so practising their newly acquired drills.

Kensington came up on the air: "Control for Bravo Whisky, over."

"Bravo Whisky, Sunray on set message, over." Iffor needed to know that Ed at the farm had been advised of their visit.

"Send over."

"Bravo Whisky for control, confirm you have advised our final R.V. that we are coming, over."

"Control. We confirm your final R.V. phoned at 1600 hours, over."

"Roger, out."

Iffor assembled his small force on the road. It was about two miles to the farm; he judged it would just be getting dark when they arrived. They moved off, Shamus and Hennie, staggered, either side of the road, the Champ with Mad Harry driving and Henry on the Bren following at fifty metres with strict orders to keep that distance and show no lights.

Iffor positioned himself in the centre of the road, an obvious target but he had to be in a position where he could spot evidence of a mine.

The government were in the process of building security fences around vulnerable farms; in Ed's case the work was still to be completed so the compound was open and unprotected.

Iffor had halted his force just short of the compound. Indicating to the Champ to stay put, he walked towards the main house with Shamus and Hennie either side of him. As he started to shout his warning to the house that the army had arrived, a single shot rang out followed by a ragged volley. Diving to the ground, he shouted, "Down!" Then, "In the house! It's the army, Ed, it's Iffor; stop shooting!"

From the house Ed shouted, "Iffor stand up where I can see you," and a beam of light from a powerful torch lit up the area.

Iffor stood and shouted back to the Champ: "Friendly fire, friendly fire, come into the compound," and turned his attention to his two soldiers. Hennie was on his feet but big Shamus was still lying face down with an ominous stain spreading around the exit wound in his back. Gently, they rolled Shamus on to his back; his eyes were open, he was trying to speak but his breathing was laboured.

Ed and daughter Verity came running from the house; she was still clutching her rifle saying, "I'm so sorry, it was me who shot him, I thought you were terrorists."

Ed was more practical. "What can I do?"

"Get him into a sitting position, it will be easier for him to breathe." Iffor looked round for the Champ as it entered the compound, shouting, "Henry, first aid kit; Harry, stay with the Bren."

The feminine side of Henry took over. "Looks like a sucking wound; we need to seal the entrance hole with a plastic cover of some sort; plastic backing on the field dressing will do."

Now that Shamus was sitting upright he was breathing a little easier. Henry applied a field dressing over entrance and exit wound. "That will have to do until we get him back to Kensington."

Joy Dix came running from the house; the two farm guards, having more sense, stayed in the house, ready to give covering fire if need be. Henry took charge. "Verity, you need a job, go inside and make a cup of hot sweet tea for Shamus, just enough for a couple of mouthfuls; Joy, you support Shamus, keep him sitting up."

Hennie said quietly, "What happened Ed? You knew we were coming in at last light; why did you shoot?"

"We didn't know you were coming; no-one told us, no-one could, both our telephone and our farm alert radio are out, batteries flat." Ed went on, "We always stand to at last light. Verity saw some figures and fired; the farm guards followed suit."

"Looks like a cock-up boss." Hennie picked up Shamus's rifle and unloaded it. "We don't want any more accidents, do we?"

Leaving Harry and Ed to try and coax some tea into Shamus, Iffor walked back to the Champ to put Mad Harry in the picture.

"Shamus is seriously wounded; I'm going to take him back to Kensington in the Champ. I'll come back for you in the morning."

Harry looked hard at him. "You're going to take Shamus back on your own?"

"Yes, no point in risking more lives."

"Well, you've got that wrong old son, we are Blue Watch—one for all and all for one and all that bollocks; we'll all take Shamus back. Now let's get him loaded, we're wasting time." Iffor didn't argue.

They put Shamus in the back between Henry and Hennie; Mad Harry drove, Iffor became gunner/operator, he needed to get a sit rep off to base as quickly as possible and have the hospital standing by. Throwing caution to the wind, they drove the Lamumbwa road at speed with headlights on main beam. Nothing mattered now but Shamus's survival.

As they passed the Gt. North Road 4 miles sign, Henry tapped Iffor on the shoulder and lifted his headphone, "We're losing him boss, his pulse is very weak."

Harry stopped the Champ. "We're at least two hours from Kensington; anyone got any good ideas."

"We could try the farm alert channel, the army monitor that and they might just have a chopper handy," Hennie's voice tailed off. Even if the army had a helicopter in the area, it would not fly at night. Nevertheless, Iffor switched the radio to the farm alert channel. "All stations farm alert, this is Bravo Whisky heading for Kensington with a serious casualty; we need an air casevac, can anyone assist, over."

Silence…

Iffor tried again, "All stations, all stations, farm alert, this is Bravo Whisky, we need an urgent air casevac, over."

To complete the transmission, Iffor said, "Bravo Whisky, nothing heard, out."

"That's it, no option but to drive like hell for Kensington," said Harry. "Hang on to your hats."

Then the miracle; Iffor had hung the headset over the butt of the Bren so now everyone heard the faint but readable, "G'day Bravo Whisky, this is Digger Digby flying into Kensington from Kariba, how can I help, over."

Iffor forced himself to speak calmly, fighting the emotion in his voice: "Digby, can you land on the North road and take our man into Kensington, over."

"No wucking furries mate; get to the turn off as quick as you can and I'll fly up the North road to meet you. When you see my landing light in the air, dim your headlights, stop in the centre of the road and come up on the air and guide me in, over."

Thanks to the combination of Digby's flying skills and the clear, light African sky, some ten or twelve minutes later Shamus was propped up on a stretcher, loaded into the aircraft and airborne en route to Kensington.

Iffor had one last message for Digby: "I'll get my HQ to have an ambulance waiting at the airstrip, over."

"No need sport, I've done this before, though not at night, I put down on the playing field behind the hospital, just get your HQ to tell them we're coming, they know the drill. Out."

A very relieved, though very angry, Iffor sent his 'situation report' and estimated time of arrival to Kensington. Phil would alert the hospital.

They arrived back in Kensington around midnight and drove straight into the MT yard at the back of the drill hall. The Colour Sergeant was waiting for them: "Bad day at the office boss?"

"You could say that," replied Iffor grimly, and climbed out of the Champ. "I'd appreciate it if you will wrap things up here. I've got to look in on Shamus."

"No need boss, I've been up to the hospital: they've drained his chest and stabilised him. He's sleeping like a baby. I told them you'd be in first thing in the morning to see him and Digby."

"Digby?" Iffor suddenly wished he didn't have to ask the question. "What in hell's name has happened to Digby?"

The Colour made him wait for an answer. "Line up with the other three, please sir, let's get these weapons cleared and put away." Iffor obeyed and waited for the Colour's command. "Unload," then, "For inspection, port arms."

As he inspected the weapons he went on, "Apparently, Digby was already short of fuel when he diverted to pick up Shamus. His engine cut out as he was landing; he had to flop down in the hospital car park; he's got two broken legs, but I left him drinking a can of Castle, so he's okay."

They handed in weapons and ammunition and dumped all the stores in the drill hall. Tomorrow would be soon enough to sort them out and hand them in; Iffor wanted to get the boys home as soon as possible.

"Lie in tomorrow lads. On parade at 0900, sort out the stores.

"Time and place for my debrief, 1100 hours, my office.

"All to attend, please Colour."

Morning came all too soon. Mrs Patel had waited up for Iffor with sandwiches and tea, and insisted he took a large Cape brandy to bed with him, but sleep didn't come easily. The Colour had made light of Shamus's wound; the bullet had exited admittedly, but Iffor knew the damage the bullet would have caused internally, especially the high velocity 7mm round that Verity used, and judging by the exit wound, the round was almost certainly soft-nosed and hollow point.

Mrs Patel was waiting in the breakfast room with tea and toast, instead of insisting on the usual fried banquet. "I thought you'd be in a hurry to get up to the hospital," she said thoughtfully.

Iffor drove to the hospital, roughly a mile past the railway station, arriving about eight, just in time for elevenses, he mused.

He went first to the ward where Shamus was, and was pleasantly surprised to see Digby in the next bed, one leg in traction, the other in plaster to the knee.

Shamus was propped up in bed, his chest swathed in bandages, a drip administered a drug of some sort into his arm, while ominously, a drainage tube led from his chest and disappeared under the bed.

Iffor sat carefully on Shamus's bed and took his hand. "Sorry about this old chap; this isn't what I had planned."

Shamus managed a smile, looked down at Iffor's hand and said, "People will talk." His head fell back on the pillow while he spent a few moments recovering from the effort of speaking, then asked, "What happened?"

"What happened old son, was a complete breakdown in communications; Ed Dix didn't know we were coming. They were 'stood to' at last light and we appeared out of the gloom; they opened fire."

Iffor didn't think it necessary to elaborate and, to change the subject, turned to Digby.

"You told me you were the nearest thing to a Vulture when it came to flying."

Digby smiled at him, "No, what I said was, I was the nearest thing to a vulture."

A nurse appeared, "I've got to throw you out, Lieutenant; the doctor would like a word with you in his office at the end of the ward."

Iffor shook Digby's hand. "This is one of those occasions when thank-you just doesn't seem enough."

"It'll do," said Digby gruffly.

With great effort Shamus held his hand out to Iffor who gripped it firmly and sincerely. "Don't bother turning up on parade today, have a lie in; see you later."

As he walked away, he heard Shamus's laboured voice, "That's— my—boss,—all—fucking—heart."

The door of the doctor's office was open, with the doctor sitting behind his desk talking on the telephone. He beckoned to Iffor to come in and take a seat.

Finished, he stood and offered his hand. "Van De Merwe, Doctor in charge. I'm looking after your boys. Now, your man Shamus," he looked through his papers in front of him, "we don't seem to have a surname."

"McGuiness," Iffor said.

"Thank-you." The doctor went on, "GSW to the chest. We've drained his chest and stabilised him, but as you probably know, the bullet will have taken dirty clothing and other debris into the wound and that is what concerns me most, so I've arranged a casevac for him to Salisbury. The chest surgeon there can open him up and have a look see and repair any damage.

"As for the pilot, broken femur and ankle. He's going to be with us for a few weeks, but he'll be okay."

"Can I assume, Doctor, that Shamus will make a full recovery?"

"That all depends on what the chest surgeon finds, but I'm hopeful. Considering that he was very close to death when he came in last night, he's doing well."

Iffor stood to leave, "Can the rest of the team come to see him?"

"For a short while only, about one o'clock. We are putting him on the evening train from New Epsom; the army have a couple of casualties supported by a medical team they are sending to Salisbury; he'll be well looked after."

Blue Watch were already in the drill hall with the Colour when Iffor arrived a little before nine. They'd brought the Champ trailer into the drill hall to re-pack it ready for the next 'off', which seemed like a good idea.

"We seem to be a man short, apart from our wounded I mean." Iffor looked quizzically at the Colour Sergeant.

"Yessir, Phil Hill, said he had something to attend to in the Watch Room, but I think he's just keeping out of your way."

Iffor glanced at his watch. "Keep them active till ten; then give them a lecture on section battle drills; eleven hundred debrief; then we'll stand them down until tomorrow morning You can give them a verbal warning order: fighting patrol on Thursday."

Eleven hundred, a sombre Blue Watch came into the training wing office.

Iffor stood behind his desk shuffling his notes and without looking up, said, "Grab a chair lads, if there aren't enough to go round get some from the orderly room.

"Colour, my compliments to Miss Patel, and ask her to join us please and keep a look out for Inspector Saxon. I've asked him to join us."

The Colour returned with both Josie and Pete Saxon in tow. Iffor sat down, indicating silence was now required. "Before we go any further, I've been to see Shamus, he's holding his own; he's being casevact to Salisbury on the evening train; he will be at home to visitors at thirteen thirty hours should you wish to visit him.

"Now down to the business at hand.

"We'll start with our comms team. Phil, perhaps you'd like to explain what went wrong at your end; please stand."

Phil had prepared his statement. "As instructed…"

"Ordered," Iffor interrupted.

Phil went on, "I phoned the Dix farm at sixteen hundred, but I was unable to make contact, the line was down. I made the entry in the log, writing on the last line of the page: 'Phoned Dix farm at sixteen hundred.' Then I turned the page and on the fresh page I wrote, 'Unable to make contact, advise Sunray when he comes up on the air.'"

He looked at Iffor. "We were keeping a listening watch, waiting for you to contact us."

"Go on," said Iffor.

"I knew it was essential that I made contact with the farm so I went around to the police station to use the farm alert radio; they told me they couldn't contact the Dix farm because someone at the farm had left the radio on transmit..."

Phil was more relaxed now. Speaking with confidence, he went on, "About fifteen minutes to six, when the shift was due to change, I went round to the police station for another try at the radio. Before I went, I turned back the page on the log so that Evil who was taking over from me would see my entry, that I had phoned the farm. I still wasn't able to raise the farm and when I got back to our Watch Room you'd already spoken to Evil. I asked Evil if he'd passed the message on to you; he said he had so I went off duty."

Evil stood up, "When I took over the radio, I looked at the log and saw the entry, 'Phoned Dix farm', I turned the page but because of the cheap paper we have to use, the pages had stuck together and I turned over two pages, to a blank page, so the message I had to pass on to you was simply, 'phoned farm'."

"Thank you, Phil, Evil. Please sit down." Iffor got to his feet. "I do not intend playing the blame game, the buck stops with me, but," he paused, and looking directly at Phil said, "I ordered you personally to pass the farm message on to me and had you done so..." He left the rest of the sentence unsaid; he was just as much to blame for Shamus being shot.

Iffor sat and shuffled his notes again, giving the team time to digest what had just been said. Then he began, "Gentlemen, our first effort in the field on Op Krait was as far as I am concerned a great success, up until our last R.V. that is. I was greatly impressed by the team in the field and by the very professional operating of the Watch Team. Phil,

I'd appreciate it if you will remain in command of the Watch Team. Here endeth my debrief; you may smoke, ten minute break, back in eight minutes please, we've other things to discuss."

The Colour came up to him during the break. "Good speech boss, you've got them on your side."

"It's called 'turning a bad situation to your own advantage'," Iffor replied, "I'm very good at it."

They resumed their seats and Iffor began, "When the terrs get to hear about our performance at the Dix farm—and they will—it will go to making them feel more confident. They will regard us as a bunch of amateurs, which of course is to our advantage. It might make them a little more ambitious, which is why we ought to take certain precautions.

"Until the Battalion gets back, I want everyone armed at all times; that means taking your weapons home with you.

"Colour, I want you to plan and rehearse a fall back plan for a possible attack on this drill hall.

"Josie, I don't want you isolated—you will move your desk into the Colour's office and be familiar with his plans.

"Inspector, you've been very patient sitting there, but I wanted you to know first-hand what went wrong at the Dix farm and I want you involved in our plans.

"If the terrorists attack this drill hall or if an assassination attempt is made, your people will be involved, so I think it will be a good idea for your officers in the station to be armed and familiar with our defence plans."

Pete stood up. "I agree with all you have said. However, we don't want to cause panic on the streets, therefore, my beat constables will continue to patrol the streets unarmed."

"Good idea," Iffor agreed. "Now gentlemen, before you go, I think the Colour has given you a warning order for operations on Thursday. 'Fighting patrol': time and place for 'O' group tomorrow morning 0800 hours. You can stand down for the rest of the day; thank-you for your patience. Colour, remain behind please…

"Bob, tomorrow and this afternoon I've places to go, things to do and people to see. I've got to formulate a plan 'B', I can't rely on my fairy godmother descending from the skies to casevac my casualties and

I've got to have a faster way of moving troops when necessary, so I'm going to ask the mine for the loan of their Islander if and when we need it; so, after my briefing tomorrow I'd like you to organise some training for the lads, weapons and range, please."

Iffor and the Colour made their way down into the drill hall where Henry was talking to Pete. As the two joined them, Henry said, "A favour please boss, it's the time of the month and I need to leave town for a while."

The Colour looked at Iffor who, like him, was unable to contain himself and broke into a fit of childlike giggling. Henry blushed. "You bastards, I mean the time is right to paint the falls; it only happens once a month, and it's got to be this evening and dawn tomorrow. I'll be back for the briefing."

"Will you be on your own when you go off painting?" Iffor asked.

Henry shook his head. "No, my friend Paul will be with me."

Iffor looked at the Colour for some support. "Should be safe enough sir, it's about two K's from Angel Falls farm."

Iffor wasn't happy, but he couldn't think of a reason to stop him.

"Okay, but I want you to take your rifle and magazines with you."

"But boss, I'm useless with a rifle and it will only get in the way."

"Them's the rules," said Iffor, then, jokingly said to the Colour, "I suppose we could give him a couple of 36 grenades."

"Now that is a good idea," the Colour said, and to Iffor's horror, the man looked serious. "Fishing," he continued. "The Falls have the finest bottle nose bream in Africa. When Henry's finished painting he can lob a tin of bully into the pool to attract the fish, then lob a grenade in amongst them. Henry, make sure you take a good landing net with you and Friday night you and the boss can come round for dinner."

Iffor went back upstairs to his office and phoned the mine manager, making an appointment to see him the following morning. His next task was to seek out Davy Jones; that wouldn't be difficult and he felt he'd earned a pint.

As he left his office, he caught a hint of Josie's perfume that still lingered. Davy would have to wait. He opened the door to her office. "Pie and a pint at the Elephant?" he asked.

"Love to, just give me a minute to powder my nose."

As they stepped into the street, she happily took his arm. "I'm glad you asked me."

They found a table on the balcony of the hotel bar overlooking the main street. While he waited for the waiter to come for their order he was able to study her as she sat side on to him: floral calf-length skirt, crisp white blouse with a loosely knotted silk scarf about her neck giving some protection from the sun; no make-up except for painted toenails contrasting with silver sandals. "Penny for them?" she asked.

"Just admiring the view and wondering if there's a man in your life, apart from me that is, not to mention Pete, Blue Watch and two companies of infantry when they come back."

The waiter came and took their order, the speciality of the house, rare beef and horseradish sandwiches.

She laughed quite sincerely and said, "I know what you mean. No, there isn't a special man around. Mummy and Daddy came to Africa to get away from the old Indian customs. They didn't want me being forced into an arranged marriage, so my only loves were Daddy and my brother."

"Brother!" Iffor was about to take a sip of beer, but he put the glass down. "I didn't know you had a brother."

"When we came to Africa," she explained, "he stayed in India to complete his education. He joined us here, expecting to take me back to India to marry a cousin I'd never even met. When Daddy refused to let me go, my brother disowned us and returned to India. I've never heard from him or of him since, so with Daddy dead, my brother back in India, no, I have no man in my life," but looking into Iffor's face she said, chuckling and in unison with him, "Apart from you, Pete, Blue Watch and two companies of infantry."

As they laughed together at their little joke he reached across the table and took her hand. Suddenly he was looking into her face and all his cares were gone; suddenly no one could possibly upset him, suddenly...

"Hello, you two, I thought I'd find you here." Pete drew up a chair and joined them.

Iffor quickly released her hand, struggling with his emotions and feelings; he hadn't had these sort of feelings since he fondled his Brno pistol for the first time prior to buying it from Foultons at Bisley.

The waiter appeared with the sandwiches. Pete turned up the corner of one of them, "Roast beef! Good, I'm starving."

Iffor's dreams of being alone with Josie were now in tatters. "Best you bring another plate of sandwiches and another round of drinks," he said to the waiter.

Pete was in buoyant mood. "I bring good tidings, lovely people—the fair and lovely Helen feels it will safer and much better for her and the lad if they move into town sooner rather than later. We are going to bring the wedding forward.

Josie got up, wrapped her arms around Pete's neck and kissed him on the cheek. "So when did all this happen?"

"I've just got off the phone to her." He looked at Iffor. "The line's been repaired. She heard about the shooting at Ed's farm and it made her realise just how vulnerable and isolated she and the boy are, so she's decided to quit while she's ahead. We'll get married, she'll get a job in town and young Jamie will go to a proper school, and we'll all live happily ever after."

"I'm absolutely delighted for you both. When does all this happen?" Iffor said, watching anxiously while Pete munched his way through the sandwiches.

"I'm not going to rush her. She'll tell me when she's ready. Then you and I will go out to the mission and collect her."

He downed his beer and beckoned to the waiter.

"Not for me," Josie stood up, "I must get back, things to do."

Iffor started to his feet.

"No," she said, "you stay and talk to Pete—he'll explode if he doesn't talk to someone."

When she'd gone, Pete became the serious policeman again. "Thanks for inviting me to your meeting this morning. I told my lads what happened to Shamus. That will stop any false rumours around the town."

He went on: "I'm having some sandbags put into the cavities behind the front office counter, our first line of defence. Agnes carries an Uzi and Sergeant Banda his Greener gun and I've dusted off my Colt 45."

"That's not an issue weapon," said Iffor. "Where did you pick that up?"

"Northern Ireland; the owner didn't need it any more—he had no hands."

"Careless!"

"Yes... arming a bomb he'd just planted."

Deep in conversation, Iffor told Pete of his plan "B" and the possibility of using the mine's Islander aircraft for casevac or moving troops in a hurry.

"Are you telling me this out of common courtesy?" said Pete, "Or are you thinking I might be able to give you some support if you're in the shit, bearing in mind I can only muster about eight constables at any given time?"

"Either way," Iffor stood to leave. "I'll feel happier with another string to my bow. Now if you'll excuse me I'm off to a meeting with a chimp and his pet man."

As Iffor entered the bar, now in uniform, the doorman in white livery and red fez came to attention and saluted. Iffor returned the salute and noticed for the first time the medals including the Burma star on his chest. Iffor paused in front of him and touched the medal. "KAR?" he asked.

The African beamed with pleasure. "Yes sir, Third Battalion King's African Rifles."

Making a mental note to invite this old soldier up to the drill hall to speak to his young Rhodesian soldiers, Iffor entered the bar and found Davy Jones exactly where he knew he would be.

Coming straight to the point, Iffor said, "Do I need to remind you that you are a signatory to the official secrets act?"

Davy sensed something important was about to be said. "No sir, I most certainly do not need to be reminded."

"Good, I might," Iffor said it again, "I *might* have need of your services. I may well ask you at some stage, day or night, to crew the Islander to assist with a casevac or re-supply. Can you do that for me?"

"Piece of piss, I did that sort of thing many times in the air force." Davy was now a changed man with a purpose in life.

Having discussed various details including code words to authenticate future operations, Iffor left, leaving Davy looking a picture of happiness and ten years younger.

Back in his office, he wrote up his orders for the forthcoming operation. Next, looking at the map, he checked his route to the mine for his meeting the following day.

He was about to leave when his phone rang. "It's the Colonel for you, Iffor," Josie said. "It's a secure line, but be careful; putting you through."

"Afternoon Colonel, Meredith here."

"Ah, Iffor, how are things with you down there?"

"Bit of a setback Colonel; I've had a casualty, friendly fire, but apart from that I'm pleased with the situation."

"Good man, now let me tell you how things are at this end. We are very much on the offensive but our resources in men and materials, particularly helicopters are very stretched. I've had to re-deploy Bravo company to Mwonza to help out Support company, so they won't be coming back to Kensington as planned, and Alpha company have been tasked to keep an eye on Faira, in Zambia, so their homecoming may also be delayed. One R.A.R (Rhodesian African Regiment), who were due to relieve us have been inserted into Kariba."

The Colonel went on, "The bottom line is, Iffor, if you get in a jam, we can't help, you're on your own. Any questions?"

"No questions Colonel. Thanks for phoning, have a good war. Goodbye."

Walking back to his hotel, Iffor contemplated his evening: dinner at the hotel, a bottle of South African wine, then an evening alone in his room with his weapons and a cleaning kit—perfect!

He entered his office next morning, in compliance with his own orders carrying his Ruger Carbine and wearing his Brno in his shoulder rig. Instead of the customary shorts, shoes and long stockings, he wore bush shirt, K.D. trousers, boots and puttees

The Colour stood and saluted. He was wearing a business-like Hi-Power on his hip with a lanyard from the pistol about his neck, the rest of the team wearing pouches and carrying rifles.

"Sit down please gentlemen, you may not smoke. Pete, Josie, glad to see you could make it." Iffor turned to the wall map behind his desk and pointed to the area west of the Great North Road and began his briefing:

"Ground: The farms to the west of the Great North Road: North Road farm; Arc Angel farm; Long Acre farm and the various African villages scattered about the area.

"Situation: Enemy forces: we still have a terrorist group in the area;

"Friendly forces: just us and the police if we are pushed.

"This gem of information was passed on to me by the C.O. yesterday afternoon. We can expect no help from New Epsom, and there will be a delay in our soldiers coming back to Kensington. We are now on our own, gentlemen.

"Mission: As before: vehicle check points and showing the flag in the area; this time we'll stay away from farms after dark.

"Execution: Phase one: Mount the patrol at the drill hall;

"Phase two: Proceed to the Great North Road crossroads and establish vehicle check point;

"Phase three: Make our way to the farms area and establish a firm base.

"Timings: We leave here 0800hrs Thursday morning.

"Orbat: Ops team Phil, Henry, who seems to be conspicuous by his absence, and Hennie. Phil, you'll have to arrange the shifts around the men you've got."

Phil nodded: "Okay boss."

"Patrol team: myself, Mad Harry, Evil, Mal Jackson and Alvin.

"Coms: Phil, you will keep a listening watch; don't contact us unless it is important. We will give you a radio check every hour or so, and I will give you a sit rep at 1600hours."

Iffor went on: "Phil, you will be responsible for contacting the farms in the area and tell them that we are in their area.

"Now gentlemen, you may smoke while I go over all that again;

"Josie, Pete, thanks for coming, I know you've work to do."

As they left the room, Iffor called after Josie: "Get a progress report on Shamus please."

After the briefing, Iffor took the Colour aside. "You've got the range jacked up?" he asked.

"Yes boss, we're using the 25 meter range—that should be sufficient."

"Fine, look Colour, I'm concerned about Henry. It's not like him to be late on parade; can you send one of your serfs round to his flat to see if he's home?"

"And if he isn't?"

"Tell Pete Saxon we've a man missing, then phone me at the mine."

PART NINE

There are two kinds of ambush, 'hasty' and 'deliberate'. The hand signal for a hasty ambush is the hand cupped over the mouth and the thumbs down indicating enemy.

IFFOR DROVE THOUGHTFULLY to the mine in his newly acquired pick-up. He should have been thinking what he would discuss with the mine manager, but his mind was on Henry. He tried to tell himself that the artist in Henry would make him forget all about time if the light was in the right place for him, but Iffor was feeling that stab of fear, that feeling of dread.

He was shown straight into the mine manager's office, a spacious affair with a large highly polished desk, behind which was the obligatory leather swivel chair. Two large comfortable armchairs, with an Indian ornately carved coffee table between, completed the furnishings. The manager left the comfort of his chair to greet Iffor.

"Tweed," he said, "George Tweed."

"…but most of my friends call me 'Harris'," Iffor interjected.

The man smiled, "Right first time, come and sit down." He indicated the armchairs. "Coffee?"

While the coffee was being served, Iffor was able to study his man: tall, upright with a military bearing, late fifties and sporting a Royal Engineers' tie.

"A fellow sapper I see." Iffor pointed at the tie.

"Ah, I thought you looked too intelligent to be an infantryman. Which regiment?"

"I was airborne sappers, after a couple of years with infantry," Iffor replied.

The manager was obviously enjoying the military banter, so Iffor encouraged him; he needed to get this man on his side.

The manager went on: "What prompted you to see the light and become a sapper?"

"It was no big deal," Iffor began and thought, I've been down this road before!

The manager looked interested, so Iffor went on, "I was in Cyprus during the Eoka days. I was sent on detachment to an engineer squadron, which turned out to be an independent parachute squadron, who were building a bridge across a river. Since it would speed up the deployment of troops in the area, the terrorists didn't like it and started doing churlish things, like ambushing troops moving stores and equipment along the only road leading to the bridging site. With insufficient men to protect convoys, the O.C. came up with a rather good idea. He put the whole area out of bounds to the locals and formed a small team; a sapper full corporal, a sapper and myself. I was a lance jack then. I was to advise on likely ambush sites.

"We were called a 'military survey team', but what really happened was, at the likely ambush site which I selected, I pretended to take bearings and make sketches while the other two laid anti-personnel mines, the number one carrot mine, behind the rocks that the terrorists might use for cover. It was ironic that we were on our way to the site, from where we were ambushed and I was wounded. Unfortunately, our driver was killed. Jamie, the sapper corporal got an M.M. for his actions that day."

"Are we talking about Jamie Dix?" the manager asked.

"Yes, my very good friend and comrade Jamie Dix," Iffor replied.

The manager pointed his finger at Iffor. "I know who you are now, I've heard all about you. You still haven't told me why you became a sapper. More coffee?"

Iffor sipped at his coffee. Although he was enjoying talking to the manager, he couldn't take his mind off Henry, but he continued, "Well, the O.C. was very impressed with our actions; when the terrorists realised what we'd done, the number of ambushes fell quite considerably. He visited me in hospital and told me if I needed a job there was always a place for me in his squadron. My battalion was sent to Borneo; I went back to England to recover, then was posted back to Winchester to train recruits for three years. So faced with the prospect of three years at the depot or joining an active service unit, I opted for the red beret and the extra three pounds and six shillings a week para pay."

Iffor couldn't help but look at his watch. He was anxious to get back and the manager realised this. "Now, tell me how we can help."

Iffor went through his plan "B" involving the mine Islander aircraft. He explained how Davy Jones would use his expertise in crewing the aircraft and the code words to initiate the operation.

The manager sat quietly nodding in approval, waiting for Iffor to finish.

"We'll help in any way we can. We rotate three pilots. I'll have them all in and brief them myself. Any requests we get from you, we will consider a priority."

They stood and shook hands. Iffor put his beret on, stood to attention and saluted, "Thank you—Colonel?" he queried.

"Yes, Colonel Royal Engineers 11th Armoured Brigade."

Iffor went into the outer office to collect his Carbine and pistol belt. The secretary was waiting for him with the message he was dreading. "Your HQ phoned; can you get back to Kensington as soon as possible and report straight to the police station?"

He parked his pick-up in the M.T. yard behind the drill hall and walked briskly to the police station. Pete was on the chair behind his desk, a civilian sitting opposite him writing a statement. The man stood up as Iffor entered the office.

"Iffor, meet Paul. He was with Henry when he was killed."

Iffor stopped short of the desk; now that he knew, he felt relieved. He stared at Pete. "You've certainly got a way with words, you thoughtless bastard."

"If there was an easier way of telling you, I would have done," Pete replied.

Agnes brought in a chair for Iffor while Paul sat looking expectantly at the Inspector. "Tell the Lieutenant what happened," Pete said, "from this morning."

Paul started, "Henry wanted to catch the light of the rising sun over Botha's pool, below the falls. While it was still dark we got up; we were camping in Botha's cave as usual. I started to start tidying up and packing up our gear and preparing breakfast. Henry went down to the pool to set up his easel and paints, then came back to get changed."

"Into female clothes I presume," interrupted Iffor.

"Yes, he said it gave him the freedom to express himself on canvas."

"Sorry, please go on."

"Anyway, from the back of the cave that we used for our sleeping quarters, I was just able to see Henry sitting on his stool waiting for the light to improve. I knew he wanted to get back to town early so I busied myself packing our gear. After half an hour or so when the sun was just rising and it was quite light, something made me look out towards the pool. Henry was walking backwards slowly and deliberately towards the cave. As I looked past him, I saw three armed men on our side of the stream advancing on Henry, and another two men crossing the stream behind them.

"I knew they couldn't see me so I stayed put. Just as Henry reached the mouth of the cave they opened up on him. The force of the bullets hitting him knocked him back into the cave. I was unarmed, I couldn't help him.

"He was able to grab his rifle which was propped up in the entrance to the cave and started shooting back at them. He turned and gestured to me to stay where I was.

"Then he must have realised how badly wounded he was. I could see he was kneeling propped up against the wall of the cave in a pool of blood; I think his femoral artery was shot through and he was hit in the body. He shouted to the terrorists in Ndebele that he was wounded and was surrendering. He asked them not to shoot as he was coming to them. Then he reached across for his ammo pouches and pulled a grenade from the pouch. I didn't know he had it with him. He pulled the pin from the grenade but held on to the arming lever, then, with an almighty effort, I really don't know how he did it, he pulled himself on to his feet and using his rifle as a crutch, he started to hobble towards the terrorists, holding the grenade in his right hand down by his side; the frock would have hidden it from view. The terrorists were now walking towards him; they were jeering at him and one of them had laid down his rifle and drawn his panga. Henry still continued to move towards them, talking to them as he did so.

"From where I was watching, I saw Henry release the arming leaver. The terrorists were only five or six feet away. He then stopped and held out his hand with the grenade in it, as if offering a gift to them. The grenade exploded! I turned away. When I looked again, Henry and two of the terrs were obviously dead, and the third terrorist was on all fours coughing up a lot of blood. The other two terrorists crossing the stream had turned and ran back into cover.

"I knew I had just one chance to escape. I left everything, ran out of the cave and along the track to where we left the Mazda. It was only when I got to the Mazda that I realised the keys were in Henry's day clothes, so I just kept on running. I eventually reached the road to North Road Farm and you can imagine how relieved I was when I found Father Sean standing beside his mini bus."

"Father Sean!" Iffor couldn't contain himself. "What the fuck was he doing there?"

Pete interjected, "Among his other pastoral duties, Sean runs a sort of employment agency; he supplies labourers to the local farms and runs a sort of taxi service, and since the labourers work from six in the morning till noon he is often out and about before dawn. Now please go on, Paul."

"Thank you. Well, Father Sean said he'd heard shooting and an explosion so he was waiting there in case he could be of help to anyone. I told him there might well be a couple of terrorists chasing me so we got into his bus and he drove me into town. I told him what had happened; he dropped me at the police station and drove off."

For a few moments, no one spoke. Iffor admired the way Paul had held his composure when delivering his story, but now he was beginning to fall apart and tears were trickling down his cheeks. Pete stood and said, "Finish writing your statement, Paul; we'll leave you in peace now," and beckoned to Iffor to join him in the outer office.

Agnes was standing behind the big desk now fortified with sandbags, her Uzi resting on the desk, but within easy reach. "Our man in there could do with a motherly touch," Pete told her, "See what you can do for him."

She nodded and picking up the Uzi waddled into Pete's office, closing the door behind her.

"Sorry about your man, he died well."

"It's only what I would have expected from him," Iffor replied. "I'll get the team together and collect the bodies and weapons."

"You can't, and you're too late anyway; it's a police matter, a murder and I've already sent Timothy Banda and a team out to the site. It's now a crime scene."

Pete saw the look of concern on his friend's face. "They'll be okay, I put Tim and two constables in the Rhino and my Detective Constable with another officer in the Rover. They should be back early evening."

"You realise this was a deliberate attack, not a chance meeting, don't you?" Iffor said. "And the terrs must have moved bloody fast to mount the attack, so someone in this town got word to them very quickly."

"I'm aware of that," said Pete, "and as part of my investigations I'll question Paul and find out who he told, and of course I'll question your lot; they all knew what Henry was up to."

Iffor went back to the drill hall and, pausing just long enough to stick his head into the orderly room to tell Josie, announced, "Henry's been killed," and went to his office.

He needed time alone, time to think, time to plan how he would break the news to Blue Watch when they came back from the range.

He went back into the orderly room. Josie was dabbing her eyes with her hankie. "Find Henry's next of kin address for me please, I'll need to write to them. Then advise Battalion of his death, as yet unconfirmed."

Josie nodded. "Cause of death?"

"Enemy action whilst on active service."

Back in his office Iffor began to draft a letter to Henry's next of kin. He knew that delay in these matters would be fatal. The letter must be written now.

Josie interrupted him. "Henry's next of kin," she said.

Iffor looked at the paper she handed him. "Good God, are you sure about this?"

"That's what he told me when he signed up."

"What surname did he use?" Iffor felt embarrassed. He should have known the surnames of all his men.

"Brown, Henry Brown," she said, and left Iffor to his task.

As he finished the letter, short but to the point, the sound of voices down in the drill hall told him the troops were back from the range. He needed to speak to them.

The Colour saluted him. "Want to inspect weapons?" he asked.

"No thank-you, just get them seated please Bob, something important to say."

When they were seated, Iffor stood for a few moments in silence just looking at them.

The manner of Henry's death made him realise just how proud he was of them, especially knowing that he was one of them. He began, "Gentlemen, a little after dawn this morning Henry was killed by terrorists. His friend Paul managed to survive, thanks to Henry."

Iffor related Paul's story to them. When he finished, he unfolded the letter he had just written. "This is the letter I have written to Henry's dad; it's on behalf of us all:

"To, Lieutenant General Sir Alec Glaxtonbury."

Surprise was complete—not a word was uttered.

> *"Dear General,*
> *I write to inform you of the death in action of the man known to us as Henry Brown, but who has nominated you as his father and next of kin.*
> *Henry was killed at first light this morning when he and a civilian with him were surprised by a gang of five terrorists.*

Although severely wounded at the start of the action, Henry fought back, killing two and wounding one of the terrorists before being killed himself.

As a result of Henry's selfless action, the civilian was able to escape.

'Harry' as we called him was part of a small but elite team engaged on a hazardous operation. He was popular and will be missed.

Confirmation of his death will follow in due course.

Yours etc

"That OK?" Iffor asked.

Mad Harry stood up. "Thanks boss, that will do. Who's bringing the body in?"

Iffor relaxed, grabbed a vacant chair and sat down among them. It was as if Henry's death had bought them all closer. "The police," he said, "and they've asked us to stay clear of the site until tomorrow; it's a police crime scene.

"Now for some good news. Shamus is on the road to recovery and is being transferred to our hospital here in Kensington in the next few days.

"The other bit of news is that the mine Islander has been put at our disposal.

"And finally, I'm bringing our estimated time of departure for Op Krait forward to 0500 hours, so everyone on parade by four. We'll load the Champ and trailer now, and please note, we'll be staying out two nights; back on Saturday.

"Our Orbat remains the same.

"Phil, you'll have to make do with what you've got unless the Colour can loan us one of his sick, lame and lazy."

"No can do, boss. They are on the morning train to New Epsom. The Colonel wants them—he needs every man he can get."

Josie had joined them. "I can help with the watch keeping," she said. "I'd like to do my bit."

"Okay with you Phil?" Iffor asked.

"Love to have her," said Phil.

Wouldn't we all? thought Iffor.

"Questions? No? Right, over to you, Colour. Get the lads loading the stores: ration packs for three days; first line scale of ammo. I'll be in my office if you need me, writing my report to the Colonel."

Iffor wanted to protect Henry from any ridicule, plus, he had to cover his own arse; he had after all given Henry his permission to go painting dressed as a woman, and he had ordered him to take his rifle and two grenades with him.

His report was brief, to the point and written in military language the army would accept:

"It was my intention to drive to Angel Falls myself to recce for a good firm base to operate from on the next stage of Op Krait.

"However, when Rifleman Brown asked for permission to go to Angel Falls to paint and fish for a few hours and since he was going to be accompanied, I agreed and asked him to make sketches of the area and select a Bivvi area.

"Since he was a member of this unit, I insisted he went armed.

"It was unfortunate that he was confronted by a group of at least five terrorists.

"In the ensuing action we know from the civilian witness, who was lucky to escape, that Rifleman Brown killed two terrorists and wounded a third before being killed himself."

He pressed the intercom and asked Josie to come in. "You just caught me," she said, "I was just leaving, time to go home."

Iffor looked at his watch. "Sorry, I didn't realise the time."

He handed her his report to Battalion. "Tart that up a bit and get it sent up to New Epsom, please… Oh, and thanks for volunteering for watch keeping duties."

She smiled that devastating smile of hers. "I'm not normally one for bribes, but I'll accept dinner at the Elephant when you get back. Shall I book a table?"

Iffor went down to the drill hall. He had to get the team away home as quickly as possible; they needed an early night.

The men were loading magazines and stuffing them into their pouches; five twenty-round magazines, a further hundred-round in the Champ for each man and a 'thirty-six' each, primed.

In Cyprus Iffor had seen too many well-meaning, but stupid officers, sending men into the field on escort duties and the like with a token ten rounds, just to comply with the order that the men should be armed. If Blue Watch got into trouble, Iffor was determined lack of ammunition would not be the problem.

He walked across to the Colour and nodded towards the men. "I'm impressed," he said. "They look as if they are beginning to take soldiering seriously."

"Couldn't agree more. They were great on the range today. Fancy a beer? The Moth club should be open by now and we can take our weapons in there. Besides, I think the boys are having a couple in there."

They made their way down to the Moth Club, dumping their weapons and equipment in the strong room provided. An elderly Askari in Khaki drill, who was employed by the club as a night-watchman, stood guard. He was armed with the old Lee Enfield number one, probably the same one he used in the war.

As they all sat around the 'committee' table, Mad Harry said, "Fiver in the kitty, lads."

Iffor frowned. "We're not making a night of this, we've got a war to fight tomorrow."

Without thinking, Mad Harry continued, "Get the beers in Harry." Then he remembered the awful truth. Harry wouldn't be around to get the beers in future—Harry was dead. He muttered an apology and turning to the barman, indicated drinks all round, Lion or Castle, it didn't matter.

The talk around the table was subdued, almost hushed, with every sentence beginning, "Do you remember when Harry did this or that?" It was only the Colour who made any remark about Harry coming from a military background.

Finding conversation difficult, Iffor was quite relieved to see Pete standing in the entrance to the bar. He patted the top of his head, the 'on me' sign, and walked back into the lobby where Iffor joined him. "Problems?" Iffor asked.

Pete nodded, "Yes, we recovered Henry's body and the bodies of two terrs. Sergeant Banda thinks a third terrorist crawled into the bush and is dead."

Pete went on, "All the weapons had been taken away, probably by the other two terrs who made a run for it when Henry's grenade exploded. And that should have given my chaps a clue."

"Clue to what?" but Iffor knew what was coming.

"Henry's body was booby trapped. Henry was lying face down and when my chaps rolled him over onto the stretcher, the grenade underneath him exploded. It killed my detective constable."

After Pete left, Iffor walked back to the table. "Sorry to piss all over your strawberries, but I've news."

"It can't possibly be good," said Evil.

"Right first time," Iffor agreed. "The police recovered all the bodies. But someone had left a grenade under Henry's body; a cop was killed."

The Colour looked hard at Iffor, probably thinking the same thing— was the grenade one of the two he had given Henry, or was it the terr's own grenade? They'd find out in due course.

Iffor had a couple more beers, but realising he was getting the taste, made his excuses. "I'm off back to my hotel, a long bath, dinner then an early night; early start tomorrow boys."

"That's a point boss," said Mad Harry, "Why so early?"

"Because, my old mucker, the terrorists have developed a rather nasty habit of finding out about our plans, so changing our plans may well catch them wrong-footed and avoid any unpleasantness. It comes under the heading, 'Know your enemy'."

Back in his hotel room, Iffor emptied his pockets on to the bed and stepped out of his uniform, leaving it on the floor knowing Mrs Patel would retrieve it and have it washed and pressed by the morning. Wrapping a towel around his waist, he made his way to the bathroom, and while he waited for the bath to fill, shaved. A shave always made him feel better, more refreshed, a little more human.

He lingered in the bath longer than he intended, allowing guilt to interrupt his thoughts: He should have seen the mine that killed Elias; he shouldn't have let Henry go to Angel Falls; he shouldn't go into the field with half-trained men; he shouldn't... Mrs Patel knocked on the bathroom door: "Dinner in ten minutes."

As he entered the dining room he was delighted to see Josie sitting at his table.

"Thought you might like some company, take your mind off things." She looked gorgeous, dressed in a deep blue sari, no make-up, just a flower in her hair. "Don't worry," she said laughing, "we're not having curry, I've asked Auntie to serve steak and salad with a bottle of Cape Red."

"I couldn't possibly have asked for more," Iffor replied.

After the dishes were served and they were alone, he said, "I'm bloody glad you're here."

"It was Auntie's idea and I agreed with her, we didn't want you to be alone after what's happened today."

They ate for a while in silence, enjoying the meal and the wine and each other.

She reached across the table and touched his hand. "None of it was your fault."

He said softly, "Darling girl, it was all my fault, but I'm a soldier, I can live with it."

She tried to change the subject but made things worse. "Can I confirm Henry's death with Battalion?" She quickly realised what she had said and tried to stammer an apology.

His turn to put his hand on hers. "Thanks for reminding me. Yes, and get the letter off to his father please."

They finished the meal and although he tried to look at his watch discreetly, she noticed. "I'm keeping you," she said, "You must have lots to do," and before he could reply added, "and anyway, I've got to wash my hair."

They parted at the foot of the stairs, he to his room and her to go and have a chat to Auntie.

His kit and clothes were laid out ready for the morning. He spent a few minutes under the shower relaxing, then climbed gratefully into bed. It was just after ten—five hours sleep would do nicely. He lay in the darkness listening to the wind blowing through the jacaranda trees in the garden and smelling their fragrance.

He went through his mental check list for the following morning, ticking off each item. Then his thoughts turned to Josie; he was getting too close for comfort—maybe he should back off a little, maybe he should... The door of his bedroom opened and Josie came in, carefully closing it behind her. She stood by the side of his bed and dropped her nightdress to the floor, standing naked in front of him.

"I couldn't sleep either," she said, and slid in beside him.

"You told me you were going to wash your hair."

"I lied," she whispered.

It seemed no matter how early Iffor arrived at the drill hall, the Colour Sergeant was always in first and always looking 'bright-eyed and bushy-tailed', this morning being no exception. "Morning boss, I've been through the check list, all okay. Phil's fully charged the radio battery and the spare. He's already up in the Watch Room waiting for your radio check."

"God! But he was up early—did he sleep here?"

"As a matter of fact boss, he did. He slept beside the Champ all night, just to be on the safe side. Oh, and he's moved a camp bed into the Watch Room—says as long as you are in the field, he'll be in the Watch Room."

Iffor switched the radio on and pressed transmit: "Bravo Whisky radio check, over."

"Control, loud and clear, any last instructions, over."

"Bravo Whisky, yes. Ask the police if the hours of curfew are unchanged and advise me on a radio check. And confirm you are okay with procedure for scrambling Islander, over."

"Control, we can confirm that, over."

"Whisky Bravo, thanks Phil, out."

The patrol team assembled around Iffor and the Champ. The Colour Sergeant had already raised the door at the end of the drill hall. "Fall in lads, let the boss inspect you."

Iffor went through his normal procedure: weapons; ammo; water; field dressings and finally the order, "Prepare to load... Load!"

As they started to climb aboard the Champ, Iffor said, "I hope you bastards are sober and had an early night."

Evil looked at him slyly, "You're a fine one to talk! Your eyes look like piss holes in the snow—you look like you've been on the nest all night."

Iffor smiled at him and hoped no one noticed his face beginning to go red.

The vehicle moved slowly out of the drill hall, through the M.T. yard gates and onto the main road leading to the Great North Road. The first blush of dawn was just beginning to make itself noticed, and the dew on the jacaranda trees only intensified its perfume. Africa was at its best this time of the morning.

As they drove, Iffor reminded his team of immediate action drills for ambush:

"It's 'shoot and scoot' or 'stand and fight'.

"Number one priority: lay down concentrated fire and get out of the killing ground; or, if the vehicle becomes disabled, stand and fight, rallying around the Bren."

As expected, the team encountered no other vehicles on the road north. Whites as well as Blacks had a healthy regard for the curfew, and so they made good time to the North Road Farm turn off, Iffor's first R.V.

As they turned off the main road, the team stopped as planned, took up an all-round defence and cooked their compo breakfast.

Iffor came up on the air: "Bravo Whisky radio check, over."

"Control, loud and clear, reference curfew, hours unchanged, first light plus one hour until last light minus one hour, over."

"Roger control, we are now three miles west of Snipe. Over."

"Control, roger out."

Iffor had given Phil a list of code words comprising game birds' names for the farms and prominent areas he would be operating in. He knew it was very unlikely that terrorists would be able to monitor his radio traffic, but old habits die hard, especially good habits.

An hour or so later they drove into 'Snipe', North Road Farm.

There was already a security fence built around the farm and compound. As they stopped at the gate, a 'Guard Force' soldier carrying an Enfield number five rifle came out of the sanger to open the gate. "Heard you were coming. Charlie's up at the main house—he'll be glad to see you."

Charlie came out to meet them: short, square, barrel chested, bush shirt opened to the navel exposing a deeply tanned grey-haired chest, shorts, boots, no socks and a Ruger Black Hawk in a cross draw holster. "Charlie Shoesmith," he said, "and am I glad to see you boys! I know it's a bit early but come in and have a beer."

Iffor started to explain to Charlie the reasons why they couldn't have a beer. Then finding himself talking to an empty veranda, muttered, "Oh bollocks, if you can't beat 'em, join 'em." He just hoped Charlie didn't have any Krait.

Charlie took Iffor aside, leaving the team tucking into the hot samosas that his wife had prepared. "Thanks for coming," he said simply, "We are beginning to feel quite isolated. Although there are three farms in the area, they are ten miles apart, so we can't be much help to one another. I've got the two Guard Force men but they can't be on duty twenty-four hours a day."

"Have you had any sightings of terrs?" asked Iffor quietly.

"I haven't, but Shadrak, my game guard thinks a game track about three miles west of here is being used regularly by just one or two men; they could be poachers, or… who knows?" he shrugged.

"When did he last see tracks?"

"Monday; I confined him to the compound after that. I didn't want your boys running into a lone armed black man." Iffor took his map out of his map pocket and spread it on a table. "Can you show me?"

Charlie ran his finger along the old Mwonza Road running parallel to the road connecting the three farms. "There, that's where the game track joins the Mwonza Road." Iffor studied the map, looking, hoping for a clue to the terrorists' hide.

Aware Charlie was watching him, he said, "You do know we haven't got a clue where our local terrs are holed up, don't you? They just seem to materialise, cause havoc, and vanish."

Iffor wanted to spend time at each farm. He wanted his soldiers to be seen by the farm workers who would spread the word, so when Charlie suggested they stay for lunch, Iffor was happy to agree. "But no more beer," he warned.

Charlie took the team on a tour of inspection and to meet the Guard Force boys.

Iffor went in search of Shadrak; he wanted to know more about the tracks on the game trail.

He found the game guard feeding the chickens.

As he approached, Shadrak turned to face him, standing tall and erect with his pride and joy, a Mauser '98 rifle held across the crook of his arm.

He greeted Iffor: "I see you N'kosi."

"I see you M'dala."

Solomnly, they shook hands. Iffor studied his man, just as Shadrak studied him.

He was probably eighty plus, dressed in an old army jumper in spite of the heat, shorts and bare footed. His Mauser looked pristine; this was the standard German rifle that was issued to the Boers during the Boer war.

They squatted in the dust, each holding his rifle in both hands in front of him, Shadrak waiting patiently and politely for Iffor to ask his questions, for why else would an officer want to speak to him?

"M'dala, how often do men use the game trail?" Iffor used the man's title rather than his name—it showed respect.

"I think it is only one man, N'kosi. He comes once, twice a month, he will come again soon."

Iffor felt the hairs on the nape of his neck beginning to rise with excitement and anticipation.

"M'dala, is this man a poacher?"

"I do not think so."

"Have you seen him?"

"No, Inkosi, but he leaves tracks. He is very careful and moves slowly. He stops often to rest. I think he is carrying something heavy."

"M'dala, can you tell me when this man will use the track again?"

"I cannot N'kosi, but if I am allowed to go back into the bush, my jackal will tell me."

"How so, old man?"

"If the jackal feeds with me he is hungry, if he does not feed with me he is following a man through the bush feeding on that man's droppings."

Both men stood up. As they shook hands, Iffor said, "Go back into the bush, find out when this man is coming and tell me. You must do this thing for me."

"I will do as you ask, Inkosi."

Iffor returned to the farm house, trying to contain his excitement. The tracks, after all, could belong to a wood gatherer or someone just as innocent.

But his soldier's instinct told him otherwise.

On the veranda, Evil was showing off the virtues of his Bren gun to the Guard Force soldiers. "Weight, nineteen pounds three ounces, rate of fire six hundred rounds a minute and comes with thirteen magazines and because of its buffering system, almost recoilless."

Eric, one of the farm guards, ran his hands over the weapon. "Beautiful bit of kit, you wouldn't fancy swopping it for my wife I suppose? I'll throw in her car as well."

"No," said Iffor before Evil could reply, "Definitely not."

Charlie beckoned Iffor to a couple of comfortable armchairs on the veranda. "Let's have a chat." When seated, he asked, "What did you learn from old Shadrak? Anything of any help?"

"Every terrorist group needs a line of communication," Iffor explained. "They need to be able to pass information back to their masters and receive information and instructions. They also need to be supplied with heavy kit that they didn't bring into the country with them: mines; SAMs; not to mention money for bribes and wages. Even terrorists get paid."

Charlie was showing interest. Iffor went on: "I think our man out in the bush making regular trips is a courier, a messenger. He needs to be stopped."

Leaning back in his comfortable colonial armchair and feeling much more relaxed, Iffor said, "I've asked Shadrak to go back into the bush and find out when our man is on the move. That okay with you?"

"I think you'll find he's already gone," said Charlie.

After a light but filling lunch of cold ham and mashed mealie meal, Iffor and team drove out of the compound and headed north towards Arc Angel farm.

A couple of miles out, he stopped the Champ: "Quick 'O' group, chaps. We are heading for Arc Angel farm; to minimise the risk of ambush or mine, we'll have two men, one either side of the road about fifty metres in front of the Champ. We'll rotate every mile or so but Evil, you stay on the Bren. I'll walk down the centre of the road sniffing."

"Got a cold, boss?" said Alvin, not normally known for saying anything even remotely funny.

"Sniffing for mines, you cunt. Now, let me impart a little titbit of information you should know about. Shadrak, Charlie's game guard, tells me a man is making regular trips from Mwonza area. He's using an old game trail that crosses the old Mwonza Road about three Ks north of Charlie's farm.

"From what I've gleaned from Shadrak, I firmly believe this man is a terrorist courier and I've asked Shadrak to go back into the bush and to tell me when our man is on the trail again. We think it will be quite soon."

"How will he do that?" asked Evil. "By the time he's found the tracks our man will be long gone."

"He's going to have a word with his jackal," said Iffor. "Apparently, they have lunch together."

"Bloody stupid question to ask," muttered Evil. "Should have known better than to ask it."

Two uneventful hours later they marched into Arc Angel farm. The farm owner had moved to South Africa to sit out the war and avoid call-up, leaving his farm manager in charge. The man who came out to greet them was totally different from the previous farmer—sixtyish, tall, slim with greying hair, dressed in check sports shirt, cravat, probably his old school colours, mole skin trousers and trader boots, '37 pattern belt and holster revealing the butt of a First World War Webley .455.

He shook Iffor's hand. "Fotheringham," he said, "Archie Fotheringham. You and your chaps are very welcome."

Iffor had already been previously briefed by Pete that this was The Right Honourable Algernon Fotheringham, Coldstream guards with an M.C.

"Bring your boys in out of the sun."

He led the way up the steps and onto the cool, shaded veranda, typical of most farms except that this veranda was fortified with sandbags. "Same at the back," he said. "There are only four of us, including the Mem Sahib, but we can give good account of ourselves. My theory is, if the terrorists know how prepared we are, they won't hit us. Can't afford casualties. They can't take them with them and can't leave them behind alive."

Iffor had to confess to himself that he hadn't really thought about that one.

The house boy, in clean white shirt and shorts but bare footed, appeared.

"Beers all round please, Kaunda," said Archie. "You boys must be thirsty after your journey."

"These boys are thirsty at any time," muttered Iffor.

Excusing himself, he said, "Radio check, must tell the folks at home where we are," and went back to the Champ, leaving Archie in his element, talking to soldiers.

Iffor hoped against hope that Josie would be doing her turn keeping a listening watch.

His luck held. "Bravo Whisky for control, radio check over."

Josie's pure, lilting voice answered, "Control, loud and clear." A pause, then, "That sounds like my Sunray."

Iffor pressed 'transmit' so she could hear him chuckle before saying, "Roger, Sunray one set. Be advised, we are firm on Woodcock. Over."

He knew she would be giggling at the word firm, and afraid of what she might say and knowing the army at New Epsom might be listening in, said, "Bravo Whisky, out."

He floated back to the veranda. The last time he felt this good was when he shot the paddy gunman in Northern Ireland.

Archie took Iffor aside. "Heard about your chap at Angel Falls, bad news. We heard the shooting. I could have taken my two farm guards to investigate, but that would have left the farm undefended and I'm responsible for my workforce and the clinic and school we have here on the farm."

"You couldn't have done anything to help," Iffor said. "You did the right thing." And he related Henry's last gallant stand, excluding his attire.

He allowed the team a second beer, then called them around him: "We'll move off in thirty minutes chaps, we'll go and have a look at Angel falls. Then, if Archie agrees, we'll come back here and stand guard tonight. Archie, you can stand your Guard Force chaps down tonight; let them get a decent night's sleep."

"I don't know about them," said Archie, "but I'll certainly sleep easier with you chaps here. I'll have a braai going when you get back; we can throw a few steaks on it."

Clear of the compound, Iffor stopped the Champ for his 'O' group.

"Same routine lads, it's only a couple of Ks to the falls. Evil, radio check please and tell them we are moving on to 'pheasant'."

At the signpost, Angel Falls 1 mile, they turned off the road. A second sign, 'Europeans advised against using this track after 2 pm' greeted them.

Harry said, "Doesn't apply to us, we're British."

They left the Champ, probably where Henry had left his Mazda. The main track reduced to a footpath.

Leaving Alvin to guard the Champ, Iffor said, "Safety off, finger on trigger, any sight or sound you are not happy with, squeeze off a shot."

The footpath led to a clearing where, in the days before the war, people would camp and enjoy the fishing and the sheer beauty of the place.

Now it was silent, the light was failing, no birds could be heard; even the sound of the water cascading over the falls seemed diminished.

Iffor nodded towards the cave that Henry had used. "Take a look please, Mal."

When he rejoined the group, Mal said, "All clear boss, what are we looking for?"

"Nothing in particular. I'd like to think the terrs will know we've been here, and I think we owe it to Henry to stand for a few moments and try to imagine him staggering out of the cave towards the terrs, leaving his trail of life's blood and offering the grenade to them as a gift."

They stood for a few moments in sombre silence, until Mad Harry said, "Tell you what boss, I've got a bottle of rum in the Champ. Why don't I go and get it and let's do the job properly."

"Okay, but for fuck's sake whistle or sing or something; remember, Alvin's at the end of the path."

"It's okay," said Mal, "Alvin will smell him long before he sees him."

Harry returned with his bottle of Liquid Sunshine and a small leather pouch containing four silver stirrup cups. "Never travel without them," he said.

Filling the cups, Harry said, "Going to say a few words, boss?"

"I think it would be better coming from you."

Harry raised his cup and looked to the sky. "Henry, we took the piss out of you a few times, but you were one of us, our mucker." Then, as an afterthought said, "And always will be. The toast, gentlemen is 'absent friends'." Solemnly they muttered the toast, draining their cups and handing them back to Harry.

"That's it chaps, back to the Champ, single file five yards apart." Iffor took the lead.

They drove back to North Road Farm in fading light, Iffor deciding it was safe enough for the five of them to ride in the Champ. The Guard Force soldier opened the gate for them to drive into the compound where Iffor lined up his troops and ordered, "Make safe."

Good to his word, Archie had a braai burning well, with a table full of the usual steaks, chops, and, of course, *Boerewors*e sausage. A couple of cool bags full of Lion and Castle stood under the table. Iffor clapped his hands to get attention. "I want you guys washed and shaved with clean weapons before we eat, and remember, you will be doing a guard duty tonight so watch the drinking."

As the team dashed off to find the bathroom, Iffor wandered back to the Champ where he relayed his situation report back to control. This time he spoke to Hennie. Then he took his wash-bag out of his Burgan, filled a mess tin with water, stripped to the waist and washed and shaved. Finished, he found a clean KD shirt to put on and turned his attention to his weapon. When the Blue Watch reassembled on the veranda, they found Iffor waiting for them 'bright-eyed and bushy-tailed'.

As darkness came, the perimeter lights came on and the house lights were doused. "This way we can see them but they can't see us," said Archie.

"Tell me about your night security," said Iffor.

"Wire is alarmed and we have trip mines, though the mines are shotgun cartridges; still, they do the job; if the terrs manage to put out the perimeter lights we have powerful torches and illuminating flares. If attacked, we fight from behind the sandbags on the veranda, two at the front, two at the back."

"Fall back plan?" said Iffor.

"Four sawn-off double-barrelled twelve bores with four boxes of buckshot inside the house; we stand in the dark and catch them coming in through the doors and windows."

"Only what I'd expect from an old Coldstreamer," said Iffor, rapidly changing his opinion of the guards. "Now, what about sentries?"

"Myself and the two Guard Force men sleep on the veranda; we have just one man on sentry watch at any given time. I suggest you do the same." Archie went on, "I have a night watchman patrolling all the other buildings in the compound. Just make your men aware of that; if my watchman wants to sound the alarm he will shout 'stand to'."

Archie and his two guards went gratefully to their beds, taking advantage of an early night. Leaving Blue Watch chatting around the dying embers of the braai, Iffor went to the Champ for a final radio check and to advise they would be away from the radio until dawn. Then he went back to his team to brief them on their sentry duties: "Stay on the veranda; you will be looking from darkness into light. Only one of us will be patrolling the veranda. If anyone needs a pee, tell the sentry.

"And finally, when you take over your watch, make ready your weapon; when you finish your watch, make safe. I will be listening—I will know if you don't."

As was his custom, Iffor took the 'dog watch', four till six. This gave him the opportunity to plan his day and to wake the men one at a time to go and shower.

He decided they would leave at 0800hrs, drive to Angel Falls, but this time they would cross the river, fan out and search for the body of the third terrorist. After that, they would drive on to Long Acre farm, spend the day there and take over the guard at night. Then back to Kensington and Josie.

They crossed the small bridge over the Lamumbwa and stopped. Iffor planned to patrol along the river until he was opposite the Angel Falls, the most likely spot to find the body. Leaving Alvin guarding the Champ, Iffor led his team single file along the river bank until they reached the waterfall. He looked across the river into the cave where Henry and Paul had made camp, trying to imagine the terrorists lying where he was now standing, watching Henry setting up his easel.

With their backs to the river and in extended line, the team moved northwards, looking for the body or a shallow grave. After only some twenty metres or so Mal stopped, and sniffed the air. "This way," he said, indicating to the right and led them to a very badly decomposed body, ravaged by animals and ants.

They were standing upwind of the breeze coming off the river; even so, the smell was overpowering. As they stood looking at the body, Iffor unzipped his flies and took out his penis. "God!" muttered Harry, "You must be desperate."

Iffor urinated into his handkerchief and tying it across his mouth and nose went forward to examine the body. He searched through the pockets looking for any scrap of paper that might be useful; then he removed the man's rifle magazines from the pouches and, finally, using his big heavy knife as an axe, chopped off a finger. A nice present for Pete, he told himself.

The team made a cursory search for a weapon but, finding nothing, they made their way back to the Champ.

Long Acre Farm was as chalk and cheese compared with the previous two farms.

Although closer to a hostile border, the owner Kirk De Witt had refused a security fence around the compound and refused to have any

Guard Force soldiers on the farm, relying instead on the belief that the terrorists would not attack him since he was 'Cape Coloured', and married to a black Zambian woman.

Iffor stopped the Champ short of the main farm building. "Radio check, please Evil, and tell them we are at 'Partridge'." The discovery of the body would go in his evening sit rep.

The houseboy came to greet them. "B'wana De Witt is not here," he said, "he is working in the fields. I am to give you tea." Iffor frowned his annoyance; he had asked Archie to phone on ahead to tell them they were coming and his own HQ had given him warning. As he pondered on his next move, Evil called to him from the Champ and offered the radio handset to him. "Sunray on set send, over."

The message was brief: "Return to 'Snipe', the jackal has spoken."

Although only some twenty miles back to Charlie's farm the journey took two hours with Iffor sitting on the bonnet of the Champ and stopping frequently to examine suspicious mounds in the road with his knife for evidence of a mine.

Charlie was waiting for them as they pulled into the compound. "There's a cold bag inside for you chaps," and to Iffor said, "Shadrak's waiting for you—he's with his chickens."

Ensuring weapons were 'made safe', Iffor found his way down to the small chicken kraal, taking with him Harry's bottle of Liquid Sunshine and the pouch of cups.

Shadrak was sitting in the shade of a thatch, nursing and talking to a hen. "I see you N'kosi."

"I see you M'dala."

Iffor sat beside the old man and filled two cups with rum. "You have news?" he asked, and waited respectfully for the man to speak. Shadrak took his time slowly sipping the rum. He would normally drink the locally made cane spirit which is like drinking petrol and putting a match to it; the Liquid Sunshine rum was a rare treat.

He held the empty cup to be filled, then began, "The jackal did not come to me—the man is in the bush, he is resting close to the river, he carries a heavy load."

Iffor knew better than to ask questions. He simply filled Shadrak's cup when it became empty. "The man will cross the Mwonza road at dawn tomorrow, I will show you where. He will travel tonight because it is a dark moon. He feels his way along the game trail with his bare feet, but he must look for the game trail on the far side of the road and for this he must have a little light."

Iffor took his map out of his map pocket. "Show me where he will cross."

The old man took a piece of straw and using it as a pointer, traced the road down from the river. "There, that's where he will cross."

Iffor used the point of his knife to trace the road from the crossing point. Fifty yards further down was a sharp left-hand bend. "Perfect," he said, "Perfect."

He could already visualise his Bren in position on the bend sighted to fire straight up the road, the killing ground. With his knife still pointing at the crossing point, Iffor said, "You can lead us there?

"Yes Bwana, I can lead you."

"What time should we be there?"

"I think midnight. He must not hear us, then we must wait."

Iffor filled his cup up again, thankful that it was so small. This had to be his last.

"M'dala, you must come to me at nine tonight, then we will leave."

Iffor left his knife on the ground while he folded his map. Shadrak picked it up to examine it. "That is indeed a fine knife."

Iffor was conscious of the rusty blade with wooden grips held together by tape that passed for Shadrak's knife and taking the knife from him said, "M'dala, you have done me great service. Come to me tonight as I ask, sober..." and as an afterthought said, "No more drink today... and tomorrow this knife shall be yours."

Back at the house, Iffor found the team tucking in to sandwiches, chicken legs and samosas. He didn't realise just how hungry he was until Charlie's wife Georgie thrust a plate at him: "Get stuck in lad, you must be starving."

Waiting until the houseboy had left the room, Iffor said quietly, "'Warning order', chaps, fighting patrol tonight, no move before twenty-one hundred." He looked at his watch. "Time and place for 'O' group fifteen hundred hours here. Okay with you Charlie?"

Charlie nodded. "I'll see you're not disturbed."

Taking his beer and sandwiches with him, Iffor went onto the veranda. He cleared his head to start thinking through his plans for the evening. Then, drawing up a table, he took out his notebook and started writing up his orders.

"Ground." He pointed his knife at the map laid out on the table. The team moved closer; he could already feel their excitement growing.

"Old Mwonza Road: Not on the map is a game trail, running parallel to the road. It crosses the road here." He let the knife-point linger, looking into their faces so he could be sure they knew what he was saying. "Fifty metres down the road is a sharp left-hand bend with a high bank." He traced the knife-point back along the road.

"Our man crosses here." He pointed to the bend in the road. "We set up our ambush here.

"Situation: As a result of information I have received..."

Evil butted in: "Would this information be from a jackal, boss?"

"Questions when I've finished please," replied Iffor.

"I firmly believe the man, who appears to be using the old game trail regularly two or three times a month, is a courier for our local happy band of terrorists. If I am right, this will be their main and probably their only line of communication, and when we close it down tonight—and we will—they will understandably, be quite upset.

"We know our man moves only at night when the moon is dark. He feels his way along the game trail with his bare feet, but," he paused, enjoying the moment, "he must have daylight to pick up the game trail on the other side of the Mwonza Road. Our man is resting by the river and will cross at first light.

"Mission: To ambush and kill this man." He repeated, "To ambush and kill this man."

Seeing a look of concern, Iffor said, "Our man falls into one of three categories; a terrorist, a poacher or a naughty boy breaking curfew. Either way, by law we can shoot him.

"Execution: Phase one: Move to the ambush site; order of march, Shadrak, Mal, myself, Evil, Alvin and Harry. On site, Evil with the Bren. Myself and Alvin will comprise the killing group; our killing ground will be the road in front of us.

"Harry, you will be the right-hand stop, you will position yourself five metres into the bush and ten metres ahead of us. Mal, you will do the same on our left.

"Your task, gentlemen, is to stop him. If he survives the ambush and runs into the bush, you probably won't be able to see him, but you will hear him; let go six or seven rounds in that direction.

"Evil, this is important: when you see our man, fire a burst of at least five rounds at him, then stop firing. Do not fire at him if he runs into the bush—you are liable to upset Harry and Mal who will be in front of you.

"Alvin, do not shoot unless in self-defence."

Iffor went back to Evil. "Evil, I will not give you a command to open fire, I will be lying beside you on your right; when I see our man I will squeeze your arm, you fire when ready. As you bring the gun into your shoulder, pick up the foresight on something light, like the sandy road. Remember, it will still be quite dark.

"Weapons made ready, safeties on. Evil, when we are in position, change lever to auto, which is forward in case you had forgotten, but I will check so don't worry too much about it.

"Dress: Combat smocks; belt and water bottle; two magazines, one on the weapon, one in your map pocket. Evil, same for you, and I will carry a third magazine.

"Timings: When I've finished, clean your weapons, sort your kit out then rest, sleep if you can until 1930; we'll have a meal of sorts, then on parade at 2000 for a final briefing and inspection. You will not shave or wash before we go out—I don't want our man smelling our soap or toothpaste. We leave at 2100.

"Right lads, have a fag, grab a beer, then back here and we'll go through all that again, only this time, I'll be asking questions."

Iffor kept the team inside the main room of the farmhouse while they cleaned and prepared their weapons. He didn't want the farm labourers seeing the activity.

After cleaning his own weapons, he turned his attention to the Bren. Although Evil had done a good job preparing the weapon, he carried out his own checks.

Between them they unloaded the three magazines, cleaned them and reloaded them.

Finally, Iffor set the gas regulator at three, set the back sight to one hundred, and declared both the Bren and Evil Jesus ready for anything.

To complete his own preparations, Iffor went to the Champ and collected his old British army Dennison smock from his Burgan and a spare face veil. He then cut a six foot length of cam net; he had to hide the silhouette of his gun group as they peered over the mound, and the cam net was made for the job.

Finally, he made a radio check with Kensington. Satisfied, he retired to the veranda, the comfort of an armchair and an enforced rest period.

The smell of the chicken and vegetable broth Georgie had prepared roused the team from their sleep. Bleary-eyed, they stumbled to the table and filled their dishes. "No booze," Iffor warned, "and not too much to eat. I don't want you bastards belching and farting when we're in position."

Eight o'clock and the team lined up on the veranda. They had already carried out their 'prepare for battle' drills.

Cam cream had been applied; floppy hats had given way to face veils that could be hung loosely over the head to break up the silhouette, and pockets searched for anything that might rattle. Shadrak had already arrived and was gratefully eating a bowl of broth.

Iffor walked down the line with his floppy hat held open. "Fags and matches in here please, they'll be waiting for you in the morning."

Satisfied after his inspection of the men, he gave his final briefing:

"Move slowly, nothing attracts like sudden movement; move quietly, our man may well have gone to ground close to his crossing point.

"Harry, Mal, select a tree that you can sit against, do not go more than ten metres ahead of us and just remember, if our man makes a run for it, he'll be charging through the bush with an AK rifle in his hands, cocked and set on full auto."

Finally, Iffor had a word with Charlie who had agreed to drive along the Old Mwonza Road in his Toyota pick-up at seven o'clock to collect the team and hopefully a body. There seemed little point in Iffor and the team hanging about, so Blue Watch moved off silently into the darkness and the chance to even up the score just a little bit.

Fifty metres short of the mound, the ambush site, their final R.V., Shadrak signalled them to stop. The team sank to the ground, adopting all round defence.

Iffor joined Shadrak who pointed ahead, "That is where we will hide," he whispered.

Iffor had to move forward two or three yards and lie down to be able to see the dark of the mound. He was tempted to go forward to recce the area but the least movement, the better. Instead, he collected Mad Harry, took him forward and placed him in position as right stop; then he collected Big Mal and put in position as left stop.

Then he took the gun group forward to take up position on the mound. Careful not to show a silhouette, Evil scraped a trench to rest the Bren, legs folded, on the top of the mound. He looked along the barrel—perfect, the gun was pointing straight up the road.

Covered with the cam net, the gun group settled down for a long wait. Deliberately, they lay within arm's reach: they had to communicate by touch rather than speech.

The first hint of light brought relief from the silence of the night. Iffor felt the tension start to grip his stomach, the same feeling he had when 'prepare for action' was shouted at them by the RAF dispatcher.

He forced himself to keep his eyes off the road, relying instead on Shadrak's animal instincts to warn him when a man was close by; he knew from experience that looking in one area long enough caused trees to start moving.

It was just light enough to make out the white sand on the road when Shadrak breathed in Iffor's ear: "He comes."

Iffor touched, then lightly gripped Evil's arm; the gun came slowly up into the shoulder.

As if in a dream, he watched as a bush stood up and materialised into a man, the man hesitated for a moment then stepped onto the road.

Iffor's grip on Evil's arm tightened, and as if in response, Evil began to take up the slack on the trigger; he had the foresight laid on the white sand in the centre of the road waiting for his target to walk into it.

The man moved slowly across the road, pausing, listening. Iffor could now see he was indeed carrying something—it looked like a... the staccato eruption of the Bren raped and spoiled a perfect innocent dawn. The man had been facing Evil when the force of the rounds knocked him onto his back.

Poacher, terrorist or just a visiting lover breaking curfew, it made no difference now, the man was dead before he hit the ground. As a matter of routine and standard operating procedure, Iffor waited thirty minutes before calling in the stops and positioning them on his flanks, then, telling Evil to keep the downed man in his sights, he moved cautiously along the side of the road to where the man lay.

Death had come swiftly—he hadn't had time to close his eyes; at least three rounds had hit him in the chest. Surprisingly, the man was well dressed, K.D. trousers, bush shirt and jacket, and wearing suede boots.

So much for Shadrak's theory of walking the trail barefooted, Iffor thought.

But the icing on the cake was the A.K. rifle with folded butt slung across his chest and a landmine, each in its carrying case, in either hand.

Retrieving the rifle, Iffor returned to the ambush site. He and Alvin then brought the body and the mines, and laid them on the road in front of their position.

"Safety catch, please Evil, and well done, bloody good shooting; well done everyone."

Harry muttered just loud enough for Iffor to hear: "Well done he says, after sending us out here without fags."

Iffor reached into his spacious smock pocket and produced a packet of cigarettes and a box of matches. "Catch," he said to Harry, "and pass them round."

Charlie was bang on time. "Heard the shooting," he said, "Couldn't wait to get here, looks like you've had some success."

They loaded the body and the mines into the Toyota and drove back to the farm. The Guard Force guard on the gate stood to attention and saluted as they drove in. Iffor returned the salute.

Charlie had laid on a braai for them with an abundance of steaks and chicken and the obligatory cold bag of beer.

But first, weapons had to be made safe and the body transferred to the Champ. Iffor knew they would have to leave promptly to get the body back to the hospital morgue as soon as possible.

As the team fell on the food and beer, Iffor took Shadrak to one side. He stripped his knife and sheath from his belt and handed it to the African. "You have served us well—will you join us?" he indicated the food.

"No, Inkosi, I must tend to my chickens."

"Go in peace M'dala."

"And you also N'kosi."

One more task before Iffor could rejoin the team: He wrote out his sit rep for control and called Evil to join him at the Champ.

"To the victor go the spoils," he said, handing Evil his notebook. "Tell control what's happened."

Face beaming, Evil switched on the radio and keyed the handset:

"Bravo Whisky sit rep, over."

"Control, send, over."

"Bravo Whisky, contact, contact, contact…"

Iffor left him to give the details to Phil and joined his group. "As and when chaps, grab a shave and wash; we must look our best when we drive through Kensington."

They didn't carry out any vehicle check points on the way back to base. Iffor wanted to get the body into the morgue as quickly as possible and more importantly, he needed to speak to Pete and hand over the weapon and mines.

They drove into the M.T. yard at midday. As usual the Colour was waiting and Iffor confessed to himself at a little disappointment that Josie wasn't waiting for him. Still, doubtless he would see her at Auntie's.

Phil and Hennie joined the team in the drill hall. "I've closed down the net, batteries on charge," said Phil. "Can we give a hand unloading stores?"

"Thanks fellas," Iffor said, "and thanks for manning the communications centre; it meant a lot to us knowing we had a dependable team back at base."

"Mines made safe?" the Colour asked.

Iffor handed him the two detonators. "Yes, and the weapon's been cleared."

The Colour inspected the captured A.K. "This is in much better condition than the usual run-of-the-mill terrorist weapon we see. This one has actually been cleaned recently. This man was someone special—he actually knows, sorry, knew what he was doing."

A growing doubt began in Iffor's mind; he'd missed something important, something so basic he couldn't blame on his tiredness.

Pete came into the drill hall, walking towards Iffor, hand outstretched. "Well done, well done you," he said.

Iffor raised one hand as if to push Pete away and put the other hand to his head, "What a cunt, what a cunt! How did I miss that?"

Pete looked hurt.

"Not you, me!" said Iffor.

"Harry, get the stores unloaded then knock off, 0800 Monday morning debrief. Pete, Colour, my office please."

Iffor gave his friends a full though somewhat brief debrief, getting on to the ambush as quickly as he could. "This is what bothered me," he said. "I was expecting a courier, a bushman, an expert in the bush, someone walking a game trail in bare feet to navigate, someone dressed in shorts and cloak. Instead, we have a well-dressed, well-nourished, well-armed man, wearing suede boots.

"Don't you see, gentlemen, he had a guide, a bushman was guiding him. Why didn't we see and shoot the guide?" He answered his own question. "Because, gentlemen, the guide had left him by the side of the road waiting for first light... Why?"

"You tell us," said Pete.

"Because once across the Mwonza Road our man was safe. Either he met another guide or a reception party or he had arrived at his destination."

"Or," interrupted Pete, "he was to be picked up by someone in a vehicle and taken to his destination."

Iffor stabbed a finger at him: "Good point, Pete, bloody good point!"

Pete stood up to go. "I'm rather anxious to get down to the morgue to see the body. It will be interesting to see what the post-mortem reveals on the contents of his stomach."

"Apart from the body…" Iffor said, getting to his feet and indicating the meeting was over, "I've got you a little present, to be precise, a finger, wrapped in a sketch map of the location of the third terrorist."

As Pete and Bob left the office, Iffor said, "Can I suggest a working breakfast at Auntie's tomorrow, nine okay?"

"Fine," said the Colour, knowing this was not a request.

"Okay by me," said Pete.

Alone, Iffor phoned battalion at New Epsom on the secure line. When the colonel answered, he came straight to the point: "We've had a good contact, Colonel, recovered one body, one personnel weapon and two landmines, no friendly casualties."

The Colonel was just as brief. "Well done, tell your team well done, get a contact report to me soon as you can."

Iffor made his way back to his hotel. He was tempted to call in at Boons bar, but common sense prevailed. He needed a shower, a meal, but more than anything, he wanted to see Josie.

In his room, he stepped out of his uniform, emptied his Burgan onto the bed and sorted out his dirty clothes. Then, towel round his waist, he walked along the landing to the shower, knowing that when he returned to his room Mrs Patel would have taken his clothes for washing.

Refreshed, and dressed in just shorts and shirt, Iffor wandered down and into the garden. He pulled a sun lounger into the shade of the jacaranda tree, ordered a plate of sandwiches and a bottle of house white and settled down to write his report to the Colonel, which Josie would send by teleprinter on Monday.

A shadow fell across him. He looked up to see Mrs Patel. "One of your men is here to see you," she said. "Shall I bring him in?" Before he could answer, Evil came striding across the lawn: "Got a few minutes, boss?"

"All the time in the world," said Iffor, "and out of uniform it's Iffor. Beer?"

Settled in a chair, beer in hand, Evil came straight to the point: "I've never killed a man before, how should I feel?"

"How do you feel?" said Iffor.

"Elated and quite chuffed."

"And that's exactly how you should feel, not because you killed a man, who after all, was only doing what he considered to be his duty. But elated and chuffed because as a soldier you did what was asked of you."

Iffor went on: "I could have asked Harry or Mal to shoot him or I could have shot him, but I decided to use you and the Bren, because that way we had a better chance of success and I knew I could depend on you. Remember, you're part of a team responsible for evening up the score, and it was the team who killed him."

Evil got up to leave. "Thanks Iffor, I feel a lot better. We're having a few beers at the Moth club tonight if you'd care to join us."

"Thanks," said Iffor, "but part of the deal I had with Josie for working in the Watch Room was to take her out to dinner tonight, if she turns up, that is. I get the feeling she's avoiding me."

Afternoon turned to evening. Iffor went back to his room to shower and shave. He still hadn't made contact with Josie, but he was confident she'd turn up.

Suited and booted and smelling like a pox doctor's clerk, Iffor came down to reception. "She's waiting for you in the garden," Auntie said.

To slow himself down, and to appear unconcerned, Iffor said, "By the way, Auntie," this was the first time he had called her Auntie and she was delighted. "By the way, I've asked Pete Saxon and my Colour Sergeant round for a working breakfast, about nine. Okay with you?"

She nodded, "That's fine."

Josie was waiting for him under the jacaranda tree, wearing a deep blue sari, gold sandals with painted toenails; plain, simple, but devastating.

Iffor sensed a change in her: no longer the sensuous woman who came to his bed two nights ago; not the giggling schoolgirl he spoke to over the radio. She was tearful, serious and very troubled.

"Dear girl," he said, "what on earth is the matter?"

"Oh Iffor, I've been such a fool, such a selfish idiot, I'm so ashamed."

She started to ramble, "I used you. I needed to find out for myself if I was still capable of love, still capable of being a woman. I tried to pass my shame on to you, I…"

Iffor stopped her there. "What on earth are you talking about?" And taking her hand said, "From the beginning; tell me all."

She dabbed her eyes and started to regain control of herself. "Were you surprised when I came to your bed the other night?"

Surprised and delighted, he said, "Delighted that you came to me, but surprised that you did. I always thought you Indian girls remained, well, chaste before marriage."

She paused for a few moments, steeling herself for what she had to tell him. She kept it brief to get it over with. "You remember I told you how upset my brother was when Daddy refused to allow me to go back to India to marry the cousin my brother had selected for me?"

Iffor nodded but wondered to himself, did he really need to know all this?

"Well, Daddy told him to leave the house, which he did, but he threatened that if I didn't marry our cousin he would see to it that I wouldn't marry at all. We thought he was just being nasty, but later that night he came back to the house and into my bedroom and raped me; he spoilt me!

"Next day he flew back to India and Mummy and Daddy were killed after they'd been to see my uncle in Zambia to decide what should be done."

In the gathering darkness, Iffor could see she was crying. She began to rock backwards and forwards in her chair. He wanted to hug her and tell her everything was all right, but she still had more to say. She turned her head away from him and said softly, "Can you understand? I had to find a man, the right man, so that I could step from the world of despair I was living in and find a new world with someone I could love, and more importantly, someone who in time could love me.

"You are the first man I have given myself to willingly; I think you are the right man."

They sat in silence, he looking into her face, she with her head turned slightly away. Then she said, "For God's sake, Iffor, say something!"

He leaned forward and gently kissed the tears from her eyes. "Apart from being very beautiful," he told her, "you are the most sensuous, exciting woman I have ever met. And now I am part of your secret, I am part of you. Now, did you book a table at the Elephants Head?"

As they swept gracefully into the dining room of the Elephants Head, Iffor was aware of heads turning and admiring glances following them. Seated at their table, he said, "Looks like you've caused a bit of a stir."

She laughed. "It's you they're looking at, not me. Word's got around about the ambush."

Determined to make this an occasion to be remembered, they spoke about everything and nothing, laughing at stupid jokes and silly comments, while, all the time Iffor found he could not stop himself from gazing lovingly and longingly into her face.

They walked back to the hotel, hand in hand, carefree and happy, enjoying the soft scented breeze and the stillness of the night.

At the foot of the stairs she said, "I'll just say goodnight to Auntie, then I'll bring a nightcap up to you."

Hurriedly she said her goodnights, put two glasses and a bottle of Cape brandy on a tray and scampered up the stairs to Iffor's room. She needn't have hurried, for Iffor was already sound asleep. She kissed her finger and touched it against his lips: "Goodnight my love, goodnight."

Iffor had a breakfast table prepared in the small residents' lounge, and got Auntie to hang a 'Private meeting' notice on the door. He was enjoying a coffee and Cape brandy when Pete and the Colour joined him. Behind them came Auntie, carrying a large oval plate loaded with *Boereworse* sausage, thick bacon and mushrooms. Godfry followed with fried eggs and black pudding.

"Tea, coffee?" enquired Auntie.

"I think two bottles of Chardonnay, please auntie. On second thoughts, make it three, I'll join them."

They ploughed steadily through their meal, enjoying the well-prepared food and the relaxed atmosphere and the presence of good friends.

Iffor said, "Auntie's watching us, for fuck's sake don't catch her eye or she'll bring us another yard of that bloody *Boereworse*."

Breakfast finished, they got down to the business in hand.

Iffor began, "I am convinced we have discovered and compromised the terrorists' line of communication. Old Shadrak, my informant, tells me the trail is used two or three times a month and has been in use for six or seven months.

"It's my belief that the terrorists are stockpiling warlike stores ready for a major escalation.

"My plan of campaign is to mount a standing patrol on the trail, denying the terrs use of the trail.

"This will mean that the terrs will have to, as a matter of some priority, establish a new L. of C."

The Colour held up a finger.

"Yes Bob?"

"The man you shot was obviously important."

"Right," said Iffor.

"And you have disrupted their L. of C.?"

"Right again."

"The point is, Iffor, the terrs will not be impressed by your actions and I feel that a four or five man standing patrol will be too exposed."

"I agree," said Iffor, "but what we must consider is that it will take quite some time for word to get back to Zambia that we are sitting on their main road. With luck we may bag another two or three couriers. Anyway, I intend to put a covert observation point in the same area as the patrol."

Pete couldn't contain himself any longer. "I have news gentlemen: the good Doctor Van De Werwe has examined the body. As I expected, cause of death was heart failure brought on by three bullets to the chest. Good shooting by the way, Iffor.

"But what is more important, my friends, was the contents of his stomach. I won't go into details, but he had eaten a substantial cooked meal within the twelve hours before his death and I'm thinking that the only place he could have had a cooked meal would be…"

"De Witt's place," finished Iffor.

"Right," said Pete.

"I've had my doubts about him for some time, but no evidence." Iffor was lost in thought for a few moments, then looking directly at his Colour Sergeant said, "Bob, would I be pushing my luck if I inserted an

O.P. overlooking De Witt's farm with radio contact to a four-man patrol? That way we can sit on the trail and keep an eye on the farm."

"They'll need at least four weeks' training for something like that," the Colour replied. "But I'll see if I can condense it into Monday."

Iffor was feeling very pleased with himself. "Okay, Bob, you have the team tomorrow for training, and brush up on their map and compass; the guys in the O.P. need to be able to give an accurate bearing on any sightings.

"I'll take them on a routine mobile patrol on Tuesday, calling on all three farms in the area, but I'll recce De Witt's place for a good hide for the O.P. and show the boys a little more of the area."

Iffor filled the three glasses with the last of the wine. "Is that it?" he asked.

The policeman spoke, "I've sent our mystery man's photo and prints to Salisbury. We should have identification tomorrow, and Father Sean's going to give our man a proper burial tomorrow."

"What's wrong with our resident clergy?" asked Iffor.

"The Catholic priest is up north on call-up and our Anglican vicar won't have anything to do with terrs, dead or alive, and anyway, Sean usually comes into town on Monday and stays overnight."

Left alone, Iffor wrote up his notes and sketched in a programme for the following week. Then he wandered into the garden. He now had the whole day to spend with Josie.

PART TEN

Preparation is your first section battle drill, heed it well, it is the most important.

MONDAY MORNING came all too soon for Iffor. Josie's lack of experience in the bedroom was more than made up for with her eagerness to learn and the first blush of dawn was beginning to appear before, contented and happy, they fell asleep in one another's arms.

"You've been at it again, you bastard," said Evil, looking into Iffor's eyes. "You've been on the nest again."

Iffor smiled and walked across to the Colour Sergeant. "They're all yours today. Let them fire their weapons and check the zeroing, then, spend some time on OPs and standing patrols; then, my old mate, I'd like you to see if you can track down a radio set for me, something here at the base. Oh, and while you're scavenging, see if you can get me a decent knife—I gave mine away; a mark five Sten bayonet would do rather well."

The Colour nodded, "I think I can get hold of both."

Iffor gathered his soldiers around him: "You're on the range with the Colour this morning. I want you to check your zeroing. Fire rounds from all five of your magazines, then reload them. I will be inspecting weapons when you get back. I'll bring you up to date with what's happening when you get back. Time and place Colour, my office, fifteen hundred."

After watching his troops depart in the old Bedford QL, he started to make his way to his office. Lots to do, he thought.

A policeman intercepted him. "Inspector Saxon's compliments sir, can you join him in his office?"

"Pull up a chair," Pete said. "Agnes, two coffees, please." Then, staring hard at Iffor, he said, "Have you been at it! You've got eyes like…"

"I know," said Iffor, "…piss holes in the snow, and what I get up to in my spare time has got fuck all to do with you."

Agnes brought in the coffees and left, carefully closing the office door behind her.

"Well," said Iffor, "Come on, you're dying to tell me something; get on with it."

Pete leaned back in his chair, savouring the moment. "It would appear that the chap you shot is none other than Samuel Kitwe."

"Never heard of him, but go on."

"Samuel Kitwe sits on the top table in the ZANU organisation. He is responsible for liaising between the two main terrorist groups ZAPU and ZANU."

Through the mists of tiredness and happy thoughts, Iffor returned to reality, excited.

"What the hell is a man like that, of that importance, doing in our neck of the woods?"

"I was sort of hoping you'd tell me," Pete answered.

Iffor thought for a moment or two. "My guess, and it is only a guess, is that he was trying to co-ordinate the efforts of both groups so they attack simultaneously in different parts of the country, thereby stretching the army even further. The mines he was carrying were probably a sweetener, and you know how fond of mines the terrorists are."

"So what do we do now?" Pete looked inquiringly at his friend.

"Well, first we've got to arrange Henry's funeral, when you release the body."

"No need," Pete said, "He's already on his way back to the U.K.; his father arranged it."

"Well, I'm going ahead with my plans to keep a standing patrol on what I believe to be the terrorists' line of communication and an OP keeping an eye on the De Witt place. We might get lucky."

"Do you still believe the terrs will carry out an attack before the Battalion get back?"

"More than ever. We've killed four of them; they've got to regain credibility. Yes, something big is brewing. And we now have an added dimension—there may well be a plan afoot to wipe out Blue Watch, attack and destroy one or two farms, thereby drawing the army away from the border area, enabling more terrorists to cross into Rhodesia."

Iffor sensed Pete was now beginning to realise how serious the situation had become. "I'll tighten the security here in town and I'll arrange for a *small*," he emphasized the term 'small', "quick reaction force to be on standby when you're out and about," he said.

Back in his office, Iffor made out his report to the Colonel, including the positive identification of the shot terrorist, then took it into Josie. "Send that off to Battalion for me please."

"In code?"

"Yes please, then phone Battalion and tell them the report is on its way and it must go direct to the CO. Then, when you've finished that, we'll go to the Elephant for a sandwich and a beer."

The team arrived back at the drill hall, noisy as ever around two.

"Good lunch?" Iffor enquired.

"Menu 'C' today," said Alvin, "Meat paste and hard biscuits followed by the house special, melted Mars Bar."

"Lucky bastards, all I had was a rare roast beef sandwich and a cold Castle."

Stores put away, weapons inspected, the team assembled in Iffor's training wing office. He revealed the identity of the shot terrorist and a broad outline of his plans for the coming week: "Phil, Hennie, I want you two in the field with me—you will man the OP."

"Are you sure we can do that boss? I mean, we've no experience of that sort of thing." Phil was speaking for the two of them.

"As my old Welsh granny used to say, and I quote," said Iffor, "'If you can't, you won't, but if you try, you might just succeed.' So there you have it, gentlemen. We'll assemble 0800 tomorrow and load stores, fuel up the champ, etc. I'll give a full briefing tomorrow. Time and place, my office at 1100; no move before 1300; be prepared to stay out for three nights. And a warning order, gentlemen, don't make any plans for next weekend."

As they stood to leave, Iffor shouted, "And remember, gentlemen!" He pointed at the blackboard and the words, IF YOU DON'T WANT YOUR ENEMY TO KNOW, DON'T TELL YOUR FRIENDS.

Mad Harry came up to Iffor. "Time you had a beer with the boys, boss, seven at the Moth club, okay?"

"I'll be there," Iffor said, wondering how Josie would take it.

After they'd all left, Iffor went into the orderly room. Josie looked up and gave him that devastating smile of hers. How the hell could he tell her he was drinking with the boys tonight? "Have Battalion confirmed they've received my report?"

"Yes, and they've told me to stand by for an important coded message."

The Colour Sergeant joined them and handed Iffor a bayonet. "As requested, one mark five Sten bayonet complete with scabbard and frog, and I've tracked down another radio set for you. It's an old 88 set that the local school cadet force use, but it's compatible with the 31 set and ideal for your standing patrol."

The teleprinter chattered into life. Iffor took the Colour's arm. "Let's wait in my office—Josie's got some decoding to do."

The Colour pointed a finger at the map on the wall. "Long Acre farm," he said. "There's a kopje 200 metres south of the farm, steep slopes at the front, gentle slopes at the rear. Difficult to attack from the direction of the farm, but a good escape route at the rear, and on a compass bearing, about a 'K' from Angel Falls which would make a good RV."

Iffor looked at the Colour Sergeant with total admiration. "You've just saved me about four hours tramping about in the bush looking for a decent position for my OP."

Josie came into the office waving a page from a message pad. "Top secret and urgent," she said, handing it to Iffor. He read it and handed it to the Colour Sergeant:

"Imperative, repeat, Imperative, you continue to disrupt enemy line of communication."

Iffor took the message and passed it back to Josie. "Stick that in the top secret file in the safe please." Turning to the Colour, he commented, "Well, that makes life easier for me."

"How so?"

"Well, I've been trying to decide whether to continue sorties into the bush or keep the team here in Kensington as a QRF ready to go to the aid of a farm under attack. I've no choice now."

As they walked down the winding, imposing staircase into the drill hall, Bob stopped and touched Iffor's arm. "Look Iffor, I know I'm under strict orders to maintain a rear link to Battalion, but I'd like to do more to help you and the team."

"Without you, we wouldn't have got this far; you've done a great job getting the team up to scratch," Iffor said, "But if you're serious, I could do with you running our OP's room. That way I can release another man into the field with me."

"Not a problem, but for Christ's sake don't let on to my wife that Josie's sharing the duty with me."

"Talking of wives," Iffor began and the Colour winced, he knew what was coming, "can she spare you for a couple of hours this evening? The boys are having a little get-together at the Moth club."

Iffor made his way back to his hotel, first stopping at the police station to tell Pete of the message from Battalion and inviting him to join him and the team at the Moth club. As he walked down the main street, feeling great, in uniform, and with his Brno slapping his right hip, he thought through his repertoire of excuses, looking for the one most suitable to allow him to drink with the boys instead of spending his last evening for a few days with her.

As it happened, Dame Fortune stepped in. He dined alone, expecting Josie to join him. Instead, Auntie came to his table and announced that Josie was having dinner with the family and then would be washing her hair.

Although this let Iffor off the hook, he knew he would spend the rest of the evening wondering if he had upset her in some way.

He was able to leave the hotel undetected before Auntie could force her 'spotted dick and custard' onto him. He wanted to get to the club early, to be able to greet the team as they arrived.

As usual, the Colour Sergeant had beaten him to it and was in deep conversation with the Inspector and Mad Harry. Before they noticed his presence, Iffor was able to hear Harry say, "I'll have money, he's shagging Josie, the lucky basta..." and stop in mid-sentence when he saw Iffor. "Hello Boss, we were just talking about you, saying what a good job you're doing."

"I heard," said Iffor, taking pleasure in Harry's embarrassment, "and yes, I think I'm doing a really good job." He smiled as sweetly as he could.

In ones and twos, the rest of the team arrived and they moved to the 'committee' table. Last to arrive, looking pale and gaunt and a lot slimmer, was big Shamus. Iffor was first across the floor to welcome him and shake his hand. The others quickly followed, eager to shake his hand and just to touch him to reassure themselves it really was him.

Mad Harry pushed his way through the throng and stood in front of Shamus as Shamus started to say, "No Harry, I'm injured." Harry wrapped his arms around him in a bear hug and lifted him off his feet, saying, "You thick Irish bastard, welcome home."

"Couldn't have put it better," muttered Evil as they sat down.

Shamus was eager to hear what Blue Watch had been up to. "I heard about Henry, but not the details."

Iffor cut across the conversation. "Come down to the drill hall in the morning and we will reveal all."

"Glad you said that boss, I'm ready for duty, ready for anything."

Iffor sat back in his chair and pointed a finger at Shamus. "Lucky for you, I'm something of a medical genius, and if I were to phone Doctor Van De Merwe in the morning, I'll have money..." He looked at Harry and watched him squirm, "...he would agree with me that you are only fit for light duties. However..." Shamus's face lit up. "...I do have a very important and useful job for you while you're convalescing. On parade at 0800, please, in uniform and the Colour will issue you with a rifle and ammunition which you will keep at home and carry with you when you are in uniform and on duty."

Pete looked at his watch.

"Expecting someone?" said Iffor.

"Yes, hope nobody objects, but Father Sean is in town, on his own, so I invited him to come over." Then, in a loud voice, he exclaimed, "Talk of the devil," and Father Sean joined them.

"Glad to see you back Shamus," Father Sean said, "I prayed for you—looks like it did the trick."

"Tenner in the kitty please, Sean," said Harry and called to the barman for another round.

"You expect a poor priest to pay for his own beer?"

"Yes."

Pete took a ten pound note from his wallet and stuffed it into the beer mug that held the kitty. "It's all right Padre, I'll pay."

"That's very good of you."

"Not at all. I'll take it out of your fee for burying the terrorist tomorrow."

"Talking of which," said the priest, "are you chaps going to come and fire a volley over him? Isn't that what soldiers do?"

"We've already done that," said Iffor, "only into him."

"He was some mother's son, perhaps a husband, a father," said Sean. "Try telling his family why he had to die."

"He was a terrorist, a thug, a murderer who terrorised his own people!" Iffor was getting angry. "Try telling Elias's family and the Dix family why their loved ones had to die."

The priest went silent and simply gestured with his hands. Then he took a notebook from his breast pocket. "Have we got a name for the man I'm burying tomorrow?"

"No." The tone of Iffor's voice contradicted what he said, "No, we haven't identified him yet."

The mood of the evening had been spoilt by the priest's appearance and the group started to break up. Bob bade one and all a goodnight and went home to his wife.

Pete and the priest became involved in conversation, while Harry and Evil wandered over to the darts board, giving Iffor a chance to sit next to Shamus. "Tell me all," he said.

"I was very lucky, the bullet went straight through me without too much damage, but it caused one of my lungs to collapse and the other one filled with fluid, so it was touch and go for a while."

"Don't I know it!" said Iffor.

Shamus went on, "In Salisbury they x-rayed me and drained me, got my lungs working again and sent me home to rest and recuperate. I've got to see our own hospital doctor every couple of days just to keep a check on me."

"So what you are telling me is that you should really be in hospital, but somehow you persuaded the doctor to allow you home to recover, and he doesn't think for one minute that you would be stupid enough to rejoin Blue Watch. Am I correct?" asked Iffor.

Shamus nodded. "I've got to help, boss."

"And so you shall," said Iffor, "and so you shall."

The priest joined them. Iffor changed the subject: "So what brought you to Africa, Shamus?"

Shamus was relieved to get away from the subject of his health. "I was in the RUC, a beat constable for 15 years, with paddies queuing up to take pot-shots at me; then one day the IRA gave me an option, leave Ireland with my family or stay in Ireland without my family, meaning of course they would kill my family if I didn't do as they suggested. I saw an advert in the police journal for security people at the mine here in Kensington, applied and got the job. But standing at the main gate all day searching people as they came and went was not my cup of tea, so I transferred to the fire and rescue here in town, which in those days was part of the mine set-up. The rest, as they say, is history."

The priest butted in: "Sorry if I upset you with my presence, Iffor. I didn't mean to cause an argument."

"S'alright Sean. No, you didn't upset me, we enjoy your company; you're most welcome any time."

"I imagine you don't go to church very often?" enquired Sean.

"I'm an atheist, if that's what you mean, but I have the utmost respect for the church and its servants." Iffor chose his words carefully—he didn't want to get involved in a theological argument; he'd only lose. "My faith is in myself, my weapons and my comrades."

"Some of whom will have faith in their God." Sean thought he'd scored a point.

"That's what I'm counting on," said Iffor. "It's what's known as 'hedging your bets'; I'm very good at it."

After the priest left, Iffor settled down to some serious drinking. He loved the atmosphere of the club, the freedom and comradeship and the incentive to drink more than was intended.

He walked back to his hotel, keeping to the centre of the road; he'd only fall off the pavement. He loved the African night, the smell of the jacaranda and jasmine, and the gentle cooling breeze that carried the sound of a distant hyena laughing at the moon.

He didn't bother with a shower, just stepped out of his clothes and into bed. As he did so, Josie, like a spectre, glided into the room. She slipped out of her nightie, but kept her knickers on. "Only a cuddle tonight," she said. "Mother Nature's paying a visit."

Gratefully, Iffor closed his eyes; all in all he thought, it hasn't been a bad day.

He opened his eyes slowly, testing the depth of pain. His first shock was Josie's face inches from his own, watching him struggling to come to terms with life. The second was Auntie walking into the room carrying a tray with a teapot and two cups on it. "Breakfast in half an hour," she announced. "Don't you two be too long in the shower."

0800 hours Tuesday: Iffor marched into the drill hall, dressed in combats, carrying his Burgan and Ruger carbine, his Brno holstered comfortably on his right buttock and the newly acquired knife on his right thigh.

As usual, the Colour had beaten him to it and was fitting a new battery to the 31 set.

"Morning boss, I'll have the other radio set for you before you leave. It's fixed frequency but compatible with the 31s; it will suit your needs.

"As per your stores list, I've loaded three extra 'chugals' of water for the OP and Phil can come and draw map and compass and binos when he's ready."

The rest of the team started to assemble with their own kit and weapons, and began loading stores into the Champ trailer. Last to arrive was big Shamus. "Morning boss, sorry I'm a few minutes late."

"You look like death," said Iffor, "you're going back to hospital, now."

As Shamus started to stammer out all the reasons why he should stay, Iffor ignored him. "Colour, use my pick-up and take him back to hospital. He can rejoin the team next week, if the doctor agrees."

Iffor left Harry in charge of the loading and went up to his office. He had intended to use Shamus on radio watch but now... He sat down to think things out.

1100 hours: The team assembled in Iffor's office for the briefing. Pete and Josie joined them, followed by the Colour Sergeant. "News of Shamus?" Iffor asked.

"Tucked up in bed, sleeping like a baby."

The briefing began. Iffor spoke slowly and clearly, watching the men's faces; he had to be certain they all understood what he was saying:

"Ground: As before: The area covering the three farms west of the Great North Road.

"Situation: The man we killed last week was a high ranking ZANU officer. We think he had rested and been fed at the De Witt's farm. We think he was using an established route. I know it is extremely likely we will have another contact.

"Mission: Let me quote you a top secret message from Battalion: 'Imperative you continue to disrupt enemy line of communication'."

Iffor paused. "Are you all with me so far?" The look on their faces told him he had their undivided attention; furthermore, they were loving it.

"Execution: We will insert a two-man covert observation point on a kopjie two hundred metres south of the De Witt farm... Phil, Hennie, that will be your job."

They looked at one another like a couple of excited school kids.

"And we will mount a standing patrol along the bank of the river from Angel Falls, past the drift and the ford, to our boundary, the old game track from Mwonza.

"The definition of a standing patrol, gentlemen, 'to watch and listen over likely enemy approach routes.'

"In the event that our OP spots a couple of likely looking customers for us, they will give us the bearing they are travelling on and leave the rest to us.

"We will insert the OP team after dark tonight.

"We will all muck in, digging in and camouflaging the hide.

"We will stay together that night and the patrol will take off just before dawn.

"Night two: At last light the patrol will join up with the OP, replenish water and give them a good night's sleep.

"OP party, if you want to take the shovel for a walk, don't go looking for somewhere secluded that offers a breathtaking view, where you can have your crap in private whilst enjoying the scenery. Stay close to the hide and ensure you leave the other man awake and alert.

"Communications: Alvin, you, the Colour and Josie will man our operations room. I was hoping that Shamus could have done that job because I would have preferred you to join the OP team."

Pete stood up. "I think I can help. Why not transfer your radio and maps to my police station. I maintain a twenty-four hour listening watch on our police radio; yours won't make that much difference. Anything urgent, your Colour Sergeant's only a phone call away, and it will mean Bob and Josie can get on with their day jobs and you can have Alvin in the field with you."

Iffor hung on to Pete's words in amazement and said, "Phil! Why didn't you think of that?"

Phil started grinning. "When you've finished with me boss, I'll start moving the radio into the station."

"Just about finished," said Iffor. "Make sure you familiarize the Colour with the procedure for scrambling the Islander and the passwords.

"Alvin, you will now join Phil and Hennie in the OP, two observing, one sleeping.

"Phil, you will have a 31 set, control will have a 31 set, my standing patrol will have the 88 set which has a very limited range so any messages I have for control will have to go through you.

"And finally gentlemen, 'Actions On', or 'What happens if?'

"Phil, if you are compromised your escape route is on a compass bearing to Angel Falls, so memorise it; we will RV with you there.

"Patrol team, if we run into trouble, 'shoot and scoot' and try to make it to one of our friendly farms.

"Remember chaps, secrecy is of the utmost importance. If our friendly farmers ask what we're up to, we are 'dominating the ground'; a good military phrase that one. It covers most things."

As Iffor stood and closed his notebook indicating the briefing was over, he saw Evil look at Harry and mouth, "Dominating the ground, Oooo."

The men left the office to go about their various tasks, the Colour to the kitchen to knock up a curry of Nineteen Forty something compo stew for lunch, Phil to transfer the operations centre and radio to the police station.

Josie walked into Iffor's office. "Since you won't be around at the weekend," she said in that way women have of saying, 'it's all right, but it isn't all right', "I'm going to go with Pete to see Helen and the twins at the Mission."

"Twins! What twins?" An alarm started sounding in Iffor's head.

"The orphaned Anglo-Indian twins at the Mission, didn't you hear about them?" She sounded much too casual and innocent for Iffor's liking. "Helen wants me to help name them, a boy and a girl." She was standing very close to him now—too close, for she knew what her fragrance did to him.

"I thought we might have them to stay with us at Auntie's for a weekend when they get a little older."

He was now holding her hand, looking up into her face and smelling her; he was beaten, "That sounds like a wonderful idea," he said.

She bent over him and lightly kissed his lips. "I thought you'd like it."

1500 hours, and they trundled into Charlie's North Road farm, grateful for the chance to get out of the vehicle and stretch their legs. With six in the Champ and Alvin being the smallest in the trailer, things were a little cramped.

"Radio check please, Phil, and tell control we've arrived at 'Essex'." Phil had given all reference points the name of English counties.

Charlie came out of his bungalow to meet them. "Bush telegraph told me you were on your way; you're just in time for a mid-afternoon beer."

It never ceased to amaze Iffor that 'bush telegraph' could travel faster than a modern vehicle.

"News from the front?" Charlie asked. He and Iffor were sitting on the veranda while the team were inside being fed and watered by Charlie's wife.

"Can't tell you too much. Just step up your level of security. If you get hit, they'll come in hard and fast."

"Tell me," said Iffor, "what do you know about the De Witts up at Long Acre?"

"Only that he's Cape Coloured, she's black Zambian and that they are very unsociable. They never mix with the farming community and I can only agree with any suspicions you may have about them. In short, I don't like them."

Shadrak came shuffling up to the veranda steps, raising his arm in salute.

"I see you N'kosi."

"The very man," said Iffor. "Excuse me please Charlie. I've got a present for Shadrak, and I need a word with him."

Charlie nodded. "Press on dear boy, press on."

Iffor took Shadrak's arm and led him away from the bungalow. "Are you well, M'dala?"

"I am well, thank you N'kosi."

They went to Shadrak's favourite tree, and shared the shade with Shadrak's chickens. The old man looked expectantly at Iffor, who in turn took the hip flask from his map pocket and offered it to him. Just my luck he thought, as a look of appreciation and satisfaction appeared on Shadrak's face, the old bastard likes malt whisky. "Tell me, M'dala, have there been any more men in the bush?"

"Indi Bwana, yes, just one. I saw him. He carried a rifle and a heavy load."

"Tell me Shadrak, why didn't you shoot him? You must know the government will give you a lot of money for his weapon and a finger."

The old man went very silent, embarrassed.

Iffor knew the answer. "Would these have helped?" he said, and reaching back into his map pocket produced four, five-round clips of Mauser ammunition, courtesy of Giles' gunsmiths in Kensington.

The old man beamed with delight. He had run out of ammunition weeks ago, but had diligently carried his weapon wherever he went, especially in the bush. The 7.92 m.m. Mauser ammunition was difficult to get hold of, but Giles had rummaged around in his 'odds and sods' box and retrieved twenty rounds for Iffor. Leaving a very happy and contented man, Iffor retrieved his flask and rejoined his men. Time to move on.

Before leaving Charlie's farm, a quick 'O' group was called.

"Since our last visit, a man in the bush has been using the game trail; this time he was spotted…"

"Not surprised," muttered Evil. "Those jackals have got fucking good eyesight."

"…by Shadrak," Iffor continued. "He was armed and probably carrying a mine, so 'make ready all weapons', and let's get switched on, it's obvious that word hasn't yet reached Zambia that their Line of Communication has been compromised. I think we are going to have good hunting."

It took more than an hour to reach Archie's farm, with Iffor calling frequent halts to 'walk' the road ahead.

To the dismay of the team, Iffor refused Archie's offer of a cold beer; he needed to press on. They 'parked up' the Champ and trailer, covering it with a cam net so it wouldn't be too obvious. From here on in, they would be on foot. If he needed the Champ, control would phone Archie.

While the team took what stores they needed from the Champ, Iffor took Archie into his confidence as much as he could. If he had a casualty, he would need the Champ quickly.

Iffor distributed the stores and equipment: The ops team: binos, map, compass, water 'chugels', radio, spare battery, cam net, shovel and insect repellent.

The patrol team: binos; radio—he carried that himself in two ammo pouches, one for the radio and one for the battery. Evil carried the Bren and five mags, one on the gun and two in each pouch. Each man, apart from his own five rifle mags, carried one bren magazine.

In their small packs they carried two twenty-four hour ration packs, washing gear, an extra water bottle and lightweight sleeping bag, and, as Iffor suspected, the odd bottle or the odd couple of cans.

With less than two hours of daylight left, they set off for the kopjie overlooking De Witt's farm.

There was just enough light for Iffor to go forward and recce the site for the Op.

Perfect, he thought. Through his binoculars he had an unrestricted view of the bungalow and compound. The forward slopes were steep and sparsely covered, the rear slope gentle and protected. As he watched the bungalow, with the people going about their tasks, he felt the thrill of adventure, the adventure he loved, whether it be in bed with Josie or here in the bush with his soldiers; he was alive, vibrant—this is what he lived for.

He called the team up to the hide and in silence they prepared and camouflaged the hide and settled for the night.

It was a little after seven next morning when the patrol reached the drift over the river and Phil's first 'contact' message came through: "Bravo Whisky for Zero one message over."

"Zero one send, over."

"Bravo Whisky, two men approaching from the north have entered the compound and have been met by De Witt and his wife and gone into the bungalow. Both black, one in shorts, one in long trousers, both wearing bush jackets, both carrying packs. We are unable to see whether or not they are armed."

"Roger, as soon as you see them leave, give me a bearing, out."

"There are three types of patrol," Iffor said as they munched their breakfast of cold bacon grill and biscuits: Fighting patrol, which includes ambushes; Recce patrol, where you avoid trouble if you can;

and a standing patrol, which is probably the most boring of the lot. We walk, stop, look and listen, boring, but, it has to be done."

Lunchtime found them in a defensive position astride the game track, west of the drift, spreading tinned meat paste on hard tack biscuits. As part of standard operating procedures, no cooking or brewing up was allowed. Fortunately, their compo packs provided a half decent lemonade powder to be mixed with water which substituted for tea.

With an hour or so of daylight left, they made their way to the base of the kopjie, arriving as darkness fell and joined Phil and his team.

Working on the assumption that any enemy in the area would be cooking their own evening meal, Iffor allowed limited cooking on a 'Tommy Cooker', knowing that a hot meal would lift spirits all round.

While the men were eating, Iffor took Phil to one side. "Any sign of the house guests at the farm?"

"No boss. They arrived about seven, lots of handshakes and hugs, then they all went inside and that's where they've stayed."

"Are your team okay in the hide?"

"Snug as bugs in Evil's underpants."

"Still in contact with control?"

"Radio check every hour, boss."

"Good, well done."

While the men were eating, Iffor went back up to the hide and spent a while watching the farm with his binoculars. The lights of the bungalow were on, but there were no perimeter lights, contrary to most farms and he could see no sign of farm guards on sentry duty.

But what concerned Iffor most was the way the bush at the rear of the bungalow had been allowed to get so close to the building. Normally, an area of about a hundred metres was cleared around the main building, giving a clear field of fire.

Either the De Witts had no fear of a terrorist attack or the thick bush so close to the house was their escape route, or both.

When he got back to the lads, a mess tin of curry and rice and a mug of steaming tea were waiting for him. He joined them sitting around the still burning 'Hexi' block that had heated the meal. Mal offered Iffor his hip flask: "Drink boss?"

Iffor sniffed the contents; his body was still suffering from the effects of that awful Indian Krait beer; he had to be careful what he drank. "Cane spirit?" he asked. Mal nodded. "You have no respect whatsoever for your body, have you?" he said, carefully pouring a measure into his tea.

Mad Harry had gone for a crap before his hour of sentry duty.

In the field Iffor felt guard duty should only last for an hour maximum. After that eyes started playing tricks with the mind.

Waking up before dawn in the African bush is the greatest pleasure known to man, or so thought Iffor as Evil kicked him hard in the ribs and muttered, "Come on you idle bastard, time to get up."

The faint pale glow of dawn gave just enough light to expose the tops of trees peeping through the ground mist and caused the dew on spiders' web to glisten like tiny diamonds. The bush was beginning to wake up as well, with birds beginning to greet one another, and down in the farm, chattering monkeys were planning their attack on the kitchen when the cook opened the windows.

The OP team crept back up into the hide to wash and shave, and breakfast on cold bacon and beans.

Iffor led the rest of Blue Watch down towards the river. In view of the drift, they found a good defensive position where they washed, shaved, and in pairs, cleaned their weapons; one cleaning, one watching and listening. Then breakfast on cold compo bacon and beans.

Ignoring call signs, Phil's calm voice came over the air: "They are on the move boss, heading towards the old Mwonza Road. They'll either head north for Zambia or south towards you, over."

"Zero one, are they the same two? Over."

"Roger zero one, but still no sign of weapons, over."

Iffor thought for a few moments. "Bravo Whisky, if we scare them and they get back to the farm, if they are carrying weapons, zap them, over."

"Roger boss. Anything else? Over."

"Yes, get sit rep off to control and tell them to call the Colour in to man the radio."

"Roger, zero one, out."

Iffor called a quick 'O' group and told them about Phil's message.

They gathered around his map. Iffor pointed to the farm with a piece of grass. "It will take them about an hour to reach the Old Road. If they turn north they are no threat to us, but if they head south, it is a question of good manners to stop them and enquire after their health. Curfew is over; we can't confirm they are armed, so all we can do is stop them and question them.

"Our battle plan chaps: we advance to a contact along the sides of the road, Mal and myself up front on the right-hand side, Harry and Evil fifty yards back on the left.

"'Actions on'. If Mal and I come under accurate fire, we'll get back to you two and we'll fight around the Bren. That's about it. Stick a bit of make-up on the face and hands, clean up the area and let's be off." Iffor made it sound flippant, but he carefully checked the camouflage and weapons before setting out.

They advanced in a staggered extended line, well away from the road, but with the road in sight, able to watch the road and keep direction.

The sun was beginning to warm up a bit, but there was still some shade in the bush which made for a pleasant stroll, apart from the heart beating just a little faster and a tense reaction to every noise and shadow, and the m'pani flies homing in on nervous sweat for their morning drink.

Iffor stopped and knelt in response to Mal's signal. He signalled 'halt' to the other two; Harry knelt, Evil lay down behind the Bren. Iffor glanced at his watch; he wasn't expecting to make contact for another fifteen minutes or so. He looked at Mal who touched his head, the 'on me' signal.

Slowly he moved to Mal's side who indicated to the more dense bush slightly to their right. He cupped an ear, indicating he had heard rather than seen movement.

Iffor put his mouth close to Mal's ear. "We'll move forward into cover; we're too exposed here. Follow me, keep a distance."

Iffor stood and cautiously advanced. He indicated to Mal to move to his right, but Mal, the old soldier, had already done that.

In spite of years of training, and even though he was expecting to come face to face with them, it still came as a complete shock to Iffor when the two men stepped into the clearing some twenty yards away. He already had the butt of his weapon in the shoulder and now brought his foresight to bear, but hesitated; he couldn't see a weapon. He lowered the muzzle slightly, realizing his mistake as he did so. The man in the shorts wasn't wearing a bush jacket—he wore the traditional cloak buttoned at the neck and concealing his hands.

Too late, far too late, Iffor saw the Sten gun that was concealed under the cloak.

The impact of the bullet hitting him and the report were simultaneous. The shock paralysed him, his legs buckled and he pitched forward. He heard himself shout, "Right and left, Mal!" The former gamekeeper fired, the two shots sounding as one, but instead of a brace of pheasants falling from the sky, both terrorists dropped and lay still.

Iffor lay on his side. He still couldn't move his legs, but he was still alive. Mal knelt beside him. "I'm here boss."

"Their weapons, get their weapons, and call the others in!"

Mal was soon back at Iffor's side with the Sten and a pistol the second man was carrying. "Both dead centre boss. One's still alive—shall I finish him?"

"No, we need a prisoner."

Harry arrived. He turned Iffor on to his back. Iffor saw the look of concern on his face as he opened the shirt. He looked at the wound, then at the shirt. "What the fuck did you have in your breast pocket?"

Iffor was beginning to 'lose it'. He felt a searing pain in his chest as he whispered, "A carton of ammo."

"Well, that's what the bullet smashed into. You've got a very nasty flesh wound, but that's what it is, a flesh wound."

Now Harry was in command. "Mal, patch up the boss, give him a drink, pick the pieces of cartridges out of the wound and put a shell dressing on it. Then see what you can do for the terr. Evil, keep a sharp lookout."

Gently, they took the pouches with the '88 set from Iffor.

Harry spoke into the handset: "Bravo Whisky message over. Send. Contact now on Mwonza Road five miles west of your location."

He paused. Phil would be writing this down. "One enemy dead, one wounded, two weapons recovered. Sunray is down, I say again, Sunray is down. Sit rep follows, wait out." He turned back to Iffor. Mal was just squeezing the tube of morphine into his thigh.

"Plan of action boss, we'll scramble the Islander to RV on the strip behind Archie's farm. We'll get the Colour to contact Archie and have him come and collect us here; risky, but we've three bodies to carry."

Iffor nodded, "Okay."

Harry was now in his element. "Zero one for Bravo Whisky sit rep over, Send."

Harry gave Phil details of the plan and ended saying, "When you have sent your sit rep off to control, pack up and strike out for the Mwonza Road. We'll pick you up. Stay in radio contact... And Phil..."

"Yes."

"Tread lightly, be careful. Roger, out."

Evil came to see how Iffor was. "You're like a fucking magnet when bullets start flying." Mal showed him the spent nine mm bullet that he had recovered along with bits of cartridge case from the wound. Evil looked at it. "I told you a bullet would just bounce off the thick Welsh bastard."

Iffor looked at Harry. In spite of the intense pain, he had some movement in his legs. "Evil has a way with words, hasn't he?"

Mal took a turn around their small perimeter, while Harry and Evil moved Iffor and the two terrorists into some shade. They heard Mal shout: "Vehicle coming, I'm going to stop it!"

"It can't possibly be Archie," Harry muttered. A few minutes later, Mal came back with Father Sean in tow.

Reactions differed, from Iffor's, "What the fuck are you doing here?" to Harry's "Sean, are we glad to see you!"

"In answer to your first question," Sean said, as he examined the field dressing on Iffor's wound with a practised hand, "I'm going about my business delivering labourers to the De Witt's farm. In case you didn't know, it's harvest time. I'm very busy ferrying my labourers around the farms at this time. Now, how can I help?"

The morphine was beginning to take effect; Iffor could take no part in the proceedings; the wounded terrorist was still unconscious.

"If you can get your chaps to walk to the farm, as the crow flies it's only an hour or so," said Harry. "You can take the two terrs, Iffor and

Mal back to Archie's farm. Me and Evil will meet up with the rest of our team and Archie can pick us up. We've arranged for the mine Islander to collect the wounded at Archie's farm."

Sean went back to the minibus to talk his labourers into walking the rest of the way. Like it or not, the priest gave them no choice and anyway, they were well used to the war interrupting their way of life.

While Sean was away, Harry laid out his sleeping bag as an improvised stretcher for his team mate. Iffor struggled into a sitting position, "I can walk, I don't need to be carried." The blood-soaked field dressing on his wound began to ooze fresh blood, Mal bandaged a second dressing over the first. "You've got a massive wound," he said, "Move around too much and you'll bleed to death. Leave it to us."

Sean gingerly drove the battered minibus with the white crosses painted on its side to their position, and they carefully loaded the casualties.

Evil relieved Mal of the Bren magazines and they parted company, Harry and Evil North to RV with Phil, the minibus south to Arc Angel farm.

Iffor dozed fitfully. The road was rutted and long and Sean seemed to be able to find every pothole. Still under the influence of the morphine, he was aware of the bus stopping and voices, in particular, Archie's voice, saying, "Don't worry old son, I'll pick your boys up."

Another thirty minutes of excruciating pain and the bus drove on to firm flat ground and stopped. The doors opened, and Davy Jones climbed in. He looked down at Iffor. "I told you, you could depend on me." Then turning to the pilot said with a voice full of authority, "We'll get the Lieutenant loaded on first."

The flight back to Kensington was no more than twenty minutes, during which Iffor was able to say to Mal, "Guard the prisoner well, no visitors, hand the terrs' weapons over to Pete when you can." Then he drifted off—the loss of blood was beginning to have a serious effect on him.

Iffor started to come to; he tried to focus on the angel looking down at him.

Shit, he thought, the bastards have posted me to heaven. Then he heard the angel speak. "He's coming round," Josie said.

Van De Werwe looked anxiously into his face. "Welcome back to the land of the living! You've been sleeping for twenty-four hours, which was just as well. I didn't want you moving around too much."

The doctor sat down on the bed. "Now then, that was quite a sizable wound you had, it took me over an hour just digging bits of cartridge case and pieces of cloth out of it. We had to give you a pint of blood; we are a bit short of your group so soon as you can, come back and replace it. The wound is too big to suture—all we can do is change the sterile dressing daily and wait for it to heal. I'll look in later; if I think you're fit enough, you can go back to Auntie's—she'll look after you better than we can."

After the doctor had left, Pete and the Colour came in. "Got a private room I see," said Pete.

"R.H.I.P." Iffor said, then for Josie's sake, "Rank has its privileges."

"About our prisoner," Pete said.

"Before we go on, someone get me a bottle, I need a pee; I'm desperate."

"Now then, let's talk about the prisoner," Iffor said, looking more comfortable and relaxed. "Pete, at all costs we've got to keep him a secret and keep him isolated."

"While you've been sleeping," the Colour said, "the Inspector and I have been scheming. Word's already out that our man died on the operating table without waking up, and Flint the undertaker will bury two coffins on Monday. We scrounged a body from the hospital morgue. The staff who came into contact with the wounded terrorist are all sworn to secrecy and they are all loyal to the good doctor. And 'our man' has been admitted to the isolation ward suffering from smallpox; that will scare the shit out of any curious Africans, and that's what the hospital staff have been told. Only the sister looking after him knows the truth.

"Agnes is guarding him, Sergeant Tim takes over at lunchtime. I've got a twenty-four hour guard on him. The doc thinks it will be a few days before we can question him."

The Colour pre-empted Iffor's next question. "The boys are all back safe and sound; I've stood them down till Monday."

"We can't do that," Iffor struggled to sit up. Josie was by his side to help him. "We've got to hit De Witt's farm, strike while the iron is hot."

"Calm down," Pete said, "stop and think. If De Witt was going to do a bunk, he'd be hacking his way through the bush to Zambia by now, and somehow, I don't think his wife is up to that. He can't leave the country legally; I've seen to that. No, I think that when we pay him a visit he will try to brazen it out. After all, he doesn't know we saw the terrorists enter and leave his bungalow, and..." his voice trailed off, "I need a warrant to search his farm and our magistrate is off fishing until Monday."

Iffor wanted to be alone, to rest, to think, but he still had questions. "Bob, did you get a sit rep off to Battalion?"

"Josie did. She thought you'd want to sit on our prisoner for a while before Battalion could take him away, so she reported: 'Bravo Whisky in contact. Sunray wounded, reports suggest two enemy killed, two weapons recovered'."

"Brilliant," said Iffor, "Brilliant! Now the lot of you piss off and let me rest."

As he got up to go, Pete said, "The Sten gun you recovered was registered to Susie Dix, thought you'd like to know."

Iffor's eyes were beginning to close; suddenly he felt very tired. The angel appeared in front of his face again. This time she said, "Sleep well, my darling, I'll come back later." Then she lightly kissed his lips.

Lunchtime in hospital is announced by a very noisy, rattling, squeaking trolley stopping outside your room and disgorging a nurse complete with tray to your bedside. "Wake up, time for lunch, doctor says you can sit in a chair to eat your meal," she said abruptly and business-like. She helped Iffor into a chair and, aware of his arm strapped to his heavily bandaged chest, cut his food into small pieces for him.

As she started to say, "You have a visitor," Davy Jones peered around the door.

"Hope I'm not interrupting," he said and came into the room and sat down.

3

Iffor looked anxiously past him.

"It's all right, I've left him at home. I've just popped in to see how you are."

"I'm fine thank you, and thanks for getting the Islander rigged so quickly."

"Well, I must confess, the Colour's phone call took me by surprise. I was still in bed but when he mentioned 'Pegasus', I was wide awake and raring to go."

Davy went on. "The Islander is a multi-role aircraft, so rigging it for casevac was a piece of piss. Anyway," he looked embarrassed, he'd come at a bad time, "I'll leave you in peace to have your lunch, see you anon," and he got up to leave.

As he went, Iffor called after him: "You did a great job, you and the pilots."

Davy turned to face him. "Does this mean I'm on the team?"

"Yes, now fuck off."

The nurse came to take his tray away and help him back into bed. For only the second time in his adult life he was wearing pyjamas, both times in hospital and both times after being shot. He settled himself and began to doze. The thought of two or three days being waited on hand and foot was beginning to appeal to him. The food was good and he could persuade Josie to bring some booze into him, and... he let his mind dwell on the thought for a moment... he had a private room.

He started to plan his seduction of Josie; she wouldn't be keen to get into a hospital bed, she'd need persuading.

Then his dream shattered as Van De Merwe came into the room. "I'll just check the dressing, then I think you can go back to your hotel and rest there. I'll come in with the district nurse tomorrow to have a look at you and she can change the dressing. Then she'll come again on Sunday to dress the wound again."

Pete appeared in the doorway. "Ready? I've come to take you home—the doc phoned me."

"That's very thoughtful of you."

"Not at all, I need a favour. I need to borrow your pick-up. I'm going to bring some of Helen's bits and pieces back from the mission. Another week or so and she'll be moving in with me."

The doctor helped Iffor to dress in the clothes Pete had brought. (Mal had taken his blood-stained uniform and weapons back to the drill hall.)

Pete sat on the bed watching Iffor struggling to dress with one hand. "I've just had a thought, why don't you come with Josie and me to the Mission on Sunday? We are back on Monday. What do you think, doc?"

Iffor started to think of a good reason why he shouldn't; he just wanted to rest in the shade of the jacaranda tree in Auntie's garden and let her look after him. Anyway, he had to have his wound dressed... Then a vision of the African doctor Grace bending over him, and with luck, showing her cleavage, dressing his wound with her long sensuous fingers, caused him to croak, "What a good idea."

"Conditions apply," the doctor said. "Take some dressings with you and complete rest. Oh, and by the time you get back, you may be able to question 'our man'."

Auntie was waiting for them at the hotel. No jacaranda tree, no bottle of wine, just straight upstairs to his bedroom. The nurses at the hospital had cleaned him up and shaved him, but he was in dire need of a bath and Auntie took upon herself this task with relish. Pete offered to help. "Thank-you, but no thank-you; another man would only get in the way. Come back later."

By the time Josie came home from the 'office', Iffor was tucked up between clean crisp sheets, and apart from being quite sore and tender, he felt great and quite pleased with himself. She kissed him passionately on the mouth—he was now glad Auntie had made him clean his teeth—then drew up a chair to the bed. "The Colonel phoned, said 'well done and get well soon'. A coded message arrived from him; it read..., hang on, I've written it down for you. I've got it here somewhere." She rummaged through her pockets: hankie, lipstick, mirror and finally, a crumpled piece of paper. "Found it," she smiled.

Iffor read the message: "Border activity increasing, Bn reserves engaged. Continue to disrupt enemy L of C."

He handed the paper back to her. "Eat it." She smiled and tore it into pieces before putting it in his waste bin.

"There was also a phone call from Selous Scouts, and a letter from Henry's father."

"Phone call first, please."

"It was from their Intelligence Officer; he said 'Congratulations on your kill, we've been after him for months'. I think he meant Samuel Kitwe—and he said if ever we need any help, we are to give him a call."

The letter read:

> *"My dear Meredith, I thank you for your letter. It was most kind and thoughtful of you. It was my wish that Henry would become a soldier in keeping with family tradition and join the family regiment, but it was not to be. However, he died a soldier's death. I loved him, I miss him and I'm damned proud of my son. If I can be of service, you know where I can be found."*

Iffor offered the letter to Josie. "I've read it, thank you," she said.

She was crying silently. "Yes, it was a moving letter," Iffor said.

"It's not the letter you bloody fool, it's you. When I heard you were 'down' or whatever terms they use, I didn't know whether you were dead or badly injured.

"When Bob told me, I felt that same stab of fear in my heart that I felt when I was told Mummy and Daddy had been attacked."

Iffor put on his best 'hangdog' look. "Sorry," he said softly.

She dried her eyes on the corner of his sheet. "You've got to rest, I'll come back later."

He sat propped up by the pillows looking out of the window without seeing anything.

He hadn't realised what her feelings were for him. He couldn't continue the relationship, he told himself. He was at least twelve years older than her; she probably wanted a husband and family while he wanted... he found himself thinking the unthinkable. He had a five-year contract with the army and he was entitled to a government bungalow; would it be so bad if she moved in with him? The very worst that could happen would be to marry her, get a dog and have children.

But that was in the future and with the job he was doing, he shouldn't be planning a future.

Now that he knew what he wanted, he could rest and get well and back into the war.

What he wanted was her.

When Auntie came in to wake him and tell him that dinner was ready, it was quite dark. She turned on the table lamp, helped him to the toilet and back into bed.

She returned a little later with a folding table which she laid across the bed. Josie followed with a tray of steaks and salad and, joy of joys, a bottle of Cape Red.

After Auntie left, Josie started to dish the food. She was wearing a sari of sorts, and having just come out of the shower was pink and glowing, and smelling of soap and scent. At first, she sat beside the bed, her plate on the bed table. "This is no good," she said as she stood up, and stepping out of her sari, she slipped into bed beside him.

"I'm not allowed to exert myself," he said.

She poured the wine. "That's all right, I'll exert for both of us."

Auntie insisted on bathing him again before she would serve breakfast. The louder he protested, the more she seemed to enjoy it.

"Why are you making such a fuss? I'm a married woman. In India we do this all the time."

He was about to mention that they weren't in India when he realised he was actually enjoying the experience, so he lay back and let her do her worst, or best.

He had the impression Auntie was enjoying it too. The thought 'threesome' skipped playfully into his mind and flirted for a moment or two, until ashamed, he drove it away, but not before a stirring caused Auntie to blush and say, "Cheekie boy," before dashing from the bathroom.

It was left to Josie to give him a hand out of the bath, dry him and help him dress—taking considerably longer than if he had dressed himself.

They had breakfast together under his favourite jacaranda tree. He found himself feeling much more comfortable with her: he was more willing to touch, and even hold her hand; talking to her gave him the excuse to look into her face, which caused havoc with his emotions.

Saturday became 'visiting day'. First the doctor and the district nurse. She smoked as she removed the bandages and dressing. "Keeps the flies away," she explained. The doctor poked and probed at the wound. "That is coming along nicely, it's healing well." And between them, with Auntie supervising, they bandaged him up again. The doctor turned to Josie, "I'm happy to let him go to the Mission tomorrow, but he mustn't exert himself." She began to giggle, then controlled herself. "I'll look after him, Doctor."

Mid-morning Evil arrived. "Chance of a beer?"

Iffor motioned to Godfry and showed two fingers. Godfry indicated the bandages around Iffor's chest: "Does this mean you won't be joining us on parade on Monday?"

"Sit down you old bastard before I set Auntie on you. How are the rest of the boys?"

"They'll be here soon, you can ask them yourself."

As he poured the beers, Harry and Mal appeared, followed minutes later by the rest of the team. Josie excused herself and cleared away the breakfast tray, but Auntie, like a mother hen, kept a discreet watch from the restaurant. She didn't want her patient tiring himself.

Once Iffor had assured them he was well on the road to recovery they went into a debrief, each critical of his own actions leading up to and during the short contact.

"What's next?" asked Harry, "Are we still active?"

Iffor beckoned to Godfry for another round. "Very much so. Battalion still want us to sit astride the terrorists' line of communication, and since the Colour is under orders to maintain a rear link, and since I'm out of action for a few days, it looks like you, Harry, my old mucker, have got the job. You take command of the team:

"I want you to spend Monday planning and preparing; into the bush on Tuesday before sparrows' fart; make a nuisance of yourselves and come back in on Wednesday after dark. On Friday, I should be fit enough to come with you. We'll patrol the Old Lamumbwa Road, visit the Dix farm and escort Helen Dix into town. She's marrying Pete, in case you hadn't heard."

After they'd gone, he was allowed the comfort of the sun lounger under the jacaranda tree, having been told quite sternly by Auntie to rest.

He allowed his thoughts to dwell on Josie. He was in no doubt that she was in love with him. He tried to define what love was, and wondered about his feelings for Josie. He knew that he had loved his wife all those years ago; that's why he let her divorce him, but what he felt for Josie, those feelings were quite new to him.

He tried to avoid thinking and worrying about Mad Harry taking the patrol out on Tuesday. He knew he had no choice, but...

He was roused from his thoughts by Bob Pearson, his Colour Sergeant: "Thought you might need this boss." He dropped Iffor's pistol belt on to the table beside him. "I've cleaned the pistol and magazines. Routine for Monday?" he asked, pulling up a chair and sitting down.

Iffor told him of his plans to send Blue Watch into the bush again under command of Mad Harry.

"They'll be all right," Bob assured him, "and anyway, it's what the Colonel ordered. Now, I'm off. Auntie said she'd have my bollocks if I stayed longer than five minutes."

Josie came to his bed again that night, but her woman's wisdom told her he must sleep. Like a mother comforting her child, she spoke softly in a mixture of English and her native tongue, telling him of her hopes and fears and her feelings for him. But if Iffor heard her, he probably thought it was a dream.

Eight sharp, Pete pulled up outside the hotel in Iffor's borrowed pick-up. He was waiting in reception with the suitcase Josie had packed for them both. Suitcase, he thought! In the old days it would have been toothbrush and razor in one pocket, clean (well, almost clean) underpants in another pocket.

Excitedly, Josie came running down the stairs: sandals, shorts and one of Iffor's old K.D. shirts knotted around her midrift, allowing her breasts the freedom from a bra.

Two hours later they drove into the Leper Mission, and were immediately surrounded by excited children accepting the sweets and chocolate Pete always brought for them. Josie, like a child about to see new-born kittens for the first time, was off looking for Doctor Grace and the twins. Iffor, feeling blissfully happy, pushed his way through the throng of children to Helen. She looked concerned, seeing his bandages. He wrapped his good arm around her waist and kissed her cheek. As he pulled away from her he felt the small of her back; it was there, the twenty-two pistol he had loaned her, in its holster. "Good girl," he whispered. She pushed him away gently and touched his bandages, "What on earth?"

"It's nothing," he interrupted. Then Pete had her in his arms, swinging her around like a child. "I think he's pleased to see you," muttered Iffor.

Josie joined them, followed by the willowy Grace. She had a bundle under both arms, each with a baby's face peering out at them. "Look what I've found," she cooed, "Aren't they gorgeous?"

Iffor sniffed, "Seen one, seen 'em all."

She kicked his shin, "Pig."

It wasn't until lunch was finished that Iffor had the chance to get young Jamie alone. "Jamie, I need someone to give me a guided tour of the mission and you're elected."

The boy was a little uncertain at first, but was soon in his element, pointing out the various buildings and introducing him to his friends. "This is my uncle Iffor, he's a soldier."

As they toured the site, Iffor became oblivious to the boy's commentary, thinking instead about the defence of the Mission when Helen had gone. He'd been toying for some time with the idea of bringing a mobile Vickers' team down from Mwonza.

The Vickers, with its range of seven miles, sited properly, could bring down defensive fire on both the Dix farm and the Mission.

"Uncle Iffor..." The 'uncle' has got to go, thought Iffor... "Mummy has told me you're my godfather, what does that mean?"

As they walked, Iffor put his arm around Jamie's shoulder. "It means old son, that if you ever need me no matter where I am, I'll come to you. It means that you and I will always be friends and we can always trust one another. And it means that you stop calling me 'uncle'; my friends call me Iffor."

Grace was waiting for him when they rejoined the group. "Let's have a look at that wound of yours." She led him to her surgery.

Iffor noted with some considerable satisfaction that he was right about her showing her cleavage. She leaned over him as he lay on her examination couch, probing and prodding. He had the distinct impression she was enjoying causing him pain. She spoke as she worked: "Helen's put you and Josie in the guest lodge tonight—does that mean you're 'going together'?"

"We share a bed," Iffor said, wincing as she poured something resembling the venom of a puffadder on his wound, and trying to change the subject, commented, "She was certainly taken with the twins."

"Probably because she knows she can't have children herself."

The enormity of what she had just said caused her to look startled, scared. "You did know, didn't you?"

"Yes," Iffor lied, "I knew."

The evening was as perfect as any evening could be, seated around the braai cooking a bush buck and listening to the Africans singing in their kraals, the African night giving the appearance of early dawn but with stars. Jamie came to him with a plate of *Boereworse*. "Thanks mate, sit down for a minute." The boy waited patiently while Iffor finished his sausage. "Do you know what the M.M. stands for on your dad's gravestone?"

Jamie shook his head. "No."

"It stands for Military Medal; your dad was given it for being very, very brave. One day your mother will give it to you, and then I'll tell you exactly what he did."

In the darkness, he could see the boy was gently crying. "Go back to your mother, lad. We'll talk more tomorrow while we're cleaning my pistol."

The end of the perfect evening, Josie led him to the guest lodge, a thatched roof on four poles with a wall three feet high affording some privacy.

To sleep on such an occasion would have been unthinkable. So they didn't.

PART ELEVEN

More damage can be inflicted by cutting downwards with the blade and ripping upwards with the serrated part of the blade when withdrawing the knife from the body

BY POPULAR DEMAND, Iffor was forced to have his breakfast in his 'bedroom' from a tray Josie brought him. A demand made by Jamie and seven or eight friends eager to help clean his pistol.

Iffor showed them the drills for cleaning the weapon, and allowed each boy to strip and assemble the weapon, watching with pride while Jamie helped those with withered hands or fingers missing because of the leprosy.

"Tell you what, boys, I'll be back next weekend with my team. Let's see if we can fire one or two weapons then."

Leaving Jamie to guard his pistol with a solemn promise not to touch it, Iffor went in search of the shower block, hoping he might find Josie there.

Reluctant as they were to leave the mission, Pete needed to get back and even though he was 'stood down', Iffor was chomping at the bit to get back and see his boys before they left for the bush.

"Everything's under control, boss," Harry said when Iffor walked into the drill hall: "Ammo; rations; water; fuel; weapons all checked; all weapons cleaned."

Iffor put his arm around Harry's shoulder and hugged him. "I've come to wave you bye-bye, not to check up on you."

The Colour came up to them. "If I can tear you two lovers apart, I need to speak to the boss. My office please, sir, if you will."

In his office, the Colour said, "Top secret, for your eyes alone," and handed Iffor the signal.

Iffor read it, sat down, and read it again. "Have you acknowledged it?" he asked.

"Yes sir. Are you going to tell the troops?"

Iffor was still looking at the signal. "Of course, it's my policy to keep them informed. Call them in; let's get this over with."

As the men assembled, Iffor said, "Sorry Harry, I shan't keep you long but this is important."

He read the signal: " 'At 0715 this morning terrorists brought down a Viscount airliner, just after it had taken off from Kariba, with a SAM. The pilot was able to make a crash landing and some thirty plus, including children survived. Reports show terrorists on the ground captured survivors and bayoneted them all after raping and sodomising all females including children. Signal ends.'

"Gentlemen, if word of this gets out before the government announces it, it can only have come from one of us and I will have to resign. Have we all got the message?"

A resounding, "yessir" followed.

"Good, carry on please, Harry."

Back at the hotel, Auntie was in the garden speaking with the doctor and 'fag ash Lil'. "Ah, here comes my patient, I think we'll have you up in your room please."

The nurse took away the bandages allowing the doctor to poke and prod at the wound while she kept imaginary flies away with her cigarette smoke.

"Though I say it myself, that's coming along very nicely—I did a good job on that. Another week of rest and you can go back on light duties."

Iffor crossed his fingers. "Yes Doctor."

The doctor waited until the nurse had finished dressing the wound and had left the room, before telling Iffor, "You can question 'our man' whenever you want."

As the doctor left, Josie came into the room. "Isn't this wonderful, we've got the rest of the day together." He told her about the Viscount tragedy, reminding her it was classified 'Secret'. She put her hand to her mouth and looked around for a chair and sat down. "That can't be true," she said, "no-one could be that wicked!"

"These bastards can," Iffor said. "I have to meet Pete and go and question our prisoner." He didn't tell her he'd already planned a sortie to Boons bar afterwards; he needed to be apart from Josie to consider the Viscount tragedy. And since Father Sean was in town to bury the 'two' terrorists, Iffor hoped he might meet up with him in Boons to thank him for his help after he'd been wounded.

A quick phone call to Pete and Iffor was on his way to the hospital. They met in the car park. "Have you heard?" Pete said.

"The Viscount? Yes, I've heard. The signal was waiting for me when I got back; bad news. How in hell's name did they manage to get hold of a surface to air weapon, and what's more important, who trained them?"

"The Cubans trained them," Pete answered, "and the weapon came in the same box of 'Bandages' that contained the rocket launcher that brought down our Beaver."

As they walked into the hospital, Pete said, "Good guy, bad guy."

"Sounds good to me," Iffor agreed. This was to be their method of interrogation, a sound plan, unless the prisoner had been trained in resistance to interrogation.

Trained or not, their plans were thrown into complete disarray when they entered the isolation ward.

The prisoner was manacled by the ankle to the bed, an armed policeman beside the bed. As they walked into the room, the policeman stood up. The Inspector nodded towards the door, "Take a break for an hour or so."

As Pete pulled a second chair up to the bed, Iffor could only stand and stare—he knew this man. The African smiled broadly revealing perfect teeth. Still heavily bandaged, he raised himself up and extended his hand. "Hello Iffor, it's been a long time."

Without thinking, Iffor took the man's hand. "Moses January, Sarn't Major Moses January. Late of the Zambian army?" he asked, "Or still serving?"

Friend or not, Iffor was now in interrogation mode, and would take advantage of their friendship by becoming mister 'nice guy'.

The African became serious, reached under his pillow and produced a scrap of paper. "That's all you will get out of me, my number, rank and name. I am a Warrant Officer in the Zambian army, and demand to be treated as such."

Mister 'nasty' leaned over the man. "You were caught inside Rhodesia's border, you were in civilian clothing, you were armed and in company with an armed terrorist. For that my friend, you will surely hang."

"How's that lad of yours?" mister 'nice' asked, "Still in school, he must be... what, seventeen now?"

Moses smiled, trying to hide the shock of his predicament. "Nearly eighteen, and still at Kafue school. Do you remember, Iffor? You said you'd try and help to get him into Sandhurst and into the British army; he wants to go into the Life Guards. He will be upset when my unit tells him I am missing."

"Your unit will tell him you are dead," mister nasty said. "We buried you and your mate this morning. We can take you into the bush anytime we like and shoot you..." he paused "...again; but this time we can promise to do a proper job."

Mister nice gently pushed his friend back into his chair. "When news of your 'death' gets back to Zambia, your son, Douglas, isn't it, will be taken from the school and sent back to his village to be brought up by relatives. No Sandhurst, no sword of honour presented while you proudly watch, no career with the British army, just a wasted life."

Moses watched him, looking for a glimmer of hope, a chance for his son.

Iffor sensed the time was right. "There is a way out of this mess for you, old son." He looked at Pete who nodded in agreement. "You can 'turn'. Many of your comrades have already done so and you can join me in the Rhodesian army, but I must tell you, we must have all the information you have about the terrorist group in this area."

"My son?"

"We will get him out of Zambia."

"Can you do this for me?"

"We have a unit which specialises in this field, the Selous Scouts. You may have heard of them."

As far as Africans can go pale, Moses went very pale.

Mister nice turned to mister nasty. "I think he's heard of them."

"I will need time to think. It will be difficult for me to betray my comrades."

"Your comrades kill and maim their own people, they kill children, they rape and bugger women, your comrades are not fit to breathe the same air as a soldier."

As they started to leave, Iffor touched Moses' arm. "You're a Nyasa, you've no loyalty to Zambia, only to yourself and Douglas. Time is short, my friend, use it well."

As they left the hospital mister nasty turned to mister nice, "Time for a beer I think."

Boons bar was surprisingly quiet for mid-afternoon. As Iffor expected, Father Sean was sitting talking to Davy Jones and Ed Dix. Pete and Iffor joined them. "Don't often see you in town," Iffor said, taking Ed's extended hand.

Ed chuckled. "I come in once a month or so, have a haircut, do some shopping, come into Boons and talk to Davy, which reminds me why I don't come into town very often. Anyway, I understand you're paying me a visit with your lads in a few days."

"That's something I don't discuss in a bar." Iffor was furious that Ed even knew about his planned visit. "Sorry," Ed muttered, "Didn't think."

"My fault," said Sean, "I was in the police station collecting my fee for the burial this morning and someone happened to mention the army might be paying me a visit at the weekend. I mentioned it to Ed. I should have known better; sorry."

Iffor sympathised with the priest and understood the predicament he found himself in.

"Don't worry too much; word will soon be out anyway. Yes, we're picking up Helen and her son and bringing them into town, As most people already know, she's marrying our handsome policeman here."

"Have you thought about the actual ceremony?" Ed asked.

"Not really, no," said Pete looking concerned.

"Fucking typical!" Iffor exclaimed.

Ignoring him, Ed said, "Why not have it at the farm, in the evening, and I'm sure Sean will do the honours."

"Delighted," said Sean.

"Can I bring Cheetah?" said Davy.

A couple or more beers later Iffor wandered back to the hotel. Josie would be waiting for him, and he was feeling quite hungry. The thought of a steak and a bottle of Cape Red under the jacaranda tree made him quicken his step.

He felt quite pleased with himself. The questioning of Moses had gone well and Pete would be getting the search warrant for the De Witt's farm tomorrow.

He decided he would call a 'coffee meeting' with Pete and the Colour in the morning to plan the visit to De Witt's. Yes, things were going well, but the Viscount disaster hovered like a black raincloud above him.

"Morning Colour, did the team get off all right?" Iffor was in uniform and the Colour saluted.

"Yessir, Harry made them sleep in the drill hall. They left at 0400."

"I suppose you saw them off?"

"Yessir, I watched as they drove off into the darkness with their new pennant flying from their radio aerial."

"New pennant?" enquired Iffor.

"Yes, it's modelled on the 'Airborne' flash you wore in the British army."

"You mean 'Pegasus', the winged horse?"

"Yes, only this is a winged pig. Apparently, some of the lads in the Moth club suggested that pigs might fly before Blue Watch could take on the terrorists."

"Did they give it a name?"

"Yes, 'PIGASUS'. We tried to come up with a motto, a battle cry like you have in Airborne, but no luck. Got any ideas?"

Iffor thought for a few moments. "Faint heart ne'er fucked a pig."

"Perfect," the Colour said, reaching for his notebook.

Shamus came shuffling up like a big bear, wearing pouches and carrying his rifle in the crook of his left arm and looking every inch a soldier.

The Colour explained. "Shamus is my quick reaction force and general dogsbody. He keeps an eye on the drill hall and takes the routine radio checks in the police station."

"Well dogsbody," said Iffor, "perhaps you would be good enough to pop round to the station, give the Inspector my compliments and ask him to join us for a 'coffee meeting' in my office."

Pete duly arrived in his starched uniform, with his big Colt holstered comfortably on his right hip. Josie served the coffee, then made to leave. "Join us please, Josie," Iffor said, "You need to know what's going on." He watched her draw up a chair and place it opposite him. She sat and crossed her legs. Thoughts of the previous night swamped his brain, causing him to refer to his notes before he could begin the meeting.

"First and foremost," he began, "have you got the search warrant yet, Pete?" Then he muttered to himself, "Not that we need it."

"I'm collecting it later this morning, and yes, we do need a warrant—we still have rule of law in this country."

Chastised, Iffor said, "When are you going to search the De Witt's place?"

"Tomorrow, and I've been told I must have army back-up. You're welcome to join me if you're up to it."

"Great!" Iffor said. "Give me your timings when you can and I'll arrange to R.V. with Bravo Whisky on the way, and Bravo Whisky can come back into town with us. Questions?"

"Can I come?" the Colour asked. "Shamus can stand in for me."

Iffor looked at Pete for an answer. "Fine with me, we've got room; I'm taking the Rhino and a Rover."

"Glad to have you with us," Iffor said, bringing the meeting to a close. "Thank you, gentlemen. Pete, you'll call an 'O' group when you're ready?"

"I think," said Pete, "for the sake of secrecy we have to move before 1000hours tomorrow and I'll brief all concerned here in the drill hall at 0900hours."

Meeting over, Iffor brought the Colour up to date with the prisoner and then drove to the hospital to have his dressing changed and another chat to Moses.

The audience with Moses did not go well. He had had time to think on his predicament. He wasn't concerned for himself; he wanted a better life for his boy, a chance to get into Sandhurst. "Iffor, you promised you would get Douglas out of Zambia, you promised to get him into Sandhurst, you said…"

"Stop." Iffor could see he was getting agitated. "I didn't promise, I said I would try."

Moses calmed down. Iffor went on: "Today, this afternoon, I will write to my friend who is a General in England. I will ask him to sponsor Douglas into Sandhurst. I know he will do this for me. I cannot ask the Scouts to get Douglas out of Zambia until you have told me about the terrorists. That is the deal, Moses, and we are running out of time."

"I will want to see the General's reply to your letter, then we will talk." He closed his eyes—the meeting was over.

As he drove back to the drill hall Iffor reflected on the situation: he was skating on very thin ice; he should have handed Moses over to Battalion for interrogation; and he most certainly should not have made a deal with a terrorist. But he was certain Moses could lead him to the terrorist organisation.

Back in his office, Iffor wrote his letter to the General. If he caught the afternoon post, the letter would be on the evening VC10 and in London by the morning. With luck he would get a reply by the weekend or the following Monday.

He told the General of the success his part-time middle-aged firemen-cum-soldiers had had, and tried to stress the importance of a positive reply to his request for sponsorship of Douglas January.

He called Josie into his office. "Post that for me," he said, handing her the letter, "Then I'm all yours for the rest of the day."

Wednesday morning by a long tradition was market day in Kensington. Traders from outlying African villages came into town, set up stalls and sold and traded everything, from fruit to wives and the occasional child. It was also the morning when Iffor could get back into the bush again.

Pete's briefing was short and to the point:

"ETD 1000hours: we R.V. with call sign Bravo Whisky midday at Arc Angel farm, then in convoy move on the De Witt's farm.

"Bravo Whisky will stop at the entrance and will be our quick reaction force. Myself, my four constables, along with Iffor and the Colour providing the military presence, will serve the warrant and search the farm.

"We will detain Mrs De Witt, her brother if he's there, and Mr De Witt.

"When we've finished the search we will arrest the De Witts for harbouring terrorists and anything else we can come up with...

"Any questions?" he asked, looking directly at his four constables.

They just smiled and nodded, happy to be taking part in an operation that may well end up in a fire fight.

A little after eleven, the small convoy turned off the Great North Road and onto the Old Mwonza Road leading to the farming community, passing the three or four small villages on the way. Iffor could not help but wonder how these villages survived. Unless they had a borehole, the nearest water was some ten miles away and work and wages were courtesy of Father Sean's labour exchange, if the farms in the area needed extra labour.

Mad Harry and the team were waiting as the police convoy drove into Arc Angel farm, standing around the bonnet of the Champ, digging in to the tray of sandwiches Archie's wife had provided. Phil was on the 31 set sending off the midday radio check and confirming Iffor's arrival. "Good to see you boss; nothing to report. Shadrak and his jackal are in the bush keeping an eye on things for us."

Harry asked, "Are we going to hit the De Witts?"

"Indeed we are," said Iffor, "indeed we are. The Inspector will brief you."

While Pete briefed Blue Watch, Iffor had a chat to Archie. "I can guess where you're going," Archie said to him, "Can I help?"

"Just make sure no one uses the phone or the radio until after we've come back down the road later this afternoon. Oh, and stay close to the phone yourself in case we have to scramble the Islander again."

The small convoy moved on to De Witt's farm, the 'mine protected' Rhino leading, followed by the police Rover, then the Champ. It was early afternoon, but complete silence: no birds singing or calling; no small animals crossing the track. It seemed the animals as well as the small villages they passed had all closed down ready for curfew, or perhaps something more sinister. Only Phil's radio check broke the silence.

They passed the usual sign 'Europeans advised not pass beyond this sign' after midday. The sign made Iffor realise just what they were up against; a mine and one or two RPD machine guns would wipe out the entire convoy in moments.

They dismounted some seventy metres short of the bungalow, leaving Harry and the team with the Champ that provided the gun-platform for the Bren.

Pete deployed his four constables on the four corners of the bungalow about fifty metres out. Then Pete, Iffor and the Colour walked as casually as they could towards the bungalow. Mrs De Witt came onto the veranda to greet them. She was quite a formidable woman, about six feet, well-built, wearing shirt, trousers and a small chequered apron giving the appearance of working in the kitchen. She carried a large chef's knife in her hand, wiping it on her apron as she watched the group walk towards her. Pete stopped at the foot of the veranda steps. "Mrs De Witt, I've a warrant to search your..."

A black man scrambled out of a window at the far end of the bungalow carrying an AK rifle and ran towards the bush. The constable, more used to stopping traffic than a fleeing armed man, put up his hand and called, "Halt," only to be cut down by a burst of fire from the fleeing man. The Colour brought his rifle from the ready position to the shoulder in one flowing movement and fired, dropping the fleeing man. For a moment or two there was complete silence; then Mrs De Witt screamed: "My brother, my brother, you've killed him!" and ran down the steps of the veranda.

The Colour was still facing the man he had shot. She grasped him from behind, her left hand grabbing his jaw, and lifted his head, exposing his neck. She was taller than him and probably stronger. She lifted the knife, intent on plunging it into Bob's neck. If Iffor had had time to draw his pistol the bullet would have killed them both. In two steps he was behind her, drawing his bayonet and plunging it up into her heart. As she started to collapse, he withdrew the knife cutting downwards, the serrated blade tearing vital organs.

De Witt appeared on the veranda, pistol in hand. He cleared the steps and faced Iffor, pistol aimed. Iffor could only watch as the pistol came level with his chest; then a dull, flat thud that reverberated in the still air, sent a four-five semi-jacketed low velocity bullet from Pete's Colt into De Witt's brain causing chaos, mayhem and sudden death.

Mad Harry strolled up, looked at Mrs De Witt's body, then at the Colour sergeant. "Lover's tiff?" he asked, and walked towards the fallen police constable, who was trying to stand, pressing his jungle hat to the wound in his side. "Walking wounded," said Pete, "he'll live."

Leaving the team and the police constables to load the bodies onto the Rover and tend to the wounded man, Pete said, "We came here to search the place, we had best get on with it."

"I'll go in first," said Iffor, "in case of booby traps."

"This is a police matter." Pete put a hand across Iffor's chest. "I go in first."

"But I'm the expert trained in these matters," said Iffor and walked up the veranda steps, casually stepping onto the pressure switch under the 'welcome' mat that detonated the phosphorus grenade inside the bungalow.

"Some fucking expert," said Pete as they stood and watched the bungalow burn down, "I wouldn't trust you with a Christmas cracker."

Phil joined them. "I've sent a Contact, wait out message. Shall I send a sit rep?"

"Yes please." Iffor took out his notebook and wrote: 'Contact at Long Acre farm at 1520hours. No further resistance from enemy; Enemy casualties three dead; Friendly casualties one walking wounded. Returning to base.'

"Get that off to Shamus and Battalion if we can reach them; if not, ask Shamus to get Josie to send it through the teleprinter."

Ammunition began to explode inside the bungalow as the flames took hold, followed by much louder explosions as grenades exploded. "No question about it," Pete gazed into the flames, "we've certainly pissed all over their strawberries today." He turned and looked at Iffor, "Do you think they'll be upset?"

"No doubt about it." Iffor relished the thought of meeting up with an angry terrorist. "I think they'll be very upset when they get to hear what happened here today."

The convoy drove back to Kensington triumphantly, though cautiously.

Iffor would have liked to stop at the two farms they passed through but he had to think of the wounded policeman, who was sitting in the champ with Mad Harry and Evil either side of him, enjoying his new status. Instead, he stopped just long enough to explain briefly what had happened.

From time to time, Iffor caught site of the new pennant flying from the radio aerial, the flying pig, Pigasus. The tide was begging to turn, he told himself. The pig was a symbol of their success.

PART TWELVE

The Infantry section comprises two groups, the Gun group and the Rifle section.

THE GOOD DOCTOR Van De Merwe was waiting for them at the hospital, alerted by Shamus. Orderlies took the dead to the morgue while the doctor fussed over the wounded constable. Two gunshot wounds just above the left thigh, both exited without causing too much damage, was the verdict. "We'll keep him for a day or two and thoroughly spoil him, then you can have him back, good as new."

Josie and Shamus were waiting for them as they drove into the drill hall. "Phone the Colonel," she said, "He's waiting for your call."

"Colonel, it's Meredith."

"Iffor my boy, had some good hunting I hear, good body count?"

"Yes Colonel, three dead terrs and a staging post on their main Line of Communication destroyed; we had one walking wounded."

"You're doing better than me, and I've got four rifle companies, which brings me to the point. I could do with you and your team up here with me."

Iffor sat bolt upright in his chair. "You can't be serious, Colonel— we are within an ace of bringing our local terrorist group to battle; we can destroy them, you can't stop us now."

"Calm down Iffor, I'm just considering my options. We are really up against here, we're lucky not to have had more casualties and we are

171

only just holding our own against the influx of terrorists trying to cross the border."

Iffor interrupted him. "I don't think my seven-man team can do a lot of good up there on the border, but we are making one hell of a difference down here."

There was a long pause, then, "Keep up the good work m'boy, speak to you soon, goodbye."

Since Mad Harry was still in command of Blue Watch, Iffor left him to put stores away, clean and inspect weapons and re-fuel the Champ.

"Stand the boys down tomorrow," Iffor told him. "Parade at 0800 on Friday. Warning order three-day patrol on Friday." He was anxious to get back to the hotel, especially after what Josie had whispered in his ear.

Thursday was developing into the sort of day God created for lovers to picnic together beside a glorious lake. Auntie had prepared a picnic hamper for them, cold chicken, samosas and a couple of bottles of Cape Red. Excitedly, Josie put the hamper, a blanket and sunshade into the back of Iffor's pick-up. A picnic on the banks of Lake Soroya just outside Bindura was more than she dared hoped for on their day off. A whole day together, just the two of them. Perfect!

They found a spot among three m'pani trees which would give shelter from the sun. Apart from one or two anglers on the far side of the lake, they were on their own. The weekend, though, would have been a different matter. Sitting on the blanket, sipping their wine, they gazed out over the lake. "Are you happy with me?" she said, "I mean, are you happy being with me?"

He took the glass from her, placed it beside his own and gently pushed her onto her back. She cupped her hands behind her head and looked up at him. "You haven't answered my question." He looked into her face for several minutes. "You know, I could quite easily spend the rest of the day just looking into your face, you really are quite beautiful." He kissed her lightly on the lips. Not being one for romantics, he didn't answer her question, but just continued to look into her face, stroking her cheek with his fingers, and wondered if Moses had come to a decision yet.

She sat up. Iffor handed her her glass and topped it up, then filled his own glass. "I have to know Iffor. Are you happy with me?"

"Darling girl, of course I'm happy with you. I'm happy that you don't ask too much of me, I'm happy that you accept me for what I am and I'm happy being able to share your secrets. But most of all, my little Indian goddess of love, I just love being with you."

He knew it wasn't the statement of love she was looking for, but it was as close as he could get.

They finished lunch and opened the second bottle. "It's so peaceful here," she said. "No-one to disturb us, it's as if you had arranged it."

"I have." Tenderly pushing her back down, he lay across her body looking into her face, "I've arranged for us to have an invisible glass dome around us when we're together. No-one can see us or hear us; we can say what we like, and do what we like. Once inside our dome, we have no cares, no problems and no worries. It's just you and me."

"Oh Iffor!" She wrapped her arms around his neck, pulling him closer. "You don't have to love me, just be happy with me."

They drove slowly, blissfully back to Kensington, enjoying the cool of the late afternoon. She knew he'd be spending the evening preparing and planning for tomorrow's patrol, but she was happy. She'd had him to herself all day and she would be sleeping with him and after the patrol he would come home to her.

Friday morning and breakfast on the patio with Josie, both were still in their dressing-gowns. At Josie's insistence, Auntie brought them pawpaw, cream and toast and at Iffor's insistence, brandy and coffee. "A lover's breakfast," he said and touched coffee cups with her.

After Auntie had changed the dressing on his now rapidly healing wound, he dressed—combats, desert boots, floppy hat—and gathered up his equipment: belt order with ammo pouches, bayonet, water bottles and shoulder rig for his Brno. His Burgan, pre-packed, was already at the drill hall, very probably already loaded into the trailer by the Colour Sergeant, who would undoubtedly be waiting for him no matter how early he arrived.

He discussed the forthcoming patrol with the Colour before briefing Blue Watch.

"I'm not going to push the team too hard on this one. It's going to be more of a 'jolly'. We'll show the flag in the area east of the Great North Road, give Dix's farm guards an evening off, R.V. with Pete at the Mission on Sunday and escort the lovely Helen back to Kensington. Then you, me and Pete and our ladies can have dinner that night at the Elephant, and with luck, Pete will pay."

With his troops, Pete and Josie seated in his office, he began his briefing with the usual de-brief of Wednesday's raid on the De Witt's farm.

"Our mission was to search the farm and arrest the De Witts, avoiding a fire fight if we could, but it was not to be. Whether or not the De Witts carried weapons on behalf of the terrorists or just gave them succour is irrelevant. The three of them were terrorists and are where they belong, in the morgue. Well done everyone, good shooting, Bob and Pete."

"You deserve some praise yourself boss," said Mad Harry. "When I saw De Witt only a couple of feet away from you with his pistol levelled at your chest, I thought you were a gonner."

The briefing was now a shambles. Josie stood up, tears streaming down her face. "Why didn't you tell me, you should have told me! You bloody fool, you could have been killed."

"It was nothing," he tried to sound casual. "De Witt was upset—he was probably having a bad day."

"It didn't improve matters when Pete whacked him in the left ear-hole with that forty-five of his," said Evil. "That must have really pissed him off."

Iffor concluded his, by now routine, but nevertheless important, briefing with a grim reminder: "The more of them we kill, the more dangerous it will be for us; they'll be after our blood. Be vigilant, watch out for one another."

Midday found the team manning a road block and Vehicle Check Point at the Great North Road/Lamumbwa turn-off junction, the site of the mine ambush. The usual assortment of vehicles passed up and down the road. The only vehicle coming from the East was Father Sean's minibus. Iffor flagged him down and went to the driver's window.

"Afternoon, Iffor. You're welcome to search me, but please don't ask me to unload my labourers—it took for ever trying to squeeze everyone in. I've got three or four of Helen's patients on board, as well as my own lot from the monastery—we're heading for Charlie's farm. He's got some work for us."

Iffor looked into the vehicle. It was impossible to count the bodies on board; all the seats were occupied and many others were seated or standing on the floor.

"Just you drive carefully," he said. "Remember, we need you for the big day."

Sean looked puzzled.

"The wedding, you bloody idiot, the wedding."

"Ah yes, the wedding," the priest said and drove off, leaving Iffor looking at the white church cross on the back of the bus, through the smoke of the non-existent exhaust and the dust of the road. A perfect point of aim for a Rocket Propelled Grenade, he thought, and wondered if the hand of God could actually stop a rocket propelled grenade.

Ed and Joy Dix were waiting for them when they drove into Lamumbwa farm a little before four. "Tom-toms told me you were on your way," he said and led them to the veranda for sandwiches and cold beers.

"Radio check please, Phil," Iffor called back to the Champ.

"On to it boss," came Phil's reply.

Verity came shyly up to Iffor. "How's Shamus?" she asked.

"He's fine and asked me to say hello to you. He'll be with us next time we visit; ask him nicely and he'll show you his battle scars."

Ed took Iffor to one side. "Heard about the De Witts," he said. "Can you tell me anything?"

"Only that the farm was a hotel for terrorists coming across from Zambia. He and his wife fed them and provided a guide for them; but not anymore," he said with a smile, "Not anymore."

A shout from Phil roused Iffor from his happy thoughts. Phil was holding out the handset and touched the crown of his head, the 'on me' signal.

"Sunray on set over."

"Hello Sunray," It was Bob's voice. "We have, as yet unconfirmed reports from North Road farm that the church bus has been ambushed with many casualties. Roger so far over."

"Roger control."

"Control, can you RV with police at scene of attack on Old Mwonza Road three miles short of farm over."

Iffor glanced at his watch. "Roger control, our E.T.A. eighteen hundred, out."

His first impulse was to gather up his troops and charge of to the R.V. like the U.S. cavalry, but he walked away from the Champ forcing himself to think.

This could well be a trap, luring him into an ambush; he must be prepared for that.

If there were wounded he would have to set up a first aid post and do what they could, and possibly scramble the Islander, but daylight would be fading fast.

Then the thought that excited him, they just might pick up a positive spoor and bring the terrorists to a contact.

"Harry, mount up, we're off."

The scene that was waiting for them was one of utter carnage. The church bus stood innocently on flat tyres on the dirt road with more bullet holes in it than one could possibly count, showing the savagery of the attack. Several bodies were hanging out of the shattered windows, evidence of failed efforts to escape. Four or five, impossible to make an accurate count, because of body parts lying around, had managed to 'make a run for it', only to be shot down twenty or thirty feet from the bus. The remainder all killed in their seats.

The A.K. round didn't just make neat round holes in the body, it also tore off limbs, heads simply exploded when hit, and stomachs ripped open with the sheer velocity of the round. The inside of the bus was black with flies.

Pete and his lads were already on the scene, collecting bodies from the bus and laying them out on the road. They would all have to be identified and handed back to families for burial, a massive task.

As Iffor climbed out of the Champ, Pete walked over to him. "It had to happen, this is their revenge."

"Have you found Sean yet?" Iffor asked softly, almost reverently.

"He's over there talking to Charlie." Pete pointed towards Charlie's armoured Land Rover. "He's alive!"

"Yes, says his God saved him."

Iffor walked across to the Rover. "How in hell's name did you escape this lot?" he asked accusingly.

"The hand of God saved me."

Evil had joined them. "The hand of God won't stop a fucking AK round."

The priest ignored him. "When the terrorists stopped me they opened fire, smashing the windscreen. I ducked below the dashboard. A terrorist opened the door of the bus and dragged me out onto the road. As I lay there, he fired two or three bullets into the ground beside my head; then he bent over me and God spoke to me through him, 'Lie still priest and live, move, and die'."

Iffor went back to the bus. His own men were giving a hand to move bodies onto the road. He called over, "Mal, have a scout around, see if you can pick up a spoor," and walked across to Pete. "We need a plan of action: if you can cope here, I'll head north. They can't have heard about the De Witts yet. My guess is they are heading for his farm—we might get lucky."

A shout from Mal took Pete and Iffor to a clearing some fifty feet from the road.

"This one's still alive," he said, "he keeps blinking."

They looked down at the African; he was one of Helen's patients, the evidence of leprosy plain to see. He couldn't speak—the side of his face had been slashed wide open with a panga and his jaw ripped away from his face. His belly was ripped open allowing his entrails to cascade onto the track where the ants were feasting on them; the gaping hole in his chest was evidence of the bullet that hit him as he was running away. This was what terrorists, Africans, did to their fellow man. He looked up at the three, still blinking his eyes but unable to move.

Iffor placed the muzzle of his Carbine between the man's grateful eyes, "Sleep well my friend," and squeezed the trigger.

They walked slowly back to the road. "Leave when you're ready," Pete said. "I've got things under control here. Charlie's sent his game guard back to the farm to collect a tractor and trailer. We'll take the bodies back to the farm; there's a cold room there. One of my constables is going to take Sean back to the monastery. He can make contact with the relatives and help with the identification, and I'm going to set up my base at the farm and start afresh in the morning."

Iffor gathered the team around the champ. "Quick 'O' group chaps. Firstly, Mal, any tracks?"

"Yes boss, surprisingly only three men headed north through the bush."

"Right lads, my guess and it is only a guess, is that these terrs are either leading us into an ambush or heading for the De Witts to rest up before heading for the border. It's unlikely they've heard about the De Witts, so that's my best guess; so unless anyone has any better ideas..." Blank stares all round. "Good, we'll drive with extreme caution up the Mwonza Road. We'll stop at Archie's farm and tell him what's what, then we'll drive to De Witt's, cam up the Champ; Evil and Hennie can set the Bren up on the old OP, covering what's left of the farm, while myself and the rest of you will set up an ambush on the game trail. I'll give you all a full briefing when we get there."

By the time they reached Arc Angel farm, light was failing rapidly and the team were already exhausted. Areas of the road that might give cover for an ambush had to be 'walked', and all soil disturbances on the road prodded with a bayonet, but Iffor was pleased with their progress, knowing they would arrive at their final R.V. when it was just getting dark, allowing them to get into position under cover of darkness.

If the rest of the bush was quiet, the area around what was left of De Witt's farm resembled a medieval cemetery at midnight on Hallowe'en.

Iffor calculated the terrorists would take at least another four hours to reach the farm, assuming they were heading there.

They parked and cammed up the Champ at the foot of the rear slope of the kopje.

Iffor gave his orders: "Change of plan chaps. Since we don't know which direction the terrs will approach the farm from—they may well circle around and come in from the rear—it's going to be pretty pointless setting up an ambush. Our best bet will be to cover the killing ground, the area around the farm, from our old O.P position with the

Bren and hope that if they do turn up they will be tempted to go into the ruins to look for food. We'll rotate throughout the night, three men up in the kopje with the Bren, one guarding our rear and two men sleeping. No cooking, no noise, and when you sleep, don't worry about waking on time, I'll do that for you."

Throughout the night, cold, but with a hunter's moon, Iffor rotated his team, relieving one man every hour on the Bren team, ensuring awareness and continuity and taking a few minutes to search the area with the binos.

As dawn changed the dark blue sky to light blue, Iffor whispered in Harry's ear, "Take over, wake me in two hours," then snuggled up against Evil for warmth. Evil opened one eye, "Bloody tart," he said and went back to sleep.

The sound of Phil making the seven o'clock radio check woke him.

"Think we could risk a brew?" Harry asked.

"Sounds good, but keep the noise down, and we'll let the boys heat their beans and bacon."

Iffor kept the routine going until midday when he took Harry to one side. "I don't think we are going to achieve anything by staying here any longer."

"Agreed," said Harry.

"We'll pack up and head back to North Road farm and give Pete a hand, then we'll head east for the Lamumbwa area and keep our appointment with the lovely Helen on Sunday, and then," he savoured the words, "home for a few beers."

Iffor led a final patrol around the perimeter of the farm in the vain hope of stumbling on the terrorists. Then they left the area heading back to Charlie's farm.

The journey south was somewhat happier with birds flying down the road ahead of them and chattering monkeys scampering across the road in front of them. Children came out of the small villages they passed and shyly waved to them, while their fathers held out bundles of charcoal hoping for a quick sale. Iffor had deemed that the road must still be 'walked', and suspicious mounds in the road prodded with a bayonet, so it was late afternoon when they rolled into Arc Angel farm.

"Half hour break, lads, and on to Charlie's farm; radio check please Phil."

The team emptied Archie's fridge of cold beers and disposed of the sandwiches as fast as Archie's wife could make them. "Thank God you're not stopping," Archie said, "I've seen white ants do more damage than you lot."

"Anything else we can do for you?" Archie asked as he and Iffor walked, beer in hand, into the cool of his living room.

"Just be vigilant, things are coming to a head. Review your own security and be ready for anything, expect the unexpected. I suggest you fortify the sangers on the main gate and strengthen your defences on your veranda; your defences should be able to stop a rocket propelled grenade, if not," he paused, "you're in a lot of trouble."

Fortified and refreshed, the team moved on to North Road farm to RV with Pete and his police. It would only be an hour's drive and Iffor had already planned to stay the night and move off at first light. Charlie's farm was just coming into view when the radio crackled into life: "Fetch Sunray, over."

"On set," Iffor answered.

The Colour came up in clear: "Iffor, they've hit the Leper Mission, many casualties, Pete's already on his way, over."

Iffor went cold with fear. He knew everything was going to go wrong, every piece of news would be bad. The terrorists had deliberately drawn Blue Watch away from the Mission area by ambushing the minibus. This was their revenge; they had won, he had lost. But now more than ever, he had to remain calm and resolute.

"Roger so far, over," Bob sounded desperate.

"Roger, Bob, I'm going to refuel at North Road farm, then head for the Mission. We shouldn't be too far behind Pete. Now this is what I want you to do. First scramble the Islander, tell Davy to rig for casevac, and to ferry you and a medical team to the Mission. Tell the crew to prepare to land on the Lamumbwa Road as close to the Mission turn-off as they can. Then call Van De Merwe at the hospital and tell him to get a team together and meet you at the airfield. Keep in contact. I'll have the Champ waiting for you when you land."

"Roger so far, over."

"Roger, out."

The team had heard the message, except for Alvin sitting in the trailer acting as 'tail end Charlie'. They reacted accordingly, refuelling the Champ and being back on the road inside ten minutes. As they drove, Iffor tried to imagine the scene when he got there so that he could start to plan, but nothing, nothing could have prepared him for what was waiting for him.

An hour or so later as they passed the Dix's farm turn-off; they could see the smoke rising from the Mission and that distinctive smell of death carried towards them on the evening breeze. Iffor convinced himself that Helen and the boy would be safe: the terrorists wouldn't dare touch them; they were revered, almost sacred; the hundred or so lepers at the mission would have given their lives defending her; no, he told himself, they wouldn't touch her.

As they turned off the Lamumbwa Road and onto the mission road, Harry, who was driving, seemed to slow down, trying to put off the inevitable scene waiting for them.

They passed men, women and children walking away from the Mission, nowhere to go, no-one to help, just anxious to get away from the hell that once had been home.

Passing the admin block, staff houses, the school and hospital, Iffor was relieved to see them all still intact. If the terrorists hadn't touched them, they wouldn't have harmed Helen, he told himself.

"God, look at that," Harry gestured towards the hospital. The veranda was crammed with bloodied people, patiently waiting their turn to be attended to by Doctor Grace. Two or three orderlies were desperately trying to help; staunching blood from gaping bullet wounds and missing limbs; ignoring the dying, saving the living.

Harry stopped the Champ next to the police vehicles. They had only just arrived themselves, the armoured Rhino slowing them down.

Iffor climbed out of the Champ and looked around at the carnage. The patients' huts were in a rough semi-circle on the perimeter of the compound with their own beer hall, shop and community centre. All were now on fire or had already burned to the ground. Bodies like discarded children's dolls were lying around the huts, some still moving, still alive. Somewhere, in one of the huts a woman was screaming for help for her children.

Iffor was amazed at the situation, with fires still burning and bodies still lying in the open some two or more hours after the attack, until he realised that, apart from a handful of orderlies, there was no one to help these disabled people.

Ed Dix was talking to Pete with his arm around Pete's shoulders. The sight sent a dagger of terror thrusting into Iffor's stomach; he knew what was coming.

Ed turned to face him. "Helen?" Iffor asked.

"Dead. And the boy; we've put them both in Helen's bungalow."

"Bring me up to date," said Iffor, now taking charge.

"Grace has set up a sort of casualty clearing station in the hospital. We're trying to get the wounded down to her, but it's taking time. We've only got two orderlies and Grace has got more than she can cope with, without us giving her more work."

Iffor turned all thoughts of Helen from his mind: things to do, lives to save.

He went across to Pete, grabbed his arm and roughly turned him to face him. "Listen mate, tomorrow we'll mourn together, but right now we've work to do. People are depending on us, we can save a few lives." He shook his friend gently. "Come on man, let's get cracking."

Iffor called the team and the police to him. "Right boys, here's the plan. Work in pairs; collect all the wounded and ferry them down to the hospital in the Rover and the Champ. Harry, you and Alvin stay with the doctor and just do what you can. Phil, stay with the radio and contact the Islander and get an ETA. Sergeant Tim, when all the wounded are recovered, get your blokes to get the dead together—put them in what's left of the community centre for now."

Turning to Ed: "Ed, can you get a mechanical digger up here from the farm? We can't possibly get all the dead back to Kensington for post mortem and identification—we'll have to bury them here in a mass grave."

"But what about identification?" Pete had come back to life.

"When it's all over," Iffor said, "we'll call a roll; those who answer will be alive, those who don't answer, we'll know where they are... Get cracking please, Ed."

"Onto it," said Ed and walked across to his Rover and farm radio.

Working in pairs, the police and army started searching the huts for those still alive. Iffor left Pete in charge while he ran down to the hospital. Treading carefully over the injured, he made his way to Grace's clinic. She had been wearing a long summer dress when the terrorists struck. This she had now tucked up into her knickers to stop it from dragging in the blood that covered the clinic floor. She wore a cloth apron obviously made by the mission children, since it had happy smiling faces painted all over it, now covered in blood. She wiped the back of her hand across her brow and looked up from the shattered body that lay on her examination table. Her expression didn't change. "Iffor, thank God you're here, thank G-g-god." Tears or sweat ran down her face, he couldn't tell which. He was overwhelmed with pity for her; he just wanted to hold her, stroke her hair and tell her everything was going to be all right, but he had to be practical Iffor, Iffor the soldier.

"I've organised for the rest of the wounded to be brought down to the hospital. Then my team will stay with you to help; they all have advanced medical training. Pete will take care of the dead."

"Thank you, my nurse Francis will tell them what to do."

"I've also arranged for the mine aircraft to bring Doctor Van De Werwe and a team out to you. The aircraft can take some of your more seriously injured back to hospital."

She paused from tidying up the stump of what was left of the man's arm and put her stethoscope to his chest. "He's gone." She beckoned to an orderly, "Take him away."

Looking at Iffor, she said softly, "You've heard about Helen?"

He couldn't answer; he turned and left.

Harry arrived with the Champ, and between them, they carried three badly burned children and laid them on the veranda decking, joining the uncomplaining queue. Arriving back at the compound, Ed ran across to Iffor. "For Christ's sake, do something about Pete. Look at him!" With total disregard for his own safety, Pete was dashing into the most fiercely burning buildings, dragging bodies out, trying to drive the torment from his soul.

"Stop him man, or he'll kill himself."

"Nothing I can do old son, nothing I can do."

Iffor looked up at the sky, turning his head to catch the sound of aero engines on the evening breeze. "If I try to stop him, he will probably shoot me."

Harry shouted across: "We've got some more for the doc, I'm going to stay with her and see what I can do. Phil can drive the Champ back."

Iffor waved a hand, "Good man."

Ed was right. Pete was intent on self-destruction; Iffor had to do something.

He ran across to Pete, grabbing his arm. "Pete, we need a plan 'B'."

Pete calmed down a little. "What's that?" he said.

"The Islander's going to land on the road at the end of the Mission track. I want you to take your Rhino, Ed and his Rover to the hospital and start ferrying wounded down to the aircraft when it lands. Liaise with the doctor and Davy Jones—he'll tell you how many the plane can take." He pushed Pete towards the Rhino. "Do it now."

Sergeant Tim came up and saluted. "The buildings are collapsing, we must stop searching the huts or we will lose men."

"Thanks Tim. Yes, call a halt. Blow your whistle and stop them."

Iffor stood in the centre of the compound, taking stock of what had happened. It crossed his mind to get the team together and try and track the terrorists, but where to start? And anyway, the team were more use here at the Mission. But he couldn't help wondering: where the hell did they come from? Where the hell did they go? Where are they holed up, probably celebrating their success? One man could tell him, and that was Iffor's next task.

The Islander came in low from the south west, circled the mission to get wind direction from the smoking huts, and touched down on the Lamumbwa Road. The white sandy surface of the road reflecting the moon and stars of the bright African night was just sufficient to give the pilots an easy landing.

Twenty minutes later the Champ brought the Colour Sergeant up to what was now Iffor's command post. He made his report: "Davy is organising the casualties with Pete; they can squeeze six stretchers and eight walking wounded into the plane; the aircraft will be back at first light for another load. The three town doctors have been told to report to the hospital along with Bill Jeffries, our retired surgeon. The two hospital ambulances will be waiting at the airstrip and the mine is sending their ambulance straight to the airstrip, and I've rounded up some odds and sods with estate cars to help out."

Hardly pausing for breath, he said, "Phil told me about Helen. Now, what can I do?"

"Help me make some sense of all this... For starters, the gang must have numbered a dozen or more, and judging by all the empty cartridge cases scattered around the place and the indiscriminate way they sprayed the huts with rifle fire, they were not worried about conserving ammunition, which means they have a re-supply dump somewhere in the immediate area. And having killed Helen, why didn't they kill Grace and her nurses? Were they under orders?"

"Let's sleep on that one boss, nothing more we can do here tonight. Let's get down to the hospital and see what we can do there."

The battered, wheezing spluttering VW Beatle brought Father Sean up to the command post. Sean got out, carrying a double-barrelled hammer shotgun.

"What do you intend doing with that?" Iffor asked.

"God's work, my son, God's work."

"Well if you intended shooting any terrorists, you're too late, they've gone. Now go and find Sergeant Tim—he'll give you a job. Oh, and avoid Pete—the bastards killed Helen and the boy."

Sometime between midnight and the next day, Iffor held a council of war, his main players, Pete, Bob, Ed, Mad Harry, the priest and Grace, squatting or sitting around a fire, burning bloodied tattered clothing among some logs. Behind them, the soft moans of the injured and the comforting words of the orderlies were the only noises in the still air. Doctor Van De Werwe and his team were still working in the small overcrowded hospital. Grace, far too exhausted to be of any further use, had been gently relieved of her responsibilities.

Hennie had come up trumps with mugs of steaming coffee laced with Cape spirit, gratefully accepted, to help deal with shivering bodies, the result of the cold African night or spent emotions, reactions from the day's events.

Iffor began: "News on the digger, Ed?"

"Leaving the farm at first light."

"Pete, have we got a body count?"

"Twenty-one confirmed dead plus those who have wandered off into the bush to die and thirty wounded; the figure will change by morning. We also have about fifty unaccounted for. Those that the terrs took with them we'll find over the next few days; the rest will eventually find their way back here."

For a few minutes, no-one spoke, most sipping the coffee and feeling the warmth flowing through their body. Then, softly and gently, Iffor said, "Tell us Grace, tell us what happened."

"They came in the afternoon—at first there were only four of them.

"When I first saw them they were walking down from the community centre. I knew at once who they were, they were all armed. David had just come out of Helen's office; he saw them and ran towards them shouting to them to go away. They waited until he was very close to them, then they shot him and carried on walking down towards the admin block. Helen came out of her office and started to run towards David, then stopped; she must have realised he was dead. The terrorists continued walking towards Helen, then Jamie came out of the school hut. He ran towards the terrorists, putting himself between them and his mother. He shouted at them not to touch his mother. They shot him too.

Helen just stood as if rooted to the spot, horrified, terrified, petrified as she watched her beloved son die. The terrorist who shot Jamie laid down his rifle, unzipped his shorts and took out his penis, making clear what they were going to do to her.

As they reached out for her, she suddenly reached under her shirt and pulled out a small silver pistol—I didn't know she had it. As the man tried to grab her, she fired three or four shots into his chest. The man simply sat down looking up at her. The others drew back and she fired another shot into the man's head; he fell back. Then, looking past the other terrorists and at the body of her son, she put the barrel of the pistol into her mouth and pulled the trigger.

The terrorists went wild. They stripped all her clothing off and slashed her with pangas and bayoneted her.

I waited for them to come for me, but then many more men appeared among the residential huts and started shooting and setting fire to the huts. I ran back into the hospital and locked the door and waited with my nurses until it was over. When the shooting and screaming had stopped, a group of them came down towards our admin block. I thought they were coming for us, but they just collected their dead man and left. There was nothing I could do to save Helen."

Now she was crying, sobbing; her whole body began to shake; shock and exhaustion were kicking in. Iffor walked across to her, picked her up and carried her to her small bungalow. Inside, he made her stand while he took her dress off. She made no move to stop him taking her bra off and held his arm for support as she stepped out of her panties. Then, picking her up, he laid her on her bed and covered her with a sheet. He sat on the bed stroking her hair, telling her how wonderful she was. Another mistake, he meant to say, 'for saving so many lives', but he didn't, so when he leaned over her to kiss her forehead, she pulled him onto her mouth. "Stay with me Iffor, please stay with me." But fate closed her eyes and she slept. Iffor covered her with a blanket, kissed her again and very reluctantly left to rejoin the others.

No-one spoke. Each with their own thoughts looked into the dying embers of the fire, each trying to blot out thoughts of the horror and the terror of the events of the day. Without a word, Pete got up and walked slowly into the night. Sean made as if to follow him, but Iffor touched his arm. "Let him be, there's nothing you can do… Ed, can you take Helen and Jamie back to your farm and start making arrangements for the funeral? That will have to be within the next thirty-six hours or so, and Ed, Pete will want to see them both."

"I'll have them ready." Ed understood what had to be done. "Give me a couple of your lads and we'll leave now; it will be better than waiting for morning."

Iffor turned to Harry. "Send Alvin and Hennie with Ed. Tell them to stay at the farm tonight and get some sleep. Ed can drive them back in the morning."

Ed stood to leave. "Is that it Iffor?"

"Yup, off you go; good luck!"

Ed walked off with Harry to collect Alvin and Hennie and the two bodies.

"As for the rest of us, we'll take it in turns to drive around the Mission to keep animals away from the dead and to look out for anyone who escaped, returning. Sean, no sleep for you tonight, I want you to set up a reception centre in the main community hut for those returning. See if you can organise some hot soup or drinks."

Sean nodded. "Okay," he said.

By dawn, a further twenty or more survivors had come back to the Mission to be rounded up by Father Sean and taken to the community centre where, with the help of a few able bodies, he had provided blankets, soup and bread. It was probably the smell of the soup that encouraged many to return.

The mechanical digger had arrived, and now Iffor put the driver to work: to select a suitable site outside the Mission, and dig a grave for a mass burial.

He wasn't disappointed with the chosen site, on sloping ground looking across the valley to the brown snake that was the Lamumbwa river. "Is this to your satisfaction?" the African driver asked.

"Perfect," Iffor replied, "perfect."

Iffor had spent the night with Pete driving and walking around the perimeter of the Mission, protecting the dead from wild animals. He knew his friend wouldn't sleep, so taking on the task of 'guard stag', meant he could keep Pete's mind occupied and allow their men a much needed rest.

As was to be expected, Pete just wanted to talk about Helen and Jamie. He coaxed Iffor into revealing memories of her, from when he and Jamie first met her, just after their return from Cyprus, the courtship which frequently involved Iffor, since by now they had already become 'family', to the wedding which proved so disastrous for Iffor as best man, and the birth of Jamie junior when Iffor become a very proud godfather.

Pete, in turn, told of the first time he met her on a routine visit to the Dix's farm. He had, of course, heard about her escape from the raid that killed her husband, and how she was now prepared for herself and her son to spend the rest of their lives working in the Leper Mission. For Pete, it was love at first sight. For Helen it took some time to recover from the shock of losing her husband before she could think of anything more than friendship with Pete. But, with a lot of patience, Pete eventually won her round, making her realise a normal married life with Pete would be better than locking herself and her son away in the Mission.

He told of the day he proposed to her. She didn't say yes; she thought it was all too soon. "That's all right, my darling," he told her, "I can wait."

But now there wouldn't be a wedding, and Pete was still waiting.

Iffor could not but notice that Pete never once spoke of revenge. Throughout the night he spoke with love and tenderness in his voice. Iffor, on the other hand, made a solemn vow to his God, 'Thor', that he would bring this group to battle and defeat them, and he would happily give his life in the attempt, if he had to.

Ed Dix's arrival with Alvin and Hennie coincided with the return of the Islander.

Davy sought him out. "We can do another lift of casualties, same as yesterday and then we'll come back for the medical team; they're needed at the hospital. And that will be all we can do—the aircraft has got to go to Salisbury to re-fuel."

"Okay Davy, thanks for what you've done and thank the pilots for me. I'll meet up with them at the Elephants Head and thank them properly."

With 'all hands to the helm', the dead were ferried to the grave and laid side by side, men, women and children. If a body could be given a name, it was duly recorded by Sergeant Tim. When all the current dead were laid to rest, the digger filled in the mass grave, a simple wooden cross was stuck into the earth as a marker and Sergeant Tim measured the site in paces and duly recorded it in his notebook.

Leaving Pete and the priest to legalise and formalise the mass burial, Iffor walked down the sloping ground to the admin block, where, he told himself, it would be a duty to wake Grace with a cup of tea, and the thrill of anticipation increased the length of his stride. His lustful thoughts were dashed when he saw Grace walking towards him, looking clean and fresh, her black skin shining like ebony. She stopped in front of him. "You look awful, you smell awful and you're a pig. I needed you last night and you left me alone." With that, she turned and walked towards her hospital calling back to him, "Use my bungalow to shower and clean yourself up, and use my bed to have some rest." The thoughts returned.

Bright-eyed and bushy-tailed, but still without the benefit of sleep, he went in search of Blue Watch, who had based themselves in the school. He found them cooking their bacon grill and powdered egg. Evil came up to him and sniffed. "You smell like a pox doctor's clerk," he said. Too late Iffor remembered the only soap in Grace's shower was heavily scented. "Have you been at it again?" he asked accusingly.

Iffor smiled at him. "You'll never know my friend, you'll never know... Listen in, chaps," he looked at his watch, just after eight, "stand down for a couple of hours, 'O' group here at 1000hours." He walked back up to his command centre where Ed, Pete and the priest were in deep conversation. The Islander, flying in from the east, was already turning into wind to land, and one of Pete's constables was driving the Rover down to the hospital to take Van De Merwe and his small team to the aircraft and home.

The priest was just leaving. "Nothing more for me to do here."

Iffor took his outstretched hand. "Bloody good effort, Padre. Well done. Ed will be in touch over the funeral."

"We've already done that," said the priest and walked away to his VW, leaving Ed to explain.

"Look Iffor," Ed said, "this is very distressing, but we can't keep Helen and Jamie lying in my cold room. It's causing too much distress among my workers. They all adored Helen. As next of kin, I've decided to have the funeral this evening. My digger's already heading back to the farm; he's going to open Jamie's grave—we'll bury Helen and the lad beside him. My carpenter will make a coffin and Martha, my housekeeper, is our African's mortician; she'll prepare the bodies. We'll have the burial at midnight. Are you two okay with that?"

Iffor and Pete just nodded, neither of them trusting themselves to talk.

"Okay, I'll get back to the farm and make the arrangements." He turned to leave, then stopped and looked at them both. "I think Jamie would like a volley of rifle fire over the grave." Then, he got into his Rover and drove off.

"What now?" said Pete.

"Now my friend, we round up all the male staff we can find and set them to rebuilding the huts. I'm sure Ed will get a working party and equipment here to help out. Then, we head off for Ed's farm, give the lads a breather and get ready for the funeral. We'll take Doctor Grace with us. Ed can run her back tomorrow. First light, we head back to Kensington."

1000 Hours, Iffor held his "O" group. Pete and his police attended.

"The plan is, boys, we can't do much more here. We've organised the staff to start rebuilding the huts, and when we get back to Kensington we'll send a relief convoy with food and blankets out to them. We could go bush bashing, looking for the terrorists that did all this, but it's more likely they would find us before we found them, and we now know there are at least fifteen of them and they would choose the killing ground."

"We can't give up on them," said Harry, "not after this."

"We're not going to, Pete and I are about to play our ace." Iffor continued: "We'll drive to the Dix's farm, rest up and attend Helen's funeral at midnight. Harry, organise a party, four men, to fire a volley over the grave."

"Right boss."

As the meeting broke up Pete said, "I presume our 'ace' is Moses January?"

"Correct," said Iffor.

The two of them went in search of Grace. They found her at the hospital, supervising her staff cleaning up, and fussing over those patients who were still lying on the veranda waiting for a spot to become vacant inside. She looked up as they stepped onto the veranda, her eyes inviting Iffor to speak.

"We're going to bury Helen and Jamie tonight at the farm; we'll take you there with us and see that you get back tomorrow."

Suddenly she looked drained and very vulnerable. As she looked around, Pete grabbed a chair and put it behind her. She sat down. "So that's it then, I really have lost them, they've both gone." She buried her face in the towel she was carrying and started to sob gently and quietly. Iffor started to reach out to her, to touch her, but Pete stopped him. "Leave her, we'll come back later."

Slowly, Harry drove the Champ and Blue Watch down the slope to the admin block and the hospital to pick up Grace. Pete had gone on ahead with his small force, leaving Iffor to clear up and give whatever help they could, which was minimal, since no white man could rebuild and replace the burned out huts like the African can. However, they were rewarded for their efforts, hearing the Africans singing while they worked, a sure sign of a new day and a new beginning. Harry stopped the Champ outside the hospital as Grace came out and onto the veranda. "I'm not coming," she said. "I can't possibly leave my patients." She turned to go back into the hospital, paused and turned to face them. "Please tell Helen I'm sorry I've missed her special day, she'll understand." Then she turned and walked slowly back to her patients. Harry sniffed and wiped the back of his hand across his eye. "Move off, boss?" he asked. Iffor grunted, not trusting himself to speak.

They drove down to the main entrance where Harry stopped the Champ, allowing them to look back at the Mission. Smoke was still rising from the smouldering huts, but now gangs of deformed and disabled Africans were tearing them down and replacing them with new ones. Already, bunches of flowers were appearing on the massed grave, prominent on the slopes overlooking the Lamumbwa valley. They moved off in silence, eager to catch up with Pete. "Safety in numbers," muttered Evil to no-one in particular.

They caught up with Pete's column a couple of miles from the Dix farm and followed him into the farm compound. A Guard Force soldier waved at them from a sanger and came to close the steel mesh gates behind them. Iffor was glad to see Ed was beginning to take his security a little more seriously.

As he climbed stiffly out of the Champ, Pete came over to him from the Rhino. "If we park our vehicles in the workshop yard," he pointed at a building with its own compound and security fence, "they'll be safe and won't interfere with our field of fire if our friends come visiting."

"Good idea," said Iffor. "Get your kit off lads. Harry, you heard the man."

Ed Dix came to greet them. "Under any other circumstances, I'd be delighted to see you, but now…" his voice trailed away.

"We okay on the veranda?" said Iffor.

"You can all sleep inside if you want," Dix replied.

"No, the veranda's fine."

Blue Watch, now joined by Pete's police, found and occupied their bed space on the spacious veranda which stretched along the front and both sides of the farm bungalow, making themselves as comfortable as was possible. As Iffor laid out his sleeping bag, he suddenly realised just how tired he was. When did he last sleep? He couldn't remember. Harry was beside him: "Get your head down for a couple of hours boss, I'll get the lads cleaning weapons and sorting their kit out for tonight. I'll call you in a couple of hours." Gratefully, Iffor took off his boots and uniform and crawled into his sleeping bag, asleep before he could zip it up.

Late afternoon, Alvin woke him with a welcome mug of steaming tea. He looked at his watch—he'd been asleep for four hours. "Ed's wife has laid on some sandwiches and tea," Alvin said and stood and watched as Iffor took a pair of shorts from his Burgan and put them on. "A favour please, boss," he said.

"Go on," said Iffor, savouring his tea after sniffing it suspiciously to make sure Hennie hadn't got at it first.

Alvin was silent for a few moments, as if looking for the right words, then said, "Before you volunteered me for the army, I spent most of my spare time at the Mission helping Helen and Grace, and so I would like to play some part in the funeral."

"Sounds good to me. What have you got in mind?"

"I'd like to read Helen's favourite psalm over her grave. If ever I was at the Mission on a Sunday, she would always ask me to read it at church. It seems appropriate to read it now."

Iffor, smiling, looked into his face, feeling a little ashamed that he knew so little about this man who was quite prepared to risk his life for him. "That is a wonderful idea, I'll tell Father Sean."

The two walked over to join Blue Watch, who were enjoying the tea and sandwiches laid out on a trestle table. Ed had decreed that beer would only be available after the funeral, when they would rejoice and not mourn.

The team were in various stages of undress, some in shorts, some with just a towel wrapped around their waist. "They've all washed their combats and cleaned weapons," Harry announced, "Do you want to inspect the weapons?"

"No thank-you, but I would like to have a look at the Bren. Perhaps you would ask Evil to bring the gun and the spare parts wallet onto the veranda when he's finished his sandwiches."

Evil appeared at Iffor's bed space on the veranda, carrying the Bren and spare parts wallet with a face like thunder. "So you want to inspect Betsy, do you?"

"No, why should I? You take very good care of her."

This was the very first time Iffor had ever heard a light machine gun called by a woman's name, but then again, Evil wasn't your average man.

Evil relaxed, smiled, "What do you want us for, then?"

Iffor found himself using Evil's name for the gun, "Betsy, like all females on occasion, needs a little extra love and attention, and that's what we're going to give her." He turned his sleeping bag over, exposing the waterproof groundsheet and sat down, inviting Evil to join him. "Could you undress her for me, please?"

Evil stripped the gun down into its component parts.

"We'll start with the gas cylinder, shall we?" said Iffor.

"It's spotless," Evil muttered.

Iffor took the two-piece cleaning rod from the wallet and fixed the wire brush onto the end, then poured oil on it and worked it into the gas cylinder. Then, replacing the wire head with a 'jag' and flanallete, repeated the procedure, finally withdrawing the flanallete and holding it in front of Evil. Normally white, it was now black from carbon deposits removed from the cylinder.

Evil looked dismayed. Iffor explained, "Like all females, Betsy needs a good servicing from time to time and that's what we are doing now." They continued, reaming out the gas ports in the gas plug, stripping the trigger mechanism, cleaning and lightly oiling the parts. Finally, satisfied, Iffor said, "Thank you Evil. Put her back together again and join the lads." Evil said simply, "Thanks boss, we must do this again sometime."

Midnight was approaching all too soon. Iffor had deliberately refrained from giving the team any form of guard duties. He wanted them to rest as much as possible, and anyway, the Guard Force lads had their routine and were very capable, and it was very unlikely that terrorists would attack such a large force.

About ten o' clock the African labourers started to assemble, standing around in small groups talking to one another. They had obviously decided who the pall bearers would be, for these men had already positioned themselves around the coffins.

Blue Watch also started to prepare themselves. They'd showered, shaved and even made an attempt at pressing their combats. As Iffor said when he looked them over, "Booted and suited, ready for any occasion."

Ed came across to speak with Iffor. "About the volley of rifle fire," he said.

"All organised, Harry's got it in hand."

"I'm sure he has, but I need to explain. I don't want the volley for Helen and young Jamie; a volley over a grave is a military thing. It's just that, only after we had buried Jamie senior, did I realise that as a soldier a volley over his grave would have been appropriate."

"I understand," said Iffor, "and I agree with you. I'm just very glad you thought of it."

Eleven o'clock, and Father Sean arrived in his battered old VW. Iffor took him to one side. "If you don't mind Padre, Alvin wants to read the 23rd Psalm and then, at the end of the ceremony, we'll fire a volley over the graves. This is for Jamie senior."

"I understand," said the priest.

At eleven-thirty, the procession started to form up. Torches, made from branches with oil-soaked hessian wrapped around the end, were lit.

Most of the African women carried candles and somewhere in the night, the old men left behind to look after the children, began to sing. Iffor had sent Harry and the firing detail on ahead. Now, with Pete, the remainder of Blue Watch and the police, they followed the Dix family and the two coffins up the slope to the family grave and the last resting place for Jamie and his family.

At Ed's request, the priest kept his service to a minimum. With a nod from Iffor, Alvin took his small Bible from his breast pocket and began to read, "The Lord is my shepherd…" It was unlikely that he could see the words, but his memory stood him in good stead.

Harry had done a good job with his firing party. They came from the slope to the "Present arms", when Harry saluted; then to the "Present in the shoulder," and "Fire!" Not one but three volleys, one for each of them, as Harry explained later.

As silence descended once more, Iffor looked down into the grave at the three coffins. This was his family, the nearest and dearest to him, and with the realisation of what he had lost, his mind gave him a glance of better times, times when he sang to the baby Jamie to get him off to sleep and he heard himself singing, softly at first then louder as his confidence grew:

> *"Holl amrantau'r ser ddywedant,*
> *Ar hyd y nos.*
> *Dyma'r ffordd I fro gogoniant,*
> *Ar hyd y nos.*
> *All Through the Night."*

The procession made its way back down to the compound, leaving half a dozen labourers to fill in the grave. Alvin caught up with Iffor. "Nice touch that," he said, "better than any hymn."

"I've just buried the last of my family, Alvin. They've all gone."

Harry had joined them and he put an arm around Iffor's shoulder. "We're your family now Iffor, me, Alvin, Evil and the rest of them; we'll look after you. Come on, let's have a couple of beers."

The party went on through the night. The Africans and Pete's police, most of whom had relatives among the farm workers, joined the group at the kraal, where Ed had laid on a kudu and a supply of 'Chibuku', the African beer. The priest had long since departed, refusing the offer of an escort from the police, and making a point of loading his old shotgun before leaving.

Blue Watch and the Dix family drank without getting drunk, the alcohol having no effect. Laughs were hollow and forced and conversations always seemed to turn to memories of Helen and Jamie. As the first glimmer of dawn appeared the Dix family said their goodnights, giving Harry the cue to say, "Come on lads, time to get our heads down," and Blue Watch made their way onto the veranda and to their own bed spaces, leaving Pete and Iffor finishing their beer and looking into the dying embers of the *braaivleis*. Pete stood up: "Feel like a stroll?" and together they walked back up to the graves.

Standing side by side, they watched as the sun brought light to the valley and warmth to the grave. From the east the morning breeze brought the smell of burning timbers from the Mission, while down in the kraal, the few Africans still on their feet sang to greet the new day.

Pete broke the silence between them. "You know, I think we've both made the same vow."

Without taking his eyes off the grave, Iffor said, "Indeed we have, my friend, indeed we have."

PART THIRTEEN

Providing you maintain a good parachute position elbows tucked in, head on chest and feet and knees together, you will walk away from most landings.

ALTHOUGH UP AND ABOUT quite early himself, Iffor let his team wake in their own time. He breakfasted on one of Joy's egg sandwiches and a mug of steaming tea. Pete joined him. "After what we've been through, can I suggest we put off interrogating Moses until tomorrow? We've both got more than enough on our plates and neither Moses nor the terrorists are going anywhere, and it will give us a chance to think through our strategy."

"What fucking strategy?" Iffor replied angrily. "Either he talks or I shoot him." He calmed down. "You're right. Beer and sandwiches in the Elephants Head at midday tomorrow; then we'll go and have a chat to him."

The smell of Joy's bacon and egg sandwiches had roused Blue Watch. In turn, they either went to the bathroom or the kitchen. Mad Harry wandered over to Iffor, sandwich in one hand, a bottle of Castle in the other. "I've told Phil, soon as he's dressed to bring the Champ over and open the radio link, okay Boss?"

"Fine, thanks Harry."

With kit loaded on to the trailer, goodbyes said, Iffor gathered the team around him.

"Back to Kensington lads, order of march: police in the Rhino leading; we bring up the rear. When we get back to the drill hall usual routine, stores, weapons and the Colour will issue a new set of combats. Then we'll stand down for a couple of days."

"When do we get to hear about the 'ace' you're going to play?" Evil asked. "We need to get after these bastards as soon as possible."

Iffor thought quickly. "My office 1500 tomorrow and I'll bring you up to date, okay?"

The team nodded approval.

"Right lads, mount up, let's get cracking. Pete's ready to move off."

Mad Harry drove the champ into the M.T. yard and on into the drill hall sometime a little after midday. It was at this stage that Iffor left it to the Colour and Harry to organise the handing in of stores and first line ammunition, and to clear and check weapons. Much as Evil would have loved to have taken the Bren home with him, Iffor had insisted he carried a rifle in town for personal protection.

Before going up to his office Iffor took the Colour to one side. "When you issue them new combats, issue them all with a bayonet and a bayonet frog."

"Bayonet!" the Colour echoed.

"Yes, the terrorists love using their bayonets; we'll match fire with fire. I wonder how a terrorist would stand up to Mad Harry bearing down on him with a fixed bayonet."

The Colour chuckled. "I'm sure there must be something in the Geneva Convention about giving Harry a bayonet. Do you want a word with them before they knock off?"

"No, just remind them, my office tomorrow at 1500 and I'll tell them what I've managed to find out from our prisoner. Oh, and when you've finished with them, come up to my office please and tell me what mundane office work I have to catch up on."

He couldn't resist looking into the orderly room and at Josie's empty desk. Selfishly, he had expected to find her there, until he realised that with the news of Helen's death, she'd be in no state to work. She'd be at the hotel waiting for him, and he knew he would have to tell her in detail about the events at the Mission and the church bus massacre.

He sat at his desk; what to do first?   Desk diary, combat diary, phone the Colonel, or... He picked up the envelope marked 'Lt, Meredith: SECRET'.

The signal was brief: Battalion's mission extended.

While trying to take on board the implications of the signal, he picked up the phone and pressed the button for the direct line to Battalion. The adjutant answered: No, the Colonel was not available; yes, they had heard about the mission raid; and yes, they had sent a PATU tracker team; and no, they hadn't been able to track the terrorists to their hide; and yes, he could speak to the Colonel if he phoned back later.

As he put the phone down the Colour came into the office waving a set of house keys and a folder. "Your bungalow," he said. "The public works department have tarted it up for you, you can move in when you want to. It's fully furnished; check the inventory and read the agreement; sign 'em both and give them back to me. It's number forty Sinioa Road, the road to the mine."

Silently, Iffor handed him the signal to read. "Where does that leave us?" he asked.

"Doesn't change a thing; we carry on just the same until the Colonel says otherwise. With luck and a few kind words," Iffor added, tapping the butt of his pistol, "Moses will come up with the goods and we can have ourselves a sizable cull or, at worst, give Battalion our intelligence and let them sort it out. Pete and I are going to interrogate Moses tomorrow at the hospital, 1200hours. Then, at 1500 I'm going to brief the team. I'd like you to be there."

"Okay boss. I'll go and tell the lads to knock off now."

Iffor dropped his Burgan off behind the reception desk where Auntie was waiting for him. "How is she, and where is she?" he asked.

"She is very quiet and withdrawn. I thought the news of Helen's death would finish her, what with losing her parents and after what her brother did to her, but she's hanging on," Auntie replied. "She is in the garden waiting for you; she has been there waiting for you since dawn."

He stepped onto the patio and looked across the lawn at her. Without looking up, she knew he was there. As he walked towards her, she stood up and held her hand out to him. Not in her mourning clothes, she had dressed in a gold and orange sari with a red scarf about her throat—her act of defiance against the men who had taken Helen from her and almost destroyed her.

He took her hand and they sat at the table. "The twins?" she asked, "did they survive?

The question threw Iffor—he hadn't given them a thought. Bluff it out or come clean?... best come clean. "Sorry Josie, I don't know. Grace didn't say they'd been killed so they must be alive. Next weekend we'll go out to the Mission and see them."

He took her other hand and looked into her eyes. Thank God she wasn't crying—he hated seeing a woman cry. She looked serene and composed, but he sensed she was on the verge of despair. In those few moments, he knew he had to bring her back from the edge of an abyss; he had to give her hope and a future and he knew what he must do. "Go and get a shawl for your shoulders, it will be quite cool when we come back."

"Where are we going?" she asked. "I won't be good company."

"You'll see. I'm just going back to the drill hall to collect my pick-up."

"Aren't you going to change?"

"No time."

And he was gone, telling himself over and over again, "I really can't believe I'm doing this."

When he got back to the hotel, he found her still sitting in the garden. "I can't go anywhere with you until you tell me everything about the attack on the Mission and Helen's death, and you must tell me the truth." She sounded more confident now, more resilient. She went on, "It's important I know the truth. I'm going to have to listen to all sorts of gossip and rumours over the next few days, I must be prepared."

Pulling up a chair close to her and grasping both her hands, he looked directly into her face as he related the events, from the attack on Sean's minibus and his escape, to Helen's funeral. He hesitated for a moment before telling her about carrying Grace to her room and putting her to bed. But even with his limited knowledge of women, he knew if he didn't tell her, she would find out sooner or later, so he told her, but in a way that made it sound like a father putting his child to bed.

They remained seated, still holding hands, still looking into one another's eyes.

"I'm so glad you told me, Iffor. I felt lost, alone, but now, you and Helen and Jamie are back in my life." Almost in a whisper she said, "With you I can cope; I'll be strong again." She stood up, "Now, where are you going to take me?"

"It's a secret," he teased. "Now you get your shawl while I have a quick word with Auntie."

Twenty minutes later they drove into the drive of Number Forty Sinioa Road,

"And this, dear heart, is home, that is if you'll move in with me and live with me."

Her response was what Iffor had expected. "I can't do that, what would Auntie say?"

"She's already said it," said Iffor, opening the pick-up door for her. "She said she's delighted, and can't wait to visit, especially when we've got the twins for the weekend."

She wrapped her arms around his neck and he gently lowered her to the ground. He felt her tear on his face. She whispered something in his ear, but he was far too preoccupied just holding her close, allowing himself to be intoxicated by her perfume.

She ran from room to room, squealing like an excited child, before finally gracefully lowering herself into one of the two armchairs in front of the big open fireplace. "This is perfect," she said, "When can we move in?"

"Well, since you decoded the signal from Battalion, you know they're not coming home just yet, so I intend getting Blue Watch back into the bush, unless the Colonel tells me differently. So I think it will have to be next weekend, after we've been to see the twins, but if you hold on to the keys, you can start moving your bits and pieces in at any time."

Back at the hotel, Auntie handed Iffor a message from Pete: 'Need some company, I've booked the three of us in for dinner at the Elephant, seven thirty.' Iffor glanced at his watch and handed the note to Josie. "We've time for a pot of Auntie's Earl Gray in the garden. Then I'll shower and change."

"So will I," Josie said.

"No!" Iffor chided her, "Stay as you are, just freshen up. You'll take Pete's mind of things, and besides, you know how much I enjoy showing you off."

By accident or design, dinner was a huge success. All conversations started with, 'Do you remember when Helen did this or that', or, 'do you remember when Helen said, whatever'. No tears or sadness, just three friends enjoying the memory of a much loved friend. As they parted on the steps of the Elephant, Pete shook hands with Iffor and gave Josie a hug. "Thanks guys, that was just what I needed."

"And me," said Josie.

"Me too," mumbled Iffor, adding, "Don't forget our date tomorrow."

"Nope! I'll be there."

She sat and watched him undress and climb into bed. Then she turned off the light, undressed and got in beside him. "Just hold me close tonight," she said, but he was already asleep

They breakfasted together in the small dining room. Dressed in floral skirt and crisp white blouse, she was ready for work at the drill hall. Iffor had tried to persuade her to have more time off, but she wouldn't hear of it. Iffor, in shorts and shirt, long socks and shoes, was champing at the bit, anticipating his meeting with Moses January. Without thinking, he spoke his thoughts aloud, causing Josie some alarm. "I hope I don't have to shoot him, he's quite a decent sort of bloke."

Pete already had the beers and sandwiches waiting on the bar when Iffor joined him at the Elephant. "News from the front?" he asked, watching Iffor drink long and hard from his glass.

"Yes, the Battalion aren't coming home just yet. It sounds as if they are really up against it. Have you got any news?"

They started munching the sandwiches. "Yes, apparently there's some obscure religious group entered the fray on the side of ZAPU; don't know much about it though."

Anxious to get to their meeting with Moses, they drank up and left and ten minutes later walked into the Isolation ward. He was no longer manacled to the bed, but sitting in a chair reading a book. The hospital had found some clothes for him, his own having been burned. Sitting opposite was a uniformed constable with 'Sam Browne' cross strap and regulation issue Webley in a shiny leather holster. He stood and saluted as Pete and Iffor entered the room. "Take a break," said Pete, "back in an hour."

Moses put away his book, watching them as they drew up chairs and sat opposite him, looking directly at him.

Pete started the proceedings. "On Saturday your pals raided the Mission at Lamumbwa, killed many innocent, disabled people and murdered our dearest friends. The Lieutenant here wants to kill you and feed you to the crocs."

Moses interrupted him. "I have already made up my mind. I will help you and tell you everything."

Iffor could hardly contain himself. "Moses, when we caught you, was that the first time you were going to make contact with the terrorists, your comrades in the bush, as you call them?"

"They are no longer my comrades, they are now my enemies. No, I had contacted them twice before."

"What was your task?"

"I carried messages in my head for them. It was also important that I stayed with them for a few days each time so they could get to know me, and I had to make myself familiar with the trail we would use when I guided them back into Zambia, after they had completed the final act of God's vengeance."

"Who came up with that phrase?" asked Pete.

Moses paused, and played his trump card. "The priest, Father Sean. He is their leader. All the raids they carried out were a rehearsal for the final act of God's vengeance, and that will come very soon." Pete and Iffor exchanged startled glances, neither wanting to believe what they had just heard, remembering clues that should have warned them, but had been dismissed from their thoughts.

Iffor didn't want to interrupt Moses' line of thought. "Why you? Why did you have to guide them out? Why a warrant officer in the Zambian army? Any bushman could have done it."

Moses offered a cunning smile. "Imagine what would happen, if a bushman, leading twenty armed terrorists, met one of those Rhodesian army patrols that frequent that area. Disaster! But if that same Rhodesian army patrol met a Zambian army warrant officer, leading twenty men in Zambian army uniforms…" He smiled and gestured with his hands, and went on, "Because the border is so fluid in that region, Zambian and Rhodesian patrols often meet up with one another. They dare not fire on one another; that would start a war. They simply exchange greetings and go on their way. I was chosen because I speak Portuguese, as do most of the terrorists, since they come from Mozambique. I had buried the uniforms in a tin chest just outside Mr De Witt's farm; he couldn't afford to have them found on his property."

Pete butted in, "I'll need a statement from you at some time." His raid on the De Witt's was now justified.

Again, Iffor couldn't contain himself, "Where are they holed up, Moses? Tell me where they are."

"At the monastery, or to be more exact, under the monastery. There is a large hall, the same size as the great hall above, in the monastery, with what used to be priests' cells leading off for sleeping accommodation. There are steps concealed behind the fireplace in the great hall which led down into the underground hall."

"But surely," Pete interjected, "surely they would have been seen using those stairs? There are two white priests on sabbatical at the monastery; they would have been suspicious."

Moses shook his head. "The white priests are IRA men rotated from Ireland to help train the terrorists and to get away from the British army, who are after them, and anyway, the terrorists always use the tunnel that goes underground from the monastery to the railway, where it crosses the river."

"That's why we could never follow their spoor," Iffor said, "They didn't go over the ground, they went under the fucking ground, the cunning bastards. Tell me," he went on, "when you were on the trail, did you walk all the way to the Mission, or did Sean meet you and take you there?"

"He would meet me near to the De Witt's farm and take me to the monastery, then drop me off there when I returned to Zambia."

The police constable knocked at the door and entered the room.

"Take a chair and sit outside," Pete said, "Make sure nobody disturbs us." The man nodded and left.

Pete and Iffor now started to discuss what they had learned: "So when Henry's mate ran from the terrorists after Henry had been killed, and ran into the priest, the priest was probably waiting to pick up his killers and take them home for breakfast," Pete said. He went on, "And whenever he was dropping off labourers to work on the farms, he probably included a couple of his own blokes to carry out a recce."

Iffor joined in, "And he very probably inserted the team that brought down the Beaver, and collected them after the attack in that old beaten up VW of his, and he must have orchestrated the ambush on his own minibus to draw me away from Ed's farm, leaving him free to hit the mission. Pete my friend, we've got them, we've got them!"

Pete was more cautious. "Tell me Moses, have you any idea when the final act of vengeance is to be?"

"No, Father Joyce never told me, but I was to lead them back into Zambia on this visit."

"You mean Father Flynn?" said Pete.

"No, his real name is Joyce, Flynn is the name he uses."

Iffor was on his feet: "Oh my good God, it can't be, it can't be him!"

Pete looked at him, alarmed, "Who Iffor, who?"

Iffor sat down again. "Don't you remember, Pete? I told you about it, the Paddies Jamie and I shot in Belfast, their name was Joyce and they had a brother in Italy studying for the priesthood. That's why he's targeting the Dix family; his final act of vengeance is going to be the destruction of the Dix farm."

"And the North Road Farm," said Moses. "They will use lorries from the Dix farm to get them there. That's the plan, and they are to wipe out your base at Mwonza before crossing into Zambia. Being in army uniform they will get very close before they attack."

"Since you won't be with them," Iffor pointed out, "do they have a fall back plan?"

"Yes, the priest's second-in-command is a Zambia army sergeant on loan to them. His name is Simeon. He will lead them back to Zambia."

"And the priest, will he be with them?"

"No, he will lead the attack on the Lamumbwa farm; then he will return to the Mission. I do not know what he will do after that."

"That's risky," Pete said.

Moses shook his head. "We do not leave any wounded alive and all the men have taken the oath, the same oath the Mau Mau used. They will be too frightened to break the oath."

They sat in stunned silence for a few moments, until the grim realisation came over Iffor: "The date Pete, what's the date?"

"Nineteenth, it's the Nineteenth of October, why?"

"Because, it was on the twentieth of October when Jamie and I killed his two brothers and cousin. He's breaking out tomorrow at dawn; tomorrow is his day of vengeance."

"They are not breaking out at dawn," Moses interrupted, "They are going to feast and leave the monastery at midnight. They will attack at dawn."

"What now?" said Pete. "Do we tell Ed to get the hell out of there and reinforce Charlie's farm? Do we get your Battalion to get some troops down to help us? What do we do, we've so little time?"

"Battalion can't help us. Even if they scramble their quick reaction force, by the time they recce and plan an attack it will be dark. They may kill a few terrorists, but the majority will simply melt into the bush, dump their weapons and become migrant blacks looking for work. No," Iffor went on, "we're on our own, it's up to us and this is our chance to kill every single one of them. Let's get back to the drill hall and do some thinking. Moses, you're coming with us."

They raced back to the drill hall, not a moment to lose, parking their vehicles outside the main entrance. Pete, Moses and the constable followed Iffor inside. "Colour!" he shouted.

From the depths of the Q.M. stores came a faint, "Sir?"

"My office please."

Iffor ushered his party into the office. "Grab a seat, I'll be right with you."

He went back along the landing to the orderly room and opened the door. "Josie, phone the mine chief executive and tell him we must have the Islander this afternoon. No matter where it is, we must have it. Then phone Boons bar and tell Davy Jones to get his arse up here as quickly as possible. Tell them the word is Pegasus.

"When you've done that, phone Blue Watch and tell them to get in here as quickly as possible and prepared for operations. Oh, and put me through to the Colonel."

Back in his office the Colour joined them and Iffor quickly brought him up to date.

He opened his council of war: "Gentlemen, you are aware of the situation, let's see if we can come up with the solution." The phone on his desk rang; he got straight to the point, "Colonel, It's Meredith, I need some help, your QRF and a chopper, if you can spare them."

"Sorry m'boy, I've just deployed my reserve platoon; the 'Lenshina' have left their Tribal Trust Land and joined up with the terrorists. Can you give me any details of your situation?"

"Not on the phone, Colonel." Iffor was aware the Zambians listened in to all military phone calls and the monastery had a phone. "I'll send you a coded sit rep."

That phone call confirmed there could be no help from Battalion.

He went back to his council of war. "That's it chaps, no help from Battalion; we are on our own. Moses, will the Inspector here be able to find the mechanism to open the door to the stairs in the monastery?"

"No, he will have to be shown."

"And you can do that?"

"Yes."

"Then you will go with the Inspector and his team."

Pete looked startled and a little uncomfortable. Iffor went on, "Chaps, I've thought of many scenarios and 'what if' situations since I've been doing this job, and one plan that passed through my mind I considered too audacious, too daring and too risky to even contemplate. However, it's perfect for this situation. The broad outline is this:

"Pete and his police will drive into the monastery as if making a routine visit. Once inside, they will go straight to the great hall where Moses will open the door to the staircase for them. Pete will call on the terrorists to surrender; they will undoubtedly tell him to fuck off (Moses will translate for him). Pete will then fire a burst from his SMG down the staircase, followed by a couple of 36's. Hopefully, this will cause a general stampede down the tunnel to the exit, where we will be waiting."

"Especially when I chuck three or four C.S. gas canisters into the cellar as well as the 36's," Pete exclaimed quite casually.

The Colour put his hand up. "If we drive in convoy, they'll know we're coming and guess what we are up to."

"That's why Blue Watch will parachute into the area at the end of the tunnel. Any more questions?... Good. Pete, go and prepare your lads; tell them no move before 1530 hours. Colour, give Pete six number thirty-sixes. Is that enough?" he asked.

"We should be able to destroy most of the monastery with those," said Pete, matching Iffor's flippancy.

"Good. Then Colour, issue another hundred rounds and a 36 each to the boys when they get here, plus one compo pack, and we'll take all thirteen mags for the Bren with us. And make sure everyone has a shell dressing, including Pete's boys and a morphine pack each."

Bob just sat looking at him. "Parachute! You're going to drop the boys in by parachute? They're not trained, you can't do it!"

"I can, and I will. And you will be with us, and you will all have sufficient training to ensure no one gets injured."

Josie came into the room, followed by Davy. "The Islander will be waiting for you from 1600," she said, "And all of Blue Watch are on their way."

"Thanks Josie. Come in, Davy."

"Gentlemen, 'O' group at 1500 hours, thank-you."

Pete and the Colour, along with Moses and his guard, left the room. No 'ifs', 'buts' or 'maybes'; the plan was risky, very risky, but neither of them could think of anything better.

"Davy, I'm going to parachute Blue Watch into the Lamumbwa valley. We know where the terrs are holed up. I want you to rig the aircraft for static lines and provide me with nine static line parachutes, ready for take-off at 1800 hours. We'll be jumping too low to worry about reserves. Oh, and I'll need you to give the boys some tuition on landing drills.

"Right boss, I'll have the aircraft and the ten parachutes ready when you arrive."

"Why ten?" Iffor asked, even though he knew the answer.

"You'll need me on the DZ to look after the parachutes and any injured."

"If we do our job right, there won't be any injured, but okay, see the Colour and draw a weapon and some combats. Consider yourself under martial law. If anyone asks, tell them you're only sixty."

Left alone, Iffor began to write up the notes for his "O" group, while down in the drill hall, the Colour issued the various stores and ammunition.

1500 hours and the cast assembled, Iffor raised the curtain. "Gentlemen, in a couple of hours' time, we are going to bring our local terrorist group to battle, but on our terms, and on our killing ground." He waited until the excited glances had been exchanged and began his now familiar briefing:

"Ground: The Lamumbwa valley, in particular the monastery.

"Situation: A group of between fifteen and twenty terrorists have been holed up under the monastery in a large cellar, able to come and go by way of a tunnel which exits under the railway at the halt. The leader is Father Sean and the two priests with him are both IRA men on the run from the British Army. It is the terrorists' intention to leave our region tomorrow morning, having first wiped out the Dix farm, North Road Farm and our unit at Mwonza, before crossing into Zambia disguised as Zambian army soldiers." He waited for this information to sink in and the realisation that this was the moment they had been waiting for, the chance to fight back.

"Mission: To kill them all, no prisoners." He repeated, "To kill them all, no prisoners will be taken." Looking directly at Pete, he said, "Except for the two bogus priests, I'm sure the British government will love to swap two high ranking IRA men for a couple of helicopters.

"Execution: Two-phase:

"Phase one: The police will drive directly to the monastery as if on a routine visit. They will force or fight their way into the main hall where our tame terrorist, one Moses January, late of the Zambian army... Stand up, Moses and take a bow." The African stood and smiled. "...will open the entrance to the stairs leading down to the cellar. Our Inspector here will call on the terrs to surrender and chuck a couple of 36's down the staircase. Since there is only room for one or two people at a time on the staircase, the terrs have only one route of escape, the tunnel leading to the halt.

"Phase two: Blue Watch will parachute into the area, the D.Z. being east of the railway. We will make our way to the railway halt and the tunnel exit, and become the stop group. Moses! Stand up and describe the entrance to the tunnel."

With his soldier's ability Moses described in detail the area of the entrance, in particular, the way the two upright supports on the southern side of the bridge lined up directly with the entrance some fifty metres away.

Iffor continued, "By jumping in, it's unlikely the terrs will see us arrive. The monastery is much lower than the railway embankment, as is our drop zone on the eastern side, and we will be jumping from 600 feet, on static lines, which will open our parachutes for us."

Harry stood up. "Are you serious! You want us to parachute in?"

"Got any better ideas?"

"Can't the Islander simply land and drop us off?"

"No, apart from the clear strips alongside the rail embankment and a clear area I've selected as our D.Z., the bush is too dense for a safe landing for the aircraft.

"Anyone else with any brilliant suggestions?"

They knew he was right, and they trusted him.

"Good, I'll carry on.

"Our order of battle: The Colour will command the gun group which will be himself, Evil and Alvin; the rest with me.

"Signals: Pete, your radio is compatible with the Islander using the 'Farm Alert' frequency. If you will loan me one of your handsets, I know the range is limited, but it will be sufficient for me to contact you at the monastery. Keep in contact with the Islander, the pilot will tell you when we've been dispatched. I'll contact you when we are on the ground. You will hold back about a mile from the monastery until we are in position. If comms fail, begin your attack at 1900hours.

"Timings: Pete, leave as soon as you can.

"For the rest of us:

"1600   Move to airfield and meet up with Davy and me for training.

"1730   Draw and fit parachutes. Pilot's briefing.

"1800   Emplane and take off.

"1830   'P' hour

"1900   We attack.

"I intend for us to drop about five hundred metres from the halt and the tunnel exit, but we can't hang about on the D.Z congratulating one another; we move on to our objective as quickly as possible... Questions?"

"Yes," said Harry, "Since it takes several months to train a paratrooper, why are we only getting an hour's training?"

"Because you're Blue Watch and because all you need to know is how to exit the aircraft and how to land. I'm asking you to step off the end of the ramp, turn into wind, and keep your feet and knees together when you land, piece of piss."

Evil stood up. "Some of the terrs may well try to escape back along the tunnel. Do we go in after them?"

"No, I won't risk lives doing that. The door to the staircase is self-sealing. It can only be opened from the outside, and we'll bring down the exit to the tunnel with grenades and seal them in. We'll get our Engineers to do a proper job of sealing the tunnel in the next day or so."

Evil sat down and the men looked expectantly at Iffor, waiting for him to say something. "Chaps, what I'm asking you to do is far beyond what would normally be expected of you and if there was any other option I would take it, but this is the only way we can wipe out these bastards once and for all. Good luck everyone, and one last thing I must tell you, the raids and ambushes on the Dix family and the raid on the Mission was in revenge for what Jamie and I did in Northern Ireland. We killed Father Sean's two brothers. I just thought you ought to know.

"Okay Colour, get them away. I'll R.V. with you at the airfield. I've got to change and grab my gear. Gentlemen, prepare for battle!"

Alone again, Iffor pressed his intercom, "Josie, come in please."

Watching her sit down, he felt an enormous pang of guilt. What he was putting her through was unimaginable. "Josie," he added, "my love, the men that killed Helen, I've got the chance to bring them to battle, but on my terms. I'll never get another opportunity like this—I've got to take it."

She wasn't really aware of what was happening since she hadn't been invited to his briefing so she just nodded. "When will I see you?" she said.

"Tomorrow, I'll be back tomorrow."

"Do what you have to do," she said. "Just come back to me."

As Iffor parked his pick-up outside the hotel, Pete in a two-Rover convoy passed him, grinning and waving. He shouted, "The Colour's got your radio."

Quickly, Iffor dressed into his combats: trousers, no shirt; he dug into the bottom of his Burgan and pulled out his old British army para smock and put that on; next, his belt with magazine pouches and water bottle followed by the shoulder rig for his Brno. Then he stuffed the pockets of his smock with two field dressings, a morphine pack, three packs of compo biscuits, two tins of compo cheese and a handful of boiled sweets. Picking up his weapons, he was now ready for anything, another adventure that he so dearly loved was about to begin.

He parked his pick-up next to the army three-tonner and dropped the keys into the airfield office. "Someone will collect it for me," he told the sole occupant.

In the hanger that the Parachute and Flying Club used for training, Davy already had the team in a semicircle around him, showing them how the 'Irvin Conical statichute' deployed. The fact that the design was based on the British army 'X' type parachute, probably the most reliable in use, made Iffor more confident in his decision not to carry reserve parachutes. Waiting until Davy had finished his first lesson, Iffor conferred with him. "Teach them flight techniques and how to steer into wind for landing, and landing techniques. I'm going to brief the pilots. Then I'll teach them the aircraft exit drills and then we'll be ready for the off."

The pilots were waiting for him in their 'ready room', charts already laid out on the table. After introductions, Iffor went straight into his brief: "We emplane and take off at 1800." Tracing a route with his finger, he said, "Fly north to the Lamumbwa valley, cross the river, then turn and fly south with the railway to starboard. Start losing height, aiming to cross the railway bridge at 600 feet. Our drop zone is below the railway embankment, 500 metres from the halt. I don't want anyone dropping into the river.

"I want you to make two passes with the ramp down. The first, I'll drop a streamer to test the wind; we'll give you any further corrections. The second pass, throttle back as much as you can, give me the red as you cross the river, then the green as we cross the D.Z."

"Why so low?" the captain asked.

"Because the ground on either side of the rail embankment is much lower, so with luck, our enemy won't hear or see us, and besides, if I dropped my novices at a 1000 feet, they'd be scattered all over the place. At least half of them would land back in Kensington. No, at 600 feet they'll be on the ground before they realise it and in a compact group... Now, let's go over the plan again."

Iffor rejoined the team in the hanger. Davy had them running up a ramp and jumping off the end. As they reached the end of the ramp, he would call, 'forward landing', or 'backward landing', 'side left', 'side right', and they would go into their landing rolls. They were all pretty puffed, but seemed actually to be enjoying themselves.

"That's it lads," Davy said, "Over to you, boss."

Iffor gathered the team around him; they were still panting hard from the unaccustomed exercise. "Let me tell you this," he began. "In the British army Parachute Brigade, because of the amount of kit we carried, and because of the type of parachute we used, we landed a lot faster and a lot harder than you will land, but the principle we used kept us from harm. That principle was, if you keep a good parachute position, head on chest, elbows tucked into the body, feet and knees together with knees slightly bent, you will walk away from most landings. Now, let's do our aircraft drills."

Obligingly, the pilots had lowered the ramp for Iffor while they went through their pre-take off checks. "This gentlemen, is the ramp you will step off into space," Iffor explained to the team gathered around him. "Inside the aircraft, down each side is a bench seat which folds back when not in use. We will emplane in the order we will jump and sit down on the bench seat and fasten our seat belts. The gun group, who will be jumping first, with the Colour leading, will sit on the starboard side; the rifle section on the port side. Davy and I will jump last, as we will be dispatching you.

"I will be in contact with the pilot on the intercom, and five minutes before the drop zone he will lower the ramp, and over the drop zone he will give me the green light and I will drop a streamer. The streamer will indicate wind speed and allow me to give corrections to the pilot. As the pilot begins a slow turn to take us back over the river, I will shout 'prepare for action'. You will all stand, fasten back the seats and hook up your static lines. Davy and I will be with you all the way to see you do it right.

"I will then check each one of you. As we approach the drop zone we will start losing height and the pilot will start throttling back the engines. I will shout 'action stations' and we will do the 'paratroopers' shuffle' to the ramp. We will go through all of this again in a few minutes, so don't worry. Coming up to the D.Z., the pilot will give me the red light followed by the green. Davy and I will be either side of Bob steadying him. I will slap him hard on the shoulder and shout 'go'. The rest of you will follow. Davy and I will jump last, we are experienced enough to catch up with you. Right, I'll put you in jumping order, we'll emplane and go through those drills."

Satisfied they had sufficient knowledge to exit the aircraft and steer into the slight wind they may encounter, and hold a good landing position, Davy led them back into the hanger to 'draw and fit' parachutes. Iffor explained and demonstrated how they would 'sling' their rifles, muzzle pointed downwards and fit the harness around the weapon, and on landing, simply turning and pressing the quick release box would release the parachute harness.

As he checked the team, the Islander's engines burst into life. "Checks completed." Iffor glanced at his watch, "Time to go, boys."

Hooked up to the dispatchers' strop above the ramp, Iffor looked anxiously at the ground below while he listened to the pilot's commentary, "600 feet, running in now, DZ in sight, DZ coming up now, now, now. Green on!" Iffor dropped the streamer and watched as it spiralled to the ground smack into the centre of the drop zone. "Perfect!" he shouted into the intercom, "Fucking perfect! Now do it again, exactly the same." He unhooked and went back into the freight bay, "Prepare for action!"

All stood and fastened back the bench seats, then hooked up.

Starting with Bob, Iffor checked, first the gun group and then the rifle group. Davy copied each move he made; there wouldn't be any mistakes. Iffor and Davy took up positions on the ramp, each hooked up to the dispatcher's strop above the ramp, Iffor listening intently to the intercom. His heart was beating much too rapidly for comfort; he tried desperately to shut out all thoughts of failure. I'll bring them all back alive, he kept telling himself. After I've settled with Sean and his crowd.

"Turning 180 degrees, 800 feet, final approach to 600 feet."

"Action stations!" Iffor shouted.

The team shuffled to the ramp, the paratroopers' shuffle.

Iffor took off his headset and hung it up. With Davy, he positioned the Colour in the centre of the edge of the ramp, the rest of the team lined up behind him. Although expected, the red light came as something of a shock, followed moments later by the green. Iffor shouted, "Go!" and slapped the spot where Bob's shoulder had been a split second earlier—the Colour had already gone. Iffor watched with relief as his parachute deployed. Immediately after him was Evil, complete with evil grin, then Alvin, followed by the rest of Blue Watch, a perfect exit. He nodded at Davy, then followed him into the slipstream, adopting a 'legs apart, lying back' position, hands across the chest, and watched as his parachute deployed. He let the wind take him towards the billowing parachutes already on the ground, leaving his turn into wind until the last moment, allowing him to land in amongst the team already on the ground.

Around him he could hear the satisfying sound of weapons being made ready. He got out of his harness and cocked his own weapon.

If the parachute jump was a means to getting troops at the right place at the right time, the added bonus was they were now completely without fear and ready for any odds and any fight.

PART FOURTEEN

Section Battle Drills: The Assault.

Charge through the enemy position firing two rounds into every enemy body, alive or dead.

THE TEAM GATHERED AROUND IFFOR. He did a quick mental head count. Davy was already gathering up the parachutes, all present. No words were necessary. He held his arms shoulder high in a 'V', Arrow formation, gun group on his right, and they moved on to their objective.

Silently, the team dropped into an all-round defensive position. Iffor and the Colour crawled forward to the near concrete upright supporting the bridge, and surveyed the area. Nothing moved. Cautiously, they moved forward to the second upright; the tunnel entrance should now be about fifty metres ahead of them. Through the sparse bush, Iffor could make out what appeared to be a cave. Bob reached into his combat jacket and produced a pair of binoculars. "Will these help?" he whispered.

Iffor looked again, this time with the binos. It had to be the entrance. Then, as if to confirm what he was thinking, a match flared in the darkness of the interior.

"Oh bollocks, I hadn't thought of that."

"What's up?"

"There's a fucking sentry inside; he's having a fag. Methinks we'll have to use caution to get into position."

Swiftly they moved back to the team for a quick brief:

"The entrance is fifty metres in front of the second upright. To the right is the river, to the left some high ground covered in gorse, which is probably why no one has discovered it. There is a sentry inside the entrance; we've got to be careful getting into position. We'll take up a loose semicircle about fifty metres out from the entrance, the gun group on our right firing directly into the tunnel with the Colour acting as right cut-off, myself on our left will be the left cut-off."

He let the information sink in and looked into their faces. No fear, a little apprehension perhaps, but that was to be expected. Now was the time for his 'eve of battle speech.'

"Chaps, our enemy outnumber us, they are bush-wise, well-armed and well trained.

"But we have surprise on our side and discipline. And we have each other.

"Fix Bayonets. Now, let's go and sort these bastards out.

"Bob, get your group away now. Take up your position where we were. That way you can fire straight into the tunnel. The rest, with me, and good luck everyone."

As they moved forward, Iffor pressed his radio key to transmit:

"Bravo Whisky in position, over."

Pete's voice was immediate, "Roger out."

Iffor positioned his men in a loose semicircle, himself on the left, tucked in on the gorse-covered hillock, the gun group on the right, close to the river with the concrete support giving some cover. Anyone escaping to the right he would nail; anyone trying to escape across the river Bob would zap. All they had to do now was wait and hope the sentry hadn't seen or heard them.

This was the hardest part, the waiting and the wondering. Would they come out cautiously? Would they charge out in panic? Had the sentry seen them and gone to give a warning? It mattered not now. In the distance Iffor heard the sound of gunfire, followed moments later by three explosions as the grenades detonated, and then half a minute later, another two explosions. Pete was obviously enjoying himself.

Iffor tried to imagine the reaction of the terrorists. Their leader Simeon would be calling for calm, telling them to collect their weapons and equipment, and probably telling them to scatter when they cleared the tunnel and R.V. after dark. They wouldn't know Blue Watch were waiting for them. After all, Simeon had posted a sentry in the tunnel. There came shouts from within the tunnel. The sentry came out, looked around and went back in to give the 'all clear.' Three men appeared; the sentry, a man Iffor took to be the leader and a man carrying a R.P.D machine-gun. They walked another five or six paces, sniffing the air and listening. The leader turned and beckoned to the rest of the group to come out. Iffor could hardly contain himself, as three five-men sections left the safety of the tunnel and stepped into the open.

Iffor breathed to Hennie beside him: "Shoot the man with the machine-gun.

"Now!

"Now!"

The terrorist pitching forward was the signal for Evil to fire a full magazine into the group. His vision had been impaired by the bush between him and his target, but that first magazine cleared a fire lane for the second magazine to cause havoc.

Total surprise, but the terrorists recovered quickly and started to return fire. A group of three or four started to back towards the tunnel entrance, firing as they went. Big Shamus stood, shouted, "Grenade!" and threw his grenade into the tunnel behind them. Phil's grenade landed amongst them.

The rifle section were now picking off those still standing. Iffor looked for a target, someone to kill. Evil was on his feet now, firing the Bren from the hip, lacing one-in-five tracer into the enemy alive or dead. The leader, Simeon, having dropped to the ground when the shooting started, was now on his feet, the bayonet of his rifle fixed, and charged to break through his attacker's line. Harry rose from his position, bayonet fixed to meet the challenge, bayonet versus bayonet. Confronted by Mad Harry rising from the ground immediately in front of him, the terrorist fatally paused. Harry parried the man's rifle knocking it across his chest. Then he stepped back a pace and thrust his bayonet up into the man's neck just below the jaw.

Withdrawing his bayonet, Harry charged into the enemy who were still standing.

To a man, Blue Watch followed, mixing it with the terrorists, with bayonet and bullet. On the right, a terrorist attempted to get to the river and escape. Throwing his weapon away, he prepared to plunge into the river. Tracer from Evil's Bren gun followed his progress, finally catching up with him and throwing him face down in the water.

A wounded terrorist was trying to get the RPD machine-gun into action. He had it in his hip and with hands slippery with blood, was trying to cock it. Iffor fired, but the man was determined and with a defiant cry he cocked the weapon. Then Hennie was on him, thrusting his bayonet into the man's chest. Iffor shot him again, this time in the head preventing his finger from tightening on the trigger.

The shooting had stopped. As with most fire fights, there was now a tranquil silence.

"Make sure they are all dead!" Iffor shouted. "Move their weapons away from the bodies."

Just ahead of Iffor a terrorist was trying to get onto his knees. He saw Iffor, smiled and attempted to wave, indicating surrender. Iffor's bullet took him above his right nipple and exited through his left shoulder blade; the second round took most of his face away. The rest of the team started clinically going about their grim business. Iffor paused and took the radio from his smock pocket, time to give Pete a sit-rep.

A shout from the Colour interrupted him: "The priest, the priest, he's getting away!"

Iffor looked to where Bob was pointing. Beyond the gorse, where the ground was slightly higher, the battered VW with the white cross on its side, was making heavy weather of the rough terrain and thickening bush. He snapped off a round into the engine; the bullet bounced off the road in front of the vehicle. Behind him someone shouted, "Cunt, the engine's in the back!" The terrain was too much for the VW, it gave up trying. Iffor watched as the priest left the vehicle and sprinted for the thicker bush only yards away. Iffor fired again and saw his man stagger, fall, regain his feet and take cover behind an m'pani tree.

Pete came up on the radio: "The priest has escaped; I'm after him in the Rover."

No time to wait for the Rover. If the priest could hide in the bush for another hour it would be too dark to look for him.

Iffor shouted to Bob as he began running after the priest: "Take over Bob, I'm going after him," and began the race of his life. As he neared the m'pani tree, caution took over. He hoped he would pick up a blood spoor, but then again the priest might be waiting for him.

He was.

Lying with his back up against the tree, leaning on his right side with his right arm underneath him, the priest watched as Iffor approached. He was bleeding badly, but Iffor couldn't see the wound. "Are you going to kill me or can we call it a draw?"

Iffor kept the muzzle of his Carbine pointed at the chest, trying to steel himself for what he must do. As a soldier, shooting a defenceless wounded man was against all the rules, but then the priest broke the rules. As if to make himself more comfortable, he pushed himself up a little, bringing his right hand into view. Iffor caught a flash of silver and a vision of Helen putting the barrel of the chrome plated pistol into her mouth. He squeezed off a round, hitting the priest in the chest.

Sean seemed to relax and he smiled. His strength left him; he coughed and blood started to trickle down his chin. Before Iffor could fire again, Pete came running up. Looking down at the priest, he said, "I promised Helen I would kill him."

Iffor looked at his friend. "Be my guest, he's still alive," and walked away.

That dull flat thud of Pete's Colt heralded the last rays of the sun. Soon it would be dark, the end of another day, the end of the terror that had stalked the Lamumbwa Valley.

Pete caught up with him and handed him the Astra pistol and holster he had loaned to Helen. "There you go, I told you I would get it back to you no matter where you were. Now, if you'll send a couple of your lads up here, I'll load the priest onto the Rover and take him back to the monastery."

Iffor made his way back to Blue Watch. The Colour had the team laying the bodies just inside the tunnel and the weapons stacked outside. Pete would now be responsible for the bodies and weapons.

The bodies would be taken back to Kensington for identification and fingerprinting. The weapons were fired into a long water trough, the bullets retrieved and sent to Salisbury to be matched with bullets taken from other terrorist raids.

"Eighteen confirmed dead, all personal weapons recovered," Bob told him.

"Nineteen," Iffor nodded towards the m'pani tree. "He made it easy for me—he had the pistol I loaned to Helen."

Suddenly, Iffor felt exhausted. He sat down against a boulder and took out his notebook. "All round defence, please Bob, and organise a guard rota, two sentries, and bring Davy and the parachutes in from the DZ. At least we'll be warm sleeping in the parachutes tonight, then tell the boys to clean weapons, relax and brew up if they can. I've got a sit-rep to send off."

The sit-rep read:

"CONTACT!

"East of Lamumbwa Monastery under rail bridge.

"Today at nineteen hundred hours. Enemy dead, nineteen confirmed body count, all weapons recovered.

"Two prisoners taken, both posing as white priests, in fact, both IRA men.

"No friendly casualties.

"Consider no further action by enemy.

"Firm on site until daybreak."

He would dictate the message to Pete who would relay it to Kensington police on the police radio. They in turn would give the message to Josie, who would encode it and send it off to Battalion. Having to go back to her office, open the safe and retrieve the Bat-Co code book and send the message by teleprinter, would have been offset by the sentence, 'no friendly casualties'. Her man was safe.

Iffor joined his team in their all-round defence position, opened his tin of meat paste and biscuits and happily munched as he cleaned his weapon. Words of praise for his men would wait until his debrief in the morning.

Iffor took the 'dog watch', four to six, with the Colour. This gave Iffor the chance to clear his head and plan for the rest of the day.

Pete would probably scrounge a three-tonner from Ed Dix to get the bodies back to Kensington. Once Pete had arrived to take charge of the bodies and weapons, Iffor could march his team back to the monastery for breakfast and a shave, and with luck, Ed would provide them with transport back to Kensington.

The beautiful new dawn flooded the valley with light and warmth and the promise of a safer existence for the residents of the valley, for the immediate future at least. Iffor roused the men in time for Pete's arrival in his Rover, followed by Ed in his long wheelbase Rover and a three-tonner in the rear.

"Didn't expect you quite this early," said Iffor, as Pete climbed out of his vehicle, followed by Moses.

"Why should the flies have all the fun—I want to get the bodies back to the hospital morgue before it gets too hot. I thought Moses would be better off with you."

"What's happening back at the monastery?" Iffor asked, "And what's happened to the two priests?"

"The priests are in custody and New Epsom are flying in a team to go through the monastery with a fine tooth comb. Me and my boys are to take the bodies and weapons back to Kensington. You are to go back to the monastery and wait for the New Epsom team to arrive. With luck, they'll give you a lift back to Kensington in the chopper. In the meantime, let's get the bodies loaded before the sun gets any higher."

As they loaded the bodies onto the truck, the Colour cleared the enemy weapons and stacked them in Pete's Rover. "There you go," he said as the last of the weapons were loaded, "Nineteen bodies and nineteen weapons."

"I suppose you want me to sign for them," Pete said.

"No, we can trust you." Words never normally used by a colour sergeant.

Pete looked at the jumble of bodies on the truck. Turning to Iffor he said, "When you came to me with your mad idea of turning Blue Watch into soldiers, I thought you were crazy and I couldn't believe I went along with you and your mad ideas. But, you did it, Iffor my old mate, you did it."

"With a lot of help from you and your lads," said Iffor.

"Not to mention Blue Watch," Evil muttered.

Ed cleared his throat, bringing silence to the group. "Gentlemen, if it wasn't for you and your courage last evening, my family and my African staff would now be lying dead in the ashes of my farm. I thank you and salute you."

Blue Watch looked down at their feet, embarrassed, not knowing what to say.

Iffor spoke: "I'd appreciate it if you will take Davy and the parachutes back to Kensington with you, please Pete."

"He can take the parachutes," Davy almost shouted, "but I'll stay with the team," and as an afterthought, "if you don't mind, sir."

"Of course Davy, after all, you are a member of the team."

Pete and Ed left with the bodies, leaving the long wheelbase Rover for Iffor to use to get his men back to the monastery and Kensington. Iffor gathered his team around him—time for a debrief: "Gentlemen, for what you did last night and over the last month or so, Rhodesia owes you a great debt of gratitude and I feel privileged and honoured to have served with you."

To have said more would have broken the spell, so he simply said, "Pack up and we'll go to the monastery for breakfast, and wait for the cavalry to arrive."

"We might find some beer there," suggested big Shamus.

"Indeed we might, my friend, indeed we might."

PART FIFTEEN

Sometimes, surrender is inevitable.

In which case, surrender with style, dignity and good grace and make the best of it.

A T THE MONASTERY, Iffor found Sergeant Banda and a constable waiting for him with the Rhino.

"The Inspector said I should wait until you arrived," he said. "Now I can go; there will be much to do in Kensington." He saluted and drove out of the courtyard, leaving Iffor and Blue Watch standing in the courtyard, looking in awe at the dark foreboding walls and towers surrounding them and looking down on them.

"I don't know how long we're going to be here lads, but first and foremost, we don't want any unpleasant surprises. Colour, organise a search of all the rooms. Moses and I will check the door to the cellar and make sure it's locked. The special branch will want to go down into the cellar; we'll open it then for them."

With all the rooms cleared, Iffor placed Phil on the gate while the rest of the team relaxed in the shade of the wall. The Colour with his nose for these sort of things went in search of breakfast in the kitchen, while Evil with his nose for alcohol went in search of beer. Thirty minutes later found them munching on ham sandwiches and drinking well-earned cold Castle beer. Iffor decided to introduce Moses more formally.

"Chaps, you may recall we had the pleasure of shooting Moses here a couple of weeks ago." Moses grinned and touched the scar beneath his shirt. "Well, he's on our side now and it was his information that brought about last night's action."

"You mean it was his fault I jumped out of that fucking plane?" Alvin said, not normally known for bad language, then with a wave at the African said, "Thanks mate."

"Moses and I served together in the Zambia Army with a special anti-terrorist unit called Dog Force. Moses and his team provided intelligence and my team provided muscle. Between us, we managed to kill Alice Chingola, leader of the Lenshina who had been causing havoc in the Fort Jameson area."

"You did not kill her," said Moses.

"Well, she was most certainly dead when I last saw her; her and her two bodyguards."

Moses smiled, shaking his head. "The woman and the men your men shot were local police pretending to be Lenshina, trying to find out where Alice was hiding. It was five or six weeks before we were told. The police liked to keep their secrets from the army. By then, you had left for Rhodesia."

All eyes turned to Iffor for his reply… "Whoops!"

"What's Alice up to now?" Iffor was already wishing he hadn't asked the question.

Moses became serious. "She is now the field commander of ZANU. Her Lenshina have joined forces with the terrorists. That way they all get pardons from the government for all the crimes they have committed."

"Alice in charge of ZANU?" Iffor shook his head in disbelief. "That's like putting a Rottweiler in charge of a cat's home."

"She sounds like a rather nasty lady," Evil said.

"Nasty! She makes Ming the Merciless look like a fucking kid's glove puppet.

"Now lads, I don't want Special Branch getting their hands on Moses here. I have done a deal with Moses and I intend to keep my part of the bargain. So, if asked, Moses is our tracker and the terrorist who gave us the information about the monastery died. Harry, take Moses under your wing, don't let any of the Special Branch talk to him."

"Right boss."

The whirring rotas of the Wessex Whirlwind heralded the arrival of the Special Branch from New Epsom. Iffor stood in the middle of the courtyard, arms outstretched, indicating to the pilot it was clear to land.

The ten-man team disembarked from the helicopter, all dressed in shorts and shirt and desert boots, but with a different array of weapons.

Their leader, under six feet, barrel chest with greying hair sprouting up from beneath his shirt and a Browning Hi-Power holstered comfortably on his hip, walked across to Iffor. "Meredith?" he enquired in a thick Afrikaan's accent, "I'm Oustaizen, Karl Oustaizen, in charge of this rabble who consider themselves to be Rhodesia's finest." Iffor accepted his firm handshake. "Any chance of a beer?" he asked, eyeing Iffor's cold Castle.

He shouted to his team: "Usual routine lads, search the place; we don't want terrorists lurking in cupboards."

"We've already cleared the area," Iffor said, "and I imagine the police before us had a good look around."

"Right," said Karl, "but my boys are professionals. We do the job properly."

Accepting a beer from Evil, Karl asked, "Can you give me the layout of this place?"

"Not really, but I can show you the concealed door that leads down to the cellars where the terrorists lived." As they walked to the great hall, Iffor volunteered information rather than waiting to be questioned: "We were lucky enough to stumble onto the terrorists' lines of communication and had some good hunting. One of the terrorists we shot a couple of weeks ago lived long enough to be able to give me the gen on this place before he died yesterday. The rest, as they say, is history, certainly for the nineteen dead and the two prisoners."

"Prisoners?" Karl looked interested.

"Yes, the two IRA men on the run from the British Army, posing as priests."

Iffor now had Karl's full and undivided attention; there would be no awkward questions about Moses. "Priests? IRA? What are you talking about?"

"The two IRA men hiding out from the British government, posing as priests and keeping their hand in by helping to train terrorists," Iffor said, giving the appearance of being totally unconcerned. "The police have taken them back to Kensington, then on to Salisbury."

They stopped walking. Iffor had just ruined Karl's day. "That's not possible," he said, "I would have known about it."

"You didn't know about twenty terrorists, led by the local priest, living here," said Iffor. His beer was going down really well now. "It's the same old story. It's us poor bloody infantry plodding about in the bush who get the results, while Rhodesia's finest go looking for clues with a magnifying glass. Any chance of your chopper giving us a lift back to Kensington?"

A radio call to Ed Dix, asking him to collect his Rover from the monastery, and Blue Watch clambered onto the Wessex. "Where to?" the pilot asked.

"Kensington airfield please cabby," Harry answered.

Back on the airfield they watched as the Wessex made its way back to the monastery.

Iffor took the Colour to one side. "I want you to take the three-tonner to the drill hall and come back with the Champ. I think it would be more appropriate for the team to drive through the town in the Champ with our pennant flying. I'm sure word must have got back to the town by now of our success. You, me, Davy and Moses can follow in my pick-up."

Bob grinned, "What a fucking good idea!"

The drive back through Kensington was not the triumphant homecoming that Iffor would have liked, but better than he expected since no-one knew they were coming. Cars hooted, shoppers came out of shops to wave and half a dozen drunks spilled out of Boons bar to raise glasses in salute, and the big Matabele doorman stood rigidly to attention and saluted. As they neared the Elephants Head Hotel, Iffor saw the Union Jack being hurriedly hoisted, and those having lunch on the veranda stood and waved.

They drove into the drill hall, where Josie was waiting for them. "Auntie phoned to say you were on your way." She was dressed in white; white skirt and shirt and sandals with a white scarf about her neck, looking clean and crisp and lovely. She gave each one of the team in turn a hug and a kiss. Iffor held on to her longer than he should have done. She smelt of exotic Indian perfume, and paradise. Moses stood to one side, but she spotted him. "And you," she said running over to him and hugging him, "There's a letter from England which might concern you."

Iffor had forgotten his promises to Moses with all that had been going on; time to do something about it.

"Colour, sort things out down here. We've got to find a home for Moses. Up to my office please, Moses, and you please, Josie."

The letter from England was on his desk. As he opened it, he said, "Get me the phone number of the Selous Scouts at Kariba and get the extension of the Intelligence Officer."

The letter was from the old General, Henry's father.

> *My dear Meredith,*
>
> *I'm so pleased I can be of service to you, after what you did for my son. I've spoken to the colonel of my old regiment and as luck would have it, he's under pressure to recruit more blacks into his regiment, and in particular a black officer. The deal is, your lad must make his way to Pretoria, where the Embassy there has a recruiting office. If they accept him, they will pay his fare to UK, where he will join his regiment. He will undergo normal recruit's training as a private soldier, then, as an Officer cadet, he will be groomed by his regiment for Sandhurst.*
>
> *I will keep you informed as to his progress.*

Iffor passed the letter across to Moses. "All we have to do now is get your son out of Zambia," he said with a wry smile.

He dialled the Scouts' number. "Meredith of the Rifles at Kensington here."

"Meredith, is what we've been hearing about you true?"

"Do you mean my astonishing good looks or the nineteen terrs we killed last night?"

"Your cull, is it true?"

"Yes, and the man who gave me the intelligence is here with me now, name of Moses January. He is a warrant officer in the Zambia Army, their 'I' section. He's eager to help and he wants to 'turn'. Now, I can either hand him over to you, or…"

The Scouts couldn't afford to let this prize go to anyone else, and the reply came, "We'll have him. What's the deal?"

"The deal is you get his son out of Zambia. He's going to join the British Army."

"Where is the boy?"

"Kafue boys' school. Can you do it?"

"Consider it done. When can we have your man?"

"Phone me back with your ETA and I'll have him waiting for you on Kensington airfield."

Iffor put the phone down and looked across at Moses, who was now grinning broadly, but still looking a little apprehensive. "Moses, I can do one more thing for you. If you don't want to join the Scouts, I'll have you back here with me when they've finished grilling you. Now I want you to go down to the end of the corridor to the duty officer's bunk, grab a shower and have some rest. I'll organise some food for you and I'll call you when it's time to go."

Alone with Josie, Iffor rose, walked around his desk and stood behind her. He put both hands on her shoulders and leaned forward smelling her hair. Slowly, he slid one hand into her blouse and down to her breast, feeling her nipple. She clutched his hand, but left it where it was. "As soon as I get rid of Moses and the team," he said, "It's you and I back to the hotel where we'll have the rest of the day and tonight together."

She stood and turned to face him, putting her arms around his neck, "We're not going to the hotel, we are going home to our bungalow. I've moved all your stuff and I've stocked up with food and alcohol. I want you to myself."

She drew away from him. "The Colonel wants you to phone him as soon as you can," she said, "but I think we can forget about it for now. I'll tell you again tomorrow."

Iffor went downstairs to the drill hall. With his usual efficiency, the Colour had already taken back all the stores and ammunition, leaving the team with their five loaded magazines to take home with them, along with their weapons. A threat still hung over the town, and in particular, the team.

"Do you want the men to fall in, sir?" the Colour asked.

"No thank you, Colour. Gather round lads, listen in. There's not much more I can say about yesterday's operation; we did a bloody good job and you should all be feeling quite chuffed with yourselves. I've arranged for the Selous Scouts to come and collect Moses. They'll look after him. I think you can all stand down until Monday morning 0800, when we'll have a full debrief and I'll discuss our future with you. Davy, that includes you."

Davy nodded his thanks and asked, "Can I hang on to this, please?" indicating his sub-machine gun.

Iffor looked at the Colour, who nodded his approval. "Yes, now you've teamed up with us you're in as much danger as the rest of the team, just don't let that fucking monkey of yours get his paws on it."

Josie came down the stairs. "The Scouts phoned back, ETA 1500."

Iffor looked at his watch. "That gives me time to write up my report for the Colonel. Colour, can you rustle up some compo stew for Moses? He's in the duty officer's bunk."

"Right sir."

Harry spoke up. "We are going to have a few beers at the Moth club later on. It would be nice if you could join us."

"Thanks Harry, but…"

"I know," said Harry, "Places to go, people to see, and a new home to move into. We understand."

Iffor and Moses, sitting in the pick-up, watched as the Lynx helicopter flew in from the west, turning into wind to land. A man wearing K.D.s leapt from the machine and bending low to avoid the rotas, ran across to them. As Iffor got out of the pick-up the man put on his distinctive grey beret with the Scouts cap badge. Noting his three pips, Iffor saluted.

"Mc'Tavish," the man said, extending his hand, "My friends call me Jock."

"That's never your real name," Iffor said, taking his hand.

"Everyone says that when they first meet me, but it is."

Iffor related the events leading up to the monastery battle and Moses' willingness to 'turn'.

"We'll look after him, providing he's prepared to play ball with us, and we've already diverted a team in the bush to go and collect his son."

Moses turned to Iffor, "My son, how will he get to Pretoria?"

Mc'Tavish responded, "We have a man who will provide the passport for him, it's all part of the deal. We'll give him a travel warrant and put him on the train to South Africa, where he'll be met by one of our colleagues from South African Special Forces who'll look after him." He added with a grin: "Bet your lot couldn't do that."

"No," said Iffor, "Our lot confine ourselves to killing terrorists."

Handshakes all round and Mc'Tavish and Moses hurried to the waiting Lynx.

I think our paths may well cross again, Iffor mused to himself.

He drove back to the drill hall, parked outside, and walked to the police station to check on the prisoners. "You've missed the Inspector," Agnes told him, "he's taken the prisoners to Salisbury."

"Escort?" Iffor enquired.

"Sergeant Banda and two constables. I am now in charge of the station."

Iffor returned to the drill hall to collect Josie. It was getting on for four o'clock, knocking off time. "Colonel's been on the phone again for you," she said. "I had to tell him you were back, wants you to phone him as soon as possible."

With sinking heart, Iffor went back to his office and phoned New Epsom. He just knew the Colonel would want to see him personally.

"Colonel, Meredith here."

"Iffor m'boy, got your sit rep, it read like something out of boy's own. It's a great boost to morale up here. Iffor, army wants a full report from me on your activities, so I want you to get your arse up here as soon as possible; tomorrow morning will do. Tea and stickies at 1000hours."

Iffor put the phone down and grinned. In army jargon, tea and stickies (cakes) meant you were in favour. If you were told, 'my office and it's not for sticky buns', you were in trouble.

Josie was waiting for him down in the drill hall. "Does he want to see you?" she asked.

Iffor nodded. "I'll have to leave at first light."

"Auntie thought you might have to go and see the Colonel, so she pressed and starched a set of K.D.'s for you. They're at home." She smiled that wonderful sweet smile of hers, pursing her full pink lips. "I just love talking about our home," she told him.

The Colour had already left to get home to his wife. Josie locked up using her own keys. "And now my gallant hero, I've got you all to myself."

The transformation of the bungalow in such a short time was nothing short of a miracle. Curtains hung at the windows, a vase of fresh flowers stood on the dining table and on the sideboard, and in a twin photo frame an Indian man and woman looked back at him. Obviously, Josie's parents.

She followed him through to the bedroom and as he sat on the bed undressing, she opened the wardrobe, showing his clothes and uniforms hanging there. "I'll run the bath and open a bottle of red," she said. "Oh, and have a shave, you need it."

She watched as he lowered himself into the bath, then, slowly, seductively, she began to undress, watching his eagerness growing as he waited for her to join him. "I have a distinct feeling," she said, "you have really missed me."

Instead of drying themselves, she laid a large towel on the bed for them to lie on and dry in the afternoon warmth. He sprawled across her, gently compressing her breast with his chest. "Happiness," he said, "is being able to just lie here looking into your face, your beautiful face." She blushed furiously and burst out laughing, breaking the spell. "Come on," she said, slapping his buttock, "Let's fire up the *braaivlies* and get some steaks cooking. I'm starving."

Josie busied herself in the kitchen preparing steaks and *Boereworse* sausage, while Iffor got to grips with the braai in his new garden. The *braaivlies* was typical, a forty gallon oil drum cut in half lengthways, four legs welded onto it and a steel mesh over the burning charcoal. As he sat watching the fire taking hold of the charcoal, he reflected on his garden. Since he would be living in the bungalow for five years, he ought to think about a gardener and perhaps a dog to keep Josie company when he was away. He'd always fancied a boxer; now was his chance. He made a mental note to make some enquiries.

Josie came into the garden with a brace of cold Castle and sat on his knee. Dressed simply in shorts and halter top, she was the promise of things to come.

"I've been thinking," he said, "we need a gardener."

"And a housekeeper," she replied.

"And how do you feel about a dog, to keep you company while I'm away, which is bound to happen?"

She drew away from and looked into his face. "Now that is a good idea. I was brought up with dogs in the family." Iffor just knew she was going to bring up the subject of the twins from the mission. He tried to think of something to say to avoid the subject, then he was saved by the bell, the doorbell.

"I'll go," Josie said and excitedly ran to the front door to receive their first visitor.

The hubbub of raised voices confirmed Iffor's worst fears: Blue Watch had arrived, complete with bulging cold bags, full of beer and steaks.

"We couldn't let you drink on your own, boss, and since you couldn't join us, we thought we would come to you; but don't worry, we'll be gone by midnight or sometime after. Weapons in the bedroom?" he asked.

"Yes, but put them on the floor please."

Josie came to Iffor, linking her arm through his. "Isn't this wonderful, having all our friends here?" Iffor smiled and nodded and just as he thought, it could have been worse, that fucking woman could be here, Auntie's voice called from the kitchen: "Let's have all the steaks in here please."

As the party got under way, Iffor was delighted and proud of the way Josie looked after their guests, the perfect hostess. He had been wondering how he could tell the team about Josie moving in with him, but here she was, the centre of attraction and everywhere at once, refilling glasses and plates and giving everyone the benefit of her dazzling smile.

Auntie had the kitchen table brought onto the lawn and loaded steaks, *Boereworse* sausage and chops and salad on it. Someone had thought to put as many beers into the fridge as they could, while Evil stood close to the fridge door watching anxiously as the stocks diminished.

The Colour Sergeant joined them. "Heard this was the only place to be on a Wednesday evening. I've got a case of Castle in the car—where do you want it?"

The doorbell rang again. "I'll get it!" Auntie shouted, and came back into the garden minutes later with the mine general manager in tow.

Iffor greeted him with a warm handshake. "Colonel, how good of you to come."

"I had to, dear boy. When Auntie phoned me and told me you were my new next-door neighbour, I had to come and welcome you."

"Neighbour!" Iffor exclaimed, "I didn't know."

"Yes, I've got the bungalow next door, a hundred yards away, but next door."

Iffor led the Colonel into the centre of the garden. "Let me introduce you to everyone. Gentlemen, gentlemen," he called for order. "We have a guest, Colonel Tweed, general manager of the mine and the man responsible for loaning us the Islander." From the team came various shouts of greeting, "Glad you could make it Harris."

"Good to see you again, Harris."

"What are you drinking, Harris?"

"I take it you've all met before," said Iffor.

"They're my drinking muckers when I can get down to the Moth club," Harris replied, "And by the way, my friends call me Harris." He took Iffor's arm and led him to a quieter corner of the garden. "I understand you had some success yesterday, a good cull as I hear it, or am I talking out of turn?"

"No," Iffor reassured him, "I imagine most of Kensington will know about it by now, and yes, we had a very good result. Nineteen dead, nineteen weapons recovered, and two prisoners who are now probably in Salisbury waiting for the government to decide whether to hang them as terrorists or exchange them to the British government for a couple of helicopters or a mobile field hospital."

"You've just lost me," Harris said.

"Our two prisoners," Iffor went on, "were IRA men, posing as priests and trying to keep out of the way of the British army, who were intent on ending their grubby little lives."

Their conversation was interrupted by Davy Jones, hand in hand with his chimp. "Fine bloody party this is, no hard boiled eggs and no more fruit left. Good to see you again Harris. I'll get down to the airfield first thing tomorrow to de-rig your aircraft."

"What did he mean?" asked Harris as they watched Davy and the ape wandering off in search of Auntie, in the hope of another banana.

"He had to rig the aircraft for dropping paratroopers and he supplied the parachutes. We jumped into the Lamumbwa valley."

Harris stared at him with a look of astonishment mingled with admiration. "You mean you and Blue Watch *parachuted* into the valley?"

"Yes, and Davy, it was the only way we could cut off their escape route. Oh, and if you haven't already heard, Father Sean was their leader. Pete Saxon killed him."

A vision of loveliness in a blue sari came and took Iffor's arm. "Excuse us Harris, the boys want to talk to him." She slid her hand down his arm and found his hand. "Thought I'd better change," she said, "you know how randy soldiers can get after a day in the bush."

"Good party boss," Evil grinned as only he could grin. "Glad you invited us—we don't often get the chance to drink with Josie, do we lads?" Mutters of approval came from the team.

"Let me have him to myself for a few days." She looked at Iffor, watching him blush furiously, "Then we'll have a proper party to celebrate our new home."

"News from the front?" Alvin asked.

"I'm driving up to New Epsom to meet with the C.O tomorrow morning. If I have anything important to tell you I'll call you in, otherwise I'll leave you in peace for a few days."

Aware that Iffor needed some well-earned rest before driving to New Epsom, Harry broke up the party around midnight, having first been assured by Iffor that he really didn't need an escort for his visit to the Colonel.

A little after six, Iffor slid out of bed and headed for the shower. The last thing he wanted was for Josie to wake and prepare breakfast, but as he finished shaving he could hear her in the kitchen. "Just tea and toast," he shouted. Back in the bedroom, she had laid out his uniform and put a duster over his shoes. As he dressed, she came in with his tea and toast. She sat on the bed beside him watching him eat. "When will you be back?" she asked.

"Just as soon as I can, but I want to call in at Ed's farm, then on to the Mission to check on the twins."

She left him to finish his meal but was waiting for him at the front door with a bunch of flowers from one of the vases. "Put these on Helen's grave and say hello for me." Then, to hide her tears she kissed him on his cheek and whispered, "Take care," and hurried back to the bedroom.

As he waited for the filling station on the edge of town to open at seven, he reflected on the previous evening: the impromptu party: meeting his neighbour, then taking his Josie to bed. I could get used to this, he mused. And in spite of recent tragedies, he realised he had never been happier.

At nine forty, he pulled up outside New Epsom Territorial Army drill hall.

Nine fifty-five he knocked on the Colonel's office door. The compulsory pause, then, "Come."

Iffor opened the door and stepped into a spacious office. Closing the door, he turned and saluted the man sitting behind the desk. The Colonel rose to his feet and walked around the desk, hand extended. "Iffor m'boy, well met, well met, come and sit down and make yourself comfortable." He indicated to the two large armchairs. "First, let me organise some tea." He opened the office door and shouted, "Serf, tea and stickies for two," then joined Iffor. "Tell me about yourself; ex-Airborne I see," eyeing Iffor's wings. The wings they both wore made them brothers under the sign of Pegasus, the Airborne Brethren.

"Yes Colonel; Sappers and infantry, British Army and Zambia Army."

"Now that is interesting," the Colonel said. "You're going to be very useful to us as this war progresses. Married, children?" he asked.

"No Colonel" Then he thought, best come clean, "But I'm sharing my bungalow with a girl who I'm rather fond of."

A knock at the door and a very young second Lieutenant came in with a tray and put it on the table between Iffor and the Colonel.

"Iffor, meet Rodney, my assistant adjutant." 'Alias' serf, Iffor thought, shaking the man's hand.

"That will be all, thank you," the Colonel said. "See that we are not disturbed." The young officer left.

"I'll be mother," and the Colonel poured the tea. "Help yourself to a sticky, the currant buns are good."

"Good of you to see me like this." Iffor cut a bun in two and spread butter over both halves. "I wanted the chance to give you my report face to face."

"Not at all, dear boy." The Colonel did the same, but added jam. "Meeting you here gives me a chance to come into town. I'm normally up front with the Battalion and my office is the tailgate of a Rover. I had a bath this morning for the first time in a couple of weeks."

Settled in his armchair, Iffor began his report, from the death of Ian Dix and his family, the massacre of the Abrahams family and Elias's death from the mine, up to the parachute drop onto the monastery.

The Colonel remained silent until Iffor had finished, making notes from time to time and putting his hand up to indicate a pause while he poured more tea.

"This chap Moses January, should I ask what has happened to him?"

"Ah, as part of the deal, I had to hand him over to the Selous Scouts for turning, and they in turn, are going to bring his son Douglas out of Zambia. I know I should have brought the prisoner up to Battalion headquarters to be interrogated by our own intelligence people, but I used my powers of detachment commander to do the deal with January and the Scouts."

"You didn't have powers of detachment commander," the Colonel looked serious. "Only I can grant that."

"It comes under the heading of A.B.I., Colonel."

The Colonel grinned, "Air Borne Initiative, good one Iffor, good one." The Colonel stood up, "Come over to the map, I'll show you our order of battle." He pointed a finger at the map. "My area of responsibility stretches from Faira in the east to Mwonza in the west, a front of some fifty miles or more, so as you can see, we are stretched very thin on the ground. Do you know the Faira area?"

"Very well Colonel. I spent my last three months with the Zambia Army in Faira, trying to stop ZAPU from infiltrating into Rhodesia and FRELIMO from infiltrating into Zambia."

The Colonel nodded thoughtfully. "And now to add to our problems, we've got these religious chaps, the Lenshina, causing trouble. Did you run into them on your travels?"

"We did indeed, Colonel. Up in Fort Jameson, my platoon ambushed and killed the woman we thought was their leader, Alice Chingola, but it turned out to be the local police special branch trying to infiltrate the Lenshina without telling us."

"Well fortunately," the Colonel said, as they returned to their armchairs, "Alice doesn't seem to be involved as yet."

"On the contrary, Colonel, Alice is now field commander of ZAPU in this region, with her tribe part of ZAPU and all their sins pardoned by the Zambia government."

The Colonel sat down heavily. "Are you sure?"

"Yes Colonel, it was in my report I sent up to you yesterday in code."

The Colonel went to the door and opened it. "Serf!" he shouted. The young officer came running along the corridor. "The report from Kensington, where is it?"

"Still being decoded, Colonel."

"Well, get it and bring it to me."

He lifted the lid of the teapot and looked inside. "Only enough for one cup, I'm afraid," and filled his cup. "Now, Iffor m'boy, I think the sooner I get you up here the better. With your knowledge of the area on the Zambia side of Faira and your knowledge of the Lenshina, you'll be invaluable to me."

Iffor knew the Colonel would be bound to try and get him up to New Epsom, so he had formulated his own plan and reasons why he should stay in Kensington.

"With respect Colonel, surely I will be more use with Blue Watch back in Kensington.

"The Battalion is stretched pretty thin as it is, and if you have to deploy a company back into the Lamumbwa valley because terrorists have been able to infiltrate into the area, you may well open the floodgates and allow more incursions."

"I appreciate what you're saying Iffor, but it is unlikely ZAPU will bulldoze another large group into the area. The risk to them would be too great. At present, they are sending small groups of two or three across and we are having some success killing them. If they sent a large force across and we engaged them, it would be a significant blow to them. And anyway, a large force would need time to re-org, recce and plan attacks on the farms and by then, we will probably have two rifle companies back in Kensington to deal with them."

Iffor countered, "They are already, very probably, sending spies down their line of communication to carry out recc'es. It's my guess that ZAPU high command in Zambia haven't yet realised their line of communication has been compromised. And anyway, when Alice gets to hear what we've done to the Lamumbwa group, she'll be hell-bent on revenge. She won't bother about planning or recc'es or escape routes. She will come mob-handed over the border at Mwonza and fall on the Lamumbwa valley like a plague of white ants."

"If that happens," the Colonel looked thoughtful, "if that happens," he repeated, "your force of what, eight men, ain't going to be much good, is it?"

Iffor changed tack, "What I have in mind, Colonel, is to continue showing the flag with routine patrols, fighting patrols and ambushes on their trail from Mwonza, and I would like to build a forward operating base at the site of De Witt's farm and fortify it. If my jackal, sorry, intelligence, tells me Alice is on her way, or if Mwonza is threatened, we can use the mine Islander to put us down on the farm landing strip. We can either defend De Witt's farm and meet Alice head on, or we can move up to Mwonza to support the company there if they are in trouble."

The Colonel was silent for a minute or so. "If you meet Alice and her tribe of what, thirty, forty men, we can't get to you for at least five hours. Even if helicopters are available, I've still got to get a sizable force together. What do you hope to achieve if you bring Alice to battle at your forward operating base?"

Iffor moved forward onto the edge of his armchair. "As I said before, the Lenshina don't bother with planning, they just barge straight in. They have no fear, they paint themselves with purple dye that protects them from our bullets. Apparently, the dye turns our bullets to water. So, with us fighting from prepared positions, we can inflict severe casualties and force them to go around us instead of over us, so more of their men will get lost in the bush. We should be able to reduce their force by about half."

"And your own casualties?" the Colonel asked.

"Probably fifty per cent."

"And you think those tactics will work?"

"They were used with some success in Korea." Iffor went on, "A forward defence location was pushed out about two hundred metres from the main line of defence and defended by about a platoon. It divided the attackers and disrupted command structure.

"It gave the Gloucesters a bit of breathing space at the Imjin River and the Middlesex used it with some success."

The Colonel was now interested, very interested. "And how will you prepare your defensive position?"

Iffor already had this planned in his head. "Sandbags and barbed wire from our own defence stores, pit props for overhead cover from the mine. Archie at Arc Angel farm will provide labour and a digger and my old friend Shadrak will put word around the villages that the De Witts have come back to haunt the place. That should keep the locals away."

"It's a good sound plan Iffor, but how do you know the terrorists will come down the Mwonza road? It would be safer for them to come through the bush."

"Because, Colonel, Alice doesn't stop to think or plan, she will take the easiest and the quickest route, the old Mwonza Road."

The Colonel settled back in his chair and closed his eyes. Without opening them, he said, "I've work to do, clear off there's a good chap and meet me for lunch at the 'Old Colonial'."

The 'Old Colonial' lived up to its name. Timber built balcony protruding from the wall, animal heads adorning the interior walls and waiters dressed in starched white uniforms. As Iffor approached the bar, he was aware of a similarly dressed officer, sitting on a bar stool watching as he made his way to the bar.

"You'll be Meredith, the Colonel told me to look out for you. I gather you're joining us for lunch."

Iffor noted the crown on the epaulettes. "Yes sir, right on both counts."

"Jack Francis, I command support at Mwonza. The Colonel suggested I should meet you."

Iffor took his hand. "Iffor," he said, then smiling at his own joke said, "but my friends call me Iffor." Now formally introduced, Iffor could use the man's Christian name. "D'you mind if we talk shop before the Colonel comes? I need to know more about your Orbat."

Jack nodded at an empty table. "I'll bring the beers over," he said.

Settled in his 'captain's chair', so typical of the hotel, he said, "What do you want to know?"

Iffor downed his beer in one and signalled to the hovering waiter for two more. "What do you have in the way of support weapons? I know you have three-inch mortars and Vickers, but how are they deployed?"

"Ah, we are a bit thin on the ground. I have three mortars, two supporting the companies here at New Epsom and one providing support for the protected villages in range of our base at Mwonza. As for my two Vickers, one is protecting the airstrip, and the other is keeping us safe from a massed attack at the police station we share with the police, as our base."

Iffor grinned sympathetically, "And there was I about to ask if we could have a mobile Vickers team down in my part of the world."

They stood up as the Colonel appeared. "I see you two have met, well done. Who's in the chair, I'm parched."

Lunch was something of an inquisition with both the Colonel and the Major anxious to learn more about Iffor's successes, whereas Iffor wanted to tell them about the tragedy of the Mission and Helen's death.

"I think, Colonel, you will agree that if we are to avoid another massacre in the Kensington area, we need a force of some description available on the ground."

"Quite right, m'boy, quite right. Now Iffor, you must try the 'prawns piri-piri', they really are delicious."

Iffor settled down to enjoy his meal. He had the Colonel's blessing to stay in Kensington; all he had to do now was persuade Blue Watch to stay in uniform for a couple more weeks.

It was after four before Iffor was able to get away, having first been introduced to the adjutant, Rupert Smithers, former Household Cavalry, who thought officers commissioned from the ranks could not possibly be 'proper chaps'. However, and reluctantly, he told Iffor he would be granted powers of detachment commander of the Kensington area and responsible for the soldiers being rotated on leave.

With a light and happy heart, he began his long drive south. Although the urge to drive straight to Kensington to be with Josie was strong, his sense of duty to visit Ed's farm and the Mission was stronger, or so he told himself.

He couldn't have chosen a better time to visit the graves. The sun was beginning to sink lower in the western sky and on the warm breeze he fancied he could hear Africans singing. The local stonemason had already added Helen's and young Jamie's names to the headstone, and a profusion of fresh flowers gave witness to the number of friends, both black and white who, like Iffor, had come to the graveside to say a few words or simply stand in silence before leaving their token of flowers.

Iffor stood and reflected; six deaths in one family, three of them his family. Had they simply been casualties of war, he could have accepted that, but to have been slaughtered in the name of revenge by a misguided priest... Iffor's thoughts were interrupted by Ed Dix who came and stood beside him.

"Now would be a very good time to promise Helen that you will never blame yourself," he said. "She would never have blamed you, so you must not spend your life blaming yourself for their deaths."

"Easier said than done, my friend, easier said than done." Iffor looked down over the Lamumbwa valley and its snaking river. "Know what Ed, this is the nearest I'll get to heaven, dead or alive."

Refusing the offer of a bed for the night from Ed, Iffor motored on to the Mission. He told himself it was important to check on the twins for Josie, and to see how the reconstruction work was coming along, but the mounting excitement at the thought of seeing Grace again made him aware of his real reason for the visit.

It was just getting dark when he pulled up outside the Mission hospital. Grace was on the veranda at a table eating her evening meal while scribbling notes on reports.

She looked up at him as he approached her. "What are you doing here?"

"I know how much you detest eating supper alone so I thought I'd come and join you, d'you mind?"

"Thursday night is fish and chip night; is that all right for you?"

"Wonderful!"

She called to her chef: "Fish and chips for the Lieutenant and a few more chips for me, please. I can't let you eat on your own," she said.

She talked all through the meal, mainly about the reconstruction of the Mission, about the various families presumed dead who had returned, and finally, without prompting from Iffor, the twins. They moved to the wicker sofa at the end of the veranda.

"So far as we know, only the girl survived; she was uninjured. The boy," she gestured with her hands, "who knows? We didn't find his body. They may have taken him with them or perhaps a wild animal took him, we just don't know. She is here in the hospital if you would like to see her; she really is very beautiful."

"Seen one, seen 'em all," Iffor muttered.

"Now," she said, "tell me about the battle. We watched you parachuting in; we guessed what you were up to. Surely, you must have heard us cheering!"

"Was that what it was?" Iffor lied. "Yes, we heard you."

Iffor recounted the battle to her, watching dismay turn to anger when he told her of Father Sean's treachery.

"Is he dead?" she asked.

"They're all dead," Iffor told her. "You can tell your people the terrorists can't hurt them again. Grace, had I taken casualties, I would have brought them here, but I couldn't warn you because the phone isn't safe."

"I understand," she said. "I'm just glad none of your men were wounded. We liked them very much."

It was quite dark now, and from the veranda they could see the glow from the cooking fires outside the huts up in the residential area. A baby cried, and as if in answer, a hyena laughed. The bush was settling down for the night.

"Drink?" Grace interrupted his thoughts. "Only Cape Brandy I'm afraid; your man Hennie the South African left it for me."

"Cape Brandy will do just fine," Iffor answered, "but only a large one."

She unwound her long legs and glided gracefully into her office, to return minutes later with a bottle and two glasses. "You'll stay the night," she asked, but it sounded more like a command.

"If the guest lodge is available," Iffor sipped his brandy with care and briefly thought back to his friend Big Ox in the Zambian army, who would down his Cape Brandy in one without wincing. The same Big Ox who, when his signaller became tired after carrying the radio set for a few miles, would tuck the signaller complete with radio under his arm and carry them both for a couple of miles.

"Yes," she said, sniffing and savouring the aroma of the brandy, even though, in Iffor's view, it smelt like a Royal Marine's body secretion after a night ashore in Malta.

"Yes," she repeated, "it is available but there's no shower, you'll have to use the shower in my room."

Iffor muttered, "That won't be necessary," but he wasn't very forceful.

"I will want to examine your injury, your old wound after you've showered. We'll finish our drinks and take the bottle back with us."

Iffor knew he was being led like a lamb to the slaughter and thought back to his section commander's course in the Brecons: "There are times when what we've taught you won't get you out of trouble and surrender is inevitable," the instructor had told them. "In which case, surrender in style, dignity and good grace and make the best of it." This was that moment, Iffor told himself, and followed her to her bungalow.

He woke with the sun shining into his face. He felt her beside him and turned towards her. Her eyes were still closed though she wasn't asleep; the sheet covered her to the waist revealing majestic breasts. Only a Zulu could have breasts like that, he told himself.

She had followed him into the shower and insisted on washing him. All the instincts and the lessons she had been taught as a young girl, brought up to please her Zulu warrior, came to the fore. In moments, she changed from a sophisticated African doctor to a young Zulu maiden intent on ravishing the man of her choice. Her cries mingled with his when he couldn't decide whether he was experiencing pain or ecstasy. Overnight, she had become a female Jekyll and Hyde, and Iffor, watching a smile appear on her face, had enjoyed every moment of it.

He didn't stop for breakfast, there wasn't time; he'd made the mistake of sharing his morning shower with her. Instead, he drove off to Ed's farm; he could scrounge a bacon sandwich there from Joy.

He drove slowly back to Kensington; he had to get his story right for Josie. Keep it simple, he told himself. He would start by telling her about the twins and the surviving girl, then he would tell how he went on a tour of inspection of the rebuilt huts and finally fell into bed in the guest lodge. He hadn't really been unfaithful, he kept telling himself. He wasn't married or engaged to Josie, they were just good friends, very good friends.

As it happened, quite typical of Josie, she asked no questions apart from the fate of the twins. She trusted Iffor and knew he would tell her about his trip when he was ready. For now, she had to feed him, he would probably want to take her to bed after lunch, then he was hers for the whole weekend. God, how she adored him.

PART SIXTEEN

A good fire trench will give room to fire your weapon and protection from the enemy.

JOSIE WAS RIGHT. After lunch, Iffor suggested a lie down on the bed. "To help digest our food," he explained.

Mid-afternoon and Iffor was awakened by the sound of a telephone ringing, quite puzzled until Josie, sprawled across him, lifted her head. "That's our phone," she said. "It's in the lounge. I'll get it, it's probably Auntie."

She walked back into the bedroom quite naked, bringing thoughts of his night with Grace back to him, thoughts he was trying to forget.

"Yes, that was Auntie, trying out our new phone. They put it in yesterday; apparently, you are 'defence priority'."

She got back on to the bed and snuggled up to him. "What shall we do this evening?" She answered her own question: "How about a night at home? Just you, me and the radio, some sandwiches and a couple of bottles of Cape Red."

"Darling girl, that will be paradise."

"Good," she said, prising herself away from him, "Then you can tell me all about your trip to New Epsom and the twin." Something Iffor was not keen to discuss.

In the cool of the evening, they sat in their very own garden—no Auntie to disturb them—listening to Radio Rhodesia forces network. The music was good, and Iffor was able to listen to the news bulletins.

She seemed always to know what to wear for the occasion. This time it was a floral skirt and one of his shirts, knotted under her breasts.

She seemed to take little interest in what he told her about the trip until he mentioned the Mission. "Tell me more about the twins," she said, "The boy, do you think he survived?"

Trying to let her down gently, Iffor said, "It's just possible that one of the African women grabbed the child when the massacre began and ran off into the bush with him. Even now, they may be being cared for in some African village."

"Oh, Iffor, do you really think so?"

"Anything is possible. I'll tell you what," he said, anxious to change the conversation, "when we start patrolling again next week, we'll put the word out around the villages that we are looking for an Anglo-Indian baby; we'll offer a reward."

She beamed happily at him. "And can we still go to the Mission on Sunday to see the girl?"

Iffor had forgotten his promise to take her to the Mission, but he and Josie would have to come face to face sometime with Grace; it might as well be sooner rather than later. "Yes of course we can, we'll go into town in the morning and get some flowers for Helen."

"And little Jamie," she said. "And I'll get some clothes for the twin."

Conversation was interrupted by the voice on the radio: "Earlier this week, a daring raid was made by Rhodesian paratroopers who were dropped into the Lamumbwa valley. Nineteen terrorists were killed with no casualties suffered by our own forces."

"The boys will be thrilled to hear they are now paratroopers," Iffor said, "Especially Davy."

He was up and about before Josie was awake, and able to prepare a breakfast of toast and coffee to have on their small patio. "Sorry," she said, "I should have been up before you, but it was so nice lying in bed listening to you in the kitchen."

"And it was so nice for me knowing you are relaxing," he said, pouring the coffee. "You've been through an awful lot lately." As he spoke his conscience began to haunt him. It wasn't my fault, he told himself, Grace seduced me, she took advantage of me.

The phrase 'lamb to the slaughter' came to mind again, making him feel even worse, and he wandered off for a shower.

Saturday morning in Kensington was normally a relaxed, happy and friendly affair, but that morning was different. There were more people about, more children in the street and fewer men carrying weapons. As they drove through town to Auntie's hotel, people waved and Iffor caught the occasional, "Well done."

"You're responsible for this," Josie said and slid across the bench seat to be closer to him, "You and your band of idiots."

"God woman, you don't know how right you are, only total idiots would have done what we did."

He left Josie with Auntie, having secured his pass into town with the promise of staying for lunch, and headed for the sanctuary of Boons bar. A few beers would restore his faith and confidence in himself. The Askari at the door saluted, "Good morning, sir!"

Although not in uniform, Iffor acknowledged the salute with a nod and inspected him. Having walked around him, he faced the man. "Good turnout," he said, "very good turnout," and walked into the bar.

The bar was in turmoil, with men shouting at one another and in particular at Davy who seemed to be the centre of things. His ape sat in his usual seat, extending his hand hopefully for a coin to anyone coming close to him.

"Gentlemen, gentlemen!" shouted Billy, "Here's the man who can tell us."

The bar went silent. "Davy here has been trying to tell us all about the Lamumbwa raid as if he was there," Billy yelled.

Iffor played to his audience. He ordered his beer and one for Davy, poured and drank it, ordered another, then turned to face the assembled crowd.

"He was," he said simply. "He jumped in with us, he jumped in front of me, I went out last."

The bar erupted, causing the Matabele to come into the bar in case of trouble. Billy waved him away. "Never doubted you for a minute," he told Davy. "Have a beer and give that fucking ape an egg."

When calm was restored, Iffor told them as much as he could about the raid, including the priest's part and saying simply that the priest was killed during the battle. Then, he warned them all to remain vigilant. "They'll be back," he told them, "And looking for blood."

Taking his beer with him, he joined Davy and the ape at Davy's table. "I don't want you giving away too much information," he told him. "We have a saying in Blue Watch, 'If you don't want your enemy to find out, don't tell your friends'."

"I understand," Davy said, "Mum's the word."

Pete Saxon joined them. "Auntie told me you would probably be here," he said. "Ready for another?" He called across to Billy, "Three Castles, please Billy, and an egg if he's allowed."

Iffor was anxious to hear about the two prisoners Pete had delivered to Salisbury, but realised he couldn't discuss it in the pub. Instead he said, "Good trip?"

"Couldn't have been better," Pete said, downing his Castle in one. "God, but I needed that."

"Another?" Iffor asked.

"No thanks, just popped in to let you know I was back and to suggest a council of war on Monday. Your office nine sharp okay for you?"

"Fine," said Iffor, "I'll warn the Colour."

As he made his way back to Auntie's, an idea began to expound in his mind. Sooner or later, soldiers would be coming back into Kensington and would start boasting having taken part in the Lamumbwa raid. He remembered when his squadron had jumped into Guernsey on exercise. Being last to jump out of the Beverly, he had missed the D.Z. and landed in the sea, to be rescued by the local lifeboat under the watchful gaze of several hundred holidaymakers on the quayside. That night they hit the town, where his friends introduced him in the first pub they went to as the guy who had landed in the sea, only to be told by the landlord, "You're the fourth tonight."

Since it was unlikely the army would recognise the efforts of Blue Watch for the monastery battle, he decided he would prepare a certificate for the team, acknowledging their part in the battle. Feeling quite pleased with himself, he entered the hotel to face Auntie and the feast he knew she would have prepared.

After a typical Saturday curry lunch, Josie took him off to buy flowers for the grave. As they walked, she slipped her hand into his. It felt good; he acknowledged her gesture with a squeeze and was quite happy walking hand in hand through the town with her, though hoping they wouldn't meet up with any of Blue Watch.

Arriving home in the late afternoon, loaded with what Josie referred to as 'essentials', along with a dozen red roses for the grave—"Helen's favourite flowers," Josie explained—they were met with a note pinned to the door: "Drinks and nibbles, my place seven o'clock." It was signed, 'Harris'. Iffor looked at his watch; time enough to relax in the garden with the newspaper, while Josie busied herself in the kitchen putting the 'essentials' into their proper cupboards. She had it in mind to leave plenty of time for a leisurely bath, time to choose and dress in her most devastating sari, so she could turn up at the Tweeds telling her hosts that she hoped she wasn't dressed too casually for the gathering.

The evening at the Tweeds' bungalow gave Iffor the chance to meet Harris's deputy and the senior pilot. Both good sound chaps, Iffor concluded, and both eager to help whenever he needed their help. "That chap Davy was a godsend for us, rigging the aircraft for your para drop," the pilot told him. "I couldn't believe it when we landed without him; it didn't dawn on me that he would actually jump in with you."

"It wasn't my idea," Iffor told him. "He just put up a bloody good case and I was glad to have him along."

"I'd like to meet him for a beer or two," the pilot said.

"He drinks at Boons bar," Iffor told him, "But whatever you do, don't get involved in a game of spoof with that fucking ape of his, he'll clean you out."

Leaving the pilot looking a little confused and bewildered, he went in search of Harris. He needed to get his help to establish his forward operating base.

Finding a quiet spot in the garden, Iffor told Harris of his plans. The ex-colonel listened intently. "Can I suggest," he said, "that instead of pit props as uprights, you use angle iron posts sunk in concrete. They can't be nicked by the locals, and if we drill corresponding holes in the uprights and pit props, you can carry the pit props with you in your trailer when you go up country, and build and dismantle your defence position as and when. You'll only need twelve pit props; overhead cover you can get from trees in the area."

"What a bloody good idea," Iffor responded. "When can I collect them?"

"Phone me Monday. Now, if you'll excuse me, I'm going to chat up that gorgeous woman of yours."

Sunday morning brought a mixture of excitement and sadness to Josie—excitement that she was going to see the twin, sadness that she had a dozen red roses to lay on Helen's grave. She had decided she would go to the grave alone; that way she could have a chat to Helen and bring her up to date with all the local gossip and the wonderful news that she had moved in with Iffor in their bungalow.

Although the threat of a terrorist attack had diminished, Iffor still kept to his standard operating procedures, taking with them his Carbine and five magazines, plus his Brno pistol. He had already made his mind up that he would teach Josie to use the Astra he had loaned to Helen, and pull rank on her to ensure she carried it at all times. For the terrorists, to kill Josie would be sweet revenge indeed.

The drive to Ed's farm was sheer enjoyment: clear blue sky, the sun not yet warm enough to bother them. She would sit close to the door of the pick-up, deep in thought; then she would move along the bench seat, hold his arm, and kissing him on his cheek would say, "I love you Lieutenant Meredith," and move back to the door to enjoy the breeze on her face and in her hair.

Ed and Joy came out to greet them as they drove into the compound. "You'll stay for lunch," he told them. "We'll have a braai."

Joy took Josie's arm and led her away, deep in conversation, leaving Ed to share a beer with Iffor in the shade of the veranda. "Any news that might concern me?" Ed asked.

"There's a rather nasty lady called Alice, who, with her tribe, is causing some concern up north. If she decides to come down to our part of the world, we could have problems, so keep your powder dry and a shot in your locker. Oh, and tell me at once if any of your chaps see an African painted purple."

"You might get to see the new owner of the monastery," Ed said, decapitating two more beers. "When you phoned to say you were coming, I called the Abbot and suggested he should meet you."

"Tell me about him."

"Well, he's about sixty-five, Polish, speaks good English and has a tattoo on his forearm, a number."

"As in concentration camp number?" Iffor suggested.

"Yes, I believe so. The four 'brothers' he has with him are also tattooed."

"Where did they come from?" Iffor asked. "How did they get here?"

Ed struggled for a moment with his emotions. "Did you read about the massacre we had just outside Umtali a few months ago? Twelve missionaries, their wives and children, were murdered by terrorists. The wives were all raped before being bayoneted, probably watched by their husbands, before they were shot or bayoneted. The children all had their throats cut. Well, the school and the clinic the missionaries ran, was in the grounds of the monastery occupied by our Abbot and his chums. After the massacre, they felt they couldn't live there with the memory of what had happened, so they packed up and started wandering around Rhodesia looking for a new home. They were up at Mwonza when they heard what had happened here and came straight down in their battered old Holden Estate car. I think they've claimed squatters' rights. They stopped off to ask for some milk and meat on their way through, and that's when I met the Abbot. They stayed for a couple of beers and that's how I got to know more about them. They seem a decent enough bunch."

Joy and her houseboy started preparing the *braaivleis*. "We'll eat early," Joy explained, "Josie's anxious to get to the Mission to see the twin."

Leaving Ed helping his wife prepare lunch, Iffor went in search of Josie. He found her at the graveside, sitting legs tucked underneath her, gazing out over the valley. He came up behind her and put his hand on her shoulder. She took his hand and rubbed it against her cheek. "You know," she spoke softly, "we really couldn't have chosen a better spot for Helen; it's perfect."

Iffor helped her to her feet. "Time for lunch," he told her, and kissed her lightly on the mouth. "Then on to the Mission."

As they walked slowly back to the bungalow, he put an arm around her slim waist, pulling her close. "My, my," she said, "you are getting romantic."

Try guilt, he thought.

They sat at the round family table, set out on the patio under a giant sun umbrella. Joy had obviously been taking lessons from Auntie. The table seemed to groan under the weight of a mountain of bushbuck steaks and chops, *Boereworse* and salads, and Joy's pride and joy, her homemade wines.

"What do you think?" she asked, as Iffor took his first tentative sip.

"Wonderful, excellent," he said, trying to smile through the pain, "Good stuff." And he decided he could forgive Hennie for forcing his Cape Spirit onto him.

The sound of an abused car engine announced the Abbot's arrival. "God!" Ed exclaimed, "I hope he hasn't brought the brothers with him; the invite was only for him." The Abbot was alone; mid-sixties, well-built, bronzed from the sun, wearing shorts, homemade sandals, a shirt that had once been a sack, and a wide-brimmed hat.

"Thought I'd dress up, since this was a formal invite," he said. "Left the robes at home; Jacob," he said, extending his hand to Iffor, "No point telling you my surname; you wouldn't remember it and you certainly couldn't pronounce it. Mind if I sit down?" he asked, looking at his hostess.

Further conversation from Jacob was out of the question until he had finally demolished what was left of the steaks and *Boereworse*. Iffor had visions of him going back to the monastery and regurgitating the food to feed his brothers.

"Tell us about yourself," Iffor said.

"Not much to tell, really. I was ordained just as the war started and served in the Polish army. I was eventually rounded up and sent to Auschwitz with several hundred thousand Jews, where somehow, I survived. While I was there, I vowed if I lived through it, I would find a corner of the world as far away from Europe as I possibly could, and eventually, my wanderings brought me to what is now Zambia and found a commune in Faira that recruited only from concentration camps. We carried our credentials with us," he said, showing a tattooed number on his forearm. He went on, "The Order embraced a vow of poverty; we had to fend for ourselves, something I was well used to."

"I remember the commune well," Iffor said, "I brought a medical team up to you once, after Frelimo had crossed the border and raided you. What happened to the commune? How did you get here?"

"We went bust, skint, flat-broke. Every time we got crops ready for reaping, either Frelimo or our local terrorists or the Angolan rebels came and helped themselves, so myself and my four friends crossed the Luangwa, and came south through the bush. He paused and added, "I don't think we've got a passport between us. Anyway," he went on, we knew we had a small commune in Umtali so that's where we headed. We'd only been there a couple of months when the terrorists attacked and killed the missionaries who were running the school and clinic. We were working in the fields when it happened; we couldn't help. Well, what we saw that day just about destroyed whatever faith we had in our fellow man, so we pinched the school station wagon, and having toured Rhodesia, headed back for Zambia. We were in Mwonza when we heard about the Lamumbwa monastery so here we are. This is bloody good wine."

Joy beamed with pleasure. "I make it myself," she said,

"Bloody creep," Iffor muttered, loud enough for Josie to kick him under the table.

"You'll have to tell me your secret," Jacob poured himself another glass. "The monastery is ideal for wine making, with its underground vaults. We're thinking of going into the wine making business and kicking the vow of poverty crap into touch." Turning to Iffor, he said, "I'm looking forward to meeting your chaps. I heard a lot about them when we were in Mwonza."

A vision of Mad Harry and Jacob getting together caused Iffor to tremble slightly and spill his wine; he made a mental note to keep them as far apart as possible.

Reluctantly, very reluctantly, Iffor took his leave of Ed and Joy and headed for the Mission. They drove in silence, both for different reasons: she thinking about happier times when Helen was alive; he wondering what reception they would get from Grace. She knew they were coming; that would help.

As they got closer to the Mission, he felt excitement growing within him, remembering his night of passion with Grace, a night unlike anything he had ever experienced before, a night, she had promised him they would consummate again.

Iffor parked the pick-up outside the hospital and they climbed the two or three steps onto the veranda. An orderly came out to greet them. "The doctor will be out shortly," she said, "Can I get you anything?"

"The baby, the twin; can I see her please?" Josie could hardly contain herself, like an excited child at Christmas.

The orderly smiled, "Of course, I'll just go and fetch her for you."

Iffor led Josie to a wicker armchair and sat her down. "While you're cooing over the baby, I'm going up to the community centre to see how things are coming along; shan't be long." But she didn't hear him; her eyes were fixed firmly on the orderly carrying a bundle in her arms.

Making his way up to the community centre, Iffor found what he had expected. The afternoon church service was over; men, women and children were dressed in Sunday best, and now was the time to get together, a time for the men to enjoy a drink. Iffor joined them and a two-pint traditional plastic container full to the brim with African Chibuku beer was thrust into his hand, as he was surrounded by happy smiling faces. He had drunk Chibuku before, so he knew what was coming: warm, a texture like cold milky, lumpy porridge and tasting of naafi tea. A woman with a fire bucket full of the stuff hovered nearby ready to 'top him up' after every mouthful. This was a mistake, he told himself. Everyone was so pleased to see him, they would keep him drinking until he fell into a coma, which wouldn't be long. He looked for a way out. Salvation came by way of the mission 'policeman' in his uniform of shorts, boots and puttees and blue shirt. Armed with only a truncheon, his task was to deal with minor squabbles and infringement of the rules. "No firearms allowed in here, sir," he said, pointing to Iffor's Brno. "You'll have to leave."

Feigning bitter disappointment, Iffor handed back his beer and left, to the howls of protest from the drinkers.

"I'll be back," he told them, "I'll be back," and whispering his gratitude to the policeman, he left and made his way back down to the hospital.

The girls were sharing a pot of tea from a tray on the coffee table between their wicker armchairs. Josie was still holding and cooing at the baby while Grace, looking thoroughly bored, sat back in her chair, completely relaxed with long ebony legs stretched out before her. He kissed Grace on the cheek, as friends do. She touched his cheek as he did so. Her smell and touch were electrifying. He drew back, holding her gaze longer than he should, hoping that Josie wouldn't notice, but she was too concerned with the baby. "Grace says we can have the baby to stay for a weekend. You don't mind, do you?"

"'Course not. Have we got a name for 'baby'?" he asked.

Grace, still looking into Iffor's face, said, "The nurses still call her Helen's baby, since Helen had all but adopted her and her brother."

"Why not call her Helen?" Iffor said softly, quite pleased with himself. "I'm sure Helen wouldn't object."

Grace suddenly took an interest. "Now that is a good idea." Laughing, she said, "Trust a man to come up with something we women should have thought of. 'Helen' it is. Iffor, I'll expect you next Friday to collect her, sorry, to collect Helen."

Iffor was already planning a trip to Battalion with an overnight stay at the Mission. "I'll be here," he said.

Anxious to get back to Kensington before dark, they took their leave. Reluctantly, Josie handed the baby back to the nurse. "See you next weekend," she cooed, "then I can really spoil you."

The drive home was filled with plans for the coming weekend. "We will have to buy a cot," she told him, "And Auntie and I will have to go shopping for baby clothes, and we will need a pram." She hugged his arm, "Oh, Iffor, isn't life wonderful?"

Monday morning Iffor held his council of war with Pete, the Colour, Josie to take notes, and a very subdued Blue Watch still smelling of alcohol.

"Pete," he began, "how did your reception go when you took your prisoners to Salisbury?"

"Great! They stuck our two friends in the top security wing of Salisbury Central Prison, and I did the rounds of briefing various departments. To say that they were all impressed when I told them a group of fifty and sixty-year-old part-time soldiers parachuted onto an enemy camp and defeated a group twice their strength, was the understatement of all time. Oh, and they were impressed by my efforts to the extent that I now outrank you, my friend."

"Tell me about the prisoners," Iffor asked. "What's happened to them?"

"They had the choice," Pete said, "Reveal all to the Special Branch team flying out from U.K to interrogate them, with a view to them being sent back to UK, but only if the information given was useful to British security forces. Or staying in Rhodesia and having a breakfast meeting with the hangman. 'Singing like Canaries', was the expression being used to describe them when I left."

"Colour, anything to say about our mission?"

"Don't pull a stunt like that again," the Colour said. "We might not be so lucky next time."

"Which brings me to the point of this meeting, chaps. I think there will be a next time, and with respect, Colour, since we will undoubtedly be outnumbered in any future engagement, it will be the unthinkable 'stunt' that will win the day for us. Here's the current situation as I see it: Terrorists are coming over the border, but only in small groups, two or three men; they lose themselves in the community until they have sufficient numbers to start causing mayhem. They probably haven't bothered sending a large force into the Kensington area because they already had a force there, at the monastery. The larger groups of terrorists seem to be content to take on the army, sapping its strength and keeping it away from the white communities, leaving these white communities open to attack.

"But we now have an added dimension—Alice Chingola. As field commander of ZAPU, she will have to prove her worth in the field at some time, and when that happens, she will cross the border mob-handed with her own tribe of fanatics and hit targets closest to her crossing point." He stood, crossed the room and pointed to the map. "Mwonza, Arc Angel Farm, North Road Farm, or Kensington itself.

"I intend to construct a forward operating base at Long Acre farm, from which we can support Mwonza if they are attacked, or we can blunt their march on the farming communities. It is unlikely we will be able to defeat them, but we can cause them to go around us instead of over us, and with luck reduce their fighting strength and confuse their command structure."

Iffor sat down again, "Questions so far?"

"Do we have a plan 'B', a fall back plan?" the Colour asked.

"We do, but it's against all military logic. We divide our force."

Bob threw up his hands in mock horror.

Iffor continued: "Dividing our force will force Alice to divide her force. We'll put the gun team up on the kopje, where they were before. They wait until Alice makes her frontal attack on our command post, then open up on her flank. She will have to send some of her force to deal with the gun. The gun team will hold on as long as possible, then withdraw to the river where we will have prepared another defensive position."

"They'll catch us and overwhelm us before we reach the river," the Colour commented.

"Then we'll just have to pull a stunt to slow them down..." Iffor replied.

"...We leave in the position some goodies, ration packs, blankets, etc., and a satchel charge filled with nails and bolts and naafi cutlery and a pound of plastic with a short fuse. That should slow them down, plus we'll be supporting you from our position. We will then fight on until it looks as if we are going to be overrun; then we'll do a fighting withdrawal back to you at the river. We will also leave a satchel charge. We'll have the Champ cammed up on the other side of the river; survivors can try and make it back to Archie's farm."

Iffor paused, letting his ideas sink in, and said, "Has anyone got any better ideas?"

The Colour remained silent. Mad Harry stood up, "Does this mean we occupy this forward operating base full time?"

"No, we'll carry on with our routine patrols at irregular intervals and rely on Mwonza to tell us when we can expect Alice. Then, gentlemen, we go like hot snot to try and beat her to Long Acre Farm."

"Do I get a role in this adventure?" Pete asked.

"Yes, you and your boys boost the defences of the farms, and set up road blocks to defend Kensington. If the Lenshina get past us, it's up to you to stop them."

Harry stood up again. "How can you be certain the Lenshina are going to come straight down the old Mwonza Road? It would be safer for them to simply infiltrate through the bush and avoid us."

"If they do that," Iffor replied, "Alice will be forever looking over her shoulder, knowing we'll be after them, and remember, the Lenshina are religious fanatics, convinced our bullets will turn to water when they hit their purple dye. No, Alice will want to defeat us before she hits the farms. I'm convinced she'll give us warning when she's on her way, to try and lure us into her killing ground. She'll probably hit Mwonza first, then us. Remember, they can't simply punch their way through the army at New Epsom—that would bring them onto the Lamumbwa Plains with sparse cover. Our aircraft would tear them to pieces. No, they'll take advantage of the thick bush west of the Great North Road, using the Old Mwonza Road or the Mwonza game trail, both of which converge at Long Acre Farm, where we'll be waiting."

Iffor began to conclude his meeting. "News from Battalion is they ain't coming home just yet, but they are sending the sick, lame and lazy back for a rest, and they will come under my command; but my orders are to send them back to the front as soon as their leave is over. I now have powers of detachment commander which means I can hire and fire."

"But you told us you had those powers when you pressed us into service," Evil said.

"I lied," Iffor grinned and stood up. "Harry, take the boys downstairs and give the Champ a little TLC, then clean the weapons. I will be inspecting them. Oh, and Harry, you can assume the rank of sergeant with immediate effect."

Alone with the Colour Sergeant, Iffor said, "Well, what do you think?"

"Well, it's good to have a sound plan rather than just carrying out routine patrols, and if we do run into trouble in the bush, it's nice to know we have a defensive position to fall back on. Now, tell me about our 'defensive position', and where do I get 'satchel charges' from?"

"The position will be a trench with protection on all sides, using pit props. By definition, a fire trench will give you room to fire your weapon and give protection from enemy fire. It will have overhead cover from the sun and a grenade trench dug around the main trench, so any grenades landing in the position can be simply dropped over the side. As for the satchel charges, we make 'em: fill a small pack with nuts and bolts and stones; wrap a pound of plastic around a primer; stick in a number twenty- seven detonator and six inches of safety fuse with a percussion ignitor on the end, and 'hey presto', one satchel charge."

"I know we haven't any explosives in our magazine, but I've got the keys to the Pioneer Platoon stores, they've got all sorts of goodies in there," the Colour said. "Shall we take a peek this afternoon?"

Alone with Josie, he planned his day. He needed to speak to Jack Francis at Mwonza and arrange a visit. He had in mind trying to get a mobile mortar team into one of the protected villages in the area, and closer to Long Acre farm, hopefully, within range. He also needed to phone the mine, and the Scouts to see how Moses was doing. "Then, light of my life," he told Josie, "you and I, and Bob and Pete will enjoy a couple of beers and some rare beef sandwiches at the Elephant."

He began to write a rough draft of a certificate of recognition for the Lamumbwa raid.

Between mouthfuls of roast beef, Iffor told the others of his progress that morning, "The mine say we can collect the uprights and props and cement whenever we want, so Bob, tomorrow morning that will be your job. Take a couple of the team as escort, use the three tonner. The Selous Scouts are delighted with the information Moses is giving them and his son should be on his way to UK later this week, and Digger is having more specialist treatment in South Africa, but he should be back with us soon."

"I've never actually been in here before," the Colour said, as he unlocked the door of the bunker. The sign on the door read 'Pioneer Platoon Keep Out'. "I shouldn't be surprised if it's booby trapped." They stepped inside, and Bob switched the light on. Iffor could feel his pulses racing; he was in familiar surrounds, a store full of explosives. "It's all here," he said, "P.E Number four, plastic explosives to you; detonators; cordtex, detonating cord to you; safety fuse."

"I know what that is," the Colour interrupted.

Iffor ignored him—he was in his element. "Percussion ignitors; trip flares; Claymore Mines, and joy of joy," he could hardly contain himself, "Beehives, six Beehives!"

"I'm really confused now," the Colour said, "What the fuck's a beehive, apart from the obvious?"

"A Beehive, my friend, is a fiendish device for blasting holes in the ground. Looking like a small beehive, it stands on its legs and blasts a steel plug into the ground to a depth of about six feet. You can then either lower a charge into the hole and detonate it, thereby loosening the earth, making it easy to shovel away; or we can simply pour concrete into the hole and sink our steel uprights into position. We shan't need any help from the farm; we can construct our defensive position ourselves."

"The boys will be ecstatic when I tell them," the Colour muttered.

Iffor hurried back to his office, fired up by his discoveries in the Pioneer Platoon stores. It had been his intention to send Blue Watch out on a routine patrol under command of Mad Harry on Wednesday, but now he realised he must get out onto the area himself for a recce of the De Witt's farm. Suddenly, he felt time was not on his side. He would take half the team out on Wednesday, back on Thursday; then up to Mwonza to visit Support Company on Friday, stopping overnight at the Mission to collect baby Helen. The thought of seeing Grace again sent a thrill of anticipation and excitement through him, and he hated himself.

PART SEVENTEEN

At night, our first line of defence, the trip flare backed up with the Claymore.

HARRY HAD ALREADY EXERCISED the authority his new rank gave him, by giving the team the afternoon off. "To celebrate my promotion," he explained to Iffor. "They'll be on parade tomorrow eight sharp."

Josie came into his office. "The railway station phoned; they're holding a package for you."

"Good, I've been expecting it. Shall we knock off early? I'll drop you at Auntie's and go on to the station to collect it, and I need to pop into the hospital while I'm down that way. I've half a good idea."

Having dropped Josie at the hotel, and collected his package from the station, Iffor found Doctor Van De Werwe in his office. "I need your help Doctor, we've been very lucky in getting our casualties back here to the hospital in time. But next time we may not have the luxury of an aircraft being available."

"What do you have in mind?" the doctor asked, pouring the tea.

"What I've got in mind is asking you to provide a decent medical kit. All we've got is a bag full of bandages, and everyone carries morphine in the field. But I need some kit that will keep a man alive until we can get him back here or to the Leper Mission, Doctor."

"Somebody will have to be taught how to use the kit," the doctor replied.

"I agree, Doctor, and since my lads, being firemen, already have advanced first aid, that shouldn't be too difficult."

The doctor was silent for a few moments. "It's a very good idea. Send your chap down to me tomorrow and we'll make a start."

Iffor parked the pick-up outside the hotel, intending to beep his horn for Josie to come, but a cold Castle in Auntie's garden beckoned to him and he went inside.

Sitting at a table in the garden, in deep conversation with Josie, was Grace. "I had to come into town for some drugs," she explained, "and thought I'd stay the night, if you can put me up."

"'Course we can," Josie said. "You'll be our very first guest, and baby Helen will be our second guest, when Iffor collects her."

Auntie appeared with the cold Castle Iffor was longing for. "You'll stay for dinner." This wasn't a request, and Iffor was quite happy to say, "Yes please." The more people there were in the garden, Iffor reasoned, the less chance of Grace getting him to herself. He'd just have to take his chances when they got back to the bungalow.

Relaxing in his chair, savouring his third or fourth beer, Iffor watched the two women in his life. Josie, petite, practical, with the delicate colouring of a beautiful orchid—she was the ideal mate for him. Grace, who he knew was watching him through her dark sunglasses—a predator, looking like a sleek black panther, recently fed.

They were engaged in a pretty pointless conversation about babies. Pointless, because Josie would look after the child in her own way, the Indian way; pointless, because Grace was most certainly not the kind of woman to have children. Her life would be devoted to the conquest and the bedding of poor idiots like himself, he mused, and looking at Josie, he told himself, she was his choice; he and Grace would have to part company.

He beckoned to Godfry for another beer. He'd tell her when he visited her on Friday, or, better still, when he left her on Saturday.

To Iffor's profound relief, when they got back to the bungalow after Auntie's feast, Grace excused herself and went to bed. "Much as I would love to stay up and chat to you two," she said, "but I've got to make an early start to be back for surgery. I'll be gone when you wake up."

"She really is very lovely," Josie said as they snuggled up in bed. Iffor rolled over, sprawling across her. He looked down into her face, her hair cascading about the delicate pink pillow. "So are you my Indian princess, so are you?"

As Iffor walked into the drill hall next morning with Josie, he was amazed to hear Harry's voice: "Blue Watch, Atten-shun!" He saluted. "Blue Watch on parade and ready for your inspection sir."

Iffor returned the salute, "Thank you Sergeant..." He looked enquiringly at Harry. He hadn't got a clue what Harry's surname was.

"Simmonds sir, Sergeant Simmonds, I believe there's a brewery in England named after me."

Ignoring that remark, Iffor inspected the troops and stood them at ease.

"This morning, chaps, the Colour is going to the mine to collect some stores. Alvin, Hennie and Shamus—you'll go with him. The rest will get the Champ fuelled up and loaded with our stores ready for our next trip into the bush. Which, gentlemen, will be tomorrow morning. Time and place for 'O' group, my office fourteen hundred hours."

He busied himself for the rest of the morning completing the certificates of recognition for Blue Watch and writing a letter to Henry's father, the General, telling him as much as he dared about the monastery fight, and enquiring about Moses's son. Then he got down to writing notes for his 'O' group until, thoroughly bored, he went down into the drill hall to see how the loading of the stores was going.

"Just about finished boss," Harry said. "Just our personal gear and first line ammo. We'll draw that when the Colour gets back. Are you coming with us this trip or do you want me to handle it?"

"Thanks Harry, I'm coming with you on this trip. I need to have another look at Long Acre Farm, De Witt's place. I'll tell you about it at my 'O' group." Although still very much in command, Iffor was quite pleased with the way that Mad Harry was prepared to relieve him of some of his duties, and was willing and indeed very capable of taking Blue Watch into the bush without him. He put his arm around Harry's shoulder: "As this war goes on, I will be depending more and more on you for bush bashing, while I'm confined to base."

A little after one, the Colour drove the three tonner with the stores from the mine into the M.T. yard.

"Problems?"Iffor asked as he climbed down from the vehicle.

"No boss, we've got everything you asked for."

"Thanks Bob, you and the boys grab a brew, 'O' group at fourteen hundred, my office."

A few minutes before two Blue Watch assembled in Iffor's office, keeping a respectful silence. The Colour was not with them. Iffor looked at his watch again: not like the Colour to be late, he mused.

Harry read his thoughts. "I'll go and find him, boss." As he opened the door to leave, two officers followed by the Colour walked in. The red tabs on the Brigadier's shirt brought Iffor and the team out of their chairs and rigid to attention. The captain with him was ignored.

The Brigadier advanced on Iffor. "Sit down gentlemen, sit down."

Iffor grabbed his beret, put it on and saluted, "Meredith sir, and this is Blue Watch."

"I know who you are and I know what you've been up to. That's why I'm here. Now, what have I interrupted?"

"An orders group sir; we're in the field tomorrow."

"Good, I'll listen in. Just ignore me, pretend I'm not here." He pulled up a chair and sat next to Evil, and looked expectantly at Iffor.

"Before I begin, gentlemen, Harry, who's our all-time genius in first aid?"

Without hesitation, Harry said, "Alvin, boss; brilliant with coughs, colds and scabby holes."

"Thank you Harry. Alvin, report to Doctor Van De Merwe at the hospital 0 nine hundred tomorrow. He'll issue you with a trauma kit, saline etc., and teach you how to use it. We've used up all our luck where casualties are concerned. We need to be better prepared."

Alvin nodded, "Right boss."

Iffor paused before going into what was now a routine briefing.

The Brigadier's aide, the captain, was looking positively embarrassed at the informality between Iffor and his men. The Brigadier didn't take his eyes off Iffor for a minute.

Iffor went into his briefing in detail, routine though it was. More for the Brigadier's benefit than the troops. "Yes," he explained, "We could take defence stores up country with us tomorrow and construct our forward operating base. But I need to look at the ground and study the map and plan properly. We can't afford any nasty surprises when the Lenshina attack. I intend to go back into the bush early next week to begin work."

The Brigadier waited until Iffor had finished, then stood beside him at his desk.

"Gentlemen, I am Brigadier Hall. I command Three Infantry Brigade, which comprises your own Battalion, Rhodesian Rifles; Rhodesian African Rifles and Rhodesian African Regiment. Two regular and one T.A. battalions. All currently deployed on the border, from Kariba to New Epsom, with Mwonza looking out for itself. It was my intention to make a speech about how impressed I am with your splendid efforts, but I think that would be wasted on men such as you.

"Sufficient to say, prior to coming here, I was going to order your commanding officer to deploy a rifle company into the Lamumbwa valley to counter the threat from the Lenshina. This would have left us with a gap in our defences, possibly allowing ZAPU terrorists to pour into the area. As it is, I think, what you chaps are planning might well slow down the Lenshina, giving me time to deploy a composite company into the area to finish them off when the time comes.

"Now Meredith, introduce me to your chaps."

Iffor's heart sank. He hadn't a clue what their surnames were apart from Mad Harry. He looked across at the Colour who simply shrugged his shoulders. Then, Harry stepped in. "Allow me sir," and led the Brigadier down the line of his standing team introducing them by Christian name and surname, finally arriving at Evil, "And this is Evil sir, Evil Jesus. He's our Bren gunner."

The Brigadier leaned towards Iffor. "Has he got a surname?"

"No sir, I don't believe he has, he's just Evil. There is just one more member of the team you should meet sir," and opening the office door he called down the corridor to Josie. "Miss Patel sir," he announced, as she came through the door looking very business-like in loose trousers and white blouse. "Miss Patel is our chief clerk and watch keeper while we are in the bush."

The Brigadier looked across at his aide, "A damn sight prettier than any of the watch keepers at headquarters, what."

The Brigadier took his leave. "We're up against it up on the border, but we're winning. Now I want you chaps to sit on the old Mwonza Road and trail as you've been doing. It's giving me what I need most of all, time."

Iffor dismissed the men. They needed to get home and pack kit ready for the 'off' next morning. "Where in hell's name did that Brigadier spring from?" he said to the Colour.

"Kariba; he parked his chopper in the school playing field; it's only a ten minute walk away."

"Well, he might have warned us he was coming."

"He did boss. He spoke to me on the phone, said my bollocks would adorn the main entrance if I told you he was coming. He's like that."

Iffor phoned his Colonel, telling him of the Brigadier's visit and giving a situation report on his own activities, and his planned trip to the Company at Mwonza. The Colonel kept the conversation brief, "Good man, good man. Keep up the good work, goodbye."

As he put the phone down the Colour walked into the office. "If you want to get away boss, I'm going to be here for a while yet, issuing kit to the first batch of sick, lame and lazy from New Epsom. No need for Josie to stay either."

Gratefully, he collected Josie and together they headed for home. "You and I, my girl, are going to change into something comfortable and have a drink. Then I'm going to show you how to use the pistol I want you to carry," he deliberately paused, "at all times."

The clear crisp warm morning air of this beautiful Wednesday morning only added to Iffor's pleasure. He was off into the bush again. The Colour was waiting in the M.T. yard and offered Josie his hand as she climbed out of the pick-up.

"Bloody creep," Iffor said, throwing his Burgan over his shoulder, "Now give me a hand and bring that package into the drill hall." He indicated the parcel he had retrieved from the station. "It's a present for old Shadrak, two hundred and fifty rounds for that old Mauser of his, and there's two fifty rounds for my Ruger. My gun dealer in Pretoria sent them up."

"That's a generous gift for the old boy." The Colour picked up the load.

"Well," Iffor replied, "if he's going to be my eyes and ears in the bush, he's entitled to be able to defend himself."

Iffor threw his Burgan on to the trailer of the Champ. "How are the boys this morning Harry, bright-eyed and bushy-tailed?"

"I don't know about that boss, quite the reverse I would say. I try not to look at them if I can help it. By the way, Alvin popped in to say cheerio. By the time we get back, he'll be a fully-fledged 'pox doctor's clerk'."

They drove slowly through the town, 'pigasus' fluttering from the radio aerial.

It was eight-thirty, shops were just opening, people stopped to wave. Iffor settled back in his seat and reminded himself of his night with Josie. Life was good.

"Just in time for lunch," Harry said as they drove into the North Road Farm. "Just hope he's remembered to put the beer on ice."

Charlie came out to greet them. "Heard you were on your way," he said.

Damn those jungle drums, Iffor thought to himself, there's no secrecy in the bush.

"Haven't had a chance to thank you lads for what you did in the Lamumbwa Valley," Charlie said.

"No need to thank us," Evil said. "A cold beer wouldn't go amiss though," and he went through his 'unload' drills with the Bren. "Oh, and we haven't had lunch yet."

Charlie ushered the team onto the veranda and into the shade. His houseboy appeared with a cold bag full of Castle. He took Iffor to the far end of the veranda. "We really are very grateful for what you did. Is it true—was the priest part of the gang?"

"Yes, and the two white priests with him, all members of the IRA and of course supporters of ZAPU."

"And Sean, the priest, was he killed along with the others?"

"Yes, but his two mates are in prison in Salisbury. They'll probably do a deal and escape the hangman."

"I see you, N'kosi," Shadrak appeared at the rail of the veranda.

"And I see you M'dala," Iffor replied, "We must talk."

Shadrak nodded and walked back to his favourite tree amongst his chickens.

"Do you mind Charlie? I need to talk to him."

"You go ahead, I'll get your heroes to tell me all about the battle."

Iffor collected Shadrak's gifts from the Champ and hurried after him. He was seated under the tree with his beloved Mauser across his knees.

Iffor placed the metal ammunition box and the chest bandolier on the ground in front of the old man. "These are for you, old friend."

The old man sat staring at his gifts for some time, afraid to touch them in case they vanished as if in a dream. He looked up at Iffor. "What must I do to earn such gifts as these?"

"You must be my eyes and ears in the bush. Go about your business for your Bwana, but look for strangers, men who are different, and a baby, a boy child."

"How shall I tell if they are different?"

"You will know them when you see them, and you will tell me."

The old M'dala nodded and with trembling fingers started to put the shiny brass cartridges into the loops of the bandolier, unaware that Iffor had left him.

"Saved you a plate of sandwiches and a beer," Charlie was waiting for him when he rejoined his men, "Did you have your chat with Shadrak?"

"Yes Charlie, I did and I hope you don't mind, but I've asked him to keep a look out for strangers when he's in the bush. In particular, men painted purple."

"These men?" Charlie asked, "Would they be from Mars?"

"No Charlie, they would be from Zambia, members of the Lenshina, who come under the heading of nasty bastards, and may start poking about in our region. Which, my friend, is why we are here." And Iffor told of his plans for the De Witts' old farm.

"Plan is, chaps," Iffor said as they mounted up, "We drive to Angel Falls for a look around and a brew, then on to Arc Angel Farm for a beer with Archie, then we'll spend the night at De Witt's farm. Sentry routine."

The sign, 'Europeans advised not to pass this sign after two p.m.' was still in place as they approached Angel Falls, and once again Evil said, "Doesn't apply to us, we're British."

Taking Mal with him, he walked down the track leading to the falls, leaving the rest of the team brewing up around the Champ. Iffor needed to concentrate on his plans, on his thinking, his 'actions on' and his 'fall back' plans. The falls would make an ideal RV for scattered troops. He sat on a rock with map, compass and notebook, taking bearings and making calculations. Mal went sniffing around, looking for tracks, suspicious or otherwise. "Someone's been living here by the looks of things, boss, and obviously injured." Mal came out of the cave carrying a bloodied piece of cloth that had been used as a bandage. "And quite recently," he added.

Iffor went into the cave with him. "No sign of a fire," Mal pointed out, "so whoever was here was roughing it and, by the looks of things, living on fish and birds and plants."

"How many?"

"Just one boss, quite young judging by the size of the feet."

They went back to the Champ, where Harry thrust a mug of steaming tea into their hands. Iffor drank gratefully, not realising just how thirsty he was, then recoiled in horror, as the scalding tea was set alight by the equal measure of cane spirit. "We didn't have any sugar," Hennie explained quite innocently.

Archie, forewarned, was waiting for them at his Arc Angel Farm. "You'll stay the night?" he asked, then answered his own question: "Of course you will. We'll have a braai, and a few beers and you can tell me all about the monastery battle."

"Archie, much as I'd love to stay, I can't. We've got to get to De Witt's place before dark. I need to recce the place."

Harry put on his very best 'hangdog' look. "Can't we go first thing in the morning, when we are nice and fresh?" he asked. "We haven't had much time together socially for a while."

"Harry, this is a standing patrol, designed to dominate the area, to show the flag and to deter terrorists, not to go on the piss at every fucking farm we come to."

"Sorry boss."

Archie was full of apologies. "I didn't want to interfere; I just thought it would be nice to be able to show our appreciation for what you're doing for us."

Iffor made his decision. "Harry, you and the boys stay put. Get your bedding sorted out and freshen up. I'll go on to De Witt's with Mal; we'll be back before dark. Phil, sit rep to base please. Tell them we're going firm here. Oh, and Harry, since when were you nice and fresh in the morning after a night on the piss?"

"Will you be safe, just the two of you?" Archie asked.

"We'll be in and out before anyone knows we're there," Iffor replied.

"Well, since I'm responsible for screwing up your plans, take my Land Rover—it's armoured—and my farm guard Dirk, he'll drive you. He hasn't been away from the farm for a month. He'll be grateful for the outing."

Archie introduced Iffor to the long-wheelbase Land Rover. "Armoured doors and sides, double thickness floor to protect you from mines, and steel mesh at the front and rear; these boys are keen on stuffing a rocket-propelled grenade up your arse, and a rear-facing seat at the back. Ah, here comes Dirk."

Walking towards them was a dark-skinned swarthy man with Latin features, medium height and build, carrying an Enfield number five jungle carbine, a fifty-round bandolier slung round his chest, wearing desert boots, no socks, shorts and shirt, and floppy hat.

"Could be Evil's grandmother," Mal said, very, very quietly.

"Thanks for inviting me along," he said, offering his hand. "I was going stir crazy stuck in this place." He had a thick Afrikaans accent, typical of the South African Boer, probably with a wealth of good bush experience.

Dirk stopped the Rover about two hundred metres short of the farm, on the edge of the clearing surrounding it. Shielding his eyes from the late afternoon sun with his hand, he looked into the sky above the farm. "All clear," he announced, "No-one around."

Mal looked curiously at Iffor, who pointed to the sky. "No birds being disturbed," he said.

Taking the chugal from where it was hung on the wing mirror, Iffor offered it first to Dirk, then to Mal, before drinking the ice cold water himself. He never could fathom out how the water in its canvas bag, hanging on the outside of the vehicle, could keep so cold.

"You two do what you have to," Dirk said. "I'll stay with the Rover and watch you from here."

Iffor and Mal walked down to the charred buildings. Every fifty or sixty yards Iffor would stop, jotting in his notebook, memorising a feature or simply getting the feel of the area. "That will have to go," he said, pointing at the burned out foundations of the farm. "Our enemy can use it as cover."

"It will be a job and a half digging that lot out," Mal said, "And it will take the best part of a day."

"Not with a ringmain of Cordex and plastic explosives," Iffor said, relishing the thought of 'blowing something up' again.

They walked back to the Rover, where Iffor talked through his thoughts and plans with the other two.

"A good plan, man, providing they don't get round behind you and cut off your escape route." Dirk rolled a cigarette, filling the paper with what looked like rhino dung. When he lit up, the smell confirmed it probably was rhino dung. "We fought a bunch similar to your Lenshina in Angola; brave as the Zulu, but no real tactical sense."

"Which is what I'm counting on," Iffor said, cursing himself for not considering the possibility of being completely surrounded by his enemy. He tore up the sketch map he had made and sketched another. This one showed his ridout a lot closer to the bush behind him. If they had to make a run for it, they would have much less open ground to cover, and fighting in the bush would put them on level terms with the Lenshina. He folded his map and put away his notebook. "We'll give this place a call sign, 'North Camp'," he said, "Now, let's be getting back."

"We haven't touched a drop, boss," Harry beamed, happy to see them return. "The shower's free; I'll make sure no one peeps. Be quick about it, the boys are dying of thirst."

As quick as he was in the shower, the boys were on their second or third bottle by the time he joined them, and the cook already had the kudu steaks on the *braaivleis*. "Went the day well?" Archie asked.

"Yes, thanks Archie. I'm planning to build a defensive position at the De Witt's farm, to take on the Lenshina, should they venture into our area, which I'm fully expecting them to do."

"Lenshina? I thought they were living up north in Fort Jameson," Archie looked concerned.

"They were until they joined forces with ZAPU. Now there's a group of them the other side of Mwonza anxious to cause mayhem and havoc."

"And the only two routes open to them converge at De Witt's farm," Archie finished.

"Correct my friend. Now let's have some food, I'm starving."

As they ate, Iffor outlined his plans to Archie. "I shall want to leave some defence stores here next week: barbed wire, sandbags, pit props and other bits and pieces. They'll slow us down if we have to lug them all the way from Kensington, and speed will be of the essence."

"Glad to be able to help. I'll fence off part of the compound for you. But if you phone me first, should you have to deploy in a hurry," Archie said, "I'll have them loaded on my armoured Rover; we'll follow you to De Witt's."

"Call sign 'North Camp'," Iffor said, "And that's a bloody good idea."

"It's the least I can do. After all, if they get past you, I'm next in line."

As the evening wore on, Iffor began to realise what a good idea it had been to spend the evening at Archie's farm. Harry and the boys were more relaxed than he'd ever seen them: drinking but not getting drunk; laughter came readily and naturally and they all seemed to carry an air of superiority. In fact, behaving like soldiers.

The *braaivleis'* fire was reduced to comforting embers, throwing a glow onto the faces of the team seated around; Harry, Evil and Archie on the steps of the veranda, the rest, on camp-chairs, all enjoying the comradeship that only a soldier could fully appreciate. "You know, you chaps," Archie broke the silence, "what you did at the monastery was brilliant. I couldn't have done it without a company of guardsmen."

"And we couldn't have done it without the boss," Harry replied.

"Amen to that," Evil said, then leaned to one side and let go one of his very own rip snorting farts.

"Common cunt," muttered Mal.

"Seriously chaps," Archie went on, "we farmers are very much in debt to you guys."

"It ain't over yet," Iffor decapitated another cold Castle. "The army is stretched to breaking point, with only a white population of some three hundred thousand to call on. And since blacks are exempt call-up we have to rely on volunteers to man our African battalions. The terrorists have a black population of several million to call on plus communist countries willing to arm them. No, Archie my old fruit, it's far from over. We won a battle, but the war goes on."

The Colour Sergeant was waiting for them when they drove into the M.T. yard behind the drill hall the following morning:

"Fall in lads, one straight line. Unload. For inspection, port arms."

Formalities completed, he turned to Iffor, "Good trip, boss?"

"Yes thanks, Bob. You, me and Mad Harry can have a chat about it later."

Right now, he wanted to get upstairs to Josie's office. He'd been savouring the thought of that first look at her since he woke up that morning. He wasn't disappointed. Wearing a sari, she was a profusion of gold, purple and lilac, looking as delicate and lovely as any orchid or English rose. He embraced her, savouring her smell, the scent of Josie. She didn't wear make-up, she didn't need to and her Indian perfume was as delicate as it was subtle. He held her at arm's length. "Miss me?" he asked.

She held his gaze, answering with her eyes, "Your messages are on your desk. O.C. Support Company wants you to phone him as soon as possible." She sat down at her desk. "If you want me to finish early today, clear off and let me do my work."

The messages on his desk were routine and unimportant. He picked up the phone and dialled Mwonza. "O.C. Support," it was Jack's cheery voice.

"Jack, it's Iffor Meredith. What can we do for you?"

"Iffor, m'boy, just want to confirm your visit to my part of the world; can you make it for mid-morning?"

"Can do; see you then, bye for now." Least said the better on the phone, was Iffor's policy. Jack would bring him up to date when they met. He went downstairs to give the team a hand unloading the Champ. Evil was sitting on his own, Bren stripped down, parts on a groundsheet. Iffor fancied he could hear Evil talking to the weapon as he cleaned it.

"That Bren is Evil's only hope of a meaningful loving relationship," Harry said. "Just look at him, he's positively drooling over the fucking thing; any minute now he'll come his duff all over the piston group."

Evil looked up, oilcan in one hand, oily cloth in the other. "If you had treated your wife with the love, care and consideration I give to this weapon, you wouldn't be on your own now, and you wouldn't be such a miserable bastard. And another thing," Evil went on, "Me and this gun might well save your life one day, so treat us both with a bit of respect."

"He loves me really," Harry said to no one in particular.

The Colour came up to them. "I'm a bit worried about Evil."

"Join the club," Harry said.

Bob ignored him. "The thing is boss, if we have to mix it with the Lenshina, Evil's going to have problems reloading the Bren on his own. I've got Captain Graham's Hi-Power Browning pistol here. I think he should carry that with him."

"Bloody good idea," Evil said. "There you go Harry, someone loves me."

"Should have thought of that myself. Thanks Bob, issue it to him along with some ammo and show him the basics."

Stores put away, water containers refilled and the Champ refuelled, Iffor gathered the team around him. "That's it lads, you can knock off. Parade 0 eight hundred Monday morning. Report to the Colour; you'll be loading defence stores on to the trailer and the three tonner."

He looked at the Colour for confirmation. "Right boss."

Iffor went on, "Warning order for operations next week. Orders group: time and place, my office O nine hundred Tuesday. No move before O four hundred Wednesday Prepare to stay out for three nights. Harry, Bob, a word."

They walked away from the main group. "I'm driving up to Mwonza tomorrow morning, but I'll leave a list of stores I want loading. Apart from defence stores, we'll need ration packs, extra water, first line ammunition, Claymores, trip flares, signal pistol and flares, and anything else you can think of. Get Mal involved; he did this sort of thing in Korea and make sure Alvin's back with us. Next week may be our only chance to rehearse our defence of North Camp before Alice decides to pay us a visit."

Josie was waiting for him in his office. "I need you to sign the travel warrants for the riflemen going back up north," she said. "They are booked on tonight's train."

Iffor did as bid. "Are they collecting them?" he asked.

"They should be here soon," she said, collecting up the documents.

"Ask them to pop in and see me for a few minutes."

Just as Iffor completed his stores list, nine soldiers filed into his office.

The only one in uniform saluted, "Corporal Adnams sir, section commander. You wanted a word with us."

"Yes, grab a chair lads, I won't keep you long."

Iffor waited for them to be seated. "I just wanted to know how things are up at the sharp end. I want to try and get a feel of things, see what you're up against."

"Well, it's a corporal's war, sir," Adnams began. "We have a platoon defensive position from where we send out section strength patrols. We always have one section in the bush as a fighting patrol, one resting and one standing by as a QRF. We rotate within the company every four days. It's pretty boring stuff actually."

"Until we get reved," one of the other riflemen said. "Then for two or three minutes it's mayhem with rounds coming at you from all directions, and us just firing at where we think the enemy may be. We rarely see them, but when we do, we kill them." The others nodded enthusiastically.

"How about rations, food?" Iffor asked.

"Bully beef and biscuits and tinned fruit. No cooking allowed. But we eat well when we get back to Battalion."

"Morale?" Iffor knew what the answer would be.

"Great sir; everyone understands why we haven't been relieved yet, and the C.O. makes a point of telling everyone what's happening."

One of the others chipped in: "We are not just a bloody good regiment sir, we are family and you and your men wouldn't have achieved what you did if you weren't close."

"Thanks lads, who are you?"

"Two Platoon A company," the Corporal said. "Three section."

"We'll have a drink together next time you're in town," Iffor said.

"We'll keep you to that." The corporal saluted and they left—back to their war, leaving Iffor to fight his war.

"Come along wench, time for home. I'm in need of a shower, a steak and a cold beer or several."

She smiled sweetly. "I'm ready, I just need my handbag."

"Handbag! I've never seen you with a handbag before!"

"I've never had to carry a pistol with me before; a holster would look a little out of place on a sari."

His Burgan was already in the back of the pick-up. He placed his Carbine in the gap between the front seats and helped her into the vehicle savouring the few moments close to her. Then they headed for home. Tomorrow was another day. He intended to make the most of what was left of today.

His journey north was boring and uninteresting until he reached the outskirts of Mwonza. Beside the sign, 'Welcome to Mwonza', was a sandbagged sanger, from which the two occupying policemen waved and grinned. He slowed in case they wanted him to stop, but they waved him on into the small town.

A casual visitor would have had cause for some alarm on seeing the first building, the post office, so heavily fortified with a sandbag ridout defending the main entrance and surrounded by barbed wire. A policeman, wearing battle order and steel helmet, loitered in the entrance chatting to an African woman, while two Europeans both carrying F.N. rifles waiting impatiently to be allowed in.

In contrast, the African store, probably run by an Indian, showed an air of normality, with African women doing last minute shopping before the weekend. Children playing 'tag' were scampering in and out of the adults or bowling an old bicycle wheel through the dusty street. A Tribal policeman stood guard over the sacks of mealie stacked outside the shop, unnecessary since no one would take away a sack without payment. And when a sack had been purchased, it was the woman who carried it the several miles back to her kraal.

Someone had done a good job fortifying the 'Cecil Rhodes' hotel. Since this was probably the only watering hole in town, Iffor reasoned, it was important that so much care had been lavished on its defences.

A 'blast wall' in front of the main entrance afforded protection from an R.P.G attack. Chicken wire frames protected the windows from grenades, and sandbags at the windows showed fire positions had been constructed inside the bar. A sign painted rifle green caused him to turn off the main street and drive a mile or so down a dusty but well-used track to the police station which also served as Support Company H.Q. Built of stone, it reminded Iffor of a French Foreign Legion fort. It had probably been used as a prison as well as a police station but now those unoccupied cells would be full of ammunition, water containers and ration packs. A weapons pit, protecting a three-inch mortar, stood between the barbed wire perimeter and the main building. This, Iffor surmised, would support the town. A Vickers gun at the rear of the building would deter all but the most determined attack on the building.

Jack Francis came out of the building to greet him. "Park your truck next to my Rhino." He pointed to his armoured car parked in the only shade available. "You're in luck, just in time for tea and stickies. Welcome to my command post," he said. "It also serves as my office." The 'office' was more like a fortified bunker: no windows, just weapons slots protected by sandbags; boxes of rifle ammunition provided fire steps and at each position a box of grenades, already opened and primed. On one wall above the desk was a large-scale map of the area covered with plastic talc on which was written grid references and call signs for target registration. They indulged in the traditional custom of 'tiffin' or 'elevenses'.

As they munched through their Danish pastries, it was Jack who did most of the talking, not as one would imagine about military matters, but about Kensington. Was the Moth Club still thriving, did the Elephants Head still serve rare beef and horseradish sandwiches, and what was showing at the open-air drive-in cinema? Iffor was more intent on how he defended his fort.

"Well, as you can see, we have a surrounding barbed wire perimeter with claymores and tripflares. Our mortar pit is protected by the sanger you passed on the way in. They have an M.A.G. machine-gun with a four-man team, occupied twenty-four hours a day. At the rear, which is the main threat, we have a Vickers team, with local protection from a M.A.G. machine-gun position. Again, these positions are occupied twenty-four hours a day. We also have a standing patrol of section strength operating about three hundred metres out. We can support them if they run into trouble, which is quite frequent."

Jack took him on a tour of the place. All the windows had been taken out and replaced with a sandbagged fire position. A box of six hundred rounds of 7.62 ammo and a box of six grenades occupied each position. "We try to maintain a normal routine," Jack said. "Sleeping, eating, cleaning weapons, and patrols of course. We only go to our fire positions when we stand to, which again, is quite regularly. We operate with one platoon on site for a week and two platoons with Battalion, one resting and one operating our mortars. Now, let me buy you lunch at the Cecil and you can tell me how we can help."

Over lunch, Iffor told of his plans to fortify North Camp. "You'll be too far out for our weapons to be of use to you, old boy. The best we can do is to give you warning when the Lenshina are on the move, then you'll have to move pretty damned quick to get to North Camp before they do."

"Aren't you tasked with supporting the protected village south west of here?" Iffor asked.

"Yes, but we can reach it from here and we've already registered targets with the Guard Force team there."

Iffor was persistent. "If you sent a Land Rover with a mobile base plate and a mortar team to the village, could you reach us?"

"With charge five and super, just about, and the Vickers might just reach you," Jack said. "But don't forget, I've got to have people alive to be of help."

"That's all I ask for," Iffor said. "Another beer?"

He delayed his departure from Mwonza for as long as he dared, enjoying the thrill of anticipation building up inside—his anticipation of a night with Grace, his proud Zulu. In mitigation, he reminded himself this would be their last meeting as lovers; somehow it helped ease his conscience. But he couldn't help but wonder how she would take the news.

"Just in time for supper," she said, as he climbed the steps onto the veranda. "You're in luck, it's fish and chips again," and she called to her chef, announcing a visitor. After supper, they sat side by side, enjoying the cool of the evening, listening to singing from the kraal on the edge of the Mission. He found her fingers, they entwined. He guessed she wanted to sit and talk for a while, which suited him. "How did you become a doctor and finish up here?" A stupid question he knew, but she gave him his answer: "As a young girl, I was living in Natal with my family, when one day my uncle came to visit. He told us of a government scheme to attract young girls from the villages to attend university in Cape Town. My parents said I was old enough to make a choice, which was being circumcised in the next few months and being a plaything for the young warriors, or being educated. So, I went with my uncle to Cape Town and became a doctor. While I was at university, my uncle clothed me and gave me money and I stayed with him during holidays. Then one night when I was seventeen he demanded payment. I had kept my clitoris, but lost my virginity." She rose to her feet. "It's getting cold, and I've got a decent bottle of Cape Red in my lodge."

She stood patiently while he patted her dry with a towel after their shower, and moaned softly as he gently rubbed scented oil onto her generous breasts, firm, uplifting with hard nipples, typical of a Zulu. Then she changed from a domineering man-eating woman to a fragile child, as he picked her up and gently laid her on the bed. At some stage during the night, clinging to him, she said, "You know this is our last night together like this, don't you? Helen would never forgive me if I came between you and Josie." He didn't answer; he just held her tighter, thankful that she had ended the relationship and not himself, and now, relieved of that awesome responsibility, he threw himself into his quest for sexual perfection.

They breakfasted together in bed, with coarse African bread and goat's cheese, and surprisingly, a half decent bottle of champagne she retrieved from her fridge. "Here's to our affair," they touched glasses. "Y'know," she said, "when I think back over my best hundred love affairs, you'll be close to the top of the list." She threw off the sheet covering them, put her glass onto the bedside table, and took his, putting it beside her own. Then she gently pushed him back onto the pillow. "There's no rush, is there?"

Maureen, the African nurse, fussed and watched as Iffor loaded the carrycot containing baby Helen into the back of the pick-up. He had erected the canopy to keep out the sun and dust, and now he anchored the cot to the seat with bungie cords. Having just been fed and changed, Maureen was certain she would sleep until they reached Kensington. Nevertheless, she opted to sit in the back with the cot instead of the comfort of a front seat. Iffor allowed himself a hug with Grace. "Thanks for a wonderful evening, the goat's cheese was fabulous," he whispered to her, before beating a very hasty retreat to the pick-up.

Having Maureen in the back was all very well, but it meant he had to stop every ten miles or so to check on her and he could imagine how anxious Josie would be getting, not to mention Auntie, who he knew would be waiting with Josie at the bungalow.

Josie! His guilt was gone, he longed to see her and to love her, and she would love him for the gift he was bringing to her, albeit that they only had the baby for the weekend.

Auntie's intuition was unnerving and unerring. As he turned onto the mine road, he could see Josie and Auntie some two hundred yards distant, come out of the bungalow to greet them. "Did you have a good trip?" Auntie asked.

The nurse answered grudgingly in N'debele. Auntie replied in the same language. A precedence had been set.

Leaving the three women to take the precious bundle indoors, Iffor parked the pick-up, collected his Carbine and Burgan and went into his bedroom to change. Then he took a cold Castle from the fridge in the kitchen, and pausing to grab the daily paper from the table in the hall, went into the garden. No-one missed him.

If Iffor was looking forward to a quiet weekend with Josie, getting to know the baby and more importantly, spending time with Josie, he was sadly mistaken. A constant stream of visitors came calling to 'Ooh' and 'Ah' over the baby, who obviously was delighted to have so many admirers after life in the Mission. Various members of Blue Watch, all posing as uncles and claiming the baby was now family, cleaned him out of beer, telling him it was quite normal to drink four or five Castles whilst wetting the baby's head, and suggesting, that in the interest of the baby's welfare, he drove into town for more beer and while he was at it, could he get some steaks for the braai?

In the cool of the late evening, after Auntie had shooed away all the guests and gone home herself; after Maureen had allowed Josie to bath the baby under very strict supervision, they sat side by side in the garden listening to Maureen crooning an African lullaby to the baby. And for Josie, this seemed the right moment to tell Iffor, "I can't have children of my own." She paused, and said very softly, "I thought you should know." He put his hand to her cheek turning her head to face him, "I know." Then they both fell silent, enjoying each other and the African night.

Sunday was a repeat of Saturday except that the baby was on display at Auntie's hotel. Maureen felt she could trust Josie well enough with the baby to go and have lunch in town with friends, leaving Josie and Iffor to face most of the Indian population of Kensington, all claiming to be an aunt or uncle.

"The baby is called Helen," Auntie would say to each group of admirers. "Josie named her after a very good friend who was killed by terrorists. She has a twin brother who disappeared after the raid."

"God, she sounds like someone out of Agatha Christie," Iffor remarked to Josie.

"Who?"

He put his arm around her waist and pulled her closer, "Tell you later."

The party was beginning to gather pace when Maureen arrived. "Has baby been fed?" A solemn nod from Josie. "Changed?" Another nod of confirmation. "Good, now we must get baby home for her bath and an early night; she has had much too much excitement."

Gratefully, Iffor agreed; he wanted to finalise his stores list for the Colour and he needed to clean his weapons. They would be taking baby back to the Mission early tomorrow; he needed an early night himself. He found himself wondering if Maureen, in the guest room with the baby, could hear him and Josie in the shower together after she had gone to bed.

Stopping just long enough to give last minute instructions and the completed stores list to the Colour, the small party headed out of town and onto the Great North Road. "We'll go straight to the Mission," he told Josie. "And call in at Ed's farm on the way home." He was aware Maureen was anxious to get the baby home.

Grace came down the veranda steps to greet them. God, Iffor thought to himself, the bitch has done this deliberately. She was dressed in tight shirt and shorts and barefooted, emphasising her long slim legs and high pert bottom. Her nipples thrusting against her shirt invited his second lingering glance.

She hugged Josie and made all the usual noises at the baby that Maureen was carrying, and led both women up on to the veranda. She looked back over her shoulder at Iffor. "Us girls are going to talk babies, find something to do."

Taking his Carbine from the pick-up, Iffor wandered up the slope towards the kraal area of the Mission. "Going hunting?" A strong accented voice stopped him in his tracks. Coming up behind him with a gang of labourers was Jacob, the new occupier of the monastery.

Iffor gestured with the Carbine, "This attracts young boys like moths to a light. Daren't leave it in my truck."

They fell into step with one another, the labourers following on behind. "You probably want to know what I am doing here."

"No, not really."

Jacob stopped and raised his hands to the sky. "This, my friend, is why we came to Africa. This is our final destination. My brothers and I are going to spend the rest of our lives in the service of these poor people here in this colony."

"And the chalk soil ideal for growing grapes for wine on the slopes overlooking the river, where the massed grave is?" Iffor asked.

"I was coming to that," Jacob said, and they started walking again. "You are right, of course. With my brothers and myself providing the brains, and our leper friends providing the muscle, we are going into production. 'Lamumbwa River Wine Estates.' How does that sound?"

"Fine, wonderful. How does Doctor Grace feel about it? She is after all in charge now that Helen has gone."

"I'm waiting for the right time to tell her; she could be difficult."

They stopped when they reached the burial ground. White painted crosses marked the graves and fresh flowers were in abundance.

"This massacre must have been quite something," Jacob said softly.

"No different from what you had in Umtali," Iffor answered.

He spent the next hour or so wandering around the newly built huts, speaking to the occupants, listening to the stories of their escape from the terrorists. All that he spoke to knew about the missing twin, but no one had any real information for him, reminding him that many bodies were burned beyond recognition.

Grace and Josie were sitting on the veranda when he strolled back to them. Maureen had taken the baby back to the small orphans' ward for feeding.

"I've explained to Grace that we can't stay, that you want to pop in and see Ed and Joy." Iffor smiled in agreement, looking at Grace and thinking, not much point in staying if I can't get into her knickers. He could tell by the way she looked at him she knew exactly what he was thinking. I hate these fucking mind-readers, he told himself.

Joy was beside herself with excitement when they drove into Ed's farm.

She grabbed his arm, leading him inside the house. "Have you heard, we are all going into the wine business. Jacob's already planted the grapes. We're all going to be rich!"

"I've tried telling her it's going to be years before our investment begins to pay off," Ed said. "But she's already sold the first crop and spent the money."

Try as she might, Josie couldn't break into the conversation. They sat around the large coffee table which stood on an impressive kudu skin, listening to Joy telling of her expectations for the future of Lamumbwa wines.

Eventually, Josie excused herself and went off to Helen's grave, where Iffor found her an hour later. "I've been telling Helen about Baby Helen," she said, burying her head on Iffor's shoulder, "And what Grace told me."

"Which was?" Iffor held her at arm's length.

"We can't adopt, we can only foster baby Helen, because we're not married. Oh, Iffor," she said, looking into his face, "I couldn't possibly simply foster little Helen. I couldn't bear the thought of someone taking her from me after a few weeks or months."

Iffor held her close, quickly considering his position. He didn't want the burden of marriage and a child at this stage, and if he did ask Josie to marry him, which he probably would at some later stage, it would have to be because he wanted to marry her and not for the sake of adopting a baby.

"Look," he said, "let's just content ourselves with having the baby staying weekends with us for the time being, and wait and see what transpires. Now let's go and say goodbye to Ed and Joy."

He loved this time of the night. The open window allowed the scent of the jacaranda and jasmine to waft into the bedroom on the gentle breeze, with the night noises of Africa audible on that same breeze. She lay asleep beside him on her back, in the crook of his arm. Now he could study her face without her giggling and becoming embarrassed. He gently moved the sheet that covered her, exposing her breasts, watching them rise and fall with her breathing. Without opening her eyes, she murmured, "Pervert," and pulled the sheet back up to her chin and snuggled closer.

PART EIGHTEEN

A sentry is the eyes and ears of his unit. If he does his job well, his unit will be safe.

"**G**OOD MORNING GENTLEMEN. Operation 'Krait' is over after the destruction of the Monastery gang. Welcome to Operation 'Pigasus'. Inspector, sorry, Chief Inspector and Davy Jones, thanks for attending this briefing."

He went over the now familiar GROUND, and on to SITUATION.

"It is confirmed a religious group of fanatics belonging to the Lenshina tribe are camped, peacefully at present, some eight or ten miles north of Mwonza inside Zambia. Since they have now sided with ZAPU, it is likely they will cross the border at Mwonza and fall on the Lamumbwa Valley, and in particular on us, for revenge after what we did to their muckers.

"Our MISSION, gentlemen, is to stop them at the only point where the two trails they will have to use, converge." He turned and pointed at the map behind him. "Here at De Witt's old place, Longacre Farm. Call sign, NORTH CAMP."

EXECUTION was once again very repetitive but very necessary. However this time Iffor paid more attention to 'Actions On', and 'what if'.

"If we are forced to withdraw to the river, it will be orderly and pre-planned.

"The Colour and I will have one of the police hand-held radios each, so when it's time for the Gun group or rifle group to go, the other group will support them. And as we leave our positions, we will fire our satchel charges. That should delay our enemy long enough for us to get into our prepared position on the far bank of the river."

He went through the formalities of command, admin and communications, finishing with casualties. "Alvin, how did your medical course at the hospital go?"

"Fine boss, I'm now a qualified surgeon and licensed to carry out abortions. Seriously though boss, we are now much better equipped and trained to deal with any casualties."

"Thanks Alvin, but remember, you are a fighting man first and foremost; casualties come second. Davy!"

"Yes boss." Davy was sitting with both arms wrapped around his sub-machine gun, certain he was going to be told to hand it back in to the Colour.

"If we need you and the Islander, it will be in a hurry. When we move out to North Camp, you move into the police station and keep in contact with us, and the mine and the pilots. Josie will tell you when. Be prepared for a 'hot' extraction of casualties and be prepared to defend yourself and the aircraft. Draw a first line scale of ammunition from the Colour.

"Finally, gentlemen, I intend to use tomorrow's sortie as a rehearsal. We'll spend three nights at North Camp, honing our skills in defence, standing patrols and sentry duties. That's it; we'll go downstairs and have a final check of stores. Then you can knock off. On parade zero three hundred tomorrow, no move before zero four hundred."

The Colour and the policeman stayed, waiting for the others to leave.

"I take it you'll want me with you tomorrow, to drive the three tonner?"

"Please Bob, if you can be spared. And I'd like you to pick me up from home. I can leave the pick-up for Josie to use. Pete, thanks for coming, I know you like to be kept up to date."

"It gives me a chance to keep my lads informed," Pete said. "They appreciate it. A lunchtime beer at the Elephant, chaps?" he asked.

"Churlish not to," Iffor answered.

After a final check of stores and equipment, Iffor dismissed the team and went back to his office for the more mundane tasks of reports, weapons and ammunition states, and a sit rep for the Colonel which had to be encoded. His phone rang. "Call for you from Kariba," Josie said. "It's a secure line."

"Meredith."

"Mornin' Meredith, thought you should know, we've had a team keeping an eye on your friends, the Lenshina. They've set up a permanent camp eight miles north of Mwonza. They appear to be being trained to use A K rifles, RPD machine-guns by a group of friendly Cubans from Angola. Alice isn't with them at present. We'll try to keep you informed."

Short, but not so sweet, not the sort of news Iffor wanted. When he'd fought the Lenshina before, they had used traditional weapons, spears, pangas with just a spattering of shotguns and modern weapons. Being trained and equipped with modern weapons would make life a little more exciting.

He asked Josie to come in. "The certificates of merit for the boys I asked you to get designed and printed, any joy?" he asked.

"They'll be ready when you get back."

Leaving Josie to get his coded sit rep off to the Colonel, he collected Bob and Pete, and wandered down to the Elephant. He deliberately hadn't asked Josie to join them; he wanted to tell of, and discuss the phone call from the Scouts.

"Do you still intend to meet them head on?" Pete asked. "It's a whole new ball game now they are better armed and trained."

Waiting until the waiter had put the rare beef sandwiches on the table, Iffor answered, "I'm hoping they'll be doped up to the eyeballs on dagga weed and still reliant on their war paint for protection from our bullets. And I'm still convinced my disciplined force will be more than a match for their undisciplined rabble."

"Never underestimate your enemy," the Colour commented quietly.

Military matters were put aside in favour of the rare roast beef sandwiches and the cold Castles. "How are you settling down in your domesticated new life with the delightful Josie?" Pete asked.

"Beats the shit out of Auntie fussing round me all the time," Iffor answered, and added: "And I get to sleep with my chief clerk."

"And Grace?" Bob asked innocently, looking quite the little angel.

"Just good friends," Iffor muttered through clenched teeth. "And talking of Grace,"—he had to change the subject—"The new Abbot of the monastery is going into the wine business and planting his vines at the Mission. It will give the lepers a new lease of life."

"If Grace gets hold of him, she will give him a new lease of life and he'll be planting more than just his vine," Pete said, just beating Iffor to the last sandwich.

Back in his office, he went over the notes from his briefing, looking for anything he might have forgotten to cover. Then he started to write a training programme for their occupation of North Camp:

How to set up a trip flare; where to site a claymore; fire lanes; fire control orders; standing patrols; duties of a sentry. So much to do, so little time.

And all the while, the Colour's words kept coming back to haunt him, 'Don't underestimate your enemy.'

He was interrupted by a knock on the door and Bob came in, followed by a tall coloured corporal. "Thought you should know boss, I've got some staff back again. Corporal Watney here," the corporal saluted, "and two riflemen lurking in my stores. The C.O. has just realised I could do with some help down here. It means when I'm away with you, we've got the corporal here looking after the shop."

Iffor shook hands with the solemn looking corporal. "You're very welcome, Corporal Watney, very welcome indeed. While you're on duty, I will want you and your riflemen to be armed at all times. The Colour will explain why."

After they had left, he locked his office, went along to the main orderly room and stuck his head round the door. "Come wench," he said, "let's go home, get dressed and come back into town for dinner at the Elephant. Then, it's an early night."

The men didn't complain about the early start; they knew it made sense to vary departure times from Kensington. Harry drove, Iffor beside him, behind the Bren, Evil in the back, quite happy now to allow someone else to take over the Bren now that he had a pistol to defend himself with. The rest of the team travelled in the three tonner with the Colour. If they've got any sense, Iffor thought, they'll be asleep by now.

Their small convoy thundered up the Great North Road, eventually turning off onto the new Mwonza Road, taking them past the two farms. In spite of his woolly pullover and para smock, Iffor was beginning to feel the cold and he knew the others would too, so he called a halt. "Get out, stretch your legs, have a pee and a fag. Keep your weapons close. We'll brew up and have some breakfast when we arrive at our final R.V."

They drove into the compound of what had previously been Long Acre Farm an hour or so later and Iffor dismounted the men.

"Remember chaps, we are in 'Injun' country, so be alert.

"Mal, you and big Shamus take a stroll around our perimeter, see if anyone's about. The rest of you brew up and have some breakfast." He took the Colour to one side and showed him his sketch map of the area.

"Our first task is to destroy what is left of the farmhouse; I don't want it to be used to give cover to an enemy.

"Our second task will be to construct our main trench with some overhead cover. Then, we'll give some thought to the Bren position up on the kopje.

"And then, my friend, we can get down to some training and preparation. You can show them how to arm a trip flare. I'm bloody useless at it."

"Have you thought, Iffor," the Colour said, "that it might be to our advantage if we let the Lenshina take cover in the ruins, *then* blow it up? We've plenty of cable."

Iffor looked long and hard at his friend. "You never cease to amaze me! That is a bloody great idea and it will save us a lot of time and effort. Let's grab some breakfast. I think I can manage a mug of Hennie's special brew."

As he munched his way through a bacon grill and beans, Iffor relished the thought of detonating ten pounds of plastic in amongst the

Lenshina as they took cover in the burnt-out building. In his mind's eye, he could see the main charge in the centre of the building, covered with rocks and stones, and a ringmain of cordtex, exploding fuse, around the outside.

Mal and Shamus joined him. "No-one around, boss."

"Thanks Mal. Now grab some breakfast, then I want you two to go back into the bush, keeping us in sight and set up a covert listening post. I'll relieve you in two hours."

Iffor gathered his team around him, explaining what he wanted of them.

He stood with the bush behind him and the farm in front of him.

To his right was the track they had driven in on, which led back to the drift over the river, about two hundred metres away.

The ground as far as the farmhouse had been cleared, but the bush had been allowed to creep up to the rear of the house—done deliberately to allow the De Witts to escape into the bush if necessary.

There were no outhouses, no servants' quarters that would normally be present on a farm, just open ground.

"Gentlemen, we will build our defences fifty metres in from the bush. That means we won't have too far to run over open ground if we have to make a run for it. You'll see that it is about a hundred and fifty metres to the farmhouse. This will be our killing range and the ground in front of us will be our killing ground, the ground of our choice. It was my intention to destroy what's left of the farmhouse, but the Colour came up with a better idea—let the Lenshina occupy it, then blow it up. Grins all round!

"We'll construct a strong point, a trench, using the angle irons, pit props and sandbags. Beyond that, our barbed wire, between the wire and the farmhouse, trip flares and claymore mines." He looked at the men around him. "Questions? No, good, let's get on with it."

Leaving the Colour to mark out the outline of the rectangular trench with mine tape, Iffor and Harry collected the beehives and demolition sets from the three tonner and set one in each corner of the rectangle.

"Anyone with a fetish for blowing things up, be my guest," Iffor said.

The team gathered round as he demonstrated: safety fuse into the number twenty-seven detonator; scarf the end of the safety fuse so it ignites easily; detonator into the hole at the top of the beehive; light the fuse and take cover.

If a midday snooze was what the local wild life had in mind, their aspirations were rudely disturbed by the four beehives exploding, firing their steel bolts into the hard ground, making it easy for Harry and the team to cement the uprights into position and dig out the loose soil of the trench.

With the Colour, Iffor walked across to the kopje, and up the slope to what was to be the gun position. "Good enough for you, Colour?"

"Couldn't be better; good field of fire, good escape route. With sandbags in front of us, and a cam net for cover and concealment, it will be like home from home."

They sat on a fallen log, looking down on the peaceful scene of what might soon become a battlefield. "Your problem Bob, will be knowing when to call it a day and fuck off. Disengaging with the enemy is probably the most difficult of all battle skills. The secret is to withdraw sooner rather than later."

Iffor went on: "You'll have a four-man gun team; you, Evil, Mal— he'll be useful, he did this sort of thing in Korea—and big Shamus. If you have a wounded man, he'll be able to carry him on his own."

"What if we have too many wounded to evacuate?" Bob asked quietly.

"We join forces and stay and fight it out. Come on, let's join the others, with luck all the hard work will be finished."

With Iffor's experience and guidance, the trench was soon completed to his satisfaction: three foot deep; two pit props as cross members already bolted to the uprights, keeping the uprights in position while the cement dried, and sandbags in front of the cross members for added protection. The cross members gave protection to the front and sides. The rear was their escape route if necessary.

"Right chaps, we'll get the barbed wire strung out on three sides, then we'll knock off for lunch and a break."

"If this is a rehearsal," Harry said, "is it really necessary to put the wire up?"

"Even as we speak," Iffor wiped his face with his face veil, "a gang may be heading our way to use the Mwonza trail back into Zambia, or Alice might be thinking, it's too nice a day to stay indoors..."

"All right boss, I've got the message."

Iffor became serious. "While we are in the field, we will use all means at our disposal to defend ourselves, and the next time we are here, we may not have time to think about what we are going to do; that's why we are going to practise it now."

The wire in position, Iffor called the two sentries in to join them for lunch.

"After lunch," he told the Colour, "you can show the boys how to site and arm the claymores and trip flares, while I go and set up the explosives in the farm ruins. Then, we'll talk through our fire plan."

The team were happy to lunch on just meat paste and biscuits, eager to get on with the business of war, eager to learn new skills. The Colour didn't disappoint them, after a demonstration allowing them the satisfaction of lying on their stomachs, withdrawing the safety pins and arming the trip flares for themselves.

Iffor allowed himself the thrill of anticipation building up inside him, as he called on the cunning he had learned in the British army when setting booby traps. He selected the position for the explosives with care, trying to imagine where his enemy would take cover. He moved slabs of concrete and burned timbers into a semicircle around the charge, giving the Lenshina a readymade firing point, inside his killing ground. He carefully covered the charge with smaller slabs of concrete. These would help conceal the charge, but would break up when the explosion occurred, for maximum effect. Satisfied with his work, he played out the cable as he walked back to the strong point, covering the cable with dirt and shrubs. It wasn't perfect, but in the heat of battle, he knew it was unlikely the Lenshina would pay much attention to the cable, even if they saw it.

He called the team around him. "Gentlemen, our fire plan:

"Twenty yards out, our barbed wire—twenty yards because that's as far as you can chuck a grenade.

"Ten yards out from the wire, three claymores fired electrically from our hand-exploders. And gentlemen, don't wait for me to give the order to fire them; if you see a sizeable group of enemy in front of one of the mines, let rip.

"Beyond the mines, our trip flares, triggered when the trip wire is tripped.

"The gun group have got two claymores and a couple of trip flares in front of their position.

"Plans for this afternoon chaps; we rest, one sentry up on the kopje with the Bren. I leave you with this thought: the sentry is the eyes and ears of his comrades; if he does his job well, his comrades can rest in safety. I'll write out a sentry roster.

"Stand to at last light."

Iffor spoke into his police radio: "Okay Bob?"

"Yes boss, we are standing to."

Iffor looked at the men standing beside him in the trench: Harry and Phil on his left, Hennie and Alvin on his right: two two-man teams, each man dressed in battle order, rifle at the ready; six primed grenades on the parapet in front of each team and a cable snaking out to the claymore in front of them. Each man full of confidence in his own and his comrade's ability, and ready for anything.

"We'll stand to for another twenty minutes. Then we'll stand down, have a meal and a couple of beers, then go into our night routine."

"Beer!" Harry exclaimed.

"Essential part of defence stores," Iffor answered.

He spoke to the Colour again: "Twenty minutes, then stand down. Let the boys cook a meal and grab some beers from the three tonner, they've earned it.

"We'll go into night routine, one man on the gun, hour at a time, the others sleeping. Stand to at dawn."

"Right boss."

"That goes for us down here," he told his team. "One man sentry, hour at a time, the others resting."

The night passed without incident, Iffor's main concern being an animal tripping a flare, but the spoor of man probably kept animals away from the ground defence area. He took the last sentry stag before dawn. As the first blush of the morning sun began to show in the east, he swept the perimeter with his binoculars one more time and then instigated the time honoured tradition of the British army at dawn, 'stand to'.

"Stand to," he called to his men, satisfied with their instant response. Up on the kopje, Iffor knew the Colour would be doing the same and taking up their stand to positions.

After the substantial compo breakfast: porridge, bacon grill and beans, washed down with a good hot brew. Iffor called in the fire section from the kopje for an orders group and to give them a chance to stretch their legs.

The men gathered around Iffor, some still drinking from metal mugs. Someone offered Iffor a mug. He accepted, sniffing suspiciously at its contents before risking a mouthful.

"I think, chaps," he started, "you'll agree that our efforts over the last twenty-four hours have made us all feel a little more confident in our ability to handle the Lenshina if they come our way."

Nods all round. "Bring 'em on," Alvin said. "We're ready for them." Again, affirmative nods all round.

"We'll go into our daytime routine now, lads. We'll have a two-man standing patrol on our perimeter, front and rear, going out at irregular intervals and staying out for different lengths of time, never more than an hour. The fire team on the kopje will ensure one man on the Bren at all times."

Harry put his hand up and asked, "Standing patrol boss?"

"A patrol," Iffor explained, "never more than four men to watch and listen over likely enemy approaches and to occupy positions the enemy may use if they attack." He chided himself for not being more explicit when he started his briefing. "There will also be a new latrine to be dug, water to be replenished, weapons to be cleaned and a wash and shave all round. Then, the Colour and I will show you how to make out 'range cards'."

Iffor walked back towards the kopje with the Colour. "Happy with things, Bob?" he asked.

"I think so boss. I'm a little concerned with my flank, so I've positioned a claymore out there, but all in all, I think things are going well."

The dull boring routine of soldiers in defence was interrupted only by meals and the standing patrols and Iffor's constant reminder, "Remember chaps, we're still in 'Injun country', keep your wits about you."

Night time routine was greeted with the prospect of a couple of beers—a welcome addition to 'defence stores' Iffor had insisted on—and the opportunity to lie in your sleeping bag looking into the night sky and enjoying the beauty of the African night.

It was with some relief that on the final morning Iffor announced, "'Pufo' time, chaps."

"Pufo?" someone queried

The Colour Sergeant volunteered the information. "Pack up and fuck off."

Leaving the Colour to wrap up the kopje position, and Harry supervising the coiling of the barbed wire, Iffor reeled himself along his cable to the explosives in the ruined farmhouse. This time he approached the farmhouse with a little less bravado and a little more caution than when he entered it on a previous occasion setting off the pressure plate which resulted in the place burning down. He gently withdrew the detonator from the primer, placed the explosive and cable into the large pack he brought with him, then retraced his steps, carefully avoiding the trip flares.

While Harry and the boys loaded the various defence stores, Iffor and the Colour disarmed the claymores and trip flares. "This is a first for me," Iffor said. Bob looked questioningly at him. "It's the first time I've made safe a trip flare without actually setting the fucking thing off."

The Colour chuckled, "Join the club!"

Leaving Bob and Harry to do a quick sweep of the area to see nothing had been left behind, Iffor ordered Phil to make radio contact with New Epsom and Battalion. "Advise Battalion we are leaving the area and heading back to base. Then advise Kensington that our ETA Kensington will be mid-afternoon. Then ask Charlie at North Road Farm to have some cold beers waiting for us. I need to chat to Shadrak."

In the cool of the early morning their small convoy set off for Arc Angel Farm, then it would be on to North Road Farm. It was still Iffor's intention to leave the defence stores at Archie's farm, and he would take

Archie up on his offer of a trailer and the armoured Rover to get the stores up to North Camp if speed was of the essence.

Archie was looking more dapper then usual: safari suit, polished shoes, Sam Browne belt and holster for his old webley, and bush hat. "I'm taking memsahib to Kensington for the weekend. Mind if we join your convoy? 'Safety in numbers' and all that, what!"

"Be my guest," Iffor said. "But we are stopping at Charlie's place for a beer or two."

"Suits me. That old bastard owes me a beer!"

Iffor's convoy, now swollen in size by Archie's World War II Jeep tucked in behind the Champ, swept past the sentry sanger and into the compound stopping in front of Charlie's bungalow. Charlie greeted them like long lost brothers; handshakes all round but with a special hug for Archie, who, after all, was his comrade-in-arms in the forefront of the war. "Beer?" he asked to no-one in particular, and was immediately surrounded by the team. Pausing long enough to tell Phil, "Sit rep to Kensington, please. Tell them where we are," he went in search of Shadrak.

Shadrak stood to greet him, chicken under one arm, his beloved Mauser resting against his tree with the bandolier hanging from the 'baling hook' of the weapon. "I see you N'kosi," he extended his hand.

Iffor gripped his hand firmly, "And I see you, my good friend," and produced the half-flask of Johnny Walker he had brought for the occasion, watching Shadrak's attention transferred from himself to the bottle.

They sat cross-legged in the dust under the tree. Shadrak took some corn from a pouch on his belt and threw a few grains to the chickens, so, well fed, they took no notice. The remainder he put into his mouth. He had learned many years ago that it was a waste of time to offer a white man a handful of corn to munch on.

Iffor unscrewed the cap on the bottle and offered the bottle to Shadrak. The old man waved it away. "It is better that you drink first," he said.

Iffor took a good swig and handed the bottle to the African. The M'dala drank deeply, then held the bottle in front of his face with both hands: "That is good N'kosi."

"It is yours, my friend." Iffor handed him the cap.

Shadrak knew why he had come. "I have news, N'kosi." He took another mouthful. "A woman follows the trail by the river. I think she is going to the village of my father; she leaves a spoor of too much blood."

"Is it her moon or is she wounded?" Iffor asked.

"She is wounded. I think she will die when she gets to the village."

Iffor's interest grew. "Was she carrying a child?"

"I do not know N'kosi, I saw no signs of a child. I knew I could not help her, so I did not try to find her."

"Keep looking for me M'dala, the man and the boy child."

Iffor rejoined his team where Charlie thrust a cold Castle into his grateful hand. "Your boys have just been telling me about your fort at the De Witt's old place. Do you think it will come to a fight?"

"Your guess is as good as mine old son, but if they do come down the Old Mwonza trail, that's where we'll stand and fight them."

Reluctantly, very reluctantly, after another hour or so, the convoy set out once more for Kensington. Iffor settled himself in his seat, looking over the Bren mounted in front of him on a sandbag. The patrol had gone well. He was pleased, and he knew the team were pleased with their own performance. He had the weekend ahead of him with Josie. Yes, the patrol had gone very well indeed.

She was waiting for him when they drove into the drill hall, as was the coloured Corporal Watney with two riflemen. "Thought you might like a hand unloading," he said. "Give you lads a chance to get off home." He turned to one of the riflemen, "Grab the guv'nor's Burgan and stick it in his pick-up." He turned to Iffor. "Good trip, sir?" he asked.

"Very good thanks, Corporal, but no hunting this time out."

"Shouldn't mind joining you on one of your patrols, if you'll have me, sir."

"Get past the Colour and you'll be most welcome. We could do with some of your experience." The man beamed with pleasure. Harry joined them and nodded at the group of soldiers gathered around Josie. "Take her home boss," he said, "I can't get any work out of those bastards while she's here, and there's no reason for you to stay."

"Thanks Harry, I'll leave you to it. Tell the boys to parade O eight hundred on Monday for a de-brief and a bit of maintenance on the Champ, then we'll have a liquid lunch at Boons."

He called to Josie, holding out his hand to her, and together they walked out into the M.T. yard to the pick-up. "And now my Indian princess, you can drive me home." As she started the vehicle, he leaned across and kissed her lightly on her cheek. "Remember the dome I conjured up when we had our picnic by the lake?" She just looked at him. "Well, it's waiting for us at home."

She didn't leave his side. She watched as he unpacked his Burgan, laying the contents on the bed ready for checking, cleaning and repacking. His Carbine and pistol he laid on the bed, to be cleaned later. Then she watched as he undressed, shaved, showered and dressed in shirt, shorts and flip-flops. "I'm all yours," he told her and wrapped his arms around her. "That is, when we've eaten and downed a couple of bottles of Cape Red."

She looked up at him, "Take a bottle into the garden and relax while I do dinner. It's only T-bone and salad, I'm afraid."

She waited until they had finished eating before she asked the inevitable question, "Any news on the missing twin?"

"No, no news on the twin," but he didn't want to tell her about the woman in the bush. He didn't want to raise any false hopes, but then again he didn't want to keep any secrets from her. Well, not too many. He went on, "But there has been a sighting of a girl, probably wounded and trying to get back to her village, but no sign of a baby."

She cleared away the dishes and took them back into the house, returning a few minutes later with a blanket and another bottle of wine. The house and garden was now in darkness. She laid out the blanket and sat down on it, patting the place beside her. Then she stretched out, lying on her back like a contented cat. He joined her, lying with his face inches from hers. "You're very daring," he said, kissing her lightly on the mouth.

"Remember our dome?" she answered. "No-one can see us, no-one can hear us?"

"You hussy!" and he started to undo the buttons of her blouse.

Iffor wasn't too upset when Josie told him they were expected at Auntie's for a curry lunch. He always enjoyed an authentic Indian curry, and it was important to Josie that he got to know her various Indian friends and relatives. "You are after all, family," she told him.

Auntie didn't waste words and came straight to the point: "You'll be having baby Helen next weekend, I expect. Make sure you give the doctor plenty of notice." Iffor looked round for some support. The last thing he wanted was the bloody baby for the weekend: he was hoping for some fishing with Mad Harry. Besides, too much of the baby and he might like to get to like her. Josie cooed, "What a lovely idea! Don't you think so, Iffor?"

Iffor smiled and nodded; the worms in his garden had a reprieve for another week. He looked around anxiously for Godfry, who was already making his way to him with a glass and a bottle of Krait on a tray. Next weekend was going to be a 'write- off', so he may as well enjoy this weekend.

Josie drove them back to the bungalow after Auntie had whispered to her, "I think Iffor's little worse for wear." She helped him undress and showered with him. Then they lay on the bed together, allowing the scented breeze to dry them.

"You will keep looking for the other twin, won't you?"

"Of course I will, my darling," he said, wishing she would go to sleep.

"That's the first time you called me 'darling'. Was it you or the beer talking?"

He had enough wit about him to remain silent for a few moments. Then he gently squeezed her hand, "It was me, my darling girl."

PART NINETEEN

In battle, fire control and fire discipline are vital if the battle is to be won.

I **FFOR SAT AT HIS DESK** observing as Blue Watch came into his office and sat down. The last to arrive was Davy Jones, in combats with his SMG slung over his shoulder. He had asked Corporal Watney to attend, since it was essential he knew what was going on, and he hoped the Colour Sergeant would give permission for the Corporal to join one of his patrols.

He began his de-brief and summary. "Gentlemen, when I arrived on the scene the terrorists ruled the roost, they dominated the ground. The only reason they didn't hit the farms was that they didn't want to sustain casualties, that's why they went for soft targets. Well, we changed all that when we wiped out our local gang at the monastery. But it is essential that we now dominate that same ground. We can't afford to relax our guard. However, I'm going to change our routine. We will continue with our standing patrols with a split force, half in the field, half resting but ready for a hot call-out. Our patrols will be regular but at irregular intervals. Alvin, there'll be no rest for you, I'm afraid. I'll need a medic with the team in the bush."

Corporal Watney stood up. "I'm a trained army medic sir, and I've got my own medical kit. I was a medic with 'A' company. I was sent here to recover from my wound."

Iffor looked at the Colour. "He was shot in the arse by a sentry when he was having a crap outside the perimeter," Bob said. "But if he wants to go into the bush, he can go."

"That makes life a little easier," Iffor said. "Our new order of battle then, gentlemen: Mad Harry, Phil, Hennie and the phantom crapper; the second brick will be Mal, Alvin, Evil and Shamus. Mal, I'd like you to assume your former army rank of corporal please. In the event that 'Alice' decides to pay us a visit while half our team are in the bush, we'll R.V. at Arc Angel farm. If we can use the Islander, we will. If not, we'll have to come up by road. The mine have agreed to loan us one of their security team's armoured Rovers. Is that right Colour?"

"Yes boss, I'm taking one of my serfs with me to collect it later on this morning. Should be back by lunchtime."

"Thank-you Colour, we'll use the armoured Rover for the team in the bush and the Champ for the cavalry. The Bren will stay with the Rover. Evil, show Phil how to clean the Bren, he'll be the gunner of his team."

Iffor looked at his watch, "Shan't keep you much longer. Last week's adventure, for my money, a total success. You all now know what the plan is, you know how to put it into operation. I feel you now have more confidence in our ability to meet any threat, and more importantly, you have more confidence in your own ability. Am I right?"

Harry spoke for them all: "Spot on, boss."

"Good. Now I've one more task." He keyed the intercom: "Bring them in please, Josie."

Josie came into the office and placed a cardboard box on Iffor's desk.

"Gentlemen," he began, "for your actions at the Lamumbwa monastery, there will be no medals. This war is being fought by corporals and squaddies, not colonels and generals. So in future when people ask 'what did you do in the war?' you will be able to show them this." He reached into the box and produced a framed certificate. "This," he said, "acknowledges your part in the parachute assault and the battle at the monastery. I've also got a certificate for Pete to hang up in his police station and a larger framed certificate to hang up in the Moth club."

The men came one by one to collect the certificates, shaking Iffor's hand and acknowledging his salute. The Colour was last. "Couldn't have done it without you Bob."

"I know that," he responded with a cheeky grin.

After a couple of minutes that allowed the men to read and admire their certificates, Iffor continued with his briefing: "Warning order Harry, standing patrol for Wednesday, leaving at sparrows fart."

Harry got his notebook out and tried to look intelligent.

"Your patrol will cover the area east of the North Road, showing the flag at the Dix farm, the monastery and the Mission. But I also want you to stop off at the kraals in the area. Let the phantom crapper do some doctoring and see if you can pick up any useful information.

"Wednesday evening at last light, I want you to establish a V.C.P at the junction of North Road and the Lamumbwa Road. You'll be looking for weapons and explosives. You'll only need one sentry on at a time. The road is straight, so the sentry will have plenty of time to see the car headlights and wake the others. If a car approaches without lights, no warning, just zap it with the Bren.

Mal, I'm going to give you a warning order for a task, otherwise the boredom will drive your lads to drink, and we don't want that, do we?"

"No boss."

"Mal, liaise with Harry, and when he comes in on Thursday, I want you to take over the armoured Rover, refuel and load your own stores, and late afternoon on Thursday, drive to the drift below North Camp and set up an ambush on the trail on the north side of the river. With luck, animals coming to drink at the river will come in behind you, so there will be less risk of an animal setting off your trip flares. You will establish your own killing ground and shoot anyone coming into your killing ground. You will withdraw at first light, which is about an hour before curfew ends, and return to base. If you want to stop off at the farms, I'll leave that to you."

Mal stood up. "Surely boss, with little risk of any terrorists being in the area, the only person we are likely to encounter is some poor bastard who's crept out of his hut to go and meet up with his fancy piece in the bush. If we open fire we are likely to kill some poor bloody innocent black."

"Precisely," Iffor said quite quietly and deliberately. "Then the locals will know the army are still in the game and on the ball. Right lads!" Iffor clapped his hands together. "Downstairs, work to be done. Harry, Mal have a chat to the Colour, see what extra kit you'll need, torches and the like. And don't forget, lads, we're having a beer at Boons at lunchtime. We'll celebrate Mal's promotion."

The Colour stayed behind. "Thought you should know boss, we've had a delivery of ammo to bring us up to scale. I can let you have number eighty-three grenades, smoke, and number eighty grenades."

"White phosphorous!" Iffor interrupted him. "Wonderful, my favourite weapon. They'll both come in bloody useful. Add them on to our first line ammunition scale."

Although it was quite normal for farmers and the like to take their rifles into Boons bar, this was the army and Iffor had to be precise:

"In a straight line with your weapons please lads. Unload. For inspection, port arms."

Iffor inspected the weapons, ensuring the chambers were empty of a live round.

"Make safe!"

Magazines were placed back onto the weapons but the weapons were not cocked.

Boons was unusually busy for a Monday, but the high-backed settle, normally occupied by Davy and his ape, was vacant, probably because most people knew that to sit there with the ape present, meant being victim to one of the his horrendous farts. The team gathered around the large table calling on Billy for beers all round. On Mal.

Evil made a point of sitting next to Iffor. "That ambush boss, at the drift, you know I won't let you down, don't you? If anyone appears in the killing ground, I'll give him a burst no matter how fucking innocent he is."

Iffor put his arm around Evil's shoulder, giving him a firm hug, "That's what I'm counting on my Evil little friend, that's what I'm counting on."

Harry was on his feet. "If you two lovebirds have finished hugging one another and whispering in each other's ear, I'd like to propose a toast:

"Gentlemen, Blue Watch!"

They downed their beers, calling on Billy for, "More ale landlord."

Iffor tapped his empty glass on the table. "May I propose another toast please, gentlemen?" He waited until he had complete silence:

"Gentlemen, Absent Friends!"

Harry broke the silence. "Are we still on for our fishing trip this weekend, boss?"

"'Fraid not, Harry. I'm going up to the Mission on Friday to collect baby Helen for the weekend. It will have to be the following weekend."

"Do you need an escort?" Alvin said. "Someone to make sure you don't run into any trouble, if you know what I mean."

"No thank-you." Iffor knew exactly what he meant.

"If you're not back by Tuesday, do you want us to come and collect you?" Alvin was now pushing his luck.

"Thank you for your concern and consideration, Alvin. I'm deeply touched, but if I'm not back by Tuesday, it will be because I'm delighting in Grace's company and drinking her cold beer in the shade of her bungalow. Whereas you, my friend, will be digging slit trenches on the south side of the drift at North Camp."

Alvin backed off; taking the piss out of Iffor was not a good move.

"As it happens," Iffor went on, "I'm taking Josie with me to collect the baby and she will be with me when I take the baby back on Monday. But Alvin, you're quite right, I should have someone with me just in case, so if you're free, I'd appreciate your company." The relief on Alvin's face was visible for all to see.

Billy appeared from behind the bar with a hammer and picture hook,

"Let's be having that certificate of yours, Davy. There's only one place for it to hang." He nailed the picture hook to the top of the settle and hung up the certificate. "That's where it belongs and that's where it stays. The drinks are on me, boys."

Another round of drinks and Iffor called a halt to the proceedings. The last thing he wanted was drunken soldiers with weapons, driving or walking home, and he wanted to get back to the drill hall to inspect the armoured Land Rover.

He stopped off at the police station. "Sundowner at my place, drinks and nibbles," he told his friend. "No need to change, come as you are."

The Colour Sergeant had the Land Rover in the drill hall. He and Corporal Watney had already removed the windscreen and made a cradle of sandbags for the Bren. "What do you think of her, Colour?"

"She hasn't got the armour that the police Rhino has got, but she's a lot faster; she'll do us boss."

Iffor went up to Josie's office. "D'ya mind if I have Pete and the Colour for a sundowner this evening?"

"Oh Iffor, what a lovely idea!" Then hesitatingly she said, "Shall I ask Auntie to organise some nibbles?"

"That, my gorgeous wondrous one, is also a lovely idea. Now tell me what's the Colour's wife's name? I've never met her."

"Michelle, and you'll love her."

He kissed her lightly on the lips and went back down into the drill hall to inspect the Rover. "Nibbles and drinks at my place this evening, if you and Michelle can make it please Bob, about sixish, an informal sundowner. Don't worry about getting changed."

Aware that the Corporal was listening, Iffor said, "That applies to you if you've got nothing else on."

"Thank you sir, but Sergeant Simmonds has asked me and my lads to join Blue Watch at the Moth club tonight."

Iffor wandered back up to his office. There were still mundane returns to be sent to Battalion, travel warrants to be signed and, more importantly, his report to the Colonel on his previous patrol. He looked at his watch, three o'clock. He reasoned, if he started on his office work now, it would be after five before he finished. But if he knocked off now… there was, after all, beer and wine to be collected from the liquor store, and whatever Auntie could knock up in the way of snacks had to be collected. He locked the office and went in search of Josie. "Come wench, we're calling it a day. Places to go, things to do and people to see."

Meeting Michelle for that first time filled Iffor with guilt and remorse. As he took her hand, he suddenly realised the dangers he had subjected her husband to. The Colour had done his bit in the bush and had earned his job in the safety of Battalion headquarters. What right did he have asking him to risk his life again? But as he studied her, aware that she was studying him, he knew he would be calling on the Colour again to put himself in harm's way.

The woman he was looking at was tall, willowy, slim with raven-black hair. He now realised why the term raven-black was used to describe a woman's hair. Hers was jet-black and shining, just like a raven's plumage. Born and bred in Rhodesia of good farming stock, she seemed the ideal match for Bob Pearson.

He took her arm and led her into the garden, only to be intercepted by Josie. "Put that woman down! Come Michelle, let me show you what I've bought for baby Helen." And the two of them wandered back into the house already engrossed in baby talk.

The three men settled themselves comfortably around the garden table, savouring the delights of a cold Castle. Still in uniform, still carrying holstered pistols, three warriors relaxing... perfect!

Iffor nodded towards the carrier bag on the table. "Present for you Pete, my old son." Pete looked at the framed certificate. "That," he said, "is bloody white of you, my chaps will love seeing that hanging in the station."

"I got your officers' names from Agnes when you weren't looking; she obviously kept my secret."

Pete chuckled. "When Agnes says her lips are sealed, they are well and truly sealed."

"Good move of yours boss, sending young Watney out on patrol with Harry's team," Bob said. "He's a good man."

"Have we got a new member?" Pete asked.

"Yes. Now, let me bring you up to date with what's been happening."

Iffor refilled their glasses before going into detail about the building of defences at North Camp. He was interrupted momentarily by Auntie's voice announcing her arrival. Her condition for knocking up a curry at such short notice was that she could serve it to the guests.

"So that's my battle plan for taking on the Lenshina, should they venture into our part of the world," Iffor said. "I've split Blue Watch into two bricks, one resting, one in the bush showing the flag. The emphasis on our patrolling is hearts and minds of the villages and kraals with our two pox doctor's clerks dishing out anti-malaria pills. And on the subject of my patrols, Pete, is the curfew still in effect?"

"Yup, sunset minus an hour, sunrise plus an hour. If you should happen to shoot anyone outside those hours, don't forget to say sorry."

The two girls joined them. "Auntie says the curry's ready, you can go and get it." Josie looked quite smug, "She says those no-good layabout men in the garden can bring our meals out to us girls."

After ensuring the three men had a second bowl of curry each, Auntie joined them in the garden where, inevitably, the conversation turned to baby Helen.

"Have you phoned Grace to arrange for the baby to come to us for the weekend?" Auntie asked, in a tone of voice normally reserved for a mother-in-law talking to her son-in-law. Iffor visibly cringed. Pete smiled the sort of smile which said, I'm single.

"No Auntie, it's my first job in the morning. Then I'll write my report to the Colonel." He looked across at the Colour. "Josie and I will be driving up to the Mission on Friday to collect the baby, okay with you?"

The Colour nodded, "Fine with me."

The evening turned out to be one of those evenings when time seemed to stand still, each one delighting in the company of the others. Even Auntie was speaking softly, and, throwing off her 'I'm in charge' routine, was showing how she really cared for those around her. Iffor noticed with some satisfaction she was into her third glass of Tia Maria. Pete would have to drive her home.

One of the nice things about Africa is that you can step out of the shower, with just a towel around your waist and into the garden, where you can pick a pawpaw fruit off the tree and eat it for breakfast. With of course a cold Castle, providing Josie didn't catch you drinking it. She joined him in the garden with a bowl of cereal. As she kissed him she smelt the fresh alcohol on his breath. "Iffor!" she chided.

"Well, fresh alcohol is better than last night's stale alcohol," he said in his defence. She sat opposite him, looking cool and seductive in a blouse and slim skirt, with a scarf about her throat.

"I'd better go and get changed into uniform or we'll be late."

"Yes, you'd better had."

"Do you want to come with me while I change? We can talk."

"No, I'll stay here and finish my coffee."

"I'll need you to pull my shirt down from inside my shorts."

"You're a big boy now, you'll cope."

He leaned over her, feeling for her nipple through her thin cotton blouse, "And I'm getting even bigger."

Leaving the pick-up in the M.T yard, they walked into the drill hall.

"Sorry we're late Colour, trouble with the car."

"Had the same trouble myself boss, don't worry about it."

Corporal Watney came shuffling up to Iffor. Started to salute, remembered he wasn't wearing a beret, and put his arm down to his side again. Sweating profusely, he looked much paler than any coloured man should normally look.

"Sir, me and my two lads aren't feeling too good this morning. Chance we could stand down for a couple of hours?"

"By the look of you, Corporal, you broke the cardinal rule of trying to match Mad Harry drink for drink last night. Am I right?"

"Sir!"

Iffor could only pity the man—he'd been in the same situation many times himself. "What do you think, Colour?"

The Colour wagged his finger at the hapless Corporal. "Get your lads back to their pits, back on parade at thirteen hundred. I've got some jobs need doing. But you, Corporal, you can knock off early this afternoon to get your kit organised. You're off into the Bundu tomorrow at sparrows'." The Corporal started to mutter his thanks, but the pale of his cheeks turned to a motley reddish, bluish, yellowish colour as he made a bolt for the bogs.

"You spoil those men, Bob."

"Only did what you would have done boss. Can't understand how they get so pissed."

Mal and his band were stood down until Thursday afternoon. Harry and his group would be in after lunch to load the trailer and fuel up the Rover, and collect stores and ammo, plus last minute instructions from Iffor.

Knowing Harry, he and his lads would sleep in the drill hall that night, ready for a dawn start. Iffor made a mental note to pop in to see them some time that night... with a bottle.

He went upstairs to his office, calling in on Josie first. He stuck his head round the door: "Has anybody told you yet today, you're wonderful."

"Go away," she said without looking up.

He completed his report to the Colonel, and pressed the intercom for Josie to come in. He handed her the report. "In code please, Josie. Class it 'classified routine'.

He phoned the Scouts at Kariba. The news wasn't good: "We've pulled our team out, old boy. The Lenshina are stepping up their own security. More patrols and sentries, and a lot more activity in the camp. Oh, and they've managed to get hold of some RPD's."

RPD! The Soviet light machine-gun: belt fed, easy to use, devastating inside six hundred metres. The scales were tilting slightly in favour of the nasties; Iffor was beginning to feel distinctly uneasy.

He put through a call to Support at Mwonza. Dick Francis confirmed his fears: "I've pulled in my standing patrol, too dangerous, and we've gone to 'Bravo state'. It's probably not necessary, but we are too thin on the ground to take chances. If they start to move, you'll be first to know," he paused. "After me, that is."

Iffor sat back in his chair, thinking hard. If he was in command of the Lenshina, he would put a fire group of two or three machine-guns on a flank, keeping the defenders' heads down and unable to return fire, while his own people strolled up to the trench and dropped some grenades in.

He cheered up. If that happened, his own gun group would take care of them. Still... He went down to the drill hall to confer with the Colour. "News from the front ain't good Bob. The Lenshina are showing signs of activity and they've taken delivery of some RPDs. Under normal circumstances, if they were clever enough to attack us with a section of machine-guns on our flank, keeping our heads down, we'd be fucked. But my plan of sticking a gun group up on the kopje is more credible now. If they do stick a fire section out on my flank, your gun team will be able to keep 'their' heads down while we concentrate on the foot soldiers."

"If they come at you over open ground, firing machine-guns from the hip, what then?" the Colour asked.

"Well, in my opinion, they'll be firing the machine-guns, not for effect, but to raise the morale of their mates as they charge across open ground. I'll be responsible for picking off the machine gunners. I can identify them better than the other chaps."

Bob looked at his watch. "If you don't mind boss, I've a dozen riflemen due any minute for kitting out before they go back to Battalion this evening, and they'll be expecting their travel documents from you."

"Christ! I'd forgotten all about that." Mounting the stairs three at a time, Iffor called to Josie. She opened the door to her office, "What's all the panic about?"

"Travel documents for the twelve riflemen on tonight's train. I'd forgotten about them."

"On your desk waiting for you to sign them," she said, sighing audibly at his incompetence.

"Have I told you yet today that you are won…" She'd already closed the door on him.

As he sat down at his desk, Josie came through on the intercom: "You owe me lunch at the Elephant, and don't forget to phone Grace about baby Helen; do it now!"

He did as bid. Grace couldn't be disturbed—just as well, he thought—but the child's nurse, Maureen, was brought to the phone. "Yes, of course you can have the baby for the weekend. As a matter of fact, I was wondering how I could get into town to see my parents, so if you can give me a lift, you can have the baby to yourselves. I'm sure you can manage."

"That's fine Maureen, but it means I won't get to hear you singing your lovely Xhosa songs to the baby." She chuckled, delighted that he had recognised her Xhosa tongue. "Another time perhaps," she said.

He was in the phoning mood now, and called Ed Dix. Ed wasn't around; Verity answered the phone. "Just to let you know that some of my chaps will be visiting you tomorrow, probably mid-morning." As an afterthought he said, "Try not to shoot any of them." Without a word, she put the phone down on him. Now why did she do that? he asked himself. Then he phoned Charlie at North Road Farm: "My boys will be in your area on Thursday night. Whatever you do, don't let Shadrak go into the bush—I don't want him wandering into my lad's ambush."

"Okay Iffor, thanks for telling me."

One last call, he told himself, then a sandwich and a cold Castle.

He got through to Boons and Davy Jones. "Davy, I've got two patrols in the field this week, stay sober and stay close to a phone. And Davy…"

"Yes boss."

"Mum's the word."

"You can depend on me boss."

As he put the phone down, Josie came into the office. "Ready? I'm starving."

He waited until they were seated on a balcony table, drinks in front of them and sandwiches ordered, before he gave her the good news. "We can have baby Helen for the weekend. Maureen's coming into town, but she is staying with her family so yo… we," he corrected himself, "can have the baby all to ourselves. Apart from Auntie, Michelle and a string of other women coming to coo over the child, he thought. Still, he told himself, they probably wouldn't miss me if I popped down to Boons for an hour or three.

"When can we collect her?" Josie asked.

"Well, that rather depends on you, my little one. If you can persuade your boss to give you the day off, we can pick her up on Friday morning."

She thought about it for a few moments, looking puzzled. "But you're my boss," she said.

"Precisely."

She smiled the smile that made his heart beat that much faster—just as it did when he was standing at 'action stations' in the Hastings when the 'red' came on. She broke into his thoughts, "You can tell me again if you want to."

"You're wonderful!"

She reached across the table, touching his hand, "And you make me very, very happy."

The arrival of the sandwiches heralded the arrival of Pete.

"Another plate of sandwiches, two Castles and an orange juice please," Iffor told the waiter. "To what do we owe the honour?" he asked Pete.

"Just came to have lunch with my two favourite people, and to thank you again for that framed certificate. My lads are cock-a-hoop over it; Timothy Banda almost smiled! Seriously Iffor, you couldn't have made a better gesture. My lads feel more involved in this war, and they want to get more involved."

"If Alice and her cronies get past me at North Camp,"—this time it was Iffor who grabbed the last sandwich—"your boys will be very involved keeping the Lenshina from destroying this town."

Josie looked concerned. "Surely it won't come to that?"

"No my sweet, they won't get past me."

But she saw the look that the two men exchanged. And she suddenly felt very afraid and squeezed his hand.

Mad Harry and his small team were waiting for him when he got back to the drill hall. "Got a bit more colour in your cheeks, I see."

Corporal Watney offered a smile of sorts; he'd heard it all before.

"We're going to load the Rover now and come back again tonight and sleep here. The Colour's going to be here in case there are any last minute bits we may have forgotten," Harry told him.

"I'll be here myself," Iffor said, "just to tuck you in and kiss you goodnight."

"Can't wait," Evil said.

"A word please, Harry," and Iffor led the way to his office.

"Grab a chair and I'll bring you up to date with the current situation."

He told Harry about his conversations with the Scouts and Mwonza.

"It looks like things are beginning to hot up, so be on your toes."

Harry nodded. "You have your primary tasks and objectives, but while the phantom crapper is doing his bit of doctoring in the kraals, keep your eyes and ears open for anything unusual.

"Right boss."

"And Harry, any situation you're not happy with, get your arse back here or call for help on your radio. We can be with you in two hours. Thanks Harry. Now send Corporal Watney up to me, please."

The tall, lanky coloured man came into the office and saluted.

"Take a seat please, Corporal." The Corporal looked distinctly uneasy; he should not have come on parade in the state he was in the previous morning. He need not have worried. "You come highly recommended by the Colour. I imagine you two go back a few years together," Iffor said, trying to put the man at his ease.

"Yessir, I've served with him for about ten years."

"Now you are off into the bush with Mad, sorry, Sergeant Simmonds tonight."

"It's all right sir, Sergeant Simmonds has told me to call him Mad Harry."

"And what else did he tell you?"

"He told me that in spite of my bush fighting experience, I was to keep my opinions to myself until he asked for them."

"Which, Corporal, is what I invited you up here to tell you myself. That's it, off you go."

The afternoon seemed to drag by. Iffor got up from his desk for yet another peer at the map on his wall, looking for inspiration. The die was cast—it was up to Mal and Harry to keep an eye on things in the bush over the next couple of days. Much as he would have liked to have been with them, he couldn't. They'd earned his trust and now he had to trust them.

The twelve riflemen had drawn their kit and travel documents, and gone off to wait for the evening train. Josie was trying to get ahead of herself, so she could take Friday off, while the Colour... the Colour came into his office.

"You wanted to tell me about your phone calls and the current situation," he said. "Can I suggest we do it down in Auntie's garden over a couple of beers? Josie can join us later."

Iffor stood, grabbing for his beret, "Colour, has anybody told you you're wonderful?"

"No sir, and I'd rather you didn't."

The two men settled themselves under one of Auntie's copious sun umbrellas, enjoying a cold beer. It wasn't strategy or tactics they needed to discuss, it was more a question of reassurance that they had the right strategy.

"What's worrying me," the Colour said, "if the Lenshina have got a couple of RPD machine-guns, the chances are they've also got a couple of RPG launchers, and that will make life really interesting. It will only take one or two of those rocket propelled grenades to knock my gun group off the Kkpje."

"I had thought about that, thank you Bob, and I'm trying hard not to think about it, if you see what I mean."

Josie appeared, flushed and breathless. "Phone the Colonel, Iffor; it's urgent."

Leaving Josie to drink his beer, he hurried back to his office. "It's Meredith, Colonel."

"Ah, Iffor my boy, good and bad news I'm afraid, but something you should be aware of. A section of nine platoon stumbled into a terrorists' forming-up position and got involved in a fire fight. They were able to whistle up the other two sections and a good battle ensued. We killed a dozen or so, but we lost six good men. The thing is, Iffor, these terrorists were obviously about to cross into Rhodesia. They were well equipped, and had plenty of food and ammunition; I'll send you a sit rep."

Iffor hurried back to the hotel, pausing only to get two bottles of 'Liquid Sunshine' rum from the liquor store for Harry's team. "Bad news Bob, Nine platoon have lost six blokes with several wounded."

"That would be 'C' company," the Colour said. "The New Epsom company."

Iffor suddenly hated himself for being relieved that it was the New Epsom company that had had the fatalities. The worst job in the army was going to tell next of kin that their son or husband had been killed.

"The thing is, Colour, they were carrying enough food and ammo for a sortie into Rhodesia. So were they intent on causing mayhem and havoc in the Lamumbwa valley... or was it a deception to take our attention away from the Lenshina?"

"Your guess is as good as mine," Bob answered. "But we must assume the worst."

"Which is?" But Iffor already knew the answer.

"It's a deception attack, and we can expect a visit from Alice quite soon," the Colour confirmed.

"I agree." Iffor beckoned to Godfry for another round of drinks. "But when?"

Pleasant as it was sitting in the garden drinking with his mate, Iffor knew Josie was anxious to get home and relax in her own garden, especially since he had volunteered to cook the evening meal. This, Iffor considered, was no big deal, since there was plenty of curry left over from the previous evening.

After dinner, they sat side by side watching the sun as it slowly began to edge towards the west. "This is the best time of day," he said reaching for her hand, "Would that it could always be this peaceful."

"Remember what you told me?" She had turned to look at him. "Inside our dome no one can interfere with us or our peace."

He got up and kissed her on the mouth. "You are absolutely right. Now my little one, I've got to go and talk to the boys before they leave. Back in an hour."

As usual, the Colour had beaten him to it and was talking to Harry. The rest of the team were laying out their sleeping bags in one corner of the drill hall. For convenience, the bags were formed in a semicircle around a couple of cases of Castle and close to the toilets. Since Bob and Harry had things well in hand, there was little point in Iffor staying. He gathered the team around him,

"Chaps, 'C' company have had a good contact at New Epsom; they hit a large bunch of terrs trying to get across the border and killed a dozen or more." He lowered his voice, "We lost six men; six good men. The point I want to make, lads, is that a large bunch of terrorists was the last thing that Point Section expected to meet up with, so expect the unexpected, leave nothing to chance, keep your wits about you."

He handed the bottle of rum to Harry. "Breakfast," he said, and left them to it.

For the first time since he had known her, albeit quite a short time, she grumbled as he dragged her out of bed, "For goodness sake Iffor, it's only just after six, surely you can wait for another hour or two before you radio Harry? He's only been on the road a couple of hours."

She was right of course, but Iffor was like a mother hen; his chicks were away from the nest and he had to check on them.

"Leave me here," she said, "and come back for me when you've made your call to Harry." Before he could answer, the phone rang.

He came back into the bedroom ant sat on the bed. "Well?" she asked.

"That was the police station, Harry's radio check."

"Well?" she asked again.

"Nothing to report."

"Breakfast in bed for me this morning, I think." She snuggled back under the covers with her back towards him, "Coffee and toast will do."

The mid-morning ritual of tea and stickies was interrupted by the phone call from the Scouts. The Colour and Josie indicated leaving the office, but Iffor waved them back into their chairs.

"Morning Meredith, Intelligence Officer Selous Scouts here. Just wondered if you have any news on the Lenshina for us."

"As I understand it," Iffor replied, "your regiment being the eyes and ears of the Rhodesian army should be doing that."

"I understand what you're saying old boy, but the Lenshina are an unknown entity for us. We don't know anything about them, not having encountered them before, and I really don't think they pose much of a threat."

"Well, I do know them, and I have encountered them before, and as far as I am concerned, they are as much a threat to the Rhodesian army as you are," Iffor put his hand over the mouthpiece before uttering, "you cunt. And another thing." Iffor was in full sail now, "The greatest authority on the Lenshina in the Rhodesian army is a member of your fucking regiment. I sent him to you."

"You mean…"

"Don't say his name. His section of Zambian army intelligence was responsible for Lenshina affairs and to my certain knowledge he infiltrated them on at least three occasions."

An idea was forming in Iffor's head. "Look," he said trying to sound more reasonable. "I need to speak to you, your Colonel and my man face to face. I think it's important."

The Scout was anxious to make amends. "I'll send a chopper for you later today; I'll advise you of ETA. Oh, and sorry about the misunderstanding."

A fool he might be, Iffor thought, as the helicopter made its approach to the Kensington airfield, but he couldn't fault his efficiency.

An hour later he was standing in front of the legendary Colonel Ron Ried-Daley. "I've spoken to your Colonel about you, Meredith. He's asked me to give you whatever help we can. Grab a chair and tell me what we can do for you." Iffor sat; the IO, a captain, remained standing.

"The Lenshina, Colonel, have joined forces with ZAPU and are being trained by Cubans."

"We were able to tell them that, Colonel," the I.O said.

Iffor went on, "Their leader, Alice, needs to assert her authority with ZAPU, and since the Zambians are totally pissed off, after what we did to their chaps in the Lamumbwa valley, it's reasonable to expect them to cross the border and cause utter fuck in the Kensington area. I'm ready for them, but the only warning I'm going to get when they start on their rampage, will be a radio message from our Support Company at Mwonza, before they are overrun, and possibly a message from the protected village, before the chaps there are slaughtered. I need notice and time, if I and my *eight* men..." he emphasised the word 'eight'... "are to have any chance meeting them on my terms and on my killing ground."

"What's the strength of the Lenshina?" the Colonel looked at the IO for his answer.

"Between twenty-five and thirty fighting men and a few hangers on, Colonel."

"Carry on please, Meredith." The Colonel liked what he was hearing.

"Moses January has infiltrated the Lenshina on at least three occasions. Although he's a Nyasa, he was brought up in Fort Jameson and speaks the local dialect, as well as Portuguese, so he wouldn't be out of place with the Lenshina. I suggest we insert him over the border to make contact with the Lenshina. He can live among them, until such time as he finds out when they are on the move, then get back to me as soon as he can."

The IO started to say something, but Iffor pre-empted him: "Moses already has a good cover story. When we caught him, he was on a mission to lead terrorists back into Zambia. He knows the route to avoid our army patrols. He simply tells Lenshina what his task was when he was ambushed by us and wounded. He will tell them he escaped and has been lying up in a kraal, recovering from his wounds."

"This chap January, will he agree to this scheme do you think?" the Colonel asked.

"He will if I ask him; I've just got his son into Sandhurst for him," Iffor replied.

"And we got his son out of Zambia," the IO said, scoring a point. The Colonel ignored the comment. "Go and fetch Moses January," he said.

Waiting for Moses gave the Colonel a chance to speak to Iffor. "That parachute drop onto the monastery, sheer genius," he said. "Especially since the average age of your chaps was what? Fifty?"

"Fifty-five, Colonel, and Mad Harry—sorry, Sergeant Simmonds— is sixty."

The Colonel silently shook his head as if in disbelief. "I suppose I can't entice you to join my regiment? I've got a vacancy for a captain."

Moses arrived before Iffor could answer. Since Iffor last saw him he was leaner, fitter and wore his uniform and Selous Scouts' beret with obvious pride. He couldn't help himself; breaking into a huge grin, he wrapped his arms around Iffor lifting him off the floor, "Iffor, we wear the same uniform again, we are brothers," which made Iffor feel even more guilty for what he was about to ask him.

Moses listened to Iffor's plan; then to the Colonel, who explained the dangers. "I will do this thing," he said simply. "It is my duty, for I am now a Selous Scout."

"When do you want him?" the Colonel asked.

"Soon as possible. I think our 'C' company contact might have been a deception, to draw forces operating further to the west to reinforce the troops at New Epsom."

The Colonel nodded approvingly. "You may be right. Anyway," he added—the meeting was coming to an end—"you can't have him for a few days; we just don't send our chaps willy-nilly into the bush. We have to prepare him, clothe him and arm him and make him look like a terrorist. We have to arrange an escape route. We'll have a standing patrol ready at an RV to bring him out if need be. How will you insert him?"

"I'll take a small patrol up to the point where we caught him. He can take it from there, and I'll arrange a method of contacting me, and I'll warn the farms in the area that we have 'friendlies' operating, so no impromptu ambushes."

"Well, that's it gentlemen. Thanks for coming, Meredith. We're all on the same side. I'll let you know when you can have trooper January; we'll fly him down to you. You'll be responsible for his security and safety."

Iffor saluted and shook the great man's hand.

"Remember what I said, Meredith. If you fancy a change, there's a slot for you here."

Iffor mused, that's the second time that's been said to me.

PART TWENTY

The morale of the soldier is the most important single factor in war

THURSDAY MORNING and Mal and his team were waiting for Harry's team to come back in. His last radio check announced he would be back by noon. It was now a little after eleven. With Mal's help, the armoured Land Rover could be unloaded, stores checked and replaced and loaded back onto the Rover, ready for Mal's excursion into the bush that evening, and the two teams would be in Boons by one o'clock enjoying a cold Castle.

The roar of the Rover coming into the drill hall through the roller door that led into the M.T. yard, gave Iffor some respite from the report he was writing for the Colonel with reference to Moses January. He'd got as far as the heading, 'Secret, Staff in confidence', and then got stuck. He wanted to sound as casual as he could about borrowing a man from Selous Scouts and sending him into the Lenshina camp. How could he say in his report, "Oh, and by the way, Colonel…"

Harry would give him inspiration; he hurried downstairs to greet him.

"Hello Harry, going away?"

Harry was lifting an empty jerrican out of the Rover. "No, we've been away, just got back, didn't you miss us?" Then, realising the joke was on him, said, "You bastard, I bet you couldn't sleep at night worrying about us. Do you want a written report boss, or…?"

"No, come up to my office when you've got the lads organised and tell me about your trip, and bring Mal with you."

Harry flopped into a chair. Iffor opened his bottom drawer and produced a bottle of Chivas Regal and three glasses. "Our secret," he said. "No-one knows about this." And he poured the golden liquid into the glasses.

"I've nothing definite to report," Harry said. "The phantom crapper did some really good work in the kraals; we stopped a few vehicles, tried the wine at the monastery, and said hello to Ed Dix and Doctor Grace. She said to say hello to you, by the way. But something's up boss; I could feel it, we all could, you could almost smell the fear in the kraals, and all the young single men have left, heading south, getting out of the area while they could. The bush telegraph has been really active, spreading doom and gloom, and we could see how grateful the Africans were for us being there, 'showing the flag' and all that bollocks. I promised we'd be back soon."

"And so you shall, my friend, so you shall. Now let me tell you what I've been up to," and Iffor revealed his plan for Moses January.

"Fuck me boss, does the Colonel now about this?" Mal exclaimed.

Iffor tapped the paper in front of him. "My report to the Colonel. I'm trying to tell him without actually telling him, if you see what I mean."

"No," said Harry.

"Nor me," said Mal.

"What time are you leaving tonight, Mal?" Iffor asked.

"Eighteen hundred boss, we'll drive off into the sunset."

"I'll be here to give you an update before you leave. Thanks guys."

Iffor returned to his report and told it just as it was. Then he wrote a letter to Colonel Ried-Daly of the Selous Scouts, thanking him for his co-operation, and detailing his plans for the defence of North Camp. And finally, a letter to the General in England asking for a progress report on Moses's son.

Having nothing better to do, Iffor went downstairs to the Colour's office. He was sitting at his desk, looking into an empty cup, while his two riflemen were pretending to count blankets. "The best thing you three can do Bob, is stand down for the rest of the day. I'll be here to see Mal on his way tonight."

"You're probably right boss, there's nothing much here to do—have a good trip tomorrow."

Tomorrow! Iffor had forgotten about the trip to the Mission. He needed to get the pick-up refuelled and Josie would need time to prepare the spare bedroom for the baby. Just the excuse he needed to call it a day himself.

Like the good soldier he was, Mal had the Bren stripped into its component parts and was inspecting it when Iffor arrived. He waited until Mal had finished with the weapon before taking him aside. "I've confirmed curfew is unchanged," he told Mal. "So by law, you are entitled to shoot anyone breaking curfew. But Mal, it will be your call, whether you open fire or not will be down to you. Now let's have a chat to the lads.

"Your patrol tonight, lads, is a fighting patrol. In that you are going to set an ambush at the drift below North Camp. Mal has plenty of experience in this sort of thing; all you have to do is listen to him and do what he tells you."

He turned to Mal, "What time are you due back in the morning?"

"I don't want to be trying to 'make safe' trip flares in the dark boss, so we'll pull out and come straight back home at first light."

"Good, so Alvin, if you still want to come to the Mission with me, we'll wait for you."

"Okay boss, looking forward to it."

Iffor gave Mal the bottle of Liquid Sunshine rum. "For breakfast," he said. "And if you think you have time, pop in to Charlie's farm, give Shadrak a drink and see if he has any news for me."

"Right boss." Then Mal stepped back a pace, came to attention and saluted—the soldier's way of saying, "Fuck off, we can manage without you."

Iffor parked the pick-up and walked the short path to his bungalow. He had already planned his evening. Get changed, a couple of beers, dinner with a bottle or two of Cape Red, listen for an hour or so to Josie telling him yet again of her plans for the weekend with baby Helen, then a shower together and an early night. Perfect, he told himself—but it was not to be.

Josie was in the garden entertaining the mine manager, Harris Tweed. He stood up as Iffor approached. "Iffor m'boy, good to see you. Just popped in to see if you have any problems with the Rover we loaned you."

"I'm delighted to see you too, Harris. No, we haven't any problems with the Rover and the boys are very happy with it. They are probably giving it more care and attention than they give their womenfolk." He held an imaginary glass out to Josie, who went scurrying in to the kitchen for a beer. He noticed that Harris was locked in mortal combat with his bottle of Chivas Regal, while Josie was talking her way through a bottle of vodka. This had the makings of a jolly evening.

They settled back in their chairs. "That idea of yours, the angle iron uprights and the pit props for cross members, was perfect for what I had in mind," Iffor told his guest. He didn't want to tell Harris too much, especially after his lectures to his men about discussing military matters with friends. But, sapper to sapper he appreciated Harris's opinions on his field defences. For Josie's sake, he made his defences sound impregnable. "We've barbed wire in front and sides, claymores and trips, a good stock of ammo and grenades, and Auntie's curry to sustain us," he joked.

The old Colonel didn't respond to the joke. "Fall back plan?" he asked.

"Fire and movement back to prepared positions across the river at the drift. The drift," he explained, "is at the end of the gentle slope from the kopje, joining with the track from the farm and crosses the shallows of the drift to the slight incline up on to the bank on the other side. Either side of that slope is a high bank which we will be defending. The river is too deep for them to cross. The drift will be our killing ground."

Iffor excused himself and went to the fridge, giving Josie a chance to engage Harris in baby talk and Auntie's new curtains for the winter. He came back into the garden, sat back, relaxed, and listened to Josie. His thoughts turned to Grace, interrupted a little while later by a thoroughly bored Harris saying goodnight.

He left Josie to walk down to Auntie's after he had parked the pick-up in the MT yard. He'd pick her up later. He was anxious to de-brief

Mal as soon as he got back in. In the meantime, he chatted to the two riflemen sent to help out the Colour. "Are you happy being here, lads?" he asked.

"We were sir," one of them answered. "Chuffed to little Naafi breaks. But after what happened to 'C' company, we want to get back into the bush. Any chance you can arrange it, sir?"

"That will be up to the Colour Sergeant, but I'll have a word with him."

The healthy roar of the armoured Rover driving into the drill hall cut short the conversation. A very dusty, but very happy Mal, climbed down from behind the Bren. "Good trip, Corporal?" Iffor asked.

"Very good, thank-you sir."

"Did you shoot anyone?"

"No boss," Mal grinned. "Not this time."

"Come up to my office and tell me about it."

"Like you suggested boss, we set the trips and our ambush with the drift behind us, so that animals coming to drink from the drift wouldn't trip the flares." He sniffed at his glass of Chivas Regal, appreciatively savouring the aroma before that first sip. "And it worked, boss. We weren't bothered by animals at all, although I think I saw, what I took to be an animal, when I went forward to disarm the trips, just as it was getting light."

"Explain," said Iffor.

"Well, it heard me rather than saw me, and it seemed to crouch and merge into the track, and then it seemed to very slowly glide across the track, which as you know is not very wide, and into the bush."

Iffor sat back in his chair, tapping his teeth with his thumbnail, something he did when deep in troubled thought. "Bollocks!" he said, "I fucked that one up."

Mal looked puzzled. "Fucked what up, boss?"

"I should have given you more information about the Lenshina. For example, when they are in the bush on a scouting mission, they wear a large cloak the same colour as a jackal, and if they think they are in any danger, they crouch down and cover themselves with the cloak. They actually think like a jackal and become a jackal and slink off into the bush. These 'discoverers' are specially selected and trained in bush craft," Iffor explained.

"Discoverers?" Mal questioned.

"It's what the Romans called the ancient Brits who worked for their army as local scouts. Alice has obviously read ancient British history which is probably why she had her warriors painted, just like the ancient Brits. She probably thinks of herself as Boadicea."

"So, what I saw, might have been a Lenshina 'discoverer'," Mal said.

"Who knows old son, who knows."

"Well, I'll know better next time." Mal handed Iffor his empty glass, disappointed when he didn't offer to refill it.

"Just so long as you don't shoot Shadrak's jackal," Iffor said.

Iffor glanced at his watch. "On the road by ten," he said. "Not bad, we'll be in time for lunch at the Mission, and it's fish and chips on Friday."

Josie sat demurely between the two men. "Alvin, you'll have to sit in the back on the way home. The baby and nurse will be in the front with Josie and me."

"That's all right boss, I'll spread my sleeping bag out and have a kip."

"Some fucking escort," Iffor muttered to himself.

Iffor was right, it was fish and chips for lunch. Grace had a large round table laid out on the veranda with chairs for herself, Iffor and Josie, Alvin and the nurse Maureen. "It will give Maureen a chance to talk to Josie," Grace explained, "and you," she said looking directly at Iffor. "You shall sit beside me and tell me what you've been up to since I last saw you."

This was one of those times when shorts were a very definite disadvantage.

Grace was also wearing very short shorts, and because everyone was crammed in around the table, Grace's leg somehow became entwined around Iffor's leg, causing him to spill ketchup over the fresh, clean white tablecloth. He glanced at Josie; she was too deep in discussion with Maureen to notice. He reached under the table to his pocket for a handkerchief, allowing his hand to stroke the inside of her thigh, returning her signal. He started to wonder if he could bring the baby and Maureen back to the Mission on his own on Monday and perhaps stay the night. A saint he wasn't! A soldier he was.

Lunch over, Grace went back to her little hospital. Josie and Maureen started to get baby Helen's bits and pieces together: nappies, powdered milk, toys and the like, while Iffor and Alvin decided on a stroll around the main compound. All was peace and tranquillity again. >From the school came the sound of children reciting their times tables; women chatted as they queued for their rations from the ration store, their children scampering excitedly around their flowing skirts.

Without a word between them, Iffor and Alvin found themselves drawn to the mass grave on the chalk slopes overlooking the great Lamumbwa River. Jam-jars containing flowers had given way to growing flowers and shrubs, all carefully cultivated. White stones marked the outline of individual graves, and pathetically, the occasional teddy bear or doll was placed beside the cross.

Iffor turned and looked towards the residential area up on the high ground, looking down on the admin block and hospital. All the burned-out huts were gone, replaced by brick homesteads. Concrete buildings housed toilets and showers; the good people, white and black, of Kensington had shown their worth and had come to the aid of the Mission.

"You know what boss," Alvin said, "when this is all over I'm going to come and live here, work with these people."

"If the wine business takes off, you could become quite wealthy," Iffor told him. "Come on, let's get back to the girls. We don't want to be travelling in the dark."

"We would be all right boss, it's only dangerous when Mad Harry's manning the road blocks."

Having first dropped Maureen off at her parents' home and Alvin at his flat above the post office, ignoring Josie's plea, "Couldn't we stop off at Auntie's for just ten minutes?", Iffor drove his precious cargo home. He had no doubt that Auntie would come visiting some time during the course of the evening, at which stage he would retire to the garden with a bottle and pamphlet ten: 'The platoon in defence'.

Weekends normally gave Iffor a chance to plan the forthcoming week. But this weekend seemed to fly by in a happy confusion of nappies, feeding and burping. "You must read baby Helen a bedtime story," Josie told him.

"But she's only four months old," Iffor protested. "We don't read to children that age."

"We do in India."

End of protest.

The highlight of the weekend was roast lamb and roast potatoes at Auntie's on Sunday. For whose benefit, Iffor thought, since Auntie spent more time with the baby than she did with her guests. But it mattered not. Godfry by now, was well-trained and poured a Krait into a glass before bringing it to Iffor and announcing, "Your cold Castle, sir."

With Josie's attention being somewhat diverted, Iffor was able to think through his plans for the coming week. He had no doubt Moses would be with him by Wednesday at the latest. Colonel Ried-Daly knew speed was of the essence. He now had to prepare the ground for Moses. He would start at Mwonza, since he would be halfway there when he returned the baby. The thought of 'having' to spend a night in the guest lodge at the Mission sent a thrill of anticipation through him, with memories of previous nights spent with Grace flooding back. This really would have to be the final time, he told himself.

He wanted to be face to face with Jack Francis, O.C. Support Company, when he told him of his plans to insert Moses through his part of the border. He had to be certain that Jack would prepare his soldiers to watch out for a lone "Selous Scout" dressed as a terrorist, 'asking to use the phone'. It was as important to him as it was to Iffor to get an early warning of the Lenshina descending on him.

He decided he would confine Blue Watch to training and preparation until Moses arrived. Then, he would take the team and Moses into the bush, leaving half a section and medic at Charlie's farm and take the other half section, including Moses, to North Camp, arriving after dark and sending Moses on his way. Then back to Archie's farm to warn him to keep his area 'sterile': no activities outside the farm by his farm guards.

Most army commanders will say, 'no matter how good your plans are, at the first shot, your plans go out of the window.' And so it was, that Josie snuggled closer when they were in bed and told him, "You can't leave me alone tomorrow night, I couldn't bear it after handing the baby back. Promise you'll come back to me."

His reassuring hug was better than any promise. "Do you want me to read you a bedtime story?" he said, "Adults do sometimes read to other adults."

"Not in India," she told him, and went to sleep.

It was a silent drive to the drill hall, Monday morning. Normally quite chatty, Josie remained silent, eyes fixed on the road ahead and not looking at the baby who gurgled quite contentedly in the carrycot on her knee. For Josie, parting with the baby was the most difficult act she could imagine. Iffor squeezed her hand. "We will have her back again, quite soon," he told her.

She couldn't trust herself to reply.

They drove into the M.T. yard and stopped in front of the roller doors to the drill hall. Iffor's beep on the horn was answered with the click of the starter for the electric motor that rolled up the doors. Iffor drove into the drill hall.

"Morning Colour, sorry it's such short notice, but since I'm halfway to Mwonza when I drop the baby off, I'm going on to Mwonza to have a chat to O.C. Support. I'll leave today's activities with you; perhaps an hour or two on the range and fire control orders. We won't go into the bush again until Moses joins us, which, I'm sure, will be mid-week."

Phoning Mwonza with his ETA received the usual reception. "Tea and stickies when you arrive," Jack told him.

The Colour, showing his high degree of common sense, suggested to Iffor, "Take the armoured Rover and leave the pick-up for Josie. Then she won't be dependent on me for a lift home." It was not so much a suggestion, more a command, which Iffor was happy to comply with, and by Zero Nine Hundred, with the baby beside him, and Maureen occupying the seat normally reserved for the Bren gunner, they headed north.

His own thoughts occupied him for a few miles. He was a bloody fool even to think about spending a night with Grace, pleasant though it would have been. He really couldn't be away from his HQ overnight, even though he was only a phone call away, he told himself. But in his heart of hearts, he knew he could never be unfaithful to Josie again.

Maureen cut through his thoughts. "You enjoyed having the baby?" she asked.

"Very much thank-you, I'm going to ask Doctor Grace if we can have her again, perhaps for a little longer."

"It's not up to the doctor, I'm the head nurse," she chided him. "And yes, you can have the baby again; it's good for the child. But you and your wife will need some help." Iffor thought it best not to pursue the fact that he and Josie were not married; she probably knew anyway.

She picked the baby out of its cot and prepared to feed it, feeling for the bottle of warm powdered milk that Josie had prepared and wrapped in a nappy.

"With both of you at work all day you should have a housekeeper, someone who will be able to help with the baby, when you have her; someone to cook your meals and wash your clothes; someone to…"

Iffor interrupted her: "Have you perchance got someone in mind?"

"My sister is looking for a job as a housekeeper," she said, and became silent, giving Iffor a chance to think.

True, Iffor thought, we do need a housekeeper, and the army would pay her wages, but Josie would have to have the last word on the matter.

"Tell her to come to the house for an interview," he told her.

"That won't be necessary," she said. "I've already told her about you, she won't need to interview you."

At this point, Iffor decided that silence was truly golden.

'Luck', or as some people call it, 'fate', smiled on Iffor again; Grace was operating and couldn't see him, but had left word, 'she would see him soon'.

He made all the usual noises one makes to a baby when saying goodbye and offered his hand to Maureen. "She, my sister, will come to you in the late afternoon," she told him. Iffor simply nodded—he had no other choice. Then, free of women and babies, he roared out of the Mission and on to the Lamumbwa road; next stop Mwonza.

"Corporal, phone Kensington and tell them their man has arrived," Jack shouted past Iffor as he walked into the OC's office. "And tea and stickies when you can, please."

"Expecting trouble?" Iffor asked, casting his eyes around the fortified office. Each window was a fire position with sandbags for protection, the fire step, a box of six hundred rounds of rifle ammo. Jack's webbing and rifle lay beside his desk.

"You could say that," Jack said. "We were hit twice over the weekend. No casualties, thank God. It keeps the boys on their toes. Now, you didn't come all this way for my Danish pastries, what gives?"

"Sometime this week, I'm going to insert a soldier into Zambia to infiltrate the Lenshina. He will be our early warning. I'd like to think he will be able to come back into your position safely when the time comes; he'll need to be able contact me."

Jack Francis leaned forward across the desk. "His name or alias?"

"Moses January."

"One of your own lads, or special forces?"

"Selous Scouts."

"Will I get to meet him?"

"Going into Zambia, no. Coming out, yes."

"Password or recognition signal?"

"What's the name of the month… January? The name of the month is… January."

"That's simple enough," Jack told him. "I've got some very good chaps here with me, thoroughly dependable; they'll look after your man. If he's compromised, what then?"

"He has an R.V. arranged with a standing patrol of Scouts; they'll get him out."

For the next hour or so, Jack brought Iffor up to date with the situation on the North East Border, or Operation Hurricane, as it was officially called. He told of 'C' company's battle with ZAPU: "The section on patrol had lost its bearings and stumbled into the terrorists F.U.P. They thought they had walked into their own platoon positions, until they realised everyone else was black. Then the fun started. They gave a good account of themselves with bayonet and rifle butt before they were overwhelmed. The other two sections arrived too late to save them."

Taking his leave, Iffor walked out of the building and into the hot dusty compound with the words, "Corporal, phone Kensington; tell them their man's just leaving," reminding him he should have done that himself.

Two of Jack's riflemen were looking over the armoured Land Rover.

"We could do with another one of these, sir," one said.

"With a mobile base-plate and the new eighty-one mil mortar!" the other one joined in.

"Try dropping Santa a line," Iffor replied, and drove off.

Back before dark, he promised himself—home and Josie.

Not quite the homecoming he had expected. He walked through the bungalow and into the garden. Josie and a young African girl were sitting on a blanket on the lawn with the mangiest of dogs Iffor had ever seen, lying between them, allowing one of the girls to plait a daisy chain around its neck, while the other fed it what was left of his steak, his supper.

"Oh, Iffor, just in time; you can give Enid a lift home. She's coming to work for us; Maureen arranged it."

"I know about the girl, what's with the dog?" he asked.

The dog, a bitch about twelve months old and, judging by its teats, recently a mother, had obviously been very neglected. She was thin, her rib bones prominent through her coat, covered in scars and sores and very obviously, a Staffordshire bull terrier. "She was waiting for me in the garden when I got home," Josie explained.

Nearly as good as Honest dad, the dog that followed me home, Iffor thought.

"Can we keep her?" she paused. "At least until she is stronger."

"Someone will come looking for her," Iffor explained. "She's probably from one of the kraals or villages around here. I would think she was kept as a breeding dog."

"Oh Iffor, that's awful, please let her stay, for a few days at least." She gave him one of those appealing looks that little girls hold in reserve for that moment when they needed something very special from their father. "Please, Iffor."

"Tell you what, I'll ask the government vet to have a look at her and have her neutered. If she can't breed, she'll be no good as a breeding dog."

Josie threw her arms around his neck. "Oh, Iffor, you are wonder…"

"Don't say it," he said.

Josie sat down again with dog. "You can name her," she said.

"You've already done that," he responded, pointing to the daisy chain around the dog's neck. "It's Daisy."

Iffor had taken another step on the road to domesticity.

He was determined to 'interview' the girl as he drove her home. Some chance! Enid got in first: "I'm eighteen, single; I live with my parents in the township. I am to call madam Josie, unless you have guests. I am to call you sir all the time. We have agreed my wages, and I shall come to work on the mine bus and catch the bus back home at night. I must ensure there is a clean uniform for you to wear, every morning."

Another fucking mind-reader, Iffor thought, and wondered if Josie would mind if he popped into Boons for a quick one after he dropped Enid off.

True to his word, but with Josie standing over him, Iffor phoned the government vet as soon as they got into work. "Don't bring her in to us, old boy," he was told. "She might have something nasty and we don't want to spread it around. I'll come out to you, lunchtime okay? About twelve thirty?" Iffor relayed the message to Josie; her eyes shone with excitement. "I'll be there," she said.

His next task was to phone the Scouts at Kariba. He needed to push them; he needed Moses in the field as soon as possible. Getting no joy from the hapless Intelligence Officer, Iffor spoke directly to the C.O.

"I'm not happy," the Colonel told him. "I could have done with more time to prepare the man. But I'm aware of your concern, so I'll fly him up to you last light. Keep him under wraps and away from prying eyes. Oh, and Meredith, look after him, he's a good soldier."

At last! This was the news Iffor was waiting for. He went to the top of the stairs and called down, "Colour, Harry, my office. Gentlemen," he said, when they were seated. "Good news! Moses arrives tonight; I'll pick him up from the airfield and bring him straight back here. The sooner we get him into the bush the better. Warning order chaps, prepare both teams for a standing patrol to the North Camp area. No move before last light today. Time and place for 'O' group, my office twelve sharp."

Harry and the Colour left to go into their own routines: vehicles to be checked over and fuelled up; rations, water and ammo to be drawn and packed; weapons to be inspected. The process whereby the men were gradually brought up to their peak of readiness in time for the 'off'.

Next step, tell the Colonel what's happening. Iffor reached for the phone.

"My man is going 'walkabout' tonight, Colonel. Can I suggest we declare the target area 'sterile'? We don't want any friendly fire incidents."

"Good idea Meredith; I'll see to it. Anything else for me?"

The Colonel sounded quite mellow and responsive, so Iffor decided to push his luck, "A little domestic situation Colonel; your chief clerk, Miss Patel and I are living together as man and wife. Thought you should know."

A few moments' silence, then, "Does Auntie know about it?"

"We have her blessing, Colonel."

"Is it serious?"

"Josie, Miss Patel, wears my shirts, Colonel."

"All right m'boy, but just remember, if your affair goes 'tits up', Josie will always have a place in my regiment but your future might not be quite so rosy."

With a sigh of relief, Iffor replaced the receiver. He'd been trying to summon up courage to tell the Colonel about Josie since she moved in with him. Now to break the good news to her. "You needn't have bothered," she told him, "I told the Colonel last week. He gave his blessing by the way."

He regarded each man as Blue Watch filed into his office. He had invited Pete, and summoned Davy. Not that it was important for Davy to be present, but to show he trusted the man with the vital information he was about to reveal: "Gentlemen, you've had your warning order.

"The ground for tonight's patrol is the farming area west of the Great North Road; the two farms and North Camp.

"Situation: I'm going to insert a special forces' soldier into the Lenshina camp as our early warning…" The men remained silent. Obviously Harry had told the men what Iffor intended, but now it was official. "…You all know the man in question, Moses January.

"Our mission tonight is to escort our man to the North Camp area and onto the old Mwonza game trail; he'll be on his own thereafter.

"Execution, chaps; Harry, you and your brick will come with me and Moses to North Camp. We'll occupy our prepared positions and sit it out till first light in case Moses has to leg it back. Mal, your team set up an ambush at the drift; you're looking for anyone coming North behind us. I don't want anyone, Lenshina or ZAPU, on the same trail as Moses.

"Timings: I'm collecting Moses from the airfield at last light. Davy, you come with me, you know the airfield better than me at night. I'll bring him back here for a final briefing, then PUFO.

"Comms: Phil, you will have the thirty-one set, Mal, the eighty-eight.

"Passwords: MONTH and JANUARY.

"Transport: Harry, we'll take the Champ; Mal, the Rover and the Bren.

"Colour, when you're happy with the loading of stores, stand the lads down. Parade again at eighteen hundred. Prepare for one night in the bush.

"Questions?"

Corporal Watney put his hand up. "Does this include me, sir?"

"Unless the Colour has need of you, yes."

The Colour nodded his agreement.

Josie hardly noticed him checking and repacking his kit. One night or a week in the bush made no difference, the kit he carried was the same either way. Her concern was the dog, 'Daisy'. The government vet, true to his word, had come and examined the dog, and had agreed that in everyone's interest the dog should be neutered. He had taken the dog back to his surgery, promising to return her, 'good as new', next morning.

"I've just got to be here when she comes home," Josie told him. "The Colour will stand in for me. Please Iffor, let me have the day off. I need to get dog food and a bed for her. After all, we can't have her sleeping on our bed... can we?"

Josie drove him into the drill hall a little before six. The already hot morning sun caused perspiration to settle on her face, giving the impression of early morning dew on a delicate orchid. He took his face veil from around his neck and gently wiped her face with it. "For luck," he said, tying it around his throat again. The team were already assembled. Hennie ambled over to the pick-up, took Iffor's Burgan and walked over to the Champ with it. "Kettle's on boss, if you fancy a cuppa," he called over his shoulder. An involuntary shudder went through Iffor, as he remembered Hennie's tea coursing down his throat like molten lava. Still, it would be a long night.

"Thank you Hennie, that would be delightful."

Josie pecked him lightly on his cheek—goodbyes had been said at home—and with a wave, drove off to spend the evening with Auntie. A typically British, "Good luck chaps," in her typical Indian accent, floated back to them.

Coinciding with the setting sun, the Scouts' helicopter clattered down onto the main runway of Kensington's airfield, and waiting just long enough to see Davy driving the Champ towards them, took off again, leaving a lone figure gazing at the side lights of the approaching vehicle. Without a word, Moses threw his small duffel bag into the back of the Champ and climbed in. "Let's go," he said simply.

His reception at the drill hall could not have been more different. The men gathered around him; handshakes, pat on the back, "good to see you again" and from Evil, "Rather you than me mate."

Iffor stood back and watched in silence. A month or so ago they had shot him and Mal, who was now thrusting a cup of Hennie's tea onto him, had wanted to 'finish him off'. The tea probably will, Iffor thought.

He stepped in to break the party up. "Moses, we are going to insert you tonight, if that's okay with you."

Moses nodded. "Fine with me. I will get changed." And he followed the Colour to his office.

The man who reappeared some twenty minutes later could not have been more different. Gone were the smart clean combats and Selous Scouts' beret and polished boots. In place, homemade sandals made from an old car tyre, civilian shorts and shirt with short sleeves underneath a tattered pullover, a belt supporting a holstered 'Stetchkina' pistol was around his waist; an old police raincoat completed his wardrobe. Somebody had done a good job with the clothes—his smell proceeded him. He put his small duffel bag into the Champ. "My uniform, bring it with you when we RV."

Iffor had the team sit down for his final briefing. He outlined his plans for Moses's benefit and emphasised the password:

"Challenge: What month is it?... January.

"If challenged: The month is... January."

Iffor joined the men sitting, leaving Moses standing beside the Champ.

"What is your name?" Iffor shouted angrily.

"I am called Moses January."

"Why have you come among us?"

"I seek rest and shelter, I have been wounded."

"You are not Lenshina."

"No, I belong to ZAPU, I was on a mission for them when I was shot. My comrade was killed, I escaped."

"What was your mission?"

"To bring the Lamumbwa comrades back into Zambia."

Hennie joined in, "You have no blood on your clothes."

"Some goatherders found me and took me to their kraal. They burned my clothes because the blood scent attracted the jackals."

Iffor called a halt. Moses had probably gone through his cover story a dozen times with the Scouts, but he wanted to give the team an idea of what Moses would be up against when he arrived at the Lenshina camp.

Standing beside Moses, Iffor said, "Look long and hard at this man and remember him. The next time you see him it may be dark; he will be exhausted and probably being pursued. Stop and think before you shoot. Remember the password. And finally fellas," he extended his hand, "Moses, welcome to Blue Watch."

"Or as our late Henry used to say," Phil commented, "We few, we happy few, we band of brothers."

"That was Shakespeare," Alvin said.

"He probably heard Harry saying it," someone muttered.

"More like a band of fucking idiots," Evil said.

PART TWENTY-ONE

If our position becomes untenable, using fire and movement, we will re-locate.

MOVING SILENTLY, SLOWLY, Iffor followed Moses through the sparse bush which surrounded the open ground around the burned-out farm. The open ground was now bathed in bright moonlight.

Harry and his brick had quietly occupied the kopje overlooking the farm. No need for trip flares; no one could cross the open ground without being seen, and no one could scramble up the side of the kopje without being heard. Three hundred metres behind them, Mal had set an ambush. Better that than hanging around the farm, Iffor had decided.

Although Moses had protested, Iffor insisted on seeing him safely to the thicker bush on the far side of the farm. And he had news for him.

Moses stopped, crouched and held out his hand, "I go alone now."

Iffor took his hand and held it for a few moments. "I have news of your son; he has passed his entrance exam and is on the next intake into Sandhurst."

Moses' teeth reflected the bright of the moon. "Thank you for telling me—I go with a light heart." He held on to Iffor's hand. "At the hospital, when you were interrogating me... would you have shot me?" The silence confirmed his judgement. "That's what I thought," he said, and was gone, leaving a shadow. With a smile on his face, Iffor made his way back to the kopje; it would be a long cold night.

Leaving Harry's brick to carry out the sentry watch; two on, two off, Iffor spent the remainder of the night intermittently dozing and peering through his binoculars into the bush, ever watchful for Moses should he have to return.

Hennie kicked his boot, bringing him instantly awake. "Mug of tea, boss, 'stand to'. It's almost dawn." Iffor took up his firing position overlooking the farm. Since Moses had not returned and no gunfire had been heard, he would wait until full light before lifting the ambush and meeting up with Mal. Then, back to Archie's farm for breakfast.

"We are getting quite good at this ambush lark," Mal told him when they met up. "Although it was quite light, we set a couple of trips with no problems. I had two awake and two sleeping, an hour at a time and even we had difficulty finding the Rover this morning, it was so well cammed up. By the way, no sign of that jackal."

With the mine-proofed Land Rover leading the way, they made their way to Arc Angel Farm. Dirk, the farm guard, was on 'point of entry' control, seeing the farm workers into the compound, his number five jungle carbine held in the crook of his arm and a fifty round bandolier hung around his chest. He flagged them to a halt: "Any news for us?"

"I'll hold a briefing after breakfast," Iffor told the man, "for you and the other guard."

Dirk waved them through and into the compound where Archie was waiting. "Tom-toms told me you were coming," he said. "Beer, anybody?" he asked, quite innocently.

Archie's chef did them proud: cold ham, eggs, mushrooms, *Boereworse* and his own home-baked bread. "Think we'll be in time for lunch at Charlie's farm," Evil said, to no-one in particular, accepting another thick slice of ham from the beaming chef.

After breakfast, Iffor took Archie and the two farm guards into the shade of the veranda. "I've got a man in the bush," he told them. "A black guy, a soldier. He's our early warning. All you need to know is that he will be dressed as a terrorist. The password, his recognition, will be 'January'. If you see such a man, challenge before you shoot. You will say, 'What is the month?' He will answer…"

"January," the guards answered in unison.

"You'll still leave the trailer loaded with your defence stores here?" Archie asked.

"Seems sensible," Iffor replied. "It keeps my options open."

"If it gets too hot for you up at North Camp, I imagine you'll drive back here and defend the farm."

Iffor shook his head. "No, it's all or nothing. If we withdraw to the farm, they would simply bottle us up with a handful of men while the main bunch wander off down to Charlie's farm. They would simply by-pass us, go around us. Whereas, now that the river is in flood, the only crossing place is the drift. They have to defeat us there to get to you."

Dirk looked at his watch. "Time for our morning patrol. We patrol the security fence," he explained to Iffor, "looking for breaks. Once in the morning and once in the afternoon. We vary the times and route and sometimes we just sit, listen and watch."

Mad Harry, bottle in hand, joined them, "Great breakfast, thanks Archie, I think Evil's just asked your chef to marry him."

"Are we nearly ready to move?" Iffor asked.

"Not yet boss, the phantom crapper's giving a lecture on 'turd strangling'."

"Hygiene, to you," Iffor explained to Dirk.

"And Alvin is at the dispensary, lancing boils, cutting toenails and giving intimate advice to the young maidens on contraception." He went on, "Phil's having a meaningful conversation with a female radio operator at Mwonza, and Hennie has just popped down to the African shop to see if he can replenish his moonshine. The last I saw of Evil, he was disappearing into the kitchen with the chef, to swop ideas with him, whatever that meant."

Iffor left him to it and went off to find Corporal Watney.

It was Archie's idea that mothers accompanied their children to the farm school. Apart from the mums getting a basic education, it meant the teacher could be on the lookout for malnutrition and diseases, and it gave visiting health workers, and people like Corporal Watney, a chance to get mums and children together for whatever advice was on offer.

Iffor watched as the Corporal went through his lecture and demonstration on personal hygiene, knowing full well that the N.C.O.

was wasting his time. Old customs and traditions would take over where Corporal Watney left off. Still, it was worth a try.

"You know sir," the Corporal said, as they walked back to the farmhouse, "the only way we will get through to these people, and the only way we can do any good medically, is to leave me here for a week."

"I see your point, Corpo... What is your bloody christian name?"

"Edwin, sir."

"And don't call me sir in the field."

"Yes sir."

"I see your point Edwin, but at this stage you're more useful to me in the bush than here on the farm, but you've given me a bloody good idea."

His brain was racing: a small team, a medic and a couple of infantry instructors. Good for relating hearts and minds and all that old bollocks, not to mention improving security and defences. "That really was a bloody good idea," he told the Corporal.

Leaving Arc Angel Farm at mid-morning, the convoy headed down the old Mwonza Road to Charlie's farm. The armoured Rover was leading with Evil behind the Bren praying that some hapless terrorist would step out onto the road and point his A.K.at them. But it was not to be, and they swept into the farm compound in time to join Charlie having his lunchtime beer.

Having acquainted Charlie and his farm guards with the Moses situation, Iffor went in search of Shadrak, having first retrieved the hip flask from his Burgan.

"I see you M'dala, are you well?"

"I am well thank-you, N'kosi," the old man said, eyeing the hip flask as he sat down under his favourite tree.

Iffor told him of 'his man' in the bush. "If you see this man you must help him."

Shadrak nodded, and accepted another drink from the flask. Iffor sensed the old man had news for him, but was savouring the moment before he revealed it. "You have news for me M'dala?"

"I have news for you, N'kosi."

The ritual of another drink, then, "The woman I told you about, the one who was wounded and followed the river, she arrived at the village of my father and then she died."

He accepted another drink, keeping the most important news until last. "She had with her a baby, N'kosi, a young baby."

"Boy or girl?" Iffor asked.

"I know not N'kosi."

"Colour?"

"I do not know N'kosi. I have not seen the child, I met a hunter from that village—he told me."

"How far is this village?"

"A full day; we must walk, there is only a game track to follow from the river."

"You can take me to this village?"

"I can N'kosi."

"Good, but it will be many days before we can go; I have to fight a battle."

"I understand N'kosi, I will wait."

Those people on the streets of Kensington stopped to look and wave as Blue Watch drove through the town. Words of encouragement reached their ears: 'Well done' and 'Keep up the good work.' The townspeople were well used to seeing military vehicles on their roads, but this was Blue Watch, their fire brigade, their own. Iffor joined with the sense of pride his men felt, and looking up at the fluttering 'Pigasus' returned the salutes.   Passing Boons Bar, Davy and the uniformed Matabele doorman stood to attention. Iffor acknowledged with another salute. Things were going well.

"The Colonel wants you to phone him as soon as you can," the Colour told him as he climbed out of the Champ.

"I'll say hello to Josie first," Iffor said.

"She's not in, boss, I was expecting her in to work this afternoon, but she phoned in 'sick'."

"What's wrong with her?" Iffor looked alarmed.

"Not her, the dog. Josie's fine."

No, the Colonel was not available, the adjutant told him, "but you can leave a message, I'll see he gets it." The tone in his voice confirmed what Iffor already knew: the adjutant despised him; commissioned from the ranks; constantly being praised by the Colonel and the Brigadier; and rumoured to be sleeping with the chief clerk.

"Let me have your message Meredith, I haven't got all day."

"Sorry old boy, top secret, Colonel's ears only."

"But I'm the adjutant," he whined.

"Just tell the old man I phoned, there's a good chap."

Iffor replaced the receiver. It felt good getting 'one over' on the adjutant. He knew the adjutant would tell the Colonel he had phoned and that the Colonel would be phoning him back... quite soon.

He busied himself with the various papers on his desk. Josie normally put them in trays marked: Secret; Very urgent; Urgent; and the last tray, 'See me'. This was for Iffor to discuss the contents with Josie, an act which made office work very pleasurable. Nothing that couldn't wait he decided. The phone rang:

"Colonel for you," the adjutant said.

"Afternoon Colonel, Meredith here."

"Iffor m'boy, what news?"

"We deployed our man successfully, Colonel. It's just a case of sitting back and waiting, though my routine patrols will continue. Can you tell me anything?"

"News is, Iffor, 'Alice' has joined her merry men. The men will be expecting some sort of action from her quite soon, so I suggest you step up your 'readiness' to 'Bravo'.

"Thank you Colonel, we'll do that. I'll keep you informed. Goodbye sir."

It was quite normal practise for the Colour Sergeant to take charge at the end of a patrol. He would ensure the vehicles were hosed down and re-fuelled; water containers rinsed out and re-filled and vital stores replaced; weapons cleaned and inspected and ammunition accounted for. Officers simply got in the way.

"A lift home boss?" Harry said, pointing at the Champ.

"Thanks Harry. Colour, parade at zero eight hundred tomorrow, then we'll have a long weekend."

The Colour saluted, "Right boss, see you tomorrow."

In films, the returning hero is met by his wife running down the garden path and throwing her arms around his neck. He stood, waiting, but it was not going to happen for him. Burgan in one hand, Carbine in the other, he watched as Harry drove back into town. Bet I know where you'll be in another hour, he thought. Lucky bastard. He walked around the house and into the garden.

"Oh, Iffor, I thought I heard you, come and say hello to Daisy." At the sound of its new name, the dog raised its head from Josie's lap and glared at him, offering a soft growl. This was not going to be love at first sight, he told himself. The man with Josie stood up, offering his hand. "Iffor, this is my uncle Abdul, he is the government vet."

The man, sixtyish, balding, dressed typically in safari jacket and shorts, and sporting a 'Smith and Wesson' Combat Masterpiece in a 'Hunter' holster, immediately impressed Iffor. "I'm not her natural uncle," he explained, "but I am family. I went to primary school with her father and I am her godfather."

"Uncle Abdul says the dog will be fine. She will have her stitches out in a couple of days; she has been spayed," Josie explained.

Abdul stayed on his feet. "You look hot, dusty and tired and in need of a shower," he said. "I'll leave you in peace," and he patted the dog. The dog 'smiled' and thumped her tail on the grass.

"Looks like you've got a rival," Josie said, smiling at Iffor.

As Iffor looked around for a chair, Josie stood and put her arms around his neck. "Don't sit down, go and have your shower and get changed, then come and relax. Enid is cooking dinner for us this evening, your favourite, Cape Red, and steak."

For me or the fucking dog? Iffor thought.

He stood behind his desk watching as his men assembled and sat down. They were all here. The police, Davy, Corporal Watney, the Colour and his two riflemen. Josie sat demurely beside him, notebook on her knee ready to take notes. "Gentlemen," he began. "Our mission to insert Moses into Zambia seems to have been successful, and I thank you for your efforts. News from the front; Alice has joined her tribe in the field. We can expect her to strike quite soon. The Colonel has ordered we go to 'Combat Readiness,' State 'Bravo'.

"This means, chaps, that we look to our personal security and the security of this base. It means you keep your kit packed and your weapon ready. It means we are able to leave this drill hall and head for North Camp within an hour of the alarm being sounded. It means no-one leaves Kensington without my say so.

"There will be no rehearsals for a quick move, gentlemen. When the siren sounds, it will be for real.

"Now for the good news, and the bad news. When the Colour has finished with you this morning, you can stand down for the weekend.

"The really exciting news is I'm changing our Or Bat, our order of battle.

"Harry, on Monday morning take your brick up to Archie's farm, collect the trailer with our defence stores and move on North Camp and start erecting our defences. Mal's brick and myself will relieve you on Tuesday morning. Thereafter we'll take it in turns, two nights at North Camp, two nights back in Kensington. Questions so far?"

Evil stood up. "I'm a little confused boss, which was the good news and which was the bad news?"

"I will continue," Iffor said. "Harry, I suggest that while you are in situ, you stick a man up on the kopje with the Bren, and the four of you spend the night on the kopje; it's easier to defend. And Harry, no heroics, any problems, you mount up and get back to the farm and wait for the cavalry.

"It might seem strange to you guys, giving you the weekend off," Iffor explained, "but I need you rested and ready for our new routine next week. Remember, we are on sixty minutes standby. I suggest we use today packing the extra kit we'll need onto the trucks, then go home and pack your Burgans, bring them back into the drill hall and load them onto the trucks. Harry, your brick will take the Rover; Mal, the Champ and trailer.

"Right chaps, that's it. Anybody got anything to say? Colour, anything?"

"Only to you, boss."

Pete stood up. "The back pay for my promotion has arrived. I'm filthy rich--'m in the chair at the Moth Club Friday night. I hope you'll all join me."

"Try keeping us away," Mad Harry said, ushering the team out of the office.

The Colour waited until they had all left. "Leaving four men at North Camp is a bit bare-arsed, isn't it?"

"Yes, it is, Bob, but the alternative is to have the full team up there for the foreseeable future, and that means the boredom of routine eating away at the efficiency of the men. Whereas four men will, as a matter of necessity, have to be on the ball twenty-four hours a day."

The Colour Sergeant looked long and hard at him, "You're a hard bastard, Meredith, but I like the way you think."

Josie was still sitting at the desk, almost unnoticed. He'd been around women long enough to know what she was thinking. He stood behind her, his hands on her shoulders. "I don't like leaving you alone," he told her, "but I must."

She touched his hand. "I know," she said, "I know."

He stood her up to face him. "When the Battalion gets back, I'll be a nine-to-five soldier, and you'll get totally pissed off having to step over me and that bloody dog, lying about the house."

"I'm all right Iffor, really I am, you just do what you have to do, and don't worry about me."

He sat her down, and turned his chair to face her. Holding her hand, he took a deep breath. "Something you ought to know," he told her, "I wasn't going to tell you because I didn't want to raise your hopes..."

"The other twin," she interrupted him, "He's alive!"

"The woman that Shadrak tracked turned up at a village with a baby; the woman died soon after. I don't know the sex or the colour of the child," he explained.

"Oh Iffor, when can you go and see the baby?"

"I can't," he told her gently, "not for a while anyway. It's a day's march from North Road Farm; I can't be cut off from my men for that time. When this is all over, then I'll go." Without a word she left and went back to her office. He would need time alone.

Things to do, places to go, people to speak to. Iffor scribbled his priorities on a memo pad: *Double the first line scale of ammunition from two hundred rounds per rifle to four hundred rounds, with two thousand rounds for the Bren; all available grenades, including smoke and phosphorus; illuminating flares and signal pistol.*

Phone the three farms, telling them to step up security.

Phone Mwonza for sit rep.

Phone Kariba for any news from the Scouts.

Take Josie to the Elephant for lunch.

The phone calls he would leave till after lunch, now... He went down into the drill hall to tell the Colour of his ammunition and ration packs requirements, and to be on hand for the questions he knew would be coming his way.

"Do you really think they will come boss, the Lenshina?"

"Oh yes Evil, they'll come. The thought of your bollocks adorning their totem poles is much too much for them to resist."

"Is Josie going to join us?" the Colour asked as they sat down at their favourite table on the veranda overlooking 'Rhodes Square'.

"Yes, but she's gone down to the butcher's for another cow for the dog and she'll probably pop into Auntie's on the way."

Iffor called to the waiter: "Two Castles please."

"Make it three," Digger said, drawing up a chair.

Iffor turned in amazement. "Digger! I thought you were still recuperating in the flesh pots of Cape Town."

"I've recuperated—more than enough Cape Brandy, thank-you. I've returned to civilisation."

"Fully recovered?" Iffor asked.

"Good as new, and they've given me a new aeroplane; I'm back at work."

"Do your travels take you anywhere close to Mwonza?" Iffor asked.

Digger immediately became suspicious. "What do you want me to look for?"

"A group of little purple men wearing cloaks," Iffor said, trying hard to appear normal.

Digger spluttered into his beer. "Fuck me, Iffor, what have you been drinking?" He leaned forward and sniffed at Iffor's face. "You've not been hitting the Krait again, have you?"

Iffor chuckled. "They really do exist, and they are a particularly nasty bunch of terrorists."

"Any other distinguishing features?" Digger asked.

"They will probably try to shoot you down if you get too close," Iffor said.

Digger finished his beer. "Got to dash, there's a girl, madly in lust with me, waiting in the bar. I'm going to give her a ride in my new aeroplane, and, if she's very good, she can fondle my 'joystick'."

"Big piss-up in the Moth club tomorrow night!" Iffor called after him.

"Be there." Digger waved in response and was gone.

Josie occupied his vacant chair. "Auntie sends her love," she told him.

"Did you tell Auntie about the baby in the village?"

"No, of course not."

"I thought you would. What did she say?"

"She said you were right, you shouldn't go off on a wild..." She waved her arm in frustration, "...something or other chase."

"Goose," said Bob. "It's 'wild goose chase'. And what's all this about a baby?"

"Shadrak's tracked down an orphaned baby," Iffor said, eyeing the plate of beef sandwiches the waiter set on the table. "In another couple of weeks I *might*," he emphasised the word, "I *might* be able to investigate, but not now, not at this time."

The afternoon dragged by. The phone calls he had to make took only some twenty minutes. The three farms thanked him for his warning and said they would step up their security. Mwonza had no news of Moses, and nothing new to tell him, and Kariba told him, "Yes, Alice had joined her men, and yes, a standing patrol was in place to R.V. with Moses should he need some help."

Bored and frustrated, he knew he couldn't knock off while the Colour and his two riflemen were rearranging the loads on the vehicles to squeeze in the extra ammo, and they wouldn't thank him if he tried to help.

He walked along the corridor to Josie's office and opened the door. "Go away," she said without looking up, "I'm busy."

Nothing for it, drastic measures were called for. "I'm just going to have a chat with Davy about next week," he told the Colour. "Shouldn't be long," and hurried along to Davy's 'office'. A game of spoof with an Orang-Utan who probably cheated, and a beer with Davy, was just what he needed.

He had given the Colour Sergeant and his team the day off, along with the rest of the team, to make it a long weekend. He would have liked to have given Josie the day off, but it had been agreed that either Bob or Josie should be on hand to take phone calls or teleprinter messages. 'Out of hours' the phone was switched through to Iffor's or the Colour's house.

They let themselves in through the side door. The only light was from the high windows. He paused, drinking in the atmosphere that had occupied the building since the mid-eighteen hundreds.

Soldiers had left the sanctuary of this building, their home, to go and fight the Zulu and the Matabele. Rhodesians had flocked to the side of the British to fight the Boer. He could imagine the hustle and bustle and the excitement as soldiers waited for the order to march down to the station and the train that would take them to South Africa and to the ship waiting to take them to the battlefields of Flanders and the Somme.

As they walked into the main drill hall, Iffor noticed how the morning sun shone directly onto the board with the names of those Rhodesians killed defending Tobruk and El Adam. And he remembered that it was to the same Ian Smith, who went with the first fledgling Rhodesian pilots to join the RAF in nineteen-forty, that he vowed his allegiance, when he took his oath on joining the Rhodesian army.

The idea he had was gathering apace in his mind, the way in which the army could retain Blue Watch: Two teams, each with a medic, taking it in turns a week at a time out in the bush calling on farms, villages and kraals, tending to medical needs and offering advice on security and defence.

Before making a presentation of the plan to the Colonel, it had to be bullet-proof, waterproof and Adjutant proof. He had the office to himself, no one to bother him. He set to with the same enthusiasm he had when he plotted to put Blue Watch into uniform. He headed the plan, 'Operation Pigasus'.

"I can't wait to see their faces when I tell Blue Watch about this," he told himself.

It wasn't until Josie came in to remind him that it was 'poetry' day, and they usually finished early, that he realised how time had run away with him.

"Poets' day," he corrected her, and showed her his presentation. "Type it out for me on Monday, three copies please."

They drove out of the M.T. yard and onto the hot dusty road. "Home James," she told him. "It's me for a hot bath and a comfortable sari." She paused thoughtfully, "Are you going to meet up with the boys at the Moth club tonight?"

"I'd forgotten about that," he lied. "I don't think so."

"I thought you would," she said. "I'll drop you off at the club, then we are spending the evening with Auntie."

"We?" he queried.

"Me and Daisy."

The Moth club was busier than usual, probably because word had got around that Pete was 'in the chair'. Even so, Mad Harry and Evil had somehow managed to commandeer the 'committee' table for the team and persuaded the barman to let them have a waiter to themselves.

Iffor found Pete at the cloakroom handing over his pistol, and joined him. They walked into the clubroom together and found Harry and Evil, to be joined moments later by Digger Digby. The rest of Blue Watch assembled over the next ten or fifteen minutes. Last to arrive was big Shamus. Digby looked anxiously for means of escape, but the six foot something Irishman stood between him and the exit. Knowing what was to come, Digby stood and offered his hand, but that wasn't enough for Shamus. Wrapping his arms around the helpless Australian, he lifted him into the air and planted a massive, slobbering, (no tongue), kiss full on the mouth, causing the hapless Aussie to squirm and struggle to escape from the Irishman's amorous embrace.

"Man, am I glad to see you!" Shamus said.

"So it would appear," Phil said. "For Christ's sake put him down, you'll give the club a bad name."

The questions began. "How are the legs, Digby?" They knew he didn't like to called Digger when he was seriously drinking.

"Good as new, except I'm an inch shorter."

"And the aircraft?"

"Gone to that big hanger in the sky—they've given me a new one."

"You've heard how me and Evil defeated the terrs at the monastery," Harry said.

"With just a little help from the rest of us," Iffor reminded him, then softly said, "I suppose you heard about Helen and her boy?"

"Bad news travels far and fast," Digby told him.

Changing the subject, Digby said, "The *Cape Town Herald* printed the story about you guys and what you're doing. They even suggested in the editorial that it would make a good book. Fancy your chances Iffor, at writing a book, I mean?"

"I'm a soldier, not a fucking author."

"Now then," Digby settled himself back in his chair, "what are you lot up to at present? Who are you annoying?"

"The guv' has got us chasing round the countryside looking for blokes painted purple, wearing cloaks, and can change into a jackal," Mal told him.

"Fuck me, I thought he was joking when he mentioned that to me!" Digby said, sitting more upright in his chair and suddenly taking more notice.

"We've also got our own jackal giving us inside information." Evil touched the side of his nose with his finger and gave his best 'knowing look'.

"You might well mock," Iffor chided him, "but that jackal gave us the information that led to a very successful ambush."

"What the fuck are you talking about?" Digby asked, only to be interrupted by the Colour Sergeant: "Mind if we join you?"   Bob Pearson and Corporal Watney pulled up a couple of chairs.

"Ah, my little coloured friend," Mad Harry said, "let me introduce you to Digger Digby, our guardian angel. Digby, meet the Phantom Crapper, our pox doctor's clerk; he's part of the team."

The young Corporal solemnly shook hands with Digby. "Pleased to meet you, sir."

"Isn't it nice to have someone around here with some manners?" Iffor sighed, and signalled to the waiter for another case of Castle.

Intent on getting to know the young man better, Digby asked enquiringly, "White mother, black father, or vice versa?"

"Both white—my sister and brother are also very white."

Digby looked at him for an explanation. The lad went on, "My grandfather was white, my grandmother was described as being delicately shaded. My colour comes from my great-grandmother and great-grandfather."

He had an attentive audience now, so he continued, "My great-grandmother taught at a mission school in Zulu Land, Kwa Zulu and fell for a fellow-teacher who was Zulu. By the time the rest of the family got to hear of the relationship, she was married to him and pregnant."

"I imagine the family had the marriage annulled," Alvin said, giving the impression he knew about such matters.

"You could say that," the Corporal answered. "They hanged him."

The evening eventually came to its happy conclusion. Pete was helped to his 'bunk' in the storeroom by one of the African waiters, the same waiter who whispered in Iffor's ear, "The memsahib is waiting outside for you, sir."

Phil walked out with him and staggered off into the warm balmy night, only to reappear minutes later muttering, "Wrong fucking way!"

The remainder of Blue Watch were 'digging in' for the night. The bar steward knew the routine: he would lock them in, go to bed and charge them for the empty bottles in the morning.

Iffor was quite happy to climb into the back of the pick-up, the front seat being the domain of the dog, who, said Josie, was asleep and shouldn't be disturbed.

He opened one eye. A searing blinding light penetrated his brain. Foolishly, he opened the other, then shut them both, avoiding the beam of brilliant sunshine illuminating his face. He turned his head and opened his eyes again, this time looking into the dim corner of the room.

As any drunk will tell you, the first of your strategies when waking up on a different and strange planet is to retrace your steps, in order to try and discover, in the first instance, 'where you are', and secondly, 'who you are.'

He thought back to the previous evening, trying to make sense of the flashbacks of discordant conversation. He was at home and had slept on his own settee. He was fully dressed except for shoes and he remembered Josie telling him his pistol was safely locked away.

The very last thing he wanted was to attempt to stand, but his bladder warned of dire consequences if he didn't make it to the bathroom in the next few minutes. He stood over the basin, legs apart pointing his penis at the centre of the water below and opened the valve. The urine came, not in one jet, as was intended, but in two streams each at right angles to his penis, missing the bowl completely and leaving ominous puddles on the floor. Bending down to wipe it up was out of the question. His eyes would probably fall out.

Looking into the mirror resolved his second problem; he recognised himself instantly, but didn't like what he saw. Josie would look after him, he told himself walking into the bedroom. She would hold him and tell him everything was all right, she would... The dog lying beside her, where he should be lying, with its head on the pillow, where his head should be, opened one eye and glowered at him, her top lip curled back exposing white fangs and a soft growl emitted from her throat. Without opening her eyes, Josie murmured, "It's all right sweetheart," and put an arm around the dog's shoulder.

Daisy smiled, thumped her tail and went back to sleep. Iffor went in search of the fridge; a cold Castle would do one of two things for him.

An hour and a shower later, and Iffor was beginning to feel human again. He thought about pulling rank on the dog and crawling into bed beside Josie, but his breath would probably put her off him for life. Instead, he put a plate of bacon and scrambled egg and a pot of coffee onto a tray and took it in to her.

With Iffor beside her in bed, she slept naked, but on her own, she preferred to wear a nightdress which was usually one of Iffor's shirts. Comfort had nothing to do with it; she knew he relished the thought of her wearing his shirt.

He sat beside her on the bed as she ate, watching the contours of her breast and her thrusting nipples under his cotton shirt. His thoughts were interrupted by the sound of the morning paper being pushed through the letterbox. The dog slid off the bed and adopted 'combat mode', ears flattened, jaw thrust forward and soundlessly advanced on the front door, gathering pace as the newspaper came into sight, and with a final bound she fell on this, her arch-enemy. Iffor could only stand and watch as the confetti which had once been his newspaper floated around the hallway. The dog, content now that she had done her duty, marched proudly back into the bedroom. "She likes a handful of biscuits for breakfast," Josie told him.

He planned his Saturday with meticulous precision and military detail.

After Josie had gone into town shopping, he would take the dog for a long walk. Well, certainly as far as the 'Harris Tweed's' house, and who knows, he thought, seeing him walking in the hot sun the Harrises might invite him in for a cold beer. The afternoon, he would rest and let Josie tend to his needs, and in the evening, he would let Josie cook supper. Steak, chips and mushrooms with a couple of bottles of Cape Red. Then, a bath together and an early night. Perfect, he thought. But first things first, he took the sausage he had cooked and went in search of the dog. He had to establish a friendly working relationship with the animal.

It was one thing agreeing to go to Auntie's for Sunday curry lunch— he was quite looking forward to that. But he was determined to have his way over the dog. "She can't come with us," he told Josie. "She has to stay here and guard the house. That's what dogs do."

"But she'll be lonely."

"Tough."

"So she can't come with us?"

"No, and that's final, my last word on the subject."

"Come, come, come," Auntie said, as they walked into the garden. "Come and sit in the shade." She called to the waiter, "Godfry, a bowl of water for the dog, the poor dear looks parched."

He saw sanity in the form of Josie's uncle, Abdul, the vet, sitting on his own, and walked over to him. "How's the dog?" the vet asked, and answered his own question, "She looks fine. I'll come and take the stitches out in the next day or so."

"Bring the bill and I'll give you a cheque," Iffor said.

"Dear boy, you're family, there is no bill. Now, have you tried our Indian beer? It's called Krait."

It was fortunate that Iffor was only into his second bottle of Krait when the policeman appeared. The message was simple: "Phone Mwonza."

Auntie took him to her private office. "Use this phone," she told him. "I'll see you're not disturbed.

"Meredith here."

"Iffor, we have a problem. My two-man forward listening post has been taken over by a platoon from 'Delta Company'. They don't appear to know anything about our plans and they are sitting on your man's exit route."

"But the Colonel promised a sterile area," Iffor protested.

"I know, I read the S.O.Ps," Jack told him. "Something else you should know, the Adjutant and the Operations officer have swopped jobs, Smithers is now in charge of operations. Time to go, bye old chap."

He went back into the garden and beckoned to Josie. "I have to go back to my office and I'll need you to encode a message for me. I've got the side door keys and the keys to my office, but not to the safe."

"The Colour's got those," she told him. "You go on ahead, I'll phone the Colour."

Bob and Josie were only minutes behind him. "Put that into code," he told Josie, handing her a message pad. "Send it 'Flash priority' and head it 'Most secret'. Copies to the Colonel and Commanding Officer Selous Scouts."

The message read: "Be advised, January's exit compromised by friendly forces."

Josie read the message back to him. "Wouldn't it be quicker to phone?" she said.

Iffor shook his head. "No, both Colonels will probably be having lunch somewhere, with orders not to be disturbed. A flash priority message will be handed to them wherever they are. And besides, Jack Francis and I said too much on the phone before. The Zambians aren't fools, they monitor all military-sounding phone traffic."

Josie went off to her teleprinter and code books. Iffor and the Colour sat down to think through this new problem. "Since Jack Francis said nothing about a contact report, we can assume that Moses hasn't been shot," Iffor began.

"Which means he is probably still in the Lenshina camp... probably screwing Alice," the Colour interrupted.

"There is one other possibility," Iffor went on, ignoring Bob's comments. "Moses might have tried to get back to us, seen our soldiers and realising they were not part of the plan, has skirted around them and crossed the border further west and will try to get to a farm to get a message to us."

"Or, he might go straight to North Camp expecting to find us there. Shall I get Harry in?"

"No, we'll stick to our original plan, they leave in the morning."

Josie came back into the office. "Both messages sent and acknowledged," she said.

Iffor sat back in his chair. "No need for you two to hang around here. Sorry to have disturbed your Sunday lunch, Bob. Josie, I'll see you later at Auntie's. I've got to wait for the phone call."

Iffor was right in his estimation: fifteen minutes to de-code the signal and find a runner, twenty minutes to find the Colonel, a few more minutes to... the phone rang. "Meredith, C.O. here. Now what's all this about?"

"What it's about Colonel, is that twat Smithers moving troops into the sterile area and compromising my operation."

The silence told Iffor he had overstepped the mark. "My apologies Colonel, I meant Captain Smithers."

"Any damage done?"

"I don't know Colonel. I don't think so."

"Leave me with it Iffor, I'll get them shifted."

"Will you advise Mwonza, Colonel?"

"Of course, goodbye."

The rest of Sunday afternoon had been something of a disaster. Iffor was still smarting over Josie winning the battle of the dog, and he had a deep sense of foreboding over Moses. And, he and Abdul had drunk too many Kraits.

As soon as they arrived the next morning, Iffor had the team assemble in his office, where he told them of the situation concerning Moses.

"We know Moses hasn't been shot, not by our side anyway, and we know his exit is now clear, so we'll stick to our original plan.

"Harry, when you get to North Camp, have a good look around your perimeter. Moses may be lying up waiting for you. Put your trips out at night, but for Christ's sake, if someone triggers one, identify your target before you open up. I can't see Moses setting off a trip flare, but you never know."

Evil whispered something in Phil's ear.

"The reason I don't think Moses will set off a trip," Iffor said forcefully, "is that when he gets close to our camp, he will find a reed or the stem of a plant and flick it out in front of him as he walks. The weight of the reed won't be enough to trigger the trip, but it will tell him there is a wire in front of him."

"Sorry boss."

As the rest of Monday dragged on, Iffor found himself wishing he had gone with Harry. He had brought his kit into the drill hall to load on to the Champ. He had cleaned his Carbine, unloaded and cleaned the magazines, then reloaded them. He spent another hour cleaning his pistol, but still, it was only mid-morning. He drew a couple of twenty-four hour ration packs, a tin of boiled sweets, another two field dressings and a radio battery from the Colour and spent the rest of the morning repacking his Burgan.

It gave him some relief when Pete walked into the drill to tell him Harry had made his first radio check and his duty operator had logged it. The Inspector was more than pleased that having the army's radio in his station and manned by one of his constables, afforded a chance to be able to help.

"You look like you need a beer," Pete told him. "Come on."

Even after a couple of beers, he still felt edgy. The business of Smithers moving troops into the sterile area had thrown him, and now he just wished he could sit huddled over the radio in the police Ops room, waiting for Harry to come up on the air. His memory took him back to Northern Ireland when he did 'watch-keeping' duties in the Ops room. He still remembered with pride, the young twenty-year old corporal section commander coming up on the air with a simple "contact, wait out", while the background noise of rifle and machine-gun fire told Iffor the section was under very heavy fire, probably from several different buildings.

"The Colour said I've got to take you home," Josie interrupted his thoughts. "You are just getting in the way here. If Harry needs you, the police will phone you."

Sleep didn't come easy that night. He knew his meeting with the Lenshina was close at hand. He had total confidence in his men, but he still had that nagging doubt; had he missed something in his planning?

Josie didn't help. "Just think Iffor," she said, "if you do find the other twin, just think, we can have them both here for weekends and holidays. Wouldn't that be great?"

He had a vision: 'I'm just popping out for a couple, won't be long';... 'But you can't, it's your turn to bath the twins.'

Despite his sleepless night, he appeared at the drill hall 'bright-eyed and bushy-tailed' and ready for the off. He'd had the devil's own job to persuade Josie to leave the dog at home with Enid. "But I know that in the Light Infantry, the Adjutant always takes his dog to work with him," she told him.

"Yes but we are Rifles, not Light Infantry, and the dog is always a labrador, and you're not the bloody Adjutant." Her pout almost made him give in, but he held his ground. He was after all, in charge.

He felt no need to hang around at the drill hall. All the kit was packed and he needed to get up to North Camp as soon as he could. A quick kiss and a wave and they were driving through Kensington under the fluttering 'Pigasus Flag'. Next stop, North Camp.

They drove through the drift and into the clearing that once was the De Witt's farm. Harry's team were packed and ready to leave. "All quiet boss, nothing to report, the trip flares are still armed and the claymores are sited and armed. No sign of Moses."

"Okay Harry, thanks. I'd like you to pop into Charlie's farm on the way back and have a chat to Shadrak. See if he's got any news for me. He's fond of Cape Spirit if Hennie's got any left. When you get back to

Kensington, prepare for a quick turn around, I may need you back here in a hurry."

After Harry had left, Iffor's men got down to settling in. First task, unload the Champ, then drive it to the far side of the drift where it would be 'cammed' and left. In the early days of the war, vehicles that had to be left unattended were fitted with 'trembler switches' and two pounds of plastic. Word soon got around that unattended military vehicles should be given a very wide berth, and since Shadrak had put the word around that De Witt's was haunted, it was unlikely the vehicle would be disturbed.

The thought of having the Champ available for a quick getaway was very tempting, but a vehicle loaded with men would be a much easier target for ten or twenty rifles to fire at than four men running zigzag through the bush. The Champ concealed, Iffor put Evil, now reunited with his Bren, up on the kopje as sentry, had Mal check the trips and claymores, while he and Shamus went to the ruins of the farmhouse to set the explosives and lay out the firing cable; leaving Alvin to prepare lunch.

Try as he might, Iffor couldn't shrug off his overwhelming feeling of unease. True, he had no evidence that a Lenshina attack was imminent. True, he would get ample warning from Moses or Mwonza, and he couldn't keep the entire team at North Camp for days on end that would affect their effectiveness.

But as the afternoon wore on, he become more convinced that his small force was, as the Colour had suggested, a bit bare arsed.

He discussed the situation with Mal. "If it helps boss, I would feel an awful lot happier if Harry's brick were up here with us," he confirmed.

Mind made up, Iffor called up the Colour on the 31 set. "Sorry Bob, but my soldier's instinct tells me to get you and Harry's brick back up here. No move before sparrows'. Over."

"Roger boss... out."

With the decision made, Iffor felt happier. He sat with his back against a m'pani tree, took out his notebook and wrote out his sentry roster and plans for the next day. He was right about his soldier's instinct; 'the game was afoot'.

PART TWENTY-TWO

A fire mission involves calling down mortar fire onto your own position with corrections, plus or minus, left or right, onto your enemy.

WEDNESDAY'S DAWN brought with it a flawless sky, and the feeling of apprehension among the men, that served to sharpen their actions as they went about their morning duties: stand-to at first light; wash and shave followed by breakfast; a general tidying up, with two men with the Bren on the kopje keeping watch. It was with some considerable relief that Iffor watched as the Colour led his small party along the track from the drift and into their position.

"You made good time, Bob."

"Well, I knew you wouldn't have shouted for us if it wasn't urgent. Oh, and while I think of it, the dog's had her stitches out. Josie told me to tell you."

Iffor allowed another brew-up, then called his orders group.

"My plans for the defence of North Camp are unchanged, except for our order of battle. Phil, I want you and the radio up on the kopje. It's better reception and if we have to fall back the gun group will move first; they'll be able to protect you. The rest of the kopje group will be, Colour, Mal, Alvin and Evil with the Bren. The rest, Harry, Shamus, Hennie and the 'phantom crapper' with me.

Bob, I want you to go up to the kopje and look to your defences. When you're satisfied, tell me on your hand radio. Then I want you to rehearse moving your men down across the drift and taking up defence positions.

Harry, while the Colour is working on his defences, I want you to take Hennie and Shamus down to the drift and improve the earth bank—that will be our protection. When you've finished that, we'll rehearse our own withdrawal back across the drift. Then, we'll have a rehearsal combining both bricks.

Questions?   No!"

He stood up and clapped his hands. "Let's get on with it! Corporal Watney, sentry duty. Anything you're not happy with, fire a shot."

Mad Harry took him by the arm and took him aside. "Message from Shadrak," he said. "The child in the village is the child you seek."

Iffor joined in with the rehearsals with a relish; time spent planning, preparing and rehearsing was seldom wasted. He explained the principals of 'pepper-potting', covering one another as they withdrew. He watched as they made the same mistakes he had made when he was training, and corrected them. Satisfied with the rehearsals, he had the men look to their own stand-to positions. Grenades primed and handy, magazines within easy reach, the hand exploders for the Claymores within easy reach and obvious.

Since lunch had comprised tinned meat paste and hard tack biscuits, they knocked off in the late afternoon to prepare a decent evening meal and enjoy a couple of beers. As the African sun began to set, they went into night routine, watching, waiting, sleeping, eating, interrupted only when Iffor's hand radio crackled into life: "There's an armed black on the edge of the clearing—it looks like Moses." Iffor walked forward as far as the wire and cupping his hands called, "What month is it?" The reply was what he expected: "January." Iffor waited at the wire, directing Moses to the 'deliberate' break in the wire, where the wire could be pulled apart, allowing one man to pass through, and led him back to the 'bivvi' area.

Iffor and his team waited patiently until Moses had washed, shaved, changed into uniform and eaten a full twenty-four ration pack as one meal, before asking questions. "I see you collected a rifle on the way back."

"The sentry had no further need of it," Moses grinned.

"The Lenshina?" Iffor asked. "What of their plans?"

"They come soon, tonight, tomorrow, perhaps the day after. But soon. They will skirt around Mwonza; they do not like the guns on legs, the Vickers. Then they will split into two groups; one group will attack the protected village and one group will come here."

"That's bloody sneaky," Iffor said.

"What's sneaky about it, boss?" Harry asked.

"What's sneaky," Iffor answered, "is that if the Battalion can scrape together a quick reaction force, who do they come to rescue, us or innocent African villagers being raped and butchered?"

"How large are these two groups?" Iffor asked.

"About thirty men in each group, with many more coming down from Fort Jameson. The government is bringing them down in buses."

"Weapons?" Iffor asked.

"Most have rifles, the rest, pangas and spears, and they have at least three light machine-guns."

Iffor ordered the protesting Moses into a sleeping bag. "Sleep," he told him. "You're no use to me until you are rested."

Then, he went to meet with the Colour at the base of the kopje, to tell him what Moses had learned. "Get a sit rep off to Battalion, Kensington and Mwonza," Iffor told him, "Keep them up to date."

Harry came quietly to Iffor's side to relieve him on watch. Iffor instinctively looked at his watch, turning the face towards the moon, O four hundred hours.

"Do you think they'll come, boss?" he asked.

"That's what they always ask in cowboy films. And I'm supposed to answer, 'I don't like it, it's too quiet'," Iffor said, then turned his head quickly to avoid looking into the trip flare as it ignited... "Stand To; Stand To!"

Harry was already firing at the cloaked, hooded men trying to clamber over the barbed wire. The rest of the team joined him leaving Moses cursing as he tried to find the zip of his sleeping bag. Iffor quickly reacted to the situation. About eight men were attacking, now reduced to three. Bob, rightly so, had held his fire. As the trip flare died, Iffor fired an illuminating flare to give more light and to give him a chance to look through his binos into the bush behind them. "No sign of any others," he told Bob on his walkie-talkie. "These are obviously a scouting party." As the flare died, so did the last of the attackers.

"A scouting party," Moses confirmed. "The rest will come at dawn."

Dawn, according to centuries of tradition, is when British Army units in the field 'Stand To' to meet an attack by enemy forces, who are always expected to attack at dawn. The reason this never happens could be because the enemy always knows the army is standing to and expecting them. In this instance though, Iffor's insistence on a dawn stand-to was rewarded by the beating of drums, sporadic rifle fire and a full blown frontal assault by about twenty Lenshina. This time the heavies, dressed in loin cloths and in the main armed with pangas and spears, were supported by a light machine-gun on their flank behind them. They came bunched around their leader, heading for the centre of the defensive barbed wire, but the defenders' accurate fire into the centre caused them to split into two distinct groups, each group heading towards the claymores. Hennie and Shamus each picked up the hand-held dynamo, the exploder, and, judging the timing to perfection, fired the claymores. The resulting small explosion and puff of black smoke was not the huge sheet of flame and massive ball of smoke that Hennie and Shamus were expecting, but the results were spectacular. Not a man was left standing.

No celebratory cheer from the defenders, just a grim-faced Iffor saying, "Well done chaps, look to your magazines."

An hour elapsed before Iffor allowed his men, two at a time, to get some breakfast and clean their weapons. Up on the kopje the Colour did the same. Moses and Iffor shared a mug of tea, while looking over the parapet and the bodies scattered in front of their wire.

"What now?" Iffor asked.

"They wait for the other group to come, then they will attack again, but this time, in force."

"And this time," Iffor said, "they will be stoned out of their tiny minds on Chibuku and dagga and flush with the success of wiping out a village of innocent defenceless people."

Iffor spoke to the Colour on the hand-held set: "Get a contact report to Battalion, please."

"Phil's already sent a 'contact wait out'," the Colour replied.

"Good man. Now, write this down and get it sent off to Battalion:

"CONTACT AT CALL SIGN NORTH CAMP
"TWO ATTACKS REPULSED
"CASUALTIES: FRIENDLY NIL
"ENEMY TWENTY PLUS CONFIRMED.
"ENEMY NOW RE-GROUPING."

Taking advantage of the lull, Iffor opened his compo 'ham and eggs' and brewed some coffee, then washed and shaved. It was now mid-morning, with the sun high and hot. The overhead cover Iffor had insisted on was now coming into its own and maintaining a comfortable temperature in the trench.

He brought the men to 'stand to' again, checking their field of fire, and dishing out three bandoliers from the reserve ammunition to each man.

"If we have to withdraw," he told them, "I will give a 'prepare to move' order, to give you a chance to stick any magazines on the parapet into your pouches.

"When I say *move*, do it exactly as we rehearsed. You are in pairs; if your mate goes down, grab him by the scruff of the neck and drag him into cover."

Harry interrupted him: "Visitors boss. Are we expecting any one?"

Iffor took up his position between Harry and Moses and reached for his binos.

"I don't think you need those, boss," Harry said, bringing his rifle into the aim.

From the bush on the far side of the clearing, figures started to appear. Cautiously and slowly and spread out, they advanced across the open ground, crouched, making difficult targets. "Christ Almighty!" Harry said. "Where the fuck did this lot come from? There must be fifty or more."

Bob came up on the air: "This lot mean business, boss. Tell me when."

"Use your own discretion Bob, I think I'm going to be busy."

They came at them, darting, crouching, firing short bursts from their automatic rifles, longer sustained bursts from the belt fed RPD light machine-guns.

This lot had learned a lesson. As they reached the wire, they picked up their dead and threw them onto the wire, giving them a platform to cross.

The fire from the defenders was slow and deadly, punctuated by the cry 'magazine!' as magazines were changed. The wire was now breached in several places, but no-one had penetrated the wire.

"Now," Iffor said. "Now!" and as if in answer the Bren opened up. With its 'beaten zone' in depth rather than width and being at almost right angles to the wire, it caused total mayhem and confusion, forcing the enemy to fall back, and for those coming up behind them, to join in their retreat. The retreat was infectious, each man trying desperately to get away from Evil's deadly cone of fire. They got as far as far as the old burnt-out farmhouse, where their leaders urged them to take cover and return fire.

"This should be good," Mad Harry said, as Iffor reached for the exploder. A quarter turn of the key was all it took to send the current along the cable to the detonator. The ground shook as a mixture of bodies, stone and timbers rose into the sky and settled in a cloud of dust.

It crossed Iffor's mind to advance with bayonets to finish the job, but he had no way of knowing how many Lenshina were still lurking in the bush, so he had to content himself looking at the carnage he had just caused.

He conferred with Moses. "That lot weren't Lenshina," he said.

"No," Moses agreed. "They were regular ZAPU. They must have been waiting on this side of the border. They will be many and they will use different tactics next time."

He passed this snippet of information to the Colour: "You can expect a concerted attack on your position," he told him. "The secret is not to leave it too late to withdraw."

"Right boss. Phil wants a word."

"Message from Battalion," Phil said. "Be advised large number of ZAPU have penetrated border west of Mwonza, probably heading your way."

"Tell Battalion they've arrived," Iffor told him.

Just as the terrorists' leaders would be discussing a change in tactics, Iffor looked to his own defences. In the centre of his trench he had his main 'fire team': Harry, Moses and the phantom crapper. On his left flank, Hennie; on the right, Big Shamus, both with sandbags protecting their head and shoulders.

"Use grenades 'as and when'," he told them. "Don't wait for my orders, and don't forget to yell 'grenade' when you chuck them.

He took his own 'Phosphorous' grenades from his smock pocket and laid them on the parapet along with a thirty-round magazine and two 36 grenades.

Tactics had changed... A 'fire team' of two RPDs, concealed in the bush, opened up on the kopje. Two light machine-guns, each with a two hundred and fifty round belt and with a rate of fire of six hundred rounds a minute, didn't need to be aimed, just pointed, and would be enough to keep Evil's head down and prevent him from winning this 'fire fight'. A mixture of Lenshina and ZAPU terrorists broke cover and with the confidence the fire team on their left flank gave them, charged on the kopje.

"Support the kopje!" Iffor shouted to Shamus. "Remainder, watch your front; watch and shoot." A totally unnecessary fire order, he told himself, but it would give his blokes confidence.

"Here they come, boys!" Harry shouted, and dropped the first two terrorists as they left the cover of the bush. Forty, fifty enemy broke cover, covering the open ground in front of the defenders with alarming speed and recklessness. Casualties meant nothing to them. "Stand calmly and shoot deadly," he heard himself say.

It was either Kipling or Corporal Jones, his musketry instructor in basic, who said that.

While Iffor's men were containing and holding their enemy's frontal assault, Bob was in serious trouble. "They're on my flank boss, time to go."

Iffor joined Shamus on the right flank, firing on the enemy charging up the steep slope to the top of the kopje.

Foresight on a target, squeeze, then move on to another target, no need to watch for results; a hit from his five-fifty six and the man wouldn't get up again. Shamus shouted: "Magazine, magazine!" as he changed mags, then carried on with his carnage. Iffor put a fresh thirty-round magazine on his Carbine and engaged the men now reaching the summit of the kopje. He heard Harry somewhere behind him shout, "Grenades!" Christ, he thought, they've breached the wire. He called back to Harry: "The phosphorous, use my phosphorous!" That would slow the bastards down. The exploding satchel charge left by the Colour sent figures scurrying back down the steep bank of the kopje. That part of the plan at least, had worked well.

He rejoined his own fire team, no casualties. The white phosphorous had worked well; the enemy had moved back away from the wire and were taking cover behind their dead, keeping a constant if inaccurate fire on the trench. Iffor looked back up to the kopje; the enemy were now moving onto the undefended position and would soon be outflanking him. It was now or never.

"Prepare to move, chaps. Prepare to move... Harry, you and the crapper first."

Pausing long enough to stuff magazines and grenades into pouches, grab a couple of bandoliers from reserve ammo, they 'rolled' over the rear parapet of the trench and with one man covering, one man running, made the safety of the bush behind them; then turned to give covering fire to the others. Hennie and big Shamus followed suit. The attackers were now on to what was happening and were beginning to react, on their feet and moving towards the trench, firing as they came.

Iffor had to be last. He knew the last man couldn't come out of this unscathed, and Moses wouldn't have left him, even if Iffor had ordered to do so.

Their accurate fire prevented the enemy from clambering into the trench, but two men were into the far end, twenty feet away. Iffor beat them to the shot, "Go Moses, for fuck's sake go!"

Moses needed no urging. He rolled out of the trench, ran twenty metres, then turned and knelt to give covering fire to Iffor. Iffor pulled the pin from the percussion ignitor leading to the 'satchel charge'. Five seconds from now, he told himself, the trench would be full of terrorists; thirty seconds from now and they would all be dead.

He ran past Moses another ten metres, stopped, knelt and fired at those terrorists now between him and the trench. "Go Moses, go!"

Moses ran past him, gaining some cover in the bush. He turned to cover his friend, his shouts suddenly drowned out by the explosion of the satchel charge, firing a deadly hail of nuts, bolts, army cutlery and broken beer bottles into the bodies of the scavenging Lenshina.

Iffor got up and started to run to join Moses. It had to happen; an A.K. round smacked into his left shoulder. He stumbled and fell, then turned at bay, holding his Carbine in his good hand, his left arm numb with shock.

Moses was beside him, pulling him onto his feet. "Run man. Run!" A second round found its mark, causing Moses to exhale sharply as the round hit him between the shoulder blades. They staggered on towards the drift, hanging on to one another for support, not really caring how close the enemy were. A tall figure loomed up in front of them. Iffor raised his Carbine; one last shot, he told himself, make it count. It was big Shamus. At his rear, Hennie had taken up a firing position behind an m'pani tree, and was giving covering fire.

"Take Moses, I'm okay," Iffor gasped. Somehow, they made the last fifty metres to the river bank and the drift, where Mad Harry had crossed to help. "Can't leave you cunts alone for a minute," he muttered, grabbing Iffor by the waist and dragging him through the shallow water to the far bank and over the earthworks, that was their defensive position. Shamus propped Moses up against the rear bank, in what little shade he could find and called to Corporal Watney: "Take care of him."

Harry sat Iffor down behind cover and examined his wound. "Straight through, boss. Six months from now and you won't know it had happened."

He put a field dressing over the larger exit wound. "That will do for now."

Then he unzipped Iffor's smock and placed the arm inside, using the smock as a sling.

Iffor took stock, and for the first time saw the Colour Sergeant at the far end of the position, lying with a large shell dressing over a chest wound, and Alvin trying to insert an angio-catheter into the chest cavity to take the pressure off Bob's lungs. Evil, with Mal as his number two, was firing short bursts into the top of the kopje, where 'nuisance' fire was coming from.

Phil, good old Phil, was giving a running sit rep to Battalion on the thirty-one set. He saw Iffor and mouthed, "Sunray's just coming." And he held the handset out to Iffor, changing his position slightly, but showing his head and shoulders above the parapet. A bullet hit him in the side of the head, killing him instantly.

Iffor took the handset, "Sunray on set, sit rep, over."

"Send, over."

"I am in contact with large enemy force, and have fallen back on the drift. I have one dead and two, three wounded, two seriously. Over."

The Colonel's voice: "Hang on Iffor, I've got a Quick Reaction Force in the air and on its way; ETA your location twelve minutes."

"Cavalry's on its way, boys," he called out and dashed back up the trench to the drift end, where Harry, Shamus and Hennie were now firing at a large group of enemy, who were getting more numerous as they came on to the drift.

"Hennie, go and support the Bren; cover Evil's flank." Keeping low, Hennie scuttled along the trench to the far end, winking at Iffor as he passed him. "Phantom," he called, "We need your rifle." The medic left Moses's side and took his place beside Harry and Shamus, "He wants to talk to you boss, he's dying."

Iffor quickly knelt beside his stricken friend and took his hand.

"What will become of my son? He will have no family."

"He will have many brothers in his regiment," Iffor told him. "The regiment will become his family."

"But he will have no father."

Arterial blood was staining his teeth and trickling down his chin. Iffor wiped the blood away from his mouth. "I will be his father, he will be my son. And when he passes out from Sandhurst, I will be there, and that night when all the guests have gone from the mess, I will tell his brother officers of the great Bull Elephant's last battle on the banks of the Lamumbwa River and wherever Douglas January goes the great Bull Elephant's reputation will also go."

Moses smiled. "See how our blood mingles," he said as blood ran down Iffor's smock and onto his own clothes. "We are truly blood brothers." And the smile on his lips died with him.

"Iffor!"... "Boss!"—two shouts at once, Mal offering him the radio handset indicating a message for him, and Harry pointing at the far bank, where purple painted Lenshina warriors wearing loin cloth and jacket were preparing for another assault on the drift. Down the slopes from the kopje came another group, probably ZAPU, ignoring Evil's shorter bursts as he tried to conserve ammunition.

"Sunray on set, over."

"Bravo Whisky, Bravo Whisky, this is Mike one one, with a mobile base plate and in range for a fire mission over."

"Mike one one, look at your map, south of Mwonza the farm marked Long Acre, a little farther south the river. Roger so far, over."

"Roger, over."

"Mike one one, we are holding the south side of the drift, the uglies are massing on the north side, about to come and wipe us out—that's where I want your bombs."

"Bravo Whisky, not a problem, I'll be listening out for corrections, out."

Handing Mal the handset, Iffor told him, "Correct the mortar fire, call sign Mike one one, and tell Evil to use whatever ammo he has left on the drift, when they charge. Hennie, back to the drift, give Harry a hand." His flank was now unprotected, but it couldn't be helped.

The drift was wide enough for a Land Rover or four men, shoulder to shoulder. This gave Iffor his edge; as the Lenshina surged across the drift, it was only the front four who posed the threat. Iffor picked up Moses's AK and with his good hand changed the magazine for a fully loaded one. His men were compelled to keep below the earth mound, because of the accurate fire from the far bank, but now Evil was raking their position with accurate fire from the Bren. This was Iffor's moment: "On your feet boys! Meet them head on, let's mix it with 'em." And standing on the mound, he fired a long withering sustained burst of thirty rounds into the oncoming tide. His men, Harry, phantom, Hennie and Shamus rose as one and met their enemy, bayonet and rifle butt against panga and rifle, so many enemy on the drift pushing forward, that the men at the front had little room to manoeuvre.

The phantom went down; Harry moved to protect him only to receive a thrusting bayonet in his belly. He dropped his rifle and pulled the bayonet away from his body. Phantom was on his feet, firing into the man's chest. Harry crumpled to the ground trying to stem the flow of blood with one hand, reaching for his rifle with the other. Phantom stood, legs apart over him, protecting him, shooting and stabbing, ignoring the spears being thrust at him. Bayonet to the body, rifle butt to the face, shooting when he could, two rounds to the chest. Hennie and big Shamus had advanced into their enemy. Side by side, shoulder to shoulder, a killing combination, but they were now surrounded and spears were being thrust into their bodies.

Theatrics, stunt, whatever, but Iffor's battle cry, "Faint heart ne'er fucked a pig!" as he charged into the fray, firing his pistol into every head in front of him, caused a momentary pause in the Lenshina attack.

The exploding mortar bomb, landing on the north bank, sent limbs from the men trying to bring a light machine-gun into action up into the air, to land in the river.

Mal was shouting into the handset: "Drop fifty, right a smidge, fire for effect." Whatever 'smidge' meant, it had the desired effect, as a pattern of mortar bombs dropped in a line along the bank, and onto and into the Lenshina attempting to storm the drift. Evil was waiting for this moment and let rip with his Bren, his last magazine, into the confusion on the drift.

Such was battle. In a moment, the enemy threatening to overwhelm Iffor's men were running for cover, away from the mortar bombs. "Drop another fifty," Mal said, and moments later another pattern drove the enemy even further back from the river.

They dragged and carried Harry back behind the mound, where the crapper examined the wound. "Looks like a 'spike' bayonet boss, a blade would have been fatal." He used Harry's field dressing to cover the wound and set up a drip. Hennie and Shamus started to dress one another's wounds.

"For you boss," Mal offered the handset.

"Bravo Whisky, this is Zulu Tango approaching your position, is this a hot drop? Over."

"Zulu Tango affirmative, enemy on north bank and still very active. I suggest you fly down the river and drop your load off on my smoke, over."

"Roger, two minutes."

The mortars came up on the air. "Bravo Whisky, that's it, that's all our ammo and we have to get out quick before the terrs are onto us. Good luck. Out."

The old Wessex Whirlwind came clattering along the river, a very easy and very tempting target for the terrorists. Iffor unhooked the smoke grenade from his webbing and lobbed it onto the bank in front of him.

"Red smoke?" The helicopter pilot asked.

"Roger, Zulu Tango."

The battle started to hot up again. With the mortars no longer a threat, the Lenshina had to defeat their enemy and ZAPU were just as anxious to flood down into the valley.

Hastily, Hennie and Shamus took up firing positions, dropping those brave enough to attempt to cross the drift.

As the Wessex came into view, flying at zero feet, following the river, some fifty or sixty rifles and RPD's opened up, all firing at the same target, the helicopter.

Iffor's men returned fire, ammo was short, Evil had abandoned the Bren in favour of the Colour's rifle.

"Bravo Whisky, we're taking hits." Smoke started to come from the engine as a section of eight men in a fast stick leapt from the helicopter onto the bank.

"Shit, we're losing oil pressure, can't take your wounded, I'm afraid."

"Roger Zulu Tango. Can you give the top of the kopje a stonk before you go? Over."

"For you darling, anything." The smoking Wessex rose into the air, giving the waist gunner a perfect view of the enemy on the kopje, which wasn't wasted.

It then ascended high into the sky, trying to conserve fuel, as Iffor's men watched the smoke trail head east towards New Epsom.

A breathless Corporal Adnam came up to Iffor. "You promised us a beer next time we met," he said. They shook hands.

"Position your section on the drift," Iffor told him. "Fight around your machine-gun, give my blokes some ammo and we'll look after the flanks." The Corporal nodded and deployed his men. His section and the MAG machine-gun were about to piss all over the Lenshina's strawberries.

The Colonel came up on the air: "Sit rep, over."

"Your section have gone firm on my position and are engaging enemy," Iffor answered. "Your helicopter was damaged, but was still airborne when we last saw it. My priority now is my wounded, two serious and three walking."

"Can you casevac, over?" the Colonel asked.

"Roger, if I can get them back to the nearest farm, over."

"Put Adnam on, over."

Iffor called to the Corporal and offered him the handset. The Corporal just answered questions, "Yes, no, count on us sir," then he handed the handset to Iffor. "Meredith, get your wounded out of there, we owe it to them, Adnams now in command and RLI are on their way, over."

Suddenly Iffor felt very, very tired—no point in protesting, he told himself,

"Roger Sunray, out to you." He turned to the Corporal, "Looks like you're the boss."

With his machine-gun and a couple of riflemen keeping the now, not quite so keen, enemy at bay, the Corporal got his men organised to collect the two vehicles and to load the wounded.

Iffor contacted Kensington: "Message for Jones, over."

"Davy on set boss, I've been monitoring your transmissions. Over."

"Davy, scramble the Islander for a casevac, two dead, two seriously wounded, the rest walking. RV at Arc Angel airstrip over."

"Onto it boss, out."

Corporal Watney touched Iffor's arm. "The wounded are stable, but need a hospital quickly. If you don't mind sir, I'll stay and keep an eye on this lot. Alvin can look after the Colour and Harry."

Iffor looked at the new commander. "Fine with me," he said.

Iffor climbed stiffly into the Champ and extended his hand to Adnams. "Hate to leave you on your own like this," he said.

"Not for long," the Corporal answered, pointing into the sky. >From the west, in perfect "Vic" formation came three Dakotas, flying at about six hundred feet. "Dropping height," Iffor said. And to confirm his remark, parachutes started to blossom over the farm, North Camp, a perfect D.Z.

The Rhodesian Light Infantry, the army's only parachute battalion had arrived as promised.

As Blue Watch drove away, the fire from Adnam's section intensified as Rhodesian soldiers drove the terrorists onto Adnam's hungry machine gun.

Iffor guessed that a company group had jumped in. A platoon was probably clearing the kopje, while another platoon was sweeping terrorists towards the drift.

A very anxious looking Davy was waiting in the shade of the Islander's wing, its engines idling. With the help of the crew and Archie, Davy's well-rehearsed plan for loading the wounded was soon completed.

"I'll see to the vehicles," Archie told him. "Tell your lads... never mind, I'll tell them myself."

As they climbed into the clear blue African sky, Iffor was able to look back to the north and to the pall of battle smoke, his battle smoke, Blue Watch's battle smoke. He made his way towards the flight deck, pausing to encourage the now conscious Colour sergeant and Harry. He stood looking over the pilots and into the future, "Thanks boys."

"Only a pleasure," the captain answered. "Only a pleasure."

EPILOGUE

And when I get to heaven and I am standing on the guardroom veranda of that great camp in the sky, the duty regimental Angel will come to me and say, "By what right do you deem to enter this camp?" And I will stand tall and proud, and I will say, "I was a British soldier." And the Angel will smile and step aside and say, "Pass, friend."

COLOUR SERGEANT BOB PEARSON and Sergeant 'Mad' Harry Simmonds survived their wounds, thanks to Corporal Watney and Alvin Turner and the good doctor Van De Merwe, who was able to get a surgical team flown up from Salisbury that same night. The rest, Iffor's 'straight through shot hole' and Shamus's and Hennie's spear wounds, were cared for by the dedicated hospital team.

The Selous Scouts collected Moses's body, to be buried in their own cemetery with full military honours, while Phil Hill with no family apart from Blue Watch, was buried in Kensington's cemetery, with those of Blue Watch still able to hold a rifle doing the honours over his grave.

Some three weeks later, the 'Rhodesian Rifles' were stood down and rested. The Colonel held a memorial service for Phil and boasted that although he had only asked for volunteers to attend, every single man of his two Kensington companies attended.

The nursing sister, Sister Kearney, insisted Iffor and his wounded comrades were admitted for four or five nights. Josie would have to attend to his letters and reports, which he dictated:

"To Battalion:

"Call sign Bravo Whisky extricated from field.

"Casualties: Two dead, two seriously wounded, three walking wounded.

"Regret, Bravo Whisky no longer a viable fighting unit."

Letter to Cadet Douglas January c\o R.M.A. Sandhurst:

> *Dear Douglas,*
>
> *It is with sad heart that I write to inform you of the death of your father, Moses January.*
>
> *Your father, my friend, was killed in action earlier today. He had left the Zambian army and was fighting for the Rhodesian Army in the most prestigious regiment of any army, the Selous Scouts.*
>
> *Before he died, I was able to promise him that I would be your family. My home, your home; my family, your family. It is my intention to attend your passing out parade at Sandhurst. After Sandhurst, before you join your regiment, you will take leave and come back to Rhodesia with me. You will meet your new family and live in your new home. I will take you to the battlefield where your father fought and died so gallantly. Then, we will go to Kariba to his grave.*

On the second day of his enforced captivity, Charlie from North Road Farm called to see Iffor. "My farm guard and I have brought your two vehicles back," he told him. "Thought I'd pop in and see you before we take them up to the drill hall."

"How are you getting back?" Iffor asked.

"Oh, we'll scrounge a lift from someone."

"Right, you can do me a big favour. Drop the Rover off at the drill hall, refuel the Champ, then come back here in the Champ. I'll get you home."

"But you can't drive with one arm."

"You drive there, I'll drive myself back—it's a straight road for chrissake."

"You're going after the other twin, aren't you?"

"With Shadrak, yes."

Iffor's 'bash through the bush to the village of Shadrak's father' went down in romantic folklore. It needed just one look to tell Iffor that this was indeed baby Helen's brother, but the villagers were reluctant to part with the infant, until Shadrak suggested they could keep the baby, but the doctor from the Leper colony would have to come and see that the baby was not stricken with leprosy. Reluctantly, they handed the baby over.

When they reached the Lamumbwa River, they stopped and Iffor fed the baby from the gourd of milk prepared by the villagers.

"He is a fine boy, Inkosi, what shall his name be?"

"His name shall be Jamie, and if you can get me back to the farm before nightfall, you shall come and dance and get drunk at my wedding."

The M'dala struggled to his feet, using his old Mauser as a prop. "Come effendi, on your feet, Shadrak has a wedding to go to."

And that, thank God, is the end.

ABOUT THE AUTHOR

A drenalin junky, former paratrooper, contract soldier, professional diver, Gwyn Fford-Osborne is now living, singing, drinking and writing in darkest Oxfordshire.

In 1954, Gwyn joined the Royal Electrical Mechanical Engineers and qualified as an armourer. Having been posted to an Infantry Battalion, he served in Germany, Cyprus and North Africa, which culminated in him being injured during the Suez Operation. After recovering, he volunteered for the Airborne Forces and was posted to the Parachute Engineer Regiment (TA) following parachute training. Following this, Gwyn contracted to the Northern Rhodesian army, which then became the Zambian Army, serving with the infantry.

On leaving the Zambia Army he had a varied career, including time as a professional diver and then many years as a publican and also made several trips to Rhodesia during their war, one of which included running alcohol to the Tribal Trust Land (his most dangerous engagement!). During the time, he was a very active member of the Territorial Army serving in the Greenjackets, Royal Auxiliary Airforce and Light Infantry. Hanging up his boots in 1992.

As one of the very few soldiers to have been commissioned from the ranks twice, Gwyn has a unique perspective on military life particularly in Africa.

Lightning Source UK Ltd.
Milton Keynes UK
178091UK00001B/104/P